THE SECRET GIFT

IAN SOMERS

Ian Somers lives in Dublin and works as a graphic designer. His first two books about Ross Bentley, *Million Dollar Gift* and *The Hidden Gift*, are also published by The O'Brien Press.

THE SECRET GIFT

IAN SOMERS

THE O'BRIEN PRESS
DUBLIN

First published 2014 by
The O'Brien Press Ltd,
12 Terenure Road East, Rathgar,
Dublin 6, Ireland.Tel: +353 1 4923333; Fax: +353 1 4922777
E-mail: books@obrien.ie.
Website: www.obrien.ie

ISBN: 978-1-84717-647-9

8 7 6 5 4 3 2 1
17 16 15 14

Printed and bound by CPI Group (UK) Ltd, Croydon, CR0 4YY
The paper in this book is produced using pulp from managed forests

The O'Brien Press receives financial assistance from

For Kevin & Lucy.

contents

MAIN GUILD TARGETS.

All high priority targets are to be exterminated with immediate effect.

Target One
Name: Elizabeth Armitage.
Code name: Queen.
Age: 35.
Nationality: English.
Gift Level: 9.
Known Gifts: Mind-Switcher (Mutated).
Status: High Priority Target.
Location: Last sighted in London on the 3rd of August.
Guild Classification: Deep Black.

Target Two
Name: Michael Huntington.
Code name: Rogue.
Age: 43.
Nationality: Scottish.
Gift Level: 8.
Known Gifts: Psychokinesis (Partial). Electro-psych (Pure). Light-Tuner (Pure).
Status: High Priority Target.
Location: Last sighted in Ireland on the 9th of December.
Guild Classification: Deep Black.

Target Three

Name: Dominic Ballentine.

Code name: Chimera.

Age: 45.

Nationality: French.

Gift Level: 8.

Known Gifts: Psychokinesis (Pure).

Status: Undetermined.

Location: Last sighted in London on the 28th of November.

Guild Classification: Deep Black

Target Four

Name: James Tucker.

Code name: Furnace.

Age: 30.

Nationality: American.

Gift Level: 7.

Known Gifts: Pyrokinesis (Pure).

Status: High Priority Target.

Location: Last sighted in Kiev, Ukraine on the 2nd of May.

Guild Classification: Deep Black.

Target Five

Name: Cathy Atkinson.

Code name: Dolittle.

Age: 20.

Nationality: English.

Gift Level: 7.

Known Gifts: Mind-Switcher (Pure).

Status: Mid Priority Target.
Location: Unconfirmed sighting in London, England on the 9th of December.
Guild Classification: White.

Target Six
Name: Amanda Ellenberger.
Code name: Singer.
Age: 51.
Nationality: Swiss.
Gift Level: 9.
Known Gifts: Precognitive (Pure), Siren (Pure).
Status: Mid Priority Target.
Location: Last sighted in Glasgow, Scotland on the 20th of November.
Guild Classification: Red.

Target Seven
Name: Joshua Carlebach.
Code name: Ranger.
Age: 22.
Nationality: Israeli.
Gift Level: 7.
Known Gifts: Emotomagnet (Pure), Light-Tuner (Pure).
Status: Mid Priority Target.
Location: Last sighted in New York, United States on the 8th of January.
Guild Classification: Black.

Target Eight

Name: Ross Bentley.

Code name: Devil.

Age: 19.

Nationality: Irish.

Gift Level: 9.

Known Gifts: Psychokinesis (Pure), Precognitive (Pure), Time-scanner (Pure).

Status: Mid Priority Target.

Location: No reported sightings in the last twelve months.

Guild Classification: Deep Black.

Target Nine

Name: Janice Powell.

Code name: Pilot.

Age: 19.

Nationality: Unknown.

Gift Level: 7.

Gifts: Space Rupter (Pure).

Status: Mid Priority Target.

Location: Last sighted in London, England on the 15th of October.

Guild Classification: White.

Target Ten

Name: Anne Wilkins.

Code name: Thief.

Age: 18.

Nationality: Welsh.

Gift Level: 8.

Gifts: Electro-Psych (Pure), Light-Tuner (Pure), Siren (Pure).

Status: Undetermined.

Location: Last sighted in Cardiff, Wales on the 10th of November.

Guild Classification: White.

CHAPTER ONE

The Attack

'Night was fast approaching and I was running out of time,' Inspector James Harper began. 'I felt we had to close in on Wilson before darkness fell; we simply couldn't risk losing him again. He was headed for the busiest part of town, I weighed up the situation with the aid of my colleague Detective Alan Dinsley, and felt that apprehending Wilson at that time was the wisest course of action to take.'

'Your wisdom led to a lot of police officers losing their lives,' Superintendent Wayne Beckett countered coldly.

'I couldn't have foreseen what happened next. I made the logical decision considering the information that I had at that time.'

'Did any of your officers object to this course of action?'

'Not that I am aware of,' Harper shrugged. 'We all understood that we'd be putting innocent lives at risk if we allowed Wilson to disappear into a crowd. Everyone knew that he had proven dangerous and elusive since his crimes were uncovered. We didn't want to lose him again. We all believed that it was the right time to apprehend him.'

'How did it all go so wrong?'

'That's a difficult question to answer.'

'How about this question instead: Do you think the terrorist attack in Liverpool that occurred last night – 1 December – was linked to Malcolm Wilson?'

'Impossible to say with any certainty.'

'Are you aware that we've already questioned a number of your officers?'

'Yes, I am aware of that.'

'Are you also aware that most of them claim this wasn't a normal terrorist attack?'

'I'm not aware of exactly what they told you. I am aware, however, that they are fine police officers and would never lie to, or withhold evidence from, a commanding officer.'

'Stop trying to butter me up,' Beckett snarled. 'The stories your officers told me are complete fiction. No one in their right mind would believe them.'

'I'm not aware of what they told you, so I can't comment on that.'

'Right, how about you tell me what happened in Liverpool last night. Give me your own version of the events. Begin with you making the decision to apprehend Malcolm Wilson. How many men did you have at your disposal and what were their positions?'

'It was exactly 6.35pm when I gave the order to close the net on him. There were a total of twenty-one police officers at the scene, including myself. Wilson was not aware of us at that point – I'm sure of that. He was on foot and was headed deeper into the city centre. We had twelve armed officers in plain clothes on the ground, following him from various distances. The rest of us occupied three cars – all unmarked. We also had the services of a marksman who was positioned nearby. Wilson took to Ranelagh Street. That route was leading him to an area of the city which is always very hectic at that time on a Friday evening. Detective Dinsley believed there was a risk of losing him in such a built-up area, particularly as it was getting dark. I concurred. That's when I told the officers on the ground to make the arrest. They encircled him moments later.'

'Who was the first to use a weapon?'

'I believe it was Officer James Burnett.'

'What is your understanding of Burnett's actions?'

'I heard the shots and thought that perhaps Wilson had tried to run and my men had opened fire. It quickly became apparent that that was not the case. I saw Burnett discharging his sidearm with my own two eyes. He never once took a shot at Wilson, who was completely surrounded at the time.'

'Explain in as much detail as possible what you witnessed next.'

'Burnett fired eight rounds. All shots were directed at his colleagues. He killed five officers in total. Two more were seriously injured.'

'He killed six officers; Officer Fiona Jennings succumbed to her injuries two hours ago.'

'I hadn't heard ...'

'Please continue, Inspector Harper.'

'Burnett took us all by surprise. It was so unexpected. Most of us failed to react in the way we should have. I think it was Richardson who finally tackled him and dragged him to the ground. That was when the ninth shot went off – the one that killed Burnett.'

'Do you know of any reason why Burnett, an officer with an exemplary record, would open fire on his colleagues?'

'I know of no reason.'

'No one ever suspected him of taking bribes, perhaps? Did he gamble or use drugs?'

'No, nothing in his record would suggest he was anything other than a dedicated professional.'

'Well, my opinion at the present is that he was working with Wilson in some capacity.'

'If that was the case, why didn't Burnett inform Wilson that we were watching him?'

'I don't know *yet.*' Beckett raised his voice. 'Now, what happened after Burnett was grounded?'

'Wilson made a dash for Church Street. A number of us – I had left my vehicle at this point – gave chase. There were a lot of civilians in the area and we didn't dare risk firing on Wilson.'

'This was when the explosion occurred, yes?'

'Yes.'

'Describe that moment for me.'

'It was powerful enough to destroy two of the buildings on the street. I was thrown to the ground by the force of it. There was a cloud of debris spewing out across the road. People were screaming. There were bodies all around me …' Harper ran a trembling hand across his forehead and swallowed hard. 'I got back to my feet and wandered into the dust cloud towards a number of stricken bystanders. I was trying to help them. It took a moment for my eyes to adjust, and when they did, I saw three of my men had been killed by the blast. I don't know how many civilians – maybe a dozen or more.'

'Did you see Wilson after the explosion?'

'No, he wasn't seen again. Oh, one other thing: I don't think it's right to describe it as an explosion.'

'Why not?'

'The buildings simply erupted. There was no blast. No flames. No bright flash.'

'That doesn't sound plausible.'

'I understand that it sounds insane, sir. But it's what happened.'

'Let's not dwell on this right now,' Beckett said impatiently. 'Tell me how the fighting started.'

'A man appeared from the rubble,' Harper said ominously. 'He walked straight towards us.'

'Describe him in as much detail as you can.'

'He stood approximately six feet nine inches tall. He had a very stocky build – exceptionally so. He wore a dark coloured jacket and beige combat trousers. Almost like tactical clothing that the special forces wear. He also wore a black hood pulled over his head that cast a shadow over his face. His eyes were … er …'

'What about his eyes?'

'His eyes were glowing,' Harper admitted. 'They were glowing bright green.'

'Glowing eyes?'

'I know how it sounds, but I'm telling you the truth. His eyes were glowing like neon. I've never seen anything quite like it before.'

'So, did this giant with glowing green eyes attack your men on sight?'

'Too right he did. Waded into us. I saw him kill two men with his bare hands.'

'And what did you do?'

'I unloaded what ammunition I had left.'

'From what distance?'

'No more than three metres.'

'How many rounds?'

'Seven shots.'

'And you missed him seven times?'

'I *hit him* seven times.'

'Why wasn't his body recovered?'

'The bullets … they …'

'They what?'

'The bullets bounced right off him. I shot him five times in the chest. I thought he was wearing a ballistic vest or something so I adjusted my aim and capped off two more rounds – both bullets struck him in the head. He remained unharmed and kept stalking forward. He whacked an officer to my left, knocking him ten feet into the air. He was about to clobber me when our sniper, who had picked up a position nearby, shot him in the back. He took some notice of that. But he still wasn't grounded by it.'

'Do you expect me to believe that a round from a high powered sniper rifle struck this man in the back, yet it failed to inflict a significant injury?'

'I don't expect you to believe it,' Harper snapped. 'I am simply telling you what I witnessed. That monster took seven 9mm rounds from me, from a distance of less than three metres, and it didn't even slow him down. I watched him toss a grown man into the air as if he was a scrap of paper. I saw the sniper's bullet bouncing off his back like it was a ping pong ball. He stumbled forward, straightened himself, then took off into the cloud of debris.'

'Impossible, I say.'

'I don't give a damn what you say!' Harper shouted. 'I trust my own eyes and I hope they never set upon that *man* again. The mere thought of him makes my blood run cold.'

'Is that all you've got to say?'

'It is.'

'I'm ending the recording at this time.' Beckett switched off a recorder that was placed between them on the desk top. He gazed at his colleague with a mixture of sympathy and puzzlement. 'Bloody hell, Jim! Is this some sort of sick joke?'

'I wish it was, Wayne. I really do.'

'You're telling me this *giant* is real?'

'He is. You have to put out a search for him immediately. Get his description to the newspapers as soon as you can.'

'Not a chance. This is being wiped off the record forever.'

'Why?'

'Because if it goes public, every man and woman involved in the operation will have to be discharged from the force on grounds of insanity.'

'I'm not insane.'

'I know you're not. Listen, go home and get some sleep.'

'Nothing will be done about this?'

'Of course we're doing something about it. Interpol are already searching for Wilson. I'll have MI5 informed of this *giant* of yours. I just hope they find a way of stopping him if they do find him.'

CHAPTER TWO

Isolation

A single hour had passed since I said farewell to Cathy and I was already feeling intense loneliness. We'd spent over a year together in a small cottage on a remote strip of the west coast of Ireland. All we'd had during that time was each other and now she was gone. All I had now were my own thoughts. I had nothing really, as most of my thoughts were in fact memories. Painful ones. I was now the loneliest person in all the world.

I'd brought her across the country to Dublin airport where she was to catch a flight to France, where her mother was living. June Atkinson had been unwell recently and Cathy said that she wouldn't be able to live with herself if she didn't go to her. At least that was the excuse. The truth was that Cathy couldn't live with me anymore. Our relationship had become stormy in recent months and all we seemed to do was argue with each other over meaningless little things.

I had to let Cathy go, no matter what her true motives were. I had to let her return to the world of the living. I, on the other hand, was to remain in the domain of the dead, for only the dead were company to me.

I brought her to the airport on the kinetibike, but couldn't enter the complex because my face was still well known and I could have been spotted which would have landed both of us in a lot of trouble with the authorities – or worse. I pulled over to the side of the road and she climbed off and fixed the straps of her haversack, saying they were digging into her shoulders. I stayed on the bike, sulking. I forced a smile when she hugged me, telling me that she would return when we'd both had a little time to think things over. She said I'd be all right. She didn't know how fragile my mind had become, though. I had hidden most of my weaknesses from her. That's what men are supposed to do, right? Men are meant to be strong. Men aren't supposed to depend on their girlfriends for strength, which is what I had been doing since we moved to Ireland.

'Keep to a routine, Ross,' she said, holding back tears. 'Don't alter your habits no matter what. Do your shopping down at the village. Don't go near any big towns. And don't do anything stupid! And don't be drinking alcohol either – you know what happens when you –'

'I'll stay out of trouble.'

'I'll miss you,' she said, stooping slightly to look into my eyes. She pecked me on the cheek and her hand massaged my shoulder. It felt like pity. 'You know that, right?'

'Yeah.'

'I'll write to you soon enough. Watch the skies for –'

'Don't say that!' I snapped. 'Don't *ever* say that to me!'

'Jesus, Ross,' she gasped, backing away from me. 'What the hell is wrong with you?'

'I'm sorry,' I said, disgusted with myself for losing my temper with her. 'Those words reminds me of …'

'Forget *him*, Ross. He's long dead. He can never return to hurt you again. He can't hurt anyone ever again.'

'I know.' I nodded nervously as I scanned the cars that droned past us. 'I know.'

'I'll be in touch. Try to keep your temper in check. And try to keep your mind off that person and the things he did.'

'Cathy,' I said as she was about to turn away. 'Is this the end of us?'

'I just need some time, Ross.'

Her final words left me cold. She couldn't say yes or no. If she didn't know whether she wanted a future with me, then I felt that our relationship was over. Neither of us spoke again. She simply walked away towards the bright lights of the airport and soon disappeared.

I instantly regretted being so short tempered with her. But anything relating to Edward Zalech set me off. In truth, lots of things set me off. My moods had been unpredictable since we left the Guild of the True. A stubborn anxiety had been living in the pit of my stomach since we fled England, and it was growing more potent as time went on. I also suffered crippling headaches on an almost daily basis. I didn't feel like myself anymore. I was becoming someone different to the person I once was.

Sadness stung my chest when I lost sight of Cathy. I really wasn't sure if I'd ever see her again. My crutch had been swiped from under me. It was time to stand on my own two feet again. There would now be a time without distraction ahead of me, and I would be forced to deal with, or capitulate to, the many horrors that haunted me.

I steered the kinetibike onto the road and twisted the right grip and moved off at a modest speed. The bike could run on psychokinetic energy, but I chose to drive with petrol that evening, as I was training myself not to use any of my gifts. I was trying to erase the person I had been while I was part of the Guild of the True. It wasn't easy. The temptation to use my powers was rarely absent. I felt feeble without them. I guess that's always the way when you give up strength. You feel weak.

At first I headed for a motorway that would lead me to the west of the country, but after a few moments I turned the bike onto a slip road and headed for south county Dublin. I felt an overwhelming urge to visit the small town that I grew up in.

It took almost an hour to reach Maybrook. I slowly traversed the maze of narrow roads and thought that the estate hadn't changed a bit as I surveyed it. I soon made my way onto the avenue and slowed to a stop outside the house that once had been my home. The windows were grimy and filled with shadows. The garden was overgrown. Litter and dead leaves were bunched up by the front door. Some illegible graffiti on the front window. One piece of Maybrook had changed quite a lot in my absence.

'Bricks and mortar,' I whispered to the night. 'Bricks and mortar that now belong to no one.'

I wondered if anyone else really knew what had transpired in the sitting room of that house the previous year. Did anyone know that one of the most evil murderers ever to walk the earth had stalked the rooms of this abandoned house? I felt ill every time I thought about what happened on that terrible night. I often wondered what Zalech said to Dad before he killed him. Had my father been brave in those final moments? Had Zalech made him suffer? Was it swift or prolonged? Had Zalech watched the house as I now watched it? Did he stand at this very spot as he prepared to enter? What was going through his mind? There were so many questions that would never be answered. Zalech had taken all the answers to the grave with him. I was the only one who kept the questions alive. Zalech and Dad only lived on in my mind.

I took one last look at the house and doubted I would ever lay eyes on it again. There was nothing for me there anymore. I drove slowly along the avenue and out of the estate onto the narrow road to the south that led to a small cemetery. I parked the bike on the roadside, awkwardly scaled the tall iron gates without using my gifts, and wandered the gravelled pathways until I found Dad's grave. I sat for a while in silence with my head resting against the headstone. I remembered the happy days, back before my mother died. I'd been close to Dad at that time. We'd shared so much and laughed all the time.

Those comforting memories were quickly consumed by the images my mind had conjured up of Zalech killing him. My skull was aching as I tried to banish the false memories from my brain.

'I know you would have given him a good fight,' I said to the grave. 'I know you wouldn't cower at his feet. It must have really pissed him off that you weren't a quivering mess. He never got the better of us. No way. We Bentleys were too good and too strong for him in the end.'

I continued talking until my emotions finally boiled over and I wept so hard my throat and chest got sore. It was only an hour since I'd said farewell to Cathy and the loneliness was unbearable. I was breaking apart. The person known as Ross Bentley, who had fought Edward Zalech and Marianne Dolloway, was gradually morphing into a nervous wreck.

My mood grew dark and I wished that I too had taken a place in the family plot next to my mother and father. I often wished for a way out of life. Why remain alive when life is so empty? I had to keep reassuring myself that the future was worth living for. But now that Cathy was gone, I really didn't see much hope for me.

There was once a time when the mere sight or thought of her would snap me from the depths of the depression. She always found ways to cheer me up when I was down. Once she transported her mind into our cat, Nightshade, and made her dance like a drunken reveller. I couldn't help but laugh. On other occasions she would remind me of all that I had achieved since entering the Million Dollar Gift.

'You're not useless, Ross,' she would insist. 'Over the last few short years you discovered your gifts, won the toughest contest ever devised, joined the Guild, saved countless lives, confronted and defeated the greatest of foes, overcame tragedy and you fell in love with the best looking girl that has ever lived!'

Sometimes the speech worked, sometimes it didn't. Whenever it failed to lift me, Cathy would speak of Sarah Fisher, and how I had rescued her from the clutches of evil. That had been the most dangerous task I'd ever been involved in. We had saved the young prophet from Edward Zalech, who was planning to sell her to JNCOR, who in turn would use her to aid their nefarious activities. It actually *did* make me feel heroic that I'd delivered her to safety. Sarah was such an innocent and loveable young girl, and it would have been a great tragedy if we hadn't gotten to her in time.

Innocent and loveable, but also unwittingly powerful and dangerous. Her sinister premonitions often played on my mind. Sometimes I'd become overwhelmed with fear when I thought back to some of the predictions I'd found in her diary. Then it would be up to Cathy to cheer me up again. Sometimes with a hug or a kiss, other times she'd reminisce of the time we first met, in the English countryside on those long summer nights.

Those were nice memories, but now they were causing me even more anxiety. Now that she was away from me, I was struggling to think of reasons to continue on. Dealing with these ugly feelings alone was what I had been dreading for the two weeks since she announced her departure. I reached my lowest point as I sat there next to the graves of my parents. You couldn't get lower than this.

I was starting to feel the tearing chill of the December night and decided I had to get going. I zipped up my jacket to the point of my chin then pushed myself off the dirt and rested a hand on the frigid marble headstone. I bowed my head and said 'sorry' before 'goodbye'. Would he accept my apology if he could hear my words? I think he would have. Dad was a good soul. He was a wiser person than I could ever hope to be.

There was no true forgiveness, though. Dad was dead and I had taken his place in the world as the lonely man, as Sarah Fisher once described him. Yes, Dad was dead, like so many of those who I had been close to in my life. Being close to me was like a fatal disease.

I scaled the gates and mounted the bike once more. The road ahead was an empty one. A life of solitude lay beyond. To reach the motorway I had to cross through the western side of Maybrook, and as I did, a warm light caught my eye. I slowed the bike and stopped by the corner of Maybrook Road. The box room light was on in the Wrights' house. It was Gemma's room. My one real friend from childhood was only a few yards away. I had once endangered her life by calling her to let her know how I was, back when I was living at the Atkinsons' house. My stupidity had put her in great danger. The calls I made that night had almost gotten me killed, too. Marcus Romand hadn't been as lucky as I was.

I wished to go to her, to talk to her, to laugh with her. I couldn't be so reckless again. She might catch that awful Bentley disease if I re-established contact.

The window was cast into darkness as the light inside was extinguished. Best to leave Gemma to her own life, I thought. I started the bike, kicked off the stand, and was about to fire the engine when the front door to the house opened and Gemma came bustling down the driveway to the pavement. She took a glance in my direction, scowled at me, then continued in the opposite direction. I knew her eyesight was awful and felt no offence. She'd always needed glasses but refused to wear them. She could never recognise people in the dark. It seemed some things never change.

'Gemma!' I instinctively called after her.

She slowed her pace and looked over her shoulder. Then she scowled again and was shaking her head as she walked away even faster than before.

'Gemma, it's me.'

She spun around and squinted at me, then smiled hesitantly, 'Ross?' She cautiously walked towards me as that lovely smile of hers widened. 'Ross Bentley? Is that you?'

'I wouldn't say that name out loud if I were you,' I replied with a snort. 'It attracts all the wrong sorts of attention.'

She hurried towards me and the glare of a streetlight illuminated her face. She looked more mature and elegant than she did when we were friends. She'd grown into a beautiful young woman.

'I don't believe it.' She rushed at me and flung her arms around my shoulders and kissed me on the cheek. 'Ross, I can't believe it's you! I thought you were dead, you moron!' I got a slap in the arm then for my troubles. 'Why the hell didn't you …'

Gemma took a stunned step backward. It was as if she suddenly went back to not recognising me. 'My God,' she whispered, 'you look very different, Ross.'

'I am … different.'

'What happened to you?' she asked as her gaze drifted across the face that was scarred by combat, hardened by conflict, and weathered by loss. 'You look five years older than you should.'

'I've lived a lot over the last couple of years,' I told her. I'd died more than I'd lived in that time, but I didn't want to sound morbid by admitting such a thing to her. 'Enough about me, how are you?'

'Don't change the subject,' she replied instantly. 'How did you get those cuts on your face?'

I slapped the tank of the bike. 'Went too fast on this hunk of junk a few months ago and fell off. I wasn't wearing a helmet.'

'Just like you fell off your skateboard and got covered in dust? Remember that?'

'Yeah,' I smiled. 'It was something like that.'

'Oh, Ross.' Tears glistened in her eyes as she stepped forward and hugged me again. 'I missed you a lot, you crazy bugger. I worried so much about you.' She released me and looked me dead in the eye. 'I thought something bad had happened to you. Then your dad died. I was so sure you'd show up for the funeral but when you didn't, I thought that the only thing that would keep you away was death.' A deep frown twisted up her pretty face. 'Why didn't you come back for the funeral, Ross? Who doesn't attend their parent's funeral?'

'I couldn't come back.'

'You do know what happened to your dad, right? How he *died*?'

'I know *exactly* what happened.'

'They never caught the person responsible.'

'Oh, he *was* caught,' I said bitterly. A shimmer of the darkness inside was revealed for an instant. The memories of fighting Zalech on that lonely country road were as close as ever. 'He paid *dearly* for what he did.'

'The way you say that makes me think that it was you who caught him.'

I said nothing.

'Did you?'

'I don't feel like talking about all that, Gemma. It's not easy for me, you know.'

'I can imagine.'

'I'm over all that now.' I forced a smile as the lie left my lips. 'I'm fine now.'

My smile must have been an unpleasant one judging by the reaction it gained from Gemma. She stood away and looked a little wary of me. This was the last thing I wanted. I didn't want to scare off the only friend I had left in the world. I couldn't remain with her for much longer either. I was endangering her by being out in the open with her.

'Are you well?' I asked.

'I am,' she said with a weary grin. 'College is fun and I've made lots of new friends. I don't work at the supermarket anymore.'

'Brilliant! I'm glad you escaped the tyranny of Mr Reynolds!'

'So am I.'

'How come you're out at this hour?' I wondered. 'Not like you to be out so late on a school night.'

'Ross, it's Saturday night …'

'Oh. I guess I've lost track of time this week.' This was another lie. I no longer paid attention to dates or times or days or months. Every day was a carbon of the previous one for me. My life was alien to the one Gemma was leading. I was in hiding from the world of the gifted. Gemma was a carefree student. There could be no friendship between us. It was far too late for that.

I reached out to her and ran my hand along her cheek.

'I've missed you, Gemma. I've really missed you.'

'You're going again, aren't you?'

'I have to.'

'Will you ever come back? I mean, will you ever come back properly?'

'I can't. I made a mistake when I left this place for London and I will be paying for it for the rest of my life. The price of my error is exile.'

'Why are you talking this way? What have you done that's so bad?'

'It's impossible to explain.'

'Can't you just tell me what's going on, Ross? I might be able to help.'

'You can't.'

'Are you on drugs or something? Do you owe money to bad people?'

'No,' I laughed. 'If only it was that simple.'

'Come here if you're ever in need of help. Even if you simply need a friend. I liked you being a part of my life, Ross. Promise me you'll come back again.'

'I will.' Another lie. I could never return. 'I promise.'

I turned the key on the dashboard of the bike. The roar of the engine gave Gemma a fright and she took a few sharp steps away from me. 'Don't ever tell anyone you know me, or even knew me, Gemma. Do me that favour. Do yourself that favour.'

She looked crestfallen as I drove away from her. I shouldn't have talked to her in the first place. I'd now tainted her memory of me. At least she wouldn't talk about me to strangers, although I doubted that my enemies would come looking for her. I was surely off the radar. I would be safe as long as I kept my head down and didn't get involved in any *mischief*, as Cathy used to say.

I ran out of petrol before long and had no money to refill the tank. I was forced to use psychokinesis to power the bike for the rest of the journey across Ireland. I didn't speed like it was possible to on a kinetibike. I didn't even break the road limits – although I wanted to. I'd always liked being a daredevil but I was in no rush to get back to the empty cottage that night.

The ride took almost four hours and I reached my home in the dead of night. I rolled the bike up the driveway that arced around the cottage, and parked it in the garage out back. I found the cottage frigid when I stepped into the kitchen. The heating always took an age to fire up, so I didn't bother trying to get it started. Instead I climbed into bed, fully clothed, and wrapped the duvet around my shoulders.

I liked the cottage for the most part, but the silence on calm nights was in some way disturbing. It was more noticeable than ever now that Cathy was gone. I felt terribly anxious. There, in the quiet darkness, I was overcome with the faces of those who were dead: Dad, Peter Williams, Marcus Romand, Marianne Dolloway, Linda Farrier, Edward Zalech, Shinji Sakamoto, and worst of all, Ania Zalech. I mourned for those close to me and was haunted by those who once opposed me. It was Ania Zalech's face, though, that was the most troubling of all. I'd never truly gotten over what happened to her. She was too young to die and I was the one who was responsible for her death. It was an accident. There was no intention on my part. I wasn't a murderer. That didn't make it any easier to deal with. I was still responsible for ending her life.

On reflection I think something snapped inside me when I killed Ania and I never got a chance to recover properly from it. June Atkinson once told me that the human mind is like any other part of the body. It can be broken like a bone. It can become strained or torn like a muscle. It can get bruised and tender like skin. And like all injuries it takes time to heal, because, according to her, the mind can repair itself over time. If my mind had been injured by what happened to Ania, then it should have been given time to heal. That didn't happen. I was immediately dragged into a lethal vendetta after her death, one that claimed the lives of my father, some close friends, and many innocents. The last blow was dealt when I seized control over Edward Zalech's mind. I had in essence become him for a brief moment. I saw the look in Peter Williams' eyes when Zalech strangled the life out of him. I saw it, but I also felt what Zalech had felt. A part of his insanity and immorality had been passed to me as I time-scanned him. It had remained in some capacity. A piece of Edward Zalech's tormented mind lived on inside my own – I was sure of it. It had all been too much for one person to deal with and now I was paying the price. My sanity was balanced on a knife edge.

I cast off the duvet and climbed out of the bed. My mind was too busy for sleep, so I wandered the house aimlessly for a while, then tried to read one of Cathy's books. I couldn't concentrate on the words and soon placed the book back on the shelf and began roaming the rooms once more.

Eventually I found myself standing in the crisp night air. Sometimes when I couldn't sleep, I found that a stroll along the nearby beach had a calming effect on me. I was free of the deathly silence when I climbed over the dunes and onto the hard sand of the beach. A wind was rolling in from the great Atlantic and the sea was at war with itself. I stood watching it for a time. White explosions were erupting from the dark depths, creating shimmering shapes that caught the moonlight. But always the black water reached out and swallowed these livid white forms. It seemed the view was reflecting my own inner struggle. My true self was trying to break free. The blackness beneath kept dragging the real me back into the shadowy depths.

I stood there until the wind gusting in from the west became too icy to face. I turned my back on the raging waves and headed for home, following my own faint footprints in the frozen sand. In all the time I'd lived out there, mine were the only footprints I ever saw. That was how remote that place was. I doubted that anyone else had walked that stretch of coast for years.

I stalked up the dunes and took one last look over the vast, violent waters. As I turned away I saw a black spot on one of the distant cliffs. I watched it for a few moments, trying to ascertain if it was a person, or simply some rogue farm animal with a death wish. Eventually it faded from sight and I was left guessing whether my mind was playing tricks on me. After all, I was on the verge of a breakdown. I'd probably be babbling to myself and foaming at the mouth within days.

It was more morning than night when I returned to my bed. A sleep terrorised by evil dreams followed.

CHAPTER THREE

The Proposal

I opened my eyes and extended my arm across the bed to find it cold. That was always the first thing I did each morning: Reach out to Cathy, pull her in tight to me and hold her. It felt strange to be alone. It was the first morning in almost a year that Cathy and I had not spent the night together.

A lonely day was surely ahead of me. Without Cathy I had absolutely no one in the entire world that I could talk to. I'd spent much of my teenage years alone and I should have been used to isolation. My life had changed, though, when I met Marcus Romand. Through him I had been introduced to the most colourful characters imaginable, I had played my part in stopping two of the most sadistic killers the world had ever seen, and I had met the girl of my dreams. All of that had been withered away over time. I was back to being the lonely weirdo who wasn't worthy of friendship.

'Enough!' I shouted out as I got out of bed. 'Enough dwelling on the past. Today is a new day. Today will be different.'

I needed to busy myself and to lighten up. I threw on some clothes and made myself a strong coffee – a little habit that I'd picked up from the time I spent in the Scottish wilderness. I took a step into the back garden and showed my face to the solemn winter sun. I was trying to figure out a plan for the day when a black shape emerged from the bushes at end of the garden. It burst from the undergrowth, across the flagstones and came towards me at a phenomenal speed.

'Nightshade, goddammit,' I shouted as Cathy's pet cat meandered past me and disappeared into the shadows under the kitchen table. 'You nearly gave me a heart attack!'

I wished Cathy had taken the stinking feline with her. The cat was my tormentor in chief. Almost every morning I found a small dead animal on the doorstep, like some sort of twisted offering. Or maybe Nightshade knew I was under a lot of strain and thought the sight of dead animals each morning would tip me over the edge. She watched me very carefully from behind a chair and made a deep noise through her nose.

Cathy had practised her mind-switching gift with the cat daily for many months and that made me feel very uncomfortable. I had learned a lot about the gift of mind-switching when I was staying at the Williams estate. Mr Williams owned an animal sanctuary and one of the inhabitants was a gorilla named Argento. Cathy had tried to tame the beast by switching her mind into his body. The more she tried, the more intelligent Argento became. It was as if a trace of human intelligence and emotion was imprinted upon him; it was disconcerting how humanlike he was. It was unnatural. And she'd only practised the mind-switch with Argento for a few weeks. Cathy had been using the same technique with Nightshade for almost a year. The cat often sat with her on the couch at night and was enthralled by the TV. She sometimes sat on Cathy's lap when she read books, and her focus was entirely planted on the pages, as if she was reading the stories with Cathy. And that wasn't the most disturbing trait that the cat had picked up – recently Nightshade had made clumsy attempts to speak.

'I should have let you freeze to death last year,' I said to her. 'I was the one who saved your life and all I get from you is guff!'

Then Nightshade did the thing that made the hairs stand on the back of my neck. She started to meow over and over again, like she was talking to me.

'Stop that,' I insisted. 'You know I don't like when you do that.'

The meowing grew louder and more intense.

'I don't care what you have to say! You can't speak like a human, you horrible little freak. That means I can't understand you, so stop it before I make you into a hat!'

The sounds coming from the cat became more and more aggressive until she was hissing wildly at me.

The strangest thing about the little confrontation was that I was lying to Nightshade. I knew exactly what she was trying to say: 'Where's Cathy?'

I usually tried my best to avoid any form of conversation with Nightshade. On that morning I quickly caved in.

'She's gone away for a while, right? No need to be getting so upset about it. I'll feed you every day and I promise I won't make you into a hat.'

This appeared to appease the cat and she left the shadows under the table and nestled into her cushioned wicker basket in the corner of the room. My life had become very odd. Was it any wonder that I was going mad?

After finishing my coffee, I had a modest breakfast, then fed the nightmarish feline before getting ready for a jog along the coast. I walked along the narrow path that led from the cottage to the beach, then went down to the water's edge and picked up the pace. I was lost in daydreams as I jogged and went a lot further than I planned to. I got tired on my return and ended up walking most of the way back. I did some stretches when I was nearing the cottage then made my way towards the dunes. That's when I noticed something out of the ordinary.

I had spotted the footprints I'd made the night before when I took a stroll to settle my nerves. The prints were still clear to see, but they were now twinned with another set of prints. These were made by someone with very big feet and a heavy build judging by how deep the impressions were. The odd thing was that these second set of prints perfectly matched my own. It was almost as if someone had picked my trail and followed me to the cottage. Anxiety was rising from the pit of my stomach when I recalled the dark shape I'd seen on the cliffs the night before. Had someone finally found me? Had the Guild tracked me down? Golding's assassins? The authorities?

'I'm being paranoid,' I cursed under my breath.

I took my time getting back to the cottage and watched out for any sign of trouble. The landscape was as empty and bleak as it always was. I was cautious when I stepped inside my home, but found it empty, just as it should have been.

The afternoon rolled in at a stubborn pace. I sat by the window in the front room and watched dark clouds rolling in from the sea. I could think of no way to entertain myself and boredom soon set in. This was followed by a tingling of nervousness that eventually evolved into an anxiety attack. I stood under a cold shower for half an hour but I couldn't shift the heavy fear pressing on my chest. I felt like I was going to die … I longed for Cathy. I longed for any friendly face. I was so alone.

The only way of combating these awful sensations was to meditate. Back when I was living with Peter Williams, I would often practise shield creation – a little psychokinetic trick that saved my life when I faced Edward Zalech. I found that creating prolonged energy shields was also a form of meditation, and that I slipped into a kind of trance that kept any anxiety at bay. I paced into the bedroom, sat on the bed, bowed my head and began to form a circular shield around my body. The anxiety soon drifted away and I was at peace once more. I was saved from myself for a while longer.

This form of meditation was great at countering anxiety and depression, but it brought about something even more difficult to deal with: hallucinations. Whenever I broke off the shield, I would see the phantoms of friends and family who were long dead. That afternoon I allowed the shield to evaporate and found myself staring at Marcus Romand. He was standing near the window, his skin opaque, his eyes luminous. He looked *almost* real. I knew, though, that my mind had created him. He was nothing more than a figment of my imagination. Was it because I was so alone that my mind conjured up these familiar shapes? Was my mind trying to save me? Or was I simply going nuts?

I spoke to Romand. He just stood there looking out the window with a tense expression on his face. My mind was breaking apart. I was still sane enough to realise I was going insane – that was a most peculiar sensation.

The hallucination soon faded and I left the cottage and went to the garage out back. I needed something to busy myself with and decided on cleaning the front garden. There were trees at the side of the cottage and the leaves they shed throughout the autumn were scattered across the front garden and in a state of slow decay. I took a leaf rake and a yard brush from the garage, went to the front garden and got to work.

After half an hour my arms were aching and I was tempted to use psychokinesis to finish the chore. I fought the urge. I'd promised myself that I would only employ my gift for meditation, or if my life depended on it – and aching arms weren't going to kill me. I dragged the rake back to the front door and took the yard brush in hand. I'd only started pushing the brush across the paving stones when I noticed a shadow by the end of the garden, next to the gate. It was a *big* shadow and there was nothing by the gate to cast it.

I retreated towards the cottage as casually as possible, and watched as the shadow crawled ominously over the path towards me. It had to be a light–tuner. That meant either the Guild or a gifted assassin had found me. I didn't want to wait to find out if it was friend or foe. I drew in energy to fuel my powers and prepared to use it to defend myself. I would have to be accurate; the gifted rarely get a second chance in a duel.

My heart was pounding hard. Sweat was leaking from the back of my neck. Anxiety was choking me. My power was rising fast. I hadn't felt like this since I struck the blow that killed Edward Zalech a year earlier. It almost felt good.

Then I suddenly relaxed. I simply shook my head and laughed as I caught the sweet scent of cigar smoke on the chilled winter breeze.

'You're losing your touch, Hunter,' I chuckled. 'A light-tuner of your experience shouldn't forget to hide his shadow when he cloaks himself. And there is always the sense of smell, you know.'

'Do you honestly think I'd make such an elementary error, Bentley?' he replied, a playfulness in his deep voice. 'I simply wanted to see if you were staying alert.'

'I have no reason to be on the alert.'

'The gifted must always remain vigilant.'

'So I've been told.' I cast the yard brush aside and rested my hands on my hips. 'What are you doing here, Hunter?'

'This is no way to greet an old friend,' he said as he became uncloaked. He was only a couple of yards away, standing next to the garden wall with his arms folded. He looked a lot healthier than he did the last time I saw him, and was wrapped up in a heavy coat that stretched down to his knees. That intimidating aura of his had also returned. 'Do you forget old friends so quickly?'

'I'll treat you as an old friend as long as you're here *only* as a friend.'

'I *am* here as a friend,' he said, stepping forward and towering over me. 'A friend who needs a favour.'

'Good Lord,' I sighed. 'I don't think I want to hear this.'

'Remember, Bentley, you owe me a favour.'

'What kind of favour?' I asked, eyeing the big Scot suspiciously.

'It's a *long* story.'

'Give me the short version.'

'I will. Let's go inside,' he motioned at the cottage with his chin, 'and I'll try to make it as short and simple as I possibly can.'

My instincts were telling me to refuse him entry. He'd only want to draw me back into the dangerous business of the Guild. And because of the tedium of my life, I'd be very tempted to allow myself to be drawn in. Did I really need this trouble entering my life once more? Could my nerves even handle a conversation about Guild business?

'Well?' he asked impatiently.

I relented and moved to the door. I owed Hunter for not taking me back to the Guild when he'd found me the previous Christmas, and the least I could do was hear him out. I pushed open the door and led him down the narrow hall to the kitchen. I gripped the back of a chair under the table and slid it out for him as he followed me inside, then stood uncomfortably by the counter, facing him as he sat.

'Moving furniture with your hands, eh?' he said with a mocking grin. 'Cathy has you house trained, I see.'

'I've gotten into the habit of hiding my gifts again. It's safer that way.'

'Safer?'

'So I don't forget myself and use them in public. I don't want to go drawing the wrong sort of attention to myself or Cathy.' I didn't want to tell them that Cathy was gone. This would only encourage him if he was here to talk me back into the ranks of the Guild.

'How very sensible of you,' he grinned. 'Where is Cranky – I mean Cathy.'

'Give it a rest,' I said over his laughter. 'For your information, she's gone away for a couple of months.'

'Oh, while the cat's away the mice shall play,' he laughed. He stretched out his left leg and rubbed his knee, wincing. 'Damned leg is acting up again. Always like this on cold days when I do too much walking.'

'You're lucky *to be* walking.' I thought back to how his legs were practically crushed in the car crash a year before. 'In fact, you're lucky to be still breathing.'

'It'll take a lot to do me in,' he boasted.

'Yeah, so I've noticed. I thought you'd have recovered fully by now – it's been a year since the accident.'

'There was nothing accidental about that crash.'

'You know what I mean.'

'It takes longer to recover from injuries once you pass forty years of age. Especially two badly broken legs.'

'You should retire if you're feeling the pace,' I said sharply. 'It's a much better way of life.'

'I'm not ready for the retirement home just yet. I've got a few good years left in me.'

'I think it's best to choose retirement before someone else chooses it for you.'

'Oh, like how Cathy chose it for you?'

'Funny.' I took the kettle to the sink and filled it. 'You want a cuppa? It's the least I can do for a weary *old* traveller like yourself.'

'I'll have a coffee if you're offering.' He took a cigar and a lighter from the inside of his coat and showed them to me. 'You don't mind if I …?'

'No. Just open a window so that –'

The window unlatched itself and was pushed open a couple of inches.

'I still use *my* gifts,' Hunter said with a wink. 'You almost looked surprised, Bentley. You're starting to think like the normal folk.'

'Normal is good. People you care about don't get murdered when your life is normal.'

'That might be true.'

'I believe it is.'

'But you're not normal, are you, Bentley?'

'Not as long as I have you around to remind me, no.'

'I'm hardly lurking around every corner.'

'Some times I get the feeling you are.'

'You always were a little paranoid.'

'Just a little.' I turned and narrowed my eyes on him. 'Was that you on the cliffs last night?'

'Possibly,' he said, trying to keep the smile from his face.

'You stalker. I thought I was losing my bloody marbles.'

'It was a little late to have this chat. I thought it would be best to do this at a decent hour.' He blew a cloud of smoke over his head and watched me carefully. 'Tell me, how have you been?'

'I'm all right.' I only now remembered that he too had lost people close to him at the hands of Zalech. Peter Williams had been his friend for over two decades. There was also Linda Farrier, who he never admitted having feelings for, but I knew her death had been hard for him to deal with. 'How about you? How have you been since all that … trouble?'

'Same as ever.'

'You must be a cold hearted swine if what happened had no effect on you.'

'I don't usually talk about it.'

'I was only asking, Hunter. It's fine by me if you'd rather keep it to yourself. I know I've not been right since all that trouble.'

'Hardly surprising. You were dragged through hell and back.'

'Dragged through hell is right. I'm not sure about the "and back" part …'

'You're still suffering?' he asked, a genuine tone in his voice for a change.

'I'm not myself, Hunter. I'm something more than I used to be.'

'What do you mean?'

'I made a mistake when I time-scanned Zalech. I held the connection between us for far too long and I think I was *in* his mind – at one with him – for longer than was safe. I think my mind adopted a part of Zalech, and that he's living on inside me …'

'Nonsense! Do you honestly believe that he is alive inside you?'

'No, not exactly. Not his conscious mind. I know that Zalech is dead. But my mind was infected by his personality in some way. I think a part of him was imprinted on me.'

'What makes you think this?'

'I'm not like I used to be, Hunter. I don't feel emotions the way I once did.'

'I think that's a natural reaction for someone who's been through as much as you have. You've lost many who you cared for, and your instincts are telling you not to feel for anyone, because you don't want to experience loss again.'

'It's not only the isolation, though. I have vengeful thoughts. There's a rage in me. It's so strong that if I show the slightest hint of anger, it will all pour out and I'll lose control of my senses and my powers, completely.'

'Again, it's natural for a young man to feel this way. We're all angry about what happened, Bentley. You're not alone in feeling this way. And it certainly does not seem to me that any sign of Edward Zalech is in you. I listen to you now, and I hear the same brave young man I once knew. The only difference now is that he has suffered loss and endured too much loneliness. There's nothing of that monster in you. Clear your mind of all that horror and focus on the future, Bentley.'

'Thanks,' I was almost embarrassed to say. 'Maybe you're right.'

'Of course I'm right,' he almost shouted. 'I'm always right. Don't you remember?'

'I don't remember you being right all the time,' I said. 'I seem to remember that you play the odds too often.'

'I'll always be a gambler.'

'Sounds to me like you're gambling again. Have you been back working as an agent? Back to your exciting life?'

'Back to the grindstone, yes. Been a bit lonely, if I'm to be honest.' There was a sudden hollowness to his voice and he wouldn't look me in the eye. He just stared out the back window at the trees bending in the bluster. Probably thinking back to that awful night when Zalech did so much damage to our lives. 'No Farrier, no Romand, no Williams. Haven't got many who I could say are on my side. A lot of those who I trained up with are either dead or have become civilised.' He'd looked back at me when he said civilised.

'You once told me that we – agents of the Guild – were destined for lonely lives.'

'It's true, is it not?'

'Partly, I guess. I count myself lucky that I'm away from all that.'

'Enjoy life while you can, that's what Marie Canavan always says.'

'She's a clever lady,' I replied. 'You should take her advice and go live the normal life – or one that you can enjoy.'

'I'd probably miss the action too much.'

'Then you have no one to blame but yourself for the loneliness you feel. If you live by the sword, Hunter, that's the way things go.'

'It seems to me like you've lost your sense of adventure.'

'Damn right I have. Can you blame me after everything that happened?'

'You've got to make the decisions that seem right to you.' He looked around the kitchen and nodded. 'I suppose you could have done worse.'

'I like this place. It's quiet. *Usually* there are no surprises. I don't have to get up at the crack of dawn. There's a hot dinner in the evening. Warm bed at night.' I brought him a cup of coffee, then took my own to the other side of the table and sat. 'It's a healthier life, Hunter.'

'If you say so. Although you don't look too healthy now that I can see your eyes up close. Looks like something is eating you from the inside out.'

'Told you, I haven't been right since I left the Guild. I'll get over it in time.' I took a sip from my coffee and leaned back in my chair. 'Right, do you want to know more about what I've been up to? I'm sure you can put it in a dossier and give it to the Council.'

'Honestly, no. I'd rather lick dog shit off a pavement than listen to you talk about yourself.'

'You're an arsehole, Hunter.'

'Lighten up,' he laughed. 'Didn't you miss my sense of humour?'

'About as much as an ingrown toenail that I used to suffer with.'

That brought a hearty laugh from the big Scot that I found infectious. I ended up laughing too, remembering the times when we joked and laughed even while facing peril.

'All right,' I finally said. 'What's this favour you've come to ask of me?'

'Oh, that!' There was a sudden flavour of enthusiasm in his voice. 'I need the assistance of someone with a…' he leaned over the table and narrowed his eyes, '*very specific* gift.'

'Let me guess: It's one of my gifts?'

He pointed his cigar at me and winked. 'Bingo.'

'Hunter, I'm retired. I want no part in any investigation, adventure, assassination or abduction that you're planning. Don't even bother asking me.'

'You haven't even heard me out.'

'You have until I finish my coffee.'

'I best get right to it, then. One of our moles working in the police service in England – who's been there for years and is always reliable – contacted the Guild after he came across some intriguing information. It seems some of his colleagues had been monitoring a man called Malcolm Wilson, who was working in the British Ministry of Finance. They believed Wilson was taking his work home with him.'

'You mean they suspected him of stealing sensitive data?'

'Yes.'

'What's that got to do with the Guild?'

'I don't know the exact details, *but* the police closed in Wilson with the intention of capturing and questioning him. This happened in Liverpool last week …'

'And ...?'

'You didn't hear about the terrorist attack in Liverpool?'

'Hunter, look where I live. I watch TV once a month and don't have internet access. The world could be at war right now and I wouldn't know about it.'

'Right, the cops tried to apprehend Wilson in Liverpool city centre, and then a massive explosion went off and he escaped.'

'Was it a coincidence?'

'We don't know. Strangely, there has been very little information available on the blast that interrupted the cops that night. Interpol were then alerted, given Wilson's description and so on, and word was put out across the wire. The Guild was monitoring the situation but weren't convinced that it was *gift* related. One week later – yesterday – Wilson shows up again. Here in Ireland. He was spotted by an off-duty police officer at a bus station in Donegal. He followed Wilson to a hotel that's way out on the north-west coast. The most secluded place imaginable.'

'A good place to lie low.'

'Precisely,' Hunter said. 'However, it seemed Wilson was out of luck. Five armed officers moved in on him yesterday afternoon. This is where the story gets interesting. The five cops go in, they have Wilson cornered in his hotel room, and it seems like his little escapade is at an end. Then, out of the blue, the most senior officer, Detective Michael Clarke, inexplicably turns his weapon on his colleagues. Blows their brains out before turning the gun on himself.'

'He took his own life?'

'He shot himself in the stomach. Wilson skipped away without a trace. An odd streak of luck, don't you think?'

'No luck involved,' I said with a shake of my head. 'I would guess that Wilson is a mind-switcher. Once he was cornered, he transported his mind into Clarke's body, then shot the others, gave himself a not immediately life threatening gunshot wound, switched back into his own body and,' I fluttered my hands at Hunter, 'walked straight out the door.'

'My hypothesis precisely.'

'Great minds think alike, Hunter,' I toasted him with my cup of coffee. 'Now, what's all this got to do with me?'

'I left out one piece of information.'

'And that is?'

'Detective Clarke didn't die. He's on death's door, yes, but is still clinging to life at a hospital that is not too far from here. I want a time-scanner to go pay him a visit.' He leaned forward and stared me right in the eye. 'I want his past read.'

'A pointless exercise,' I replied instantly. 'You already know what happened. Scanning back to the event won't shed much light on the subject. Not enough to warrant such a risk.'

'Wrong. You haven't put as much thought into this as I have, Bentley. You see, if you scanned Clarke back to the event, you wouldn't be reading *his* mind, you would be reading *Wilson's*. And I would very much like to get inside that man's mind.'

'Why?'

'There are a number of reasons that I thought would be glaringly obvious.'

'Such as?'

'You may pick up his intentions to go to a specific place. I can then go to that location and capture him.'

'That's a long shot. What are the chances that he was thinking of a future destination in the middle of gunning down a bunch of cops?'

'I think it's possible. You could also get some sense of who he is working for.'

'What makes you think he's working for someone?'

'He was stealing very valuable information, Bentley. My guess – actually it's more than a guess – is that he was stealing for someone who was paying him a lot of money.'

'This smells like the work of Paul Golding.' I got up and started pacing about the kitchen. 'It absolutely *stinks* of him. That rules me out. Listen, I hate Golding more than anyone, you know that, but I'm smart enough to know that fighting him, or even investigating him, can land you in hot water. *Scalding* water!'

'Stop being so melodramatic.' Hunter took a sip of coffee before continuing. 'Personally, I don't think it's the work of Golding.'

'You're just saying that to get me on side.'

'No, I'm not. Golding's isn't very active at the moment.'

'What the hell is that supposed to mean? Golding Scientific is a massive corporation that is constantly active all over the world.'

'The corporation's legal activities are carrying on as normal, yes. The illegal side to Golding Scientific, though, is as quiet now as it's been for twenty years.'

'And why is that?'

'He's been relocating the sensitive sections of his operation. Remember we uncovered his base in Iceland? Yes, that lit a fire under his arse. Right now he doesn't want to be drawing attention to it. He's also very busy preparing, I would imagine.'

'Preparing for what?'

'War.'

'What war?'

'The Guild have made a decision to go all out to destroy Golding. They'll be making their move soon. I'm sure Golding expects it.'

'Why now?'

'The Guild have been eager to do this for a very long time. The incident with Zalech, along with the discovery of the clothing that counters psychokinesis, has forced their hand. They have been carefully planning out their strategy for the last year and now they are gearing up for a major assault. The Council and Sterling have gone into hiding – this happens when we declare war – to protect them if things go bad.'

'When will it happen?'

'A month from now. Maybe two.'

'I don't want to know any more about this.'

'You asked.'

'No, you came here as a friend who needed a favour. You wanted me to read some dying cop's mind and now we're discussing a war that's brewing. I don't like the way this conversation is going, Hunter.'

'Let's get back to the matter at hand then, shall we? Now you know why I don't suspect Golding. But if it isn't Golding, who is it?'

'Could be anyone,' I said. 'Could be some pariah state … mafia … tabloids …'

'This Wilson guy is a damned good mind-switcher. He's been well trained to use that gift. He's also been working in a highly scrutinised area within the British government for three whole years.

This guy didn't lose his house on a card game and decide to do this to pay up some debts. He's a spy, Bentley. A gifted spy. I need to know who he was gathering intelligence for. Because no mafia, red top or backward nation can train a mind-switcher. Anyone who has the smarts to train someone like Wilson and place him in the British Ministry of Finance is worthy of investigation.'

'If I were to help – and I haven't decided to do it yet – it would be for one day. No more than that. I scan Clarke, tell you what I saw, and that's it, I'm out. I'll have done you the favour I promised last year.'

'That's all I'm asking.' He smiled a smile that I did not like. It was the kind of smile my dad showed when he was fishing and felt the first pull on the rod. 'Just one day, Bentley. That's all I ask.'

'That's all you'll get.'

'Are you up to it?' he wondered. 'You had some injuries when you left the Guild.'

I knew he wasn't asking about my physical injuries. He wanted to know if my sanity was holding together after losing my father.

'I don't sleep much, Hunter.'

'I know that feeling. And you used to wonder why I drank whiskey every night.'

'Does it help?'

'Some nights it does. Some nights nothing helps. Some nights all you can think of is the past and the people – good and bad – who live in the past.'

'I still have Ania Zalech's face seared into my brain. And Romand's …' I finished my cup of coffee and let out a long sigh. I had been trying so hard to conquer all the loss and stress. Now I was being asked to return to the Guild. It was only one day, but I knew from experience that one day in the Guild can stay with you forever.

'You're finished your cup of coffee,' Hunter pointed out, 'and I'm finished giving you the short version of a long story. What say you?'

'I'm still considering it.'

'It's a simple job, Bentley. We'll be in and out of the hospital in fifteen minutes flat.'

'Can you promise that no one else in the Guild will know I'm involved?'

'I can assure you the Guild will not find out about this. No one will. It'll be just you and me. Just like the good ol' times.'

'If anyone ever found out …'

'Oh, come on! Would you listen to yourself. "If anyone ever found out." What happened to the brave young man that I used to know?'

'He died on a country road twelve months ago.'

'That was Edward Zalech.'

'He took part of me to the grave with him – the reckless and adventurous part. What remains is what you see. I'm just a normal person trying to live out a peaceful life.'

'Whatever you say.' Hunter dropped the cigar end into his cup, a dirty old habit of his, and leaned back in his chair. 'Scan the cop for me. You can go back to peace and solitude after that.'

'I'll do it. You just remember this: I'll be gone out of there like a bat out of hell if there is the merest hint of trouble.'

'There won't be any trouble.'

'Official duty as an agent for the Guild means your life will be in constant danger – your words to me last year when we went to track down Sarah Fisher.'

'That doesn't apply in this instance.'

'Why's that?'

Hunter leaned forward and grinned. 'Your involvement in this case isn't official.'

'You always have a smart answer, don't you?'

CHAPTER FOUR

War Stories

We spoke for a while longer before I went to my room to gather some warm clothes and my hiking boots. I knew from experience that investigations often involve sitting in a car for many hours. In winter that can become an uncomfortable business if you're not correctly attired.

I put on my heaviest woollen sweater, thermal socks and a fur-lined leather jacket. Then I grabbed my hiking boots from under the bed and sat before slipping my feet into them. I was already beginning to question my decision to accompany Hunter to the hospital. I was no longer an agent of the Guild. Only twelve months earlier I fled the organisation and swore never to return to it. What was I thinking? I was on the verge of madness because of my previous stint in the Guild and now I was going off on some crazy investigation with Hunter, of all people, without even considering the consequences. Could I be sure that this simple time-scan was safe? The search for Sarah Fisher had seemed a simple task with no obvious threats.

I rubbed my chest as the familiar tide of anxiety crept up from the depths of my stomach. I heaved in breaths and hunched over, staring into the black holes of the empty boots. This was one of those moments. A crossroads in life. Safety lay on one side, danger and excitement lay opposite. I was reminded of the moment when my great friend and mentor Marcus Romand was urging me to leave the Golding Plaza hotel with him. This decision felt as important as the one I made that night.

Then I wondered if this was really was a crossroads in life. Were there really two options and two outcomes? I had thrown caution to the wind and gone with Romand. It led me on a path of destruction, loss and violence. Along that road I had also forged the greatest friendships I had ever known, made countless discoveries about myself and the world, and had fallen in love. Perhaps the balance of stability and danger was level in both accompanying Hunter and remaining hidden to the world. Perhaps that same balance lies in every single decision a person makes.

I sat up straight and took a deep breath to chase away the fear inside me. I then realised that I had been almost completely free of worry while I talked to Hunter about the investigation. In fact, I had felt full of life and excitement for the first time in many months. It was only when I was alone, and doubting myself, that the anxiety returned. It seemed a little danger chased the blues away. Perhaps I could do myself a big favour by accompanying Hunter for a few hours. Despite the danger that was involved, time-scanning the detective was a more appealing prospect than spending the following twenty-four hours moping around the cottage with no one to talk to except Nightshade.

I slipped my feet into the boots and watched the laces tie themselves up as if they had a life of their own. Using the gift again felt good. It made me feel alive once more. I stood and zipped up my jacket and took another deep breath. I could see no sense in hiding. I'd been isolated for far too long. I owed Hunter a favour and would repay it. That's how I justified walking out the door with him.

'Have you got a mode of transport?' I asked as we strode from the cottage.

'No, I was planning on walking the entire fifty miles to the hospital.' Hunter rolled his eyes and shook his head. 'Of course I have a mode of transport. Remember, I've been doing this sort of thing since before you were born.'

'No need to be so smart!' I barked. 'You're a bloody weirdo, Hunter. It wouldn't surprise me if you'd been bussing around the country.'

'Wouldn't catch me dead on a bus,' he replied arrogantly. 'I have a 4x4 parked a few miles away.'

'A few miles?'

'I didn't want you to see me coming. I thought you might have locked yourself away in the cottage if you had.'

'Did you steal this 4x4?'

'I hardly went out and bought one,' he snorted. 'You should know the way I operate by now, Bentley.'

'I know you all too well. I know you're the most reckless person I've ever met. And when you're out and about in the real world you act like a common criminal. Which makes me more than a little wary of partnering up with you again.'

'*I'm* reckless? Look who's bloody talking!'

'I'm not as reckless as I used to be. I've changed.'

'So you keep telling me. Even though it took less than an hour to convince you to join me on this little escapade. You're as reckless as ever.'

'I'll end up turning back if you keep saying that.'

'No, you won't.'

'I might.'

'You won't.'

The 4x4, which looked strikingly similar to Hunter's old Defender, was parked on the side of the road, a mile outside the nearest village. We climbed in and he sent a shot of electricity from his hand that sparked around the broken ignition and fired the engine. He lit a cigar and blew smoke in my face and laughed before shifting gear and flooring the accelerator. The 4x4 lurched forward, almost breaking my neck, and we were on our way into the unknown. Only now did I remember how much I hated travelling with Hunter.

'Slow down,' I hollered over the growl of the engine. 'You shouldn't be driving so fast in a stolen vehicle.'

'You need to get out more, Bentley. You're starting to sound like an old granny.'

'If the police see you speeding they'll run a check on the registration plate and realise that this old banger is stolen.'

'So?'

'So, we don't want to get arrested.'

'Arrested!' He broke into a fit of laughter. 'We won't get arrested, you fool. Can you imagine the police trying to capture me?'

'I know they wouldn't stand a chance. My point is that we don't want to draw attention to ourselves.'

'I'll cloak the vehicle if a squad car appears. Try to calm down, will you?'

'Sorry,' I replied. I really was starting to sound like an old granny. 'Maybe I don't have the nerve for this type of work anymore.'

'That's a crock of shit, Bentley, and you know it.'

'It's not. My hands are bloody shaking here.'

'That's because you ran away after the trouble last year. You suffered a lot at the hands of that lunatic, and understandably it instilled in you a great deal of fear. The trouble is you ran away and never faced down your fears. You know what happens to a person when they run away from their fears?'

'I have a feeling you're about to tell me.'

'Their mind blows the fear out of all proportion. They become obsessed with that fear. Everything starts to represent that fear. They become fearful of doing the most mundane tasks, like leaving the house or walking along a busy street. They start to lose their sanity. Sound familiar?'

'Maybe.'

'I believe that is the road you're on. You haven't lost your mind entirely yet, but you will eventually. This exercise might help you overcome the fear and make you feel like the person you once were.'

'We'll see.'

'Trust me, this little sortie will make you feel a whole lot better about your life.'

'Hunter, I need to ask you one question: Is this simply an attempt to coax me back into the Guild?'

'I wouldn't do that.'

'Honestly, why on earth would you call on me to do this? Surely there are better suited people in the Guild to partner you?'

'Bentley, I don't like telling you this, but in all my years with the Guild I have not come across a better human being than you. And you're also a damn good investigator. And there's few in this world who I'd want by my side in a fight. As for the Guild, there's been a lot of changes over the last year. I don't like the way it's being changed. People are becoming very secretive. I've been forced to the fringe of the day-to-day dealings. I don't have many who I can call on to help me when I'm out of my depth. That's why I searched you out. I need to work with someone I can trust.'

'That's all nice to hear, Hunter. It doesn't seem right, though, that someone like you wouldn't be at the heart of the Guild's war plans. Why on earth are you out here in the middle of nowhere chasing down a phantom like Wilson? You should be one of the leaders in the war against Golding.'

'I haven't exactly been popular since the incident in Portsmouth. I think some of my colleagues are trying to force me out of the Guild because of it. In all honesty, there are lots of people in the Guild who have been looking for an excuse to stab me in the back.'

'I suppose it's understandable.' I thought back to the tsunami that struck Portsmouth and the carnage it caused. So many people had lost so much, and Hunter and I were partly to blame because we had followed Zalech without informing the Guild. 'I remember you and I were convinced we'd be expelled after that disaster. Remember that?'

'How could I forget,' he sighed. 'There is more to it. The Guild is going through a change at the moment. There's a war coming and when it's finished there will be a lot of jostling for power and position. At least that's the way I see it. A lot of veterans like me are getting the cold shoulder in anticipation of that power struggle.'

'You think there's going to be a change in leadership?'

'Not likely. There's no one on this earth who could dislodge Jim Sterling. The Council and the ranks of senior agents is another thing entirely. There are lots of ambitious people who are watching those positions with envious eyes. People who don't want to wait until agents like me are ready to retire.'

'I'm glad I walked out on the Guild when I did. Sounds like it's becoming very different from the vision that Jonathan Atkinson once had.'

'Cathy told you about all that?'

Cathy rarely mentioned her father, and when she did, it certainly wasn't about his work with the Guild. He'd practically rebuilt the entire organisation in the early 1990s, after he'd overthrown the previous Council, and their maniacal leader Brian Blake – who'd murdered Hunter's aunt. I'd found all this out by snooping around Hunter's home the year before.

'Did she?' Hunter persisted.

'Yeah. How else would I have known?' I gave a nervous smile. He'd kill me if he knew I'd found out about his past from nosing around his home. 'Anyway, the Guild seems to be taking to a dark road. Maybe Jim Sterling wants it to go that way.'

'Sterling is an honourable man,' Hunter said, almost insulted that I had questioned the leader of the Guild. 'I won't hear a bad word about him.'

'It might not matter how honourable he is if the new Council turns on him.'

'As I said, there's no one on earth who could shift him.'

'Why? You used to complain that he never got his hands dirty and that he rarely left the Palatium. How do you know he's so powerful if he never gets involved in the action?'

'Sterling is the leader. Leaders don't do the ground work, Bentley. Haven't you ever played chess?'

'I played against my dad when I was a kid.'

'Seems like you've forgotten the methodology of the game.'

'I'm simply making the point that he might not be as powerful as he boasts. Therefore, he could be overthrown by one or more of these ambitious agents you mentioned.'

'I know what that man is capable of. He's as strong as any gifted person I've ever known.'

'Well, my gifts are very strong, but I'm also terrified of carrying out the most basic of missions. Sterling mightn't have the bottle for a fight.'

'Jim Sterling has fought the deadliest foe imaginable and lived to tell the tale. I'm quite sure he'll be able to contend with a few arrogant agents who fancy a promotion.'

'Who is this foe you speak of?'

'Never mind,' he grunted. 'It's of no importance now.'

I'd only ever seen Hunter react like that once before. It was when I quizzed him about the Kematian – the great terror that had once threatened the Guild and almost destroyed it.

'He faced the Kematian, didn't he?'

'I told you it wasn't important.'

'Come on, Hunter. Did he fight the Kematian or not?'

'You're a real nag, Bentley, you know that!'

'Tell me and I'll shut up.'

'Yes,' he sighed, 'Jim Sterling faced the Kematian.'

'Where and when? I thought the Kematian disappeared a long time ago.'

'He did.' Hunter flicked his cigar end out the open window then rolled it up, as if someone might hear him. 'How much do you know about the story?'

'I know the Kematian's real name was James Barkley, and that apparently he was once a good man. He had banded together with other young gifted people back in the 1980s and they were planning to set up their own organisation – something like the Guild. From what I heard, Barkley was supremely gifted and that's what brought him to Paul Golding's attention. Golding tried to hire him and Barkley refused. That's when Golding decided to kill him.'

'Yes,' Hunter nodded, 'this is fairly typical of Golding's attitude towards the gifted; if they're not willing to join him, then they're his enemy and should be eliminated.'

'He's a disgusting individual!' I spat. 'I wonder how many gifted have died because of him.'

'Too many,' said Hunter soberly. 'Do you know what happened when Golding tried to have Barkley assassinated?'

'He hired a mageleton to track Barkley down. I can't remember all of what Romand told me, but somehow the mageleton found Barkley and his friends on a small island in south-east Asia. She created a tsunami that swept over the island, destroying it and killing all of Barkley's friends. Barkley flew into a rage, and in that moment he achieved a higher power. It became known as the sixteenth gift. The problem was that his mind couldn't handle such an immense gift and it drove him completely insane. Apparently he went on to commit many atrocities. There was also talk of him raising the dead …'

'Accurate enough,' Hunter said. 'Except for one detail.'

'And that is?'

'Not all of Barkley's friends were killed. One survived.'

'Jim Sterling?' I gasped.

'Aye. And he faced what his old friend had become.'

'Wow,' I breathed. 'And I thought I'd been in some spectacular fights. How did Sterling survive? What gifts does he have?'

'That's enough of the history lesson. Remember, you don't want to know anything about the true gifts or of the Guild anymore.'

'I don't want to be a part of the Guild. That doesn't mean I don't want to know about the single most dramatic moment in the history of gifted people.'

'I'd be expelled from the Guild if they knew I had shared that piece of information with you. The story of the Kematian is top secret. Try to keep that little anecdote to yourself, eh?'

'Who am I going to tell, my cat?'

'I don't even want your cat knowing about any of that.'

'Suit yourself.'

In the silence that followed I realised my heart was racing. The story of the Kematian was thrilling to me still, even over two years after I first heard about it. I imagined Sterling and Barkley on a decimated and isolated island using their immeasurable powers against one another, in what was probably the most important gifted duel there had ever been. Despite my apprehension in working with the Guild, I still had a thirst for knowledge of the gifted world. Ever since Romand gave me the first glimpse into the history of the Guild I'd had an insatiable desire for knowledge.

I wondered then if the gifted of future generations would read of how Romand and I had fought Marianne, about the search for Sarah Fisher and how pivotal it turned out to be; would they learn of my conflict with Edward Zalech, and of how I had created a new technique of psychokinesis to destroy him.

'Stop dwelling on the past,' Hunter said, snatching me from my thoughts. 'Mind on the present.'

'All right,' I replied, 'do you have a plan this time or are we jumping in with our eyes closed as usual?'

'This should be simple enough as long as we can get into the hospital room without being noticed,' Hunter said. 'The authorities think this unfortunate detective is a madman because of what happened with Wilson. So, despite him being on death's door, they will have at least two armed guards stationed at the hospital.'

'Will they be in our way?'

'I'm not sure. I'm guessing they would be posted outside the room. If that is the case, I will cloak us both and we'll slip into the room without being noticed. Then you'll be free to work your magic while I keep watch.'

'What if there's a guard in the room?'

'I think that's unlikely. I have some experience of situations such as this; they never have a guard in the room.'

'What happens if they notice us, despite our cloak?'

'They won't.'

'There's always the possibility!'

'You're going out of your way to be awkward now.'

'I'll blame you if we're caught.'

'Of that I have no doubt.'

I gazed out the window at the shimmering grasslands around

us, the dark hills to the east, the rolling grey clouds that caressed their peaks. It was a grim afternoon. Not too different from the day when Hunter and I travelled across Scotland to begin the search for Sarah Fisher. That inspired a horrible sensation in my stomach. Anxiety was never far away and I had to fight it back by turning my thoughts to matters unrelated to Edward Zalech. I tried to think of something else and only succeeded in dwelling an even darker image. The sinister figure of the Kematian filled my mind. I was amazed to hear that Jim Sterling had actually faced him and lived. That gave me some hope that the world would survive if he ever returned. The memory of the scribbled drawing in Sarah Fisher's diary dashed my hope again. I'd always felt since seeing that drawing that the Kematian still lived, and would someday return to terrorise us all. I'd never been very fond of Sterling, but now I hoped he'd stay alive and well for a long time to come.

The longer the silence lasted, the more that old nagging fear was rising in me and I was questioning my decision to join Hunter on this investigation again. I had to stop myself from thinking of darkness and dread. I needed something else to ponder as we made our way north along the coast.

'When did you go back to working for the Guild?' I asked to break my grim chain of thought. 'Last time I saw you I doubted that you'd be up for anything more strenuous than housekeeping.'

'Can you seriously picture me as a housekeeper?' he said with a smile. 'I'm still troubled by my injuries but I wasted no time in getting back to work. As soon as I could manage a sprint I was looking for a new investigation to work on.'

'Have you worked on any thrilling cases?'

'My first few tasks were routine searches for gifted children. They all turned out to be dead ends – all thanks to modern technologies.'

'What do you mean?'

'The Guild have a few people who monitor the internet for signs of gifted children – you know, strange and wonderful stories that can't be explained – so strange that they don't make it into the main-stream. This method of identification has reaped some reward, but more often than not they're false alarms. The kids I searched for had featured in online videos displaying impressive powers. All of the videos were doctored. How on earth can youngsters make convincing recordings of themselves disappearing or making objects move?'

'Simple computer programs, Hunter. I think you should stick to the old fashioned methods of investigation.'

'That's what I told those idiots at the Palatium.'

'I guess I was lucky I never revealed my identity in the videos I used to make.'

'Very lucky. You might have ended up like Marianne Dolloway if you had made yourself known in those silly skateboarding videos.'

My life had been no picnic since the Million Dollar Gift, but I was rather fortunate not to have been subjected to the type of life Marianne had endured. The mere thought of being manipulated into becoming a violent murderer like her sent a shiver down my spine.

'That's all you've been doing this last year?' I asked.

'No. After those wild goose chases, I was sent out on proper investigations.'

'Tell me about them.'

'Oh, you wouldn't be interested. You're out of the Guild, remember? You wouldn't like knowing about what goes on in the gifted world.'

'Shut up and tell me, Hunter.'

'I knew you'd come around quick enough,' he said, grinning at me. 'You're too adventurous to be cooped up in a cottage for the rest of your life. You need action, Bentley, if you want to feel alive!'

'Are you going to tell me about your cases or keep giving me half-arsed motivational speeches?'

'All right, all right. I guess there are two noteworthy cases. The first one seemed innocuous when I was first told about it. There were reports of a teenage girl in Cardiff who was walking into jewellery stores, post offices, banks and supermarkets and leaving with the contents of the registers or vaults.'

'A girl on her own?'

'Yes, that's why it came to the Guild's attention. The reports indicated that during each robbery she would enter the premises and suddenly everyone in the building would fall asleep. Then she'd clean out the registers. And no one could identify her.'

'What about cctv footage?'

'All cameras inexplicably went on the blink just as she entered each of the buildings.'

'Sounds like the work of an electro-psych.'

'That's what I thought. And I was right, she was an electro-psych. I'm the most powerful with that gift and that's why I was given the task of apprehending her. I was confident that she wouldn't present much of a challenge when I caught up with her.'

'What about all the people falling asleep?'

'That's a little trick a lot of electros can use. You shoot an electrical pulse into a person's brain and it brings about a temporary coma. Larger amounts of electricity can lead to permanent coma.'

'How did you find her?'

'The good old-fashioned way.'

'You beat people up so they'd give you information?'

'Yep,' Hunter smiled. 'You see, she took some very expensive diamond rings when she looted one of the jewellery stores. The kind that are difficult to sell on. Only a few shifty dealers would be willing to take them off her hands. I knew of one such scumbag and paid him a visit. He was tough, I'll give him that – I electrocuted him on and off for two hours before he gave me her name.'

'As I said earlier, you're not much better than a common criminal.'

'Violence is necessary when dealing with hardened thugs. That's why they're so rampant these days; cops aren't heavy-handed enough.'

'You're also a fascist.'

'Anyway, enough of all that. I got her name and tracked her down to a very upmarket apartment on the outskirts of Cardiff. She was living the high life thanks to her many crimes and never expected someone would actually be able to find her. I slipped into her place in the dead of night and created an orb of live electricity around her, so she couldn't move. I thought this would be fine, a young electro wouldn't be able to break out of such a finely constructed cage – I was very wrong.'

'She had more than one gift, right?'

'Right …' A shade of embarrassment shot across his face. 'The girl was also a siren. She let out a scream that almost left me with permanent hearing loss. I couldn't hold her and she proceeded to use a mixture of electro-psyching and pitch-shifting against me. The fight lasted more than ten minutes – which as you know is like an eternity in a duel – before I got the better of her.'

'I would have paid to see a girl knock you about,' I laughed.

'I doubt you would have done any better.'

'What did you do with her?'

'I drafted her into the Guild.'

'You see, nothing better than a criminal. You even hire criminals these days.'

'It was either that or execute her on the spot, Bentley. What would you have done?'

The serious work of Guild agents was again brought home to me. I'd found his story amusing but the result of his tussle with the thief was a life or death situation for a teenage girl.

'Well?' Hunter persisted. 'Would you have killed her?'

'No,' I admitted. 'I would have done the same as you.'

'Then you're no better than me.'

'Maybe. What was the other case you mentioned?'

'There was a report that a family had been killed over in Belgium. Ballentine and I went to look at the crime scene.'

'You and Ballentine working together? That family must have been real important.'

'The mother and two of her sons were partially gifted. Although they weren't affiliated to any organisation, it was still something we had to take very seriously. That's why two senior agents were sent.'

'How did the family die?'

Hunter took a long time to answer. This meant he wasn't sure if he wanted to tell me or not.

'Tell me, Hunter. I can handle it.'

'They were burned.'

'You saw the bodies?'

'The cops removed the bodies a day before we got there. Our job was to look over the charred remnants of the apartment for clues to who was responsible.'

'Did you find what you were looking for?'

'The apartment was burned, yes, but not in the way it would have been if a natural blaze had occurred.'

'Was a pyrokinetic involved?'

'I would say so.'

'You're not telling me what you really uncovered, Hunter.'

'One of our moles got a copy of the autopsy report. Seemed the family had been tortured with fire ...'

I thought of Rebecca Dunlow, a newspaper reporter who had died at the hands of a twisted killer with the gift of pyrokinesis. Hunter and I had found her lifeless body lying on the bathroom floor of her terraced house in Newcastle. It was a memory that still gave me chills.

'It all sounds very familiar,' I said.

'Nothing more than a coincidence. There are lots of gifted people who are sadistic. We both know that all too well.'

'How similar were the deaths to Rebecca Dunlow?'

'Not similar enough to suggest any link. I still believe Dunlow fell foul of Ania Zalech.'

'Don't mention that name to me.'

'Calm down, Bentley. I told you to face your fears.'

'I'd rather not think about her.'

There was a moment of silence before I decided to quiz Hunter about the terrorist attack that he had mentioned back at the cottage.

'Tell me more about what happened in Liverpool. Were the gifted involved?'

'I can't say for certain. The strangest part of the whole affair is that there's been no information to be had. It's like the entire police force has conspired to bury the report and the majority of the witness accounts. It should have been all over the news for weeks on end, but there was no more than two days' coverage. The story simply died because there was nothing coming from the cops.'

'Sounds like a cover-up.'

'It does indeed.'

'Did they even arrest anyone for it? Question suspects?'

'No one.'

'Perhaps Wilson was responsible for the whole thing? Seems plausible to me. He was being chased, probably panicked and used a gift to ignite the buildings. In the ensuing panic he escaped.'

'I fear there's more to it than that. I'm sure all will be revealed soon enough.'

'Then our little sortie might not be as straightforward as you claimed. Especially if Wilson has the ability to blow up buildings.'

'Now don't go getting cold feet, Bentley. There's no clear link. And remember, Wilson is not going to be anywhere near this hospital. That's the last place he'll be. All we have to do is scan the detective and find out any information that might be lying dormant in his mind. The most resistance we'll face is one or two cops who won't even know we're there.'

'And if I get the information you're looking for, what then?

'We shake hands and say goodbye.'

'I know that. But what are you going to do next?'

'You're not interested, remember?'

'I'm just making conversation.'

'You're best out of this, Bentley. The Guild might find out about this if you follow me. If they do, they will torment you to rejoin their ranks.'

'Maybe they'll need help in the time ahead ...'

'What do you mean by that?'

'Gifted people blowing up buildings in major cities, a war with Golding Scientific looming, and then there are Sarah Fisher's predictions about the Kematian and the great darkness that was to come.'

'Human history is littered with struggles, wars and tragedies. I have no doubt that such events will occur once again. The important thing is that people who are honest and good are willing to stand up to tyrants. Good will always win the day.'

'Do you really believe that?'

'Eventually good always prevails in any conflict.'

'You know something, Hunter ...'

'What's that?'

'You're not a fascist, after all.'

'Of course I'm not!'

'But you are a common criminal.'

CHAPTER FIVE

The Dying Detective

It was dark by the time the town came into view. Nerves tickled my stomach as the distant twinkling lights gave way to busy roads, bustling stores and noisy bars. I was practically trembling by the time we'd reached the road on the far side of the town that led to the hospital. Hunter, on the other hand, was perfectly calm as he steered past the entrance to the hospital grounds. He slowed the 4x4 for a moment, took a cursory glance across the car park and the front of the four-storey building, then pressed his foot on the accelerator and continued along the road.

'Seems quiet enough,' he said, taking a turn off the main road to a small housing estate. He parked the 4x4 at the end of the row of houses and killed the lights and engine. 'Let's not hang about. This is a quiet area and people who live in quiet areas tend to notice when a stranger parks near their home.'

'Why don't you park this bucket of bolts somewhere less conspicuous? A little further along the main road and we'd be in the middle of nowhere and we'd raise no suspicion.'

'I'd rather have the vehicle relatively close to the hospital. Just in case we need to make a hasty exit.'

'You were lying through your teeth when you said this mission would be safe.'

'I'm just being cautious,' he smiled as he opened the door and stepped onto the pavement. 'Nothing wrong with that.'

I pushed open the door and took a step into the cool evening air. It was colder than I expected and I felt the skin on my back tingle. I fastened up my coat then followed Hunter as he walked back towards the main road. The doubts about the mission were never far from my mind, but as soon as we'd left the vehicle there was a new confidence in me, and an anticipation of what lay ahead. The sense of danger had shattered the anxiety and depression, and hauled the real Ross Bentley to the fore. I stopped next to Hunter on the corner, close to the main road, and we nodded and smiled to one another. It was just like the year before, when we were agents hunting a killer through the streets of Newcastle. I never thought I'd enjoy feeling that way again.

'Will you use your gift to cloak us both before we enter the grounds or shall we wait until we get to the main doors?'

'We're already cloaked. There's close circuit cameras all over that car park and I don't want us showing up on any security footage.'

The strangest thing about the invisibility cloak that light-tuners, like Hunter, can weave around you is that you cannot tell if you are invisible or not. I could still see my hands, arms, body and feet as clearly as ever, and Hunter too for that matter, but we were invisible to everyone else. I'd been cloaked a number of times before and it always felt nerve-racking because it's actually hard to believe that others can't see you.

'No sign of police,' I said, scrutinising the car park.

'I told you there'll only be a couple of them inside. Hopefully they'll be in the canteen filling up with stale doughnuts and cheap coffee.'

Hunter looked along the road, then told me to follow him closely as he made his way towards the car park. We went completely unnoticed as we traversed the labyrinth of vehicles and dodged through the visitors who were near the main entrance of the building. No human eyes could see us. Robotic eyes, however, did catch us out; the automatic double doors clunked open as we approached and a nurse behind the desk stared at the space we occupied. Hunter slowed his pace, as did I, and we moved forward to the desk without making a sound.

Without warning, Hunter raised his right hand and used psychokinesis to knock over a stack of files from a shelf behind the nurse. She spun around in her swivel chair and cursed under her breath as scores of files scattered across the floor. As soon as she'd left her seat to gather them up, Hunter was leaning over the counter and flicking through the register. He was leading me to the stairwell by the time the nurse returned to her seat.

'Where are we headed?' I whispered as soon as we entered the empty stairwell.

'Top floor,' Hunter answered quietly as we took to the steps. 'According to the register there's two guards stationed here – as I said there would be. The two on duty have been here for almost five hours, which means they'll probably be half asleep by now.'

'I wouldn't count on it.'

'Stop being so pessimistic and come on.'

We quickened our pace as we made our way up the staircase to the top floor. The corridor was empty and practically silent as we entered. This accentuated our footfalls as we moved past a series of private rooms. Hunter appeared to be wandering aimlessly until we caught sight of one of the police officers. He was standing at the entrance to the adjoining corridor and sipping from a paper cup.

'It's a safe bet that our dying detective is somewhere on the corridor that cop is guarding,' Hunter whispered to me. 'I want you to lead the way.'

'Why me?' I whispered back.

'Because you're a precog, Bentley; you'll sense trouble before I do.'

'All right,' I said, starting off towards the uniformed guard. 'Here goes nothing.'

'This will be a piece of cake,' Hunter whispered over my shoulder. 'I'm right behind you.'

'I know you are. I can smell your foul breath!'

I eased forward, never taking my eyes off the guard for a second. I even slowed my breathing as I neared him. I tried to coax my precognitive gift from its dormant state, so that I would have some warning if the guard noticed us. It was useless, though, as much as I tried, the gift that I had neglected for over a year could not be woken. I couldn't let this minor failure stop me, and so I kept edging forward, and thankfully the guard didn't notice us filing past him and turning onto the adjacent corridor. Then the second guard came into view. He was sitting on a chair right outside the last door on the corridor. It seemed this wouldn't be as easy Hunter claimed it would be.

When we got halfway down the hallway, a good distance from both guards, I paused and looked to Hunter. 'Well, genius, how do you suppose we get past *him*? Have you a gift that allows us to pass through locked doors like ghosts?'

'Shut up, Bentley,' he hissed. 'I've done this a thousand times before.'

'I doubt that. I think you've done this once or twice before and probably got lucky on both occasions.'

'Be silent!' he insisted. 'Get back up against the wall and stay still.'

'What are you going to do?'

'Watch and learn, boy. Watch and learn.'

Hunter lifted both his arms and pointed towards the end of the hall, then leaned forward as he rotated both wrists like he was snapping an invisible twig. Suddenly two of the iron legs of the chair the guard was sitting on caved in. The chair quickly collapsed under his weight and he fell to the floor – making an almighty racket.

Hunter backed up against the wall next to me and started easing himself along in the direction of the felled guard, who was sprawled on the polished floor and using some very colourful language.

'Look at this crap they give us to sit on!' the guard hollered to his partner, who was hunched over laughing at his misfortune. 'I don't get paid enough for this as it is! I could have put my back out!'

He grabbed the broken chair and paced along the corridor, obviously intending to give someone a piece of his mind. Hunter and I stalled as he paced past us, still cursing under his breath about his damned job. Once he reached the far end of the corridor we made our move by swiftly crossing to the last door. Hunter took a look at the two guards remonstrating at the opposite end then eased the door open and pulled me inside.

'Right, you better not waste any time,' he said as he quietly shut the door behind us. 'Those two should be distracted for a few minutes, not much more than that.'

The room was small and bland, as most hospital rooms are. There was one window, opposite the door, with the curtains half pulled over it, and there were machines either side of the bed, in place of the flowers and "get well soon" cards that ought to have been there. In the centre of it all was Detective Clarke, lying perfectly still on a narrow bed. The only hint of life was a machine that bleeped to indicate his heartbeat.

I walked to the side of the bed and saw that the detective was much younger than I expected – no older than thirty. For some reason I'd imagined him as an overweight slob with silver hair and a creased face. The man that lay before me was athletic and had strong features, someone who had been cut down in his prime.

This threw me off slightly. I imagined that he might have a young wife and children who were forbidden to visit him. I wondered if their memories of him were forever tainted because he had unwittingly gunned down five of his fellow officers. Everyone probably believed him to be a callous murderer, when in fact he was nothing of the sort. This was a young man who put himself in danger every time he left for work. And that made me feel selfish for how I'd acted over the previous year. This man had no super power, yet he faced villains day in, day out. I was supremely gifted and was often too afraid to get groceries in the town near my home. The detective, and those like him, had no defence against the gifted villains of the world. It was up to people like Hunter and me to stop men like Malcolm Wilson. I now felt like a coward for hiding out in the cottage for so long. I really was standing at a crossroads in life.

I loomed over the unconscious detective then placed my hand on his pallid forehead. The last time I'd carried out a time-scan, my entire life had been altered. I'd become one with Edward Zalech and part of who he was had been passed into me. Even his mechanical laughter still echoed in the darkest reaches of my brain whenever I meditated. Time-scans were incredibly dangerous, but sometimes they could save lives. That last time-scan of Zalech's mind had brought me to the brink of insanity. It had also saved Cathy's life. It had been worth the sacrifice. This would also be worth the risk if it led to the capture of the mysterious Malcolm Wilson.

The detective's skin was cool and damp when I laid the palm of my left hand on his forehead. One wouldn't have to be gifted to sense he was at death's door. I shut my eyes and concentrated on the physical connection between us. The time-scanning gift slowly rose and I felt a shade of the man's inner self reaching my thoughts. I sank into a trance and my mind felt like it was floating down my arm and into the detective's head. I felt cold when our minds touched. I was sensing that the life within him was dwindling. He was almost dead – as was his brain and the precious memories within it.

Without warning there was a bright flash and my eyelids peeled back to reveal a medical team lurching down on me. Lights were being shone in my eyes. This was the detective's last conscious memory. I heard the voices of the nurses who hurried about the room. I felt the agonising pain in the stomach and across the ribs. Something cold was pressed against the chest.

This was of no use to me. I started to rewind through the detective's memories. As I went further back through time, there were flashbacks of being in the back of an ambulance. I heard a woman screaming. The detective was staggering through a hallway in a hotel, blood on his hands as they clutched his stomach. A door. A hotel room. Several dead men lying on the floor, their heads blown apart, blood sprayed over the walls. I slowed the time-scan to a complete stop, so that there was a still image before my eyes.

The detective had just fallen to the floor, the pistol still in his hand, a searing pain in his stomach, his murdered comrades lying either side of him. He had turned to the only door in the room and there was a man passing into the hallway beyond. The man was looking over his shoulder and grinning. Malcolm Wilson now had a face. He was slender, dressed in a black suit, had sharp facial features and his raven hair was slicked back. Wilson had just used his gift to kill five men and had casually walked away, but not before turning to laugh at the sole survivor as he crashed to the floor.

The bastard, I thought. There was no doubt now that this was a cold-hearted killer who had to be stopped. I was glad I'd play a part in his downfall.

Now, with renewed determination, I continued scanning into the past. It didn't take long for the entire experience to be altered. I had now scanned to the point where Wilson's mind had taken over the detective's body. I was scanning Wilson's actions and feelings and thoughts.

There was no hesitation in killing the five detectives. Hardly any feeling, except a slight hint of amusement that they were gunned down by their colleague's hand.

I slowed the scan once more and then a thought came to me. Wilson was lifting the gun, just about to fire the first shot, when he pondered his next move. I had caught him. He would never have guessed a time-scanner would have rummaged through his wicked thoughts and plans.

Wilson was thinking about travelling to Dublin once he was out of the hotel and the cops were all dead or immobilised.

'What's the point in hiding when the cops keep tracking me down!' Wilson thought. 'It's high time I visited Brofeldt!'

This was followed by a fragmented thought – one that he was barely conscious of. He pictured the street that Brofeldt lived on. A hotel called The Windmill stood tall over a busy street. A block of apartments stood opposite. Wilson was a crafty killer, no doubt about it, but he wasn't as crafty as I was. I'd just as good as caught him.

'Ross!'

'Hang on, Hunter! Give me a few more seconds.'

'Ross, are you all right?'

Light was spilling into the hotel room, chasing the figures of the detectives into nothingness. Wilson's mind became distant and intangible, moving further and further away from the time-scan. The light became painful to look upon and I fell back and landed in long grass. What the hell was going on? I raised my hands and pressed them against my temples. My skull felt like it was shattered into a million pieces.

'Ross, are you all right? Speak to me.'

'It's okay, Romand,' I replied. 'Just a headache.'

I looked up to see my old mentor reaching down and dragging me to my feet. I looked around, seeing the Atkinson house in the distance, the lush fields stretching for miles, the warm summer sun on my face, and my dead mentor holding me steady.

He stooped to look me dead in the eye and frowned. 'Don't worry. These headaches will pass in time. This can happen to some of the gifted wh–'

'Bentley, snap out of it,' Hunter demanded. He was dragging me away from the bed towards the cabinet near the window of the hospital room. I could barely think straight and was still looking around the room for Romand.

'Snap out of it,' Hunter whispered in my ear as we stood next to the cabinet, hiding us from the door. 'We're in big trouble, Bentley. Wake up.'

The word trouble did bring me round. The room sharpened into focus. My thoughts were my own once more – and were in the present and not the past. The vision of Romand and the Atkinson house quickly fizzled away and I became instantly aware of loud voices in the corridor outside.

'What the hell is going on?' I asked.

'Keep your voice down,' Hunter whispered as he jabbed me in the shoulder. 'There's something going on outside!'

'Outside ...?'

I could hear raised voices in the hallway. The cops were shouting out orders: 'Stop where you are,' and 'Hands in the air'. It appeared an unwelcome visitor had decided to pay their last respects to Detective Clarke.

I was about to suggest to Hunter that we try to escape through the window when one of the cops outside screamed at someone to get down on their knees. This was followed by the other cop barking more orders. Then there was a heavy thump before a single gunshot, which was followed by another thump. Then silence.

Hunter told me to remain silent then waved one arm in the air as he weaved a cloak to render us both invisible. Seconds later the door swung inward and a tall, slender woman with mahogany skin, high cheekbones and bright green eyes entered the room. She had the look of a model but her clothes looked distinctly military – heavy desert boots, beige combat trousers, a black tactical jacket and what looked like a metal gauntlet wrapped over her right hand and forearm.

She waited in the doorway for a moment and glanced about the room with cautious eyes. By now I figured she wasn't on our side; Hunter hadn't recognised her and that meant she wasn't a Guild member. We were in the company of an enemy assassin.

I looked to Hunter as the woman moved towards the bed. He gave me a short shake of his head, indicating that we weren't to intervene. I was experienced enough to know why he was going to allow her to carry out her work. We were in a life and death situation and we would gain the advantage if we knew what gift she had. The only way to do this was to allow her to use her gift on the detective. We were sacrificing the stricken man, but it would probably save *our* lives.

It didn't take long to identify her gift. She flicked out one hand, and in an instant my precognitive gift was unexpectedly awoken from its long slumber as I sensed that she was about to use psychokinesis to crush the detective's skull. I acted out of instinct, rather than bravery or common sense, and fired a shot of kinetic energy directly at her. The lamps in the room were blown by the force of my attack, casting the room into shadow. There was still enough light to see that I had saved the detective, but had failed to injure the mysterious female assassin. She had somehow deflected my attack, which is probably why the lights were smashed.

Hunter sprang into action as soon as she made for the door, and brushed me aside as he pounced forward. His invisibility cloak faded as he prepared to attack and the assassin turned to face the big Scot as he bore down on her. She hadn't the time to strike him before he fired enough electricity at her to ground an elephant. I was expecting her to be fried. Instead, she simply raised her right arm and the cloud of electrical sparks was drawn into the gauntlet that she was wearing. This took us both by surprise and allowed the assassin to go on the offensive.

She shot a wave of energy across the room that threw Hunter up against the wall. I was still feeling drained from the time-scan and wasn't able to protect myself. The wave of energy stuck me in the chest and I was blasted against the window frame. I crumbled to the floor with pains shooting across my back and shoulders. The air was knocked out of my lungs and I struggled to draw breath. I tried to raise myself off the floor but all I succeeded in doing was falling flat on my face.

Hunter took the fight to the assassin by using his light-tuning gift to create a sphere of blinding light above the bed that quickly filled the small room. The assassin was momentarily stunned and Hunter attacked with his other gifts. This should have been enough for him to gain the upper hand, but thanks to the unusual gauntlet, the mysterious killer seemed almost immune to his repertoire of offensive manoeuvres.

I heaved in a deep breath and grabbed hold of the window sill to lift myself from the tiled floor. By the time I was upright Hunter was pinned to the wall and was unable to move. The assassin was using a crush layer of psychokinetic energy against him – a very advanced technique – and he couldn't withstand it much longer. I felt terribly weak. My legs could barely hold my weight and I was struggling to summon my gifts.

I had to help Hunter in any way that I could. I summoned energy into my body and released it in the direction of the assassin. I thought it would be just enough to catch her attention. This was why I was so shocked to see her catapulted through the concrete wall into the corridor, her body a mangled mess of limbs, bones and blood. What was happening to me? I had lost all control over my gifts. One minute I couldn't muster enough strength to get off the floor, the next I was able to attack with a power I didn't think was possible.

Suddenly there was an crippling pain in my head and I had some sort of blackout. The last thing I remembered was Hunter picking me off the floor and dragging me out into the corridor past the remains of the woman.

CHAPTER SIX

A Killing in St Petersburg

When I came to we were in the 4x4 driving hard along a dark country road. I sat up straight and examined the rear view mirror to see if we were being chased. We weren't. Ours was the only vehicle in sight.

'What happened to me back there?' I asked Hunter.

'I was hoping you would tell me,' he replied without taking his eyes off the winding road ahead. 'You were acting real strange during the time-scan, mumbling to yourself, and twitching all over like you were having a nightmare. Then after you killed the assassin you lost consciousness and started mumbling again.'

'What was I mumbling about?'

'You kept repeating a name ...' Hunter took a deep breath as he looked to me. 'You were calling out for Romand.'

'It must have been a dream. It had to have been.'

'What?'

'Back when I time-scanned the detective, I found myself in the fields at the back of Atkinson's house with Romand. I fell to the ground with a crippling headache and he was telling me everything would be all right. It was so real, like a memory, but it's not a memory at all. I don't remember it ever happening.'

'Bentley, I hope this doesn't sound selfish, but you'll have to contemplate this little mystery at another time. There are more pressing matters at hand.'

'You're damn right there are!' I said, pointing a finger at him. 'You said this would be a straightforward task with little or no risk involved. All I had to do was scan a dying man and we'd be on our way home. Then out of nowhere there's an assassin killing cops and she almost killed us. And by the way, I got lucky with the shot that killed her. Real lucky. I can't even figure out how I did it. I was barely able to stand, let alone kill someone. I can't understand how I managed to summon the strength to kill her. Tonight has been an absolute disaster.'

'Calm down.'

'No, I will not calm down. That was not an attack by some lone amateur. She had the better of us – both of us – and we were extremely fortunate to have walked away from that hospital. That woman was a highly trained assassin.'

'I couldn't foresee an assassin of that quality being sent there,' Hunter said as he repeatedly thumped the steering wheel. 'Hell, I didn't think that anyone would want to kill that man.'

'You got it wrong, Hunter. We stepped into something much more important and dangerous than it seemed. I should have known Golding was involved in this. In fact, I did say he would be involved.'

'Golding? Why do you think Golding is involved?'

'You saw that contraption on her arm. It sucked up electricity and psychokinetic energy like a vacuum cleaner. There's only one place that produces hi-tech weaponry for the gifted. Golding Scientific. I told you Golding wouldn't be keeping a low profile. He never does.'

'I'm still not convinced he was behind the assassination.'

'Allow me to convince you. Here's my new hypothesis: Golding must have employed Wilson and placed him in the British Ministry of Finance. When Wilson was found out and went on the run, Golding sent out assassins to protect him. That's what happened in Liverpool. Wilson was told to keep a low profile, which is why he ended up in the west of Ireland, but by chance he was spotted by the police. When they tried to arrest him, he used his gift to kill them. Golding then sent in assassins to clean up Wilson's mess by making sure that detective would never recover and make a statement about what really happened in the hotel. It all makes sense to me now.'

'You have a vivid imagination, Bentley.'

'Face it, Hunter. I was right and you were wrong.'

'Perhaps I was ...'

'There's no perhaps about it! And I swore to myself that I would never take another human life after what happened last year. I don't want to be a killer. I left all that behind when I left you and the Guild behind. Then you're back in my life for one day and look what it's cost me. I have another death on my conscience. Damn you, Hunter!'

Hunter looked defeated for the first time since I met him. A young assassin had almost killed him, his assessment of the situation surrounding the detective had been so flawed that it almost cost us our lives, and he placed me in a situation that forced me to kill a young woman.

I was furious with him for dragging me into such a perilous circumstance, but there was no point in rubbing his nose in it. Hunter was a proud and brave man and he didn't need me, of all people, picking out his weaknesses. After all, I'd made some huge mistakes in the past that had almost gotten him killed, yet he never gave me a hard time about it. I tried to contain my sense of anger and remorse, and to break a very uneasy silence that was growing.

'I guess no one would have predicted an assassin would show up,' I said as calmly as I could. 'It was just bad luck on our part. It's not entirely your fault.'

'No,' Hunter said. 'I messed up. I should have suspected Golding would be involved. Maybe you were right about me retiring. I wouldn't have been so foolish a couple of years ago.'

'Only you know if it's time to hang up your spurs,' I replied. 'You've sacrificed a lot for the Guild over the years. You shouldn't sacrifice your life for them by remaining on this investigation alone. It's dangerous. As soon as we've parted company you should contact the Palatium and tell them Golding is behind all this, and that skilled assassins with fancy new toys are running with Wilson. I'm sure they'll send help.'

'I'll think about it.'

'You'll what?' I asked incredulously. 'Have you a death wish or something? You have to call for assistance. You can't face these people on your own, Hunter.'

'I will only call for assistance after I know more about the case and who Wilson really is and what he wants.'

'You're as stubborn as a mule!'

'No, I'm patient. Now, tell me what you saw when you time-scanned that detective. Did you get inside Wilson's mind?'

'For a brief moment, yes.'

'And ...?'

'Wilson is not simply a spy. He's a twisted murderer who takes a casual sort of pleasure in taking people's lives. He actually found it amusing when he saw the puzzled expressions on those detectives' faces as their friend inexplicably turned his weapon on them and started shooting. Why on earth are so many gifted people deranged?'

'I've always believed that the human mind isn't fully capable of handling these powers. The gifts are unnatural. In some cases people can deal with having a gift and go on to live relatively normal lives. Others can't handle being so different and snap.'

'I think there's a good chance that I might be snapping. I've had a real hard time dealing with it all this last year, Hunter. I didn't tell you before, but I've been seeing things.'

'Seeing things? What things?'

'Ghosts ... I know there's no such thing. What I'm seeing must be hallucinations brought on by the stress of what happened last year. My mind is seriously screwed up.'

'It's natural to have nightmares after what you've been through.'

'But that's just it. These visions of people from my past aren't confined to sleep. I see them when I'm wide awake.'

'Such things are known to happen to gifted youngsters as they develop their gifts. You have to remember, Bentley, that we know very little of what causes the gifts in people, and what effects the gifts have on the human brain – especially when the gifts are growing stronger and being used more often. It will pass, I'm sure of it.'

'I hope it passes soon, otherwise I might end up like Wilson!'

'That won't happen and you know it. You're just feeling sorry for yourself right now and you need to get your head straight. Now, did you see anything else when you were reading Wilson's thoughts?'

'Wilson felt frustrated that the police had tracked him down, despite him being in hiding, and believed that he would be better off going to Dublin to meet the *others*.'

'Please tell me you picked up on a name.'

'A name and location. He pictured Windmill Street in Dublin city centre.'

'And the name?'

'Brofeldt.'

'Well, well, well,' Hunter smiled confidently. 'This gets more and more intriguing.'

'What are you smiling about?'

'I'm smiling because there's a very good reason to be smiling. You see, Bentley, I knew I was right all along about Golding not being involved in this. I bloody well knew it!'

'Please explain.'

'I can safely say we are talking about *Elina* Brofeldt. And if we are, and if she is indeed in cahoots with Wilson, that would rule out any possibility of Golding being involved.'

'Why?'

'If you knew about Brofeldt's life, you would know she would never work with Golding.'

'Give me the short version of the long story.'

'Elina Brofeldt …' Hunter sighed. 'Where do I even begin to tell her story …? I suppose she'd be almost thirty by now. She grew up in a small town in Finland, had no siblings, lived alone with her father – not sure what happened to her mother –'

'Spare me the family history, Hunter. Why does she hate Golding so much?'

'Elina is a most brilliant mind-switcher. Usually it takes a mind-switcher decades to fully come to terms with their gift. Elina was different. She had practically mastered the power to transport her mind as a young teenager. She's also pyrokinetic, but it's not very strong in her. Her true talent was always in placing her thoughts into the bodies of other people and animals. This is what got her noticed back in the mid-nineties, when she was thirteen years old. She'd been using her gifts to make her pet dog do some rather impressive tricks – so impressive that she and her dog were featured in a number of newspapers. That's when she first appeared on the radar. The story was soon noticed by a Guild agent based in Denmark and he flew over to Finland to keep watch over Elina in case she got into trouble, or if trouble came looking for her.'

'I'm guessing trouble came looking.'

'Yes, and sooner than the Guild had anticipated. She'd already been forced to flee her home by the time our Danish agent reached her.'

'Why had she run away?'

'A gang of Golding's thugs went to her house and tried to *persuade* her to join the corporation. Golding's tactics back in those days were quite heavy-handed to say the least. They didn't bother with talent shows in the good ol' days.' He turned to me and gave me that familiar look of disapproval that everyone in the Guild gave me whenever my involvement in The Million Dollar Gift was mentioned. 'She was lucky, though. Elina's father was a Finnish ranger and he had the smarts to fend off Golding's team and to smuggle Elina out of the town. The two of them were on the run for three months, across Finland and into Russia, before they were cornered in a bus station near St. Petersburg. A fight broke out and Elina's father was shot dead. Luckily for Elina, Golding's henchmen were chased off by a combination of local men and a couple of security guards. Our agents finally located her some days later and smuggled her from a hospital and brought her to England for her own protection and for training.'

'So why did she leave the Guild?'

'I only met her a handful of times over the years, so I won't claim to know her mind. By all accounts, Elina was an impatient and over-ambitious person. She felt that because of our gifts and the sacrifices we all make for society, gifted people should be wealthy and powerful, above the law, politics and societal rules in general. Obviously this doesn't fit in with the ethos of the Guild and she decided to leave.'

'Where did she go?'

'I don't know for certain. The Guild tried to keep tabs on her but she soon went underground and hasn't been heard of for more than seven years. There was a rumour, however, that she was working for some agency in the US. There was talk back then that the Americans had set up a specialist agency – made up entirely of gifted people – and that she was a part of it.'

'Do you think the rumours were true?'

'Probably not. Elina's too greedy to be working for governments because the hours and the wages suck. I believe she's been operating in the private sector, or for some criminal organisation.'

'Not Golding's organisation?'

'I'm certain that she would never work for Golding. She hates him as much as anyone in this world because of what happened to her father.'

'I still think that assassin was working for Golding Scientific.'

'Possibly. Either way, this all raises more questions than it answers.'

'I'm just glad I'm out of it now.'

Hunter said little more after that. He lit his cigar and puffed heavily on it, as he often did when he was contemplating a difficult investigation. It was almost 4am when he parked the 4x4 outside my home. I asked him to come inside with me for a coffee or bite to eat but he grumbled about there being no time to waste. He was disappointed in me for not offering to help with the investigation, I could see it in his eyes, and it made me feel terrible about myself. I felt like a coward for leaving him alone, but I had made a decision after my father's death that I would never return to working for the Guild. I had suffered enough. It was best for me to quit while I was ahead.

Before we said farewell, Hunter handed me his phone and told me to use online maps to locate Windmill Street. I told him he should join the rest of the world in the twenty-first century and learn how to use the internet himself. He just grunted at me. It took only a couple of minutes to find the street through an online map. He simply muttered something akin to 'thanks' before shifting the gear stick into first.

'I'll take that as your way of telling me to get out,' I said crossly.

'Take it whatever way you want,' Hunter replied without looking at me. 'Have a nice life, Bentley. I'm sure you'll have no regrets when you die of old age.'

'I saved your life back there at the hospital,' I shouted at him as I pushed the door open and stepped out onto the road. 'The least you could do is –'

He used his gift to pull the door shut as soon as I got out. Within a second the 4x4 was screeching away along the narrow road and I was left standing there in the cold darkness shouting profanities at the night. I didn't turn to my home until the rear lights of the vehicle had melted into the night.

I didn't bother using a key to open the front door. I was angry and used my power to force the lock and to push the door open. I stomped through to the kitchen, still cursing under my breath, still disgusted by the way Hunter had sped off. How could anyone be so damned rude? I'd done him the favour I promised him. I had time-scanned the detective. I had produced the lead that he could not uncover by himself. I had saved his life. And after all that he dismisses my concerns for his safety and basically tells me to bugger off before nearly running me over.

And that wasn't the worst of it. That thing he'd said. I couldn't get those words out of my mind.

'I'm sure you'll have no regrets when you die of old age.'

By saying that, and not allowing me to respond, he'd taken the moral high ground and left me standing there like I'd betrayed him or something. Actually, the more I thought about it, what he'd said was even worse than any insult. What he'd said had gotten under my skin, and after half an hour of moping around the cottage I was tormented by it. Did it mean I was selfish? Cowardly? Was it some old Guild insult? Oh, if you die of old age it means you aren't a real warrior of the Guild. Only those who met death during combat were honourable. That's the way I interpreted it.

An hour later I was lying in my bed listening to silence. Hunter's last words were still on my mind. Did I want to be lying in a bed like this when my body had finally capitulated to the ravages of time in ultimate indignity, unable to walk, talk, feed or breathe? Would I, in those final moments as I clung to life for the sake of living, picture the brave men and women of the Guild who lived lives of adventure, who had cast aside fear for the embrace of courage as their doom approached? How lonely and small I would feel as I desperately searched out another breath of air tainted by the stench of my own death.

One cannot easily trade war and action for the long limp on into obscurity. Hunter knew that sentence would torment me. It wouldn't simply pass with that night. Day by day that image of the elderly and infirm Ross Bentley dying in a bed would eat at me and become more and more ravenous.

'Swine,' I sighed. 'What an absolute swine of a man!'

My thoughts were filled with Hunter's words, the vision of Romand that I'd had during the time-scan, the twisted motives of Wilson, and the struggle and killing of the unnamed assassin at the hospital. I don't know what time it was when I eventually surrendered to fatigue, but I do know what time I woke up, and I remember what woke me.

I'd had a nightmare about killing the woman at the hospital and broke free of it by sitting up and pulling in a deep breath. I found myself staring at the clock by the window and it read 8am. Standing next to the clock was the ghostly figure of Romand. Another hallucination. A figment of my mind that somehow acted outside of the confines of my consciousness. He turned to look at me then faded quickly, like a wisp of smoke.

It was my mind playing tricks on me. I knew that. But still it was like he'd visited me from the great beyond with a silent message: I am dead. I was a warrior who fought to save you. I went out on my shield and all that I could have been was stolen from me. Would you allow another to share my fate? My greatest friend Hunter fights alone while you lie here hiding.

I was acting like a coward. I'd been acting like a coward for months. Being so damned cowardly had almost driven me mad. I couldn't wander an empty house while Hunter was off tracking down assassins. I feared for his safety and I didn't want him having all the fun to himself. And I didn't like that he'd had the last word. I'd made up my mind before I even climbed out of bed. I was going to follow Hunter. I was going to help him stop Wilson and Brofeldt from completing whatever diabolical plot they had concocted.

I dumped a bag of dried cat food in the back garden and figured Nightshade would be smart enough to open it. There was enough to keep her fat for a couple of weeks. I wouldn't be gone that long anyway. I figured a few days at most would be enough time to find and capture Wilson and Brofeldt.

I didn't bother packing supplies or even a change of clothes. I simply locked up the cottage and headed for the shed at the back of the property. It was time to give the kinetibike a proper run – without petrol.

CHAPTER SEVEN

The World's Most Expensive Fish

I reached the centre of Dublin city around 11am and slowed the kinetibike and allowed it to run on petrol instead of psychokinetic power. I'd pushed the bike to its limits on the motorways that dissected the country and it had held up pretty well, despite not being used properly for more than a year. I, on the other hand, hadn't held up as well as expected; travelling on a bike at 500kmph through an icy downpour for more than two hours had left me numb and aching from head to toe. I was understandably a little dizzy as I drove along the packed streets of the city. I almost fell off at one point, while I was stopped at a red light. I used my power to stabilise the bike and to stop me hitting the road. This was noticed by a child sitting in the backseat of a car next to me. She just stared at me through the window and smiled when I winked at her. It was a good thing her parents hadn't seen this little psychokinetic cameo. I would have to be more careful and not push myself as hard as I had that morning.

By noon I'd driven up and down Windmill Street four times and had failed to spot Hunter. It was pointless to keep doing laps so I opted to park the bike in an underground car park nearby and to continue my search on foot. The pavements were bustling with people and it made the search next to impossible. By 1pm I was loitering in the doorway of an empty store and scanning the shoppers as they filed past. I waited there for a long while and used the time to examine the buildings on both sides of the road. Further along the pavement was the Windmill Hotel. It was just like I had seen it in the time-scan; four storeys of grey concrete with tall windows spanning the ground floor. There were lines of department stores either side of it. The other side of the road was dominated by two large office buildings, with a number of small bars and restaurants breaking the monotony. In the centre of this, directly facing the hotel, was a modest apartment building. I figured that if Wilson was hiding somewhere on the street it would be either in the hotel or the apartment building. I suspected it was the latter – I'd gotten a sense of that during the time-scan.

Before long I'd lost patience and decided to make my way to the hotel, in the hope that Hunter might be there. After all, it would be the best place to keep watch for Wilson. I walked slowly along the pavement, trying my best to look casual while shielding my face from the apartment block across the road. Then, as I moved close to the entrance of the hotel, I felt my precognitive powers rising and warning me of some contact or attack – I couldn't tell which. Before I had time to turn, my arm was grabbed and a tall man moved to my side.

'The most famous gifted person on the planet, out in the open, hanging about in the shadow of an apartment block where two assassins are holed up.' Hunter shook his head as he looked down at me. 'I take back everything I said about you being a good agent, Bentley.'

'I wouldn't be out here risking my neck if you hadn't stormed off last night like a moody little girl, so don't blame me for being reckless.'

'Shut up. I stormed off for a good reason.'

'What reason?'

'I'll tell you later. We need to get off this street before we're seen.'

'Nobody recognises me anymore, Hunter.'

'I suppose the general public like to forget internet sensations who embarrass themselves while the entire world watches.'

'Shut up, Hunter!'

'Don't you like my jokes, Bentley?' the big Scot grinned. 'Anyway, I wasn't referring to you being noticed by a couch potato, I meant if Wilson or Brofeldt are watching the street.'

He released my arm and walked ahead to the revolving glass doors of the hotel. I followed him after I'd looked around the street to make sure I wasn't being followed. No one was watching me. Nothing appeared to be out of place.

I pushed through the entrance and caught up with Hunter as he approached the desk. There weren't many people hanging around the foyer. Just a couple of elderly tourists studying a paper map and two younger tourists sipping coffee by the window that overlooked the busy street. Everything was as it should have been.

'I need a room for two,' Hunter said gruffly to the clerk. He rummaged in his trouser pockets then placed a few crumpled-up notes on the counter. 'Is that enough?'

The clerk, who was a young man with sharp eyes and a narrow face, looked at him, then at me, then the money and grinned.

'Seems like you two are in a big hurry to get into a room,' he said, trying to hide his amusement.

'What's that supposed to mean?' Hunter asked, leaning forward over the counter and staring down at the young man. 'What are you implying?'

'Oh, nothing, sir,' the clerk said as he typed into a computer that was hidden under the counter. 'Name?'

'Mr Smith. And that is my er …' Hunter looked over his shoulder at me and frowned. 'This is my son.'

'Of course he is,' the clerk said with a smirk. Then he glanced at me and his face went long with recognition. 'Hey, I know you, don't I?'

'I don't think so, mate,' I replied, inclining my head in a ridiculous attempt to hide my face. 'You must have me confused with someone else.'

'I do know you.' The clerk pointed at me and nodded. 'You're in a boy band, aren't you?'

'Oh … yeah, you got me there. Listen, I'd appreciate it if you didn't tell anyone that I'm staying here. You might have hordes of people outside this hotel if you do. Believe me, it's happened to me before.'

'Mum's the word,' the clerk said with an exaggerated wink. 'No wonder you two want your stay here to be incognito.'

'What's that supposed to mean?' Hunter growled. 'I don't like your tone one bit.'

'This is my protector,' I said to the clerk. 'He's a very short-tempered man. That's what makes him such a good bodyguard. Now, could we get a key?'

'Certainly.' The clerk swiped the notes off the counter and

replaced it seconds later with some loose change and a key. 'Room 408.'

'Does it overlook the street outside?'

'As a matter of fact it does. Would you prefer a room overlooking the car park out back?'

I took the key and nodded to him as courteously as I could. '408 will do just fine.'

'What a little shit,' Hunter moaned as we crossed the lobby and took to the staircase. There was an elevator in the reception area but agents never used them. The staircase was always the safer route to take. 'Winking and giggling at us like that. He should be more careful of who he laughs at!'

'You know what he was thinking, right?'

'I know exactly what he was thinking! Let's not speak of it again, eh?'

'Agreed.'

We scoped the place out as best we could as we made our way to the fourth floor. It was prudent in such situations to know where the fire exits, dead ends, hiding places and cameras were located. Room 408 was on the top floor, at the end of a long hallway with no fire exits nearby. Hunter didn't like it. I liked it less; there was no easy way out if we found ourselves in a fight.

The room was small and had that unimaginative vibe that all hotel rooms have. There were two very narrow beds, a small bathroom, a TV that you had to pay to watch and a desk with a kettle and two cups on it. None of this mattered. The important thing was the large window facing the road which was exactly what we needed. From there we could watch for any sign of Wilson and Brofeldt. Hunter pulled two chairs from the side of the desk and placed them by the window. I had the feeling we'd spend most of our time sitting on them as we held vigil over Windmill Street.

'Are you tired?' Hunter asked as he set down a haversack next to the window. 'You should get some rest now if you need it.'

'Sleep is the last thing I want.' I sat next to the window and studied the road and the pavements outside. It was near impossible to identify any faces from our lofty position. We did, however, have a perfect view of the block of apartments across the street. 'Hopefully these two won't keep us waiting. This chair will be torture after a couple of hours.'

'Let's not invest in hope, Bentley.' Hunter sat next to me and stretched out his left leg with a groan. 'This could take an hour or a week. We'll just have to be patient.'

'What's in the haversack?'

'Spare clothes, cigars, whiskey, binoculars and a laptop.'

'I didn't think you knew how to use a laptop.' I had a chuckle at his expense before returning my gaze to the street. 'And what happens if we do spot them? What then?'

'We'll watch them at first. We have to know what they're up to before we contact the Guild.'

'Can we handle these two if things don't go according to plan?'

'Of course we can. Wilson and Brofeldt might pose a serious threat to normal people, but we're the gifted soldiers that spies like them have nightmares about.'

'I somehow doubt that. Wilson doesn't seem like a man who fears much.'

'We'll see about that when the time comes.'

'I guess we will,' I replied, before lifting Hunter's laptop from the floor. I powered it up and connected it to one of the many wifi signals available.

'What are you doing?' Hunter wondered.

'I want to see what's being said about the incident at the hospital last night.'

There was a lot being said. The internet was alive with news reports and vague theories about what had happened the previous night.

'What does it say?' Hunter asked. 'Are there any details?'

'They're claiming it was the work of terrorists.'

'That seems to be the excuse for everything these days.'

'Damn it,' I hissed as I read through one of the reports. 'Detective Clarke died during the night.'

'That's hardly surprising. He was on death's door when we got there.'

'I thought I'd saved him.'

'You did for a short time. It isn't your fault, Bentley.'

'It still upsets me, though. Clarke is yet another innocent person who was killed because of the struggles of the gifted.'

'Get used to it,' Hunter said. 'He won't be the last.'

'I had a feeling you'd say that.'

Nothing out of the ordinary happened during the first few hours of our stakeout and I decided on having a shower as darkness crept over the city and the lights of the street below pained my eyes. It wasn't like the penthouse bathroom of the Golding Plaza in London but it was a welcome change to the unpredictable plumbing of my isolated cottage. I returned to the room to find Hunter hunched over, with his legs crossed and staring at the building through a pair of binoculars. He looked ridiculous.

'You know, some woman is going to notice you staring through those things and call the police.'

'Highly unlikely, seeing as though I have an invisibility barrier set up in front of the window. No one outside can see anything in this room other than darkness.'

'Always thinking ahead, eh.' I sat next to him and examined the road below. 'See anything out of the ordinary yet?'

'Nothing.' He raised the binoculars and scanned the windows of the apartment block. Some were filled with shadows, others were warmed by lamps. There was no one in sight. 'It's only a matter of time.'

'Crafty spies,' I sighed. 'You know, my father used to read spy novels all the time. I've read a few myself.'

'I sense the coming of an outlandish theory …'

'Well, now that you mention it, I do have a new theory. I was thinking while having a shower that perhaps the rumours about Brofeldt were true. What if she was, and still is, working for a secret American agency. Maybe Wilson is also working for them. In spy novels governments are always spying on each other. Maybe the Americans hired Wilson and Brofeldt to pry into the British government's financial dealings. How about that?'

'The spy novels you read were obviously based on the cold war,' Hunter replied without taking his eyes from the binoculars. 'I'm quite sure the Americans would be capable of using computers to hack into the British databases instead of planting mind-switchers directly into their departments. These people are too rare and valuable to be put in harm's way when a computer can do their work more efficiently. No, there's some other explanation. There's something more sinister at work here.'

'I think it's a more likely scenario than Wilson and Brofeldt working for criminals.'

'I would rule out both,' Hunter said. He handed the binoculars to me and leaned back in his chair and lit a cigar. 'I can't figure it all out right now. I need more information. There is, however, another possibility that I have been mulling over.'

'And that is?'

'That Wilson and Brofeldt are only two of a whole host of spies who are working together. Enough spies to do more than simply spy. Enough spies to *influence*. That's what mind-switchers are best at. They influence the minds of others.'

'You think there's a bunch of them placed in government agencies and using their gifts to influence the decisions of more important people?'

'That's my current theory, yes.'

'Seems plausible,' I nodded. 'It leads us back to the same question: Who are they working for?'

'They could be working for themselves. Perhaps they are a group of individuals with a common cause or bond. They could be fanatics who believe they can bring about great change in the world if they could seize control of a powerful government. Groups of people don't always need a leader, Bentley.'

'It helps to have a leader, Hunter. That way they stay focused.'

'Having a leader can be construed as having a weakness. When there is a leader, people become dependent upon him or her, and if the leader is suddenly removed, the group can be left in disarray. Remember we discussed the game of chess? Yes. Kill the king. End the game.'

'The Guild has a leader. Does that make us weak?'

'*Us*?' He glanced at me and smiled.

'You know what I mean.'

'Not in the Guild's case, no. We have a very strict structure set up in our organisation. If our leader was to fall, then the Council would elect a new person within hours.'

'Who would get the vote if Sterling was killed?'

'I don't know. Not me at any rate. But this talk is folly, Sterling is probably the most difficult person in the world to kill.'

'Oh yes, I forgot you seem to think he's infallible.'

'Not infallible. Just wise and powerful, very well protected and very well hidden. Even I don't know where he is right now.'

'Maybe Wilson and Brofeldt are working for someone just as powerful. It's not impossible, is it?'

'Let's hope it is. I would not like to think there's an enemy out there who is so strong with the true gifts.'

'You know, all these theories go to mud when we consider the assassin at the hospital. That gadget she had on her arm … There would have to be some serious financial backing and experience to invent and construct something like that.'

'All will become apparent in time.'

I looked through the binoculars and moved my tunnelled gaze from one window of the apartment block to the next. Still nothing to see, unless you considered a man jogging on the spot or a woman drying her hair as worth looking at – although the woman was rather hot.

'I've been meaning to ask you something,' I said, turning back to the big Scot, who was still enjoying his cigar. 'Why did you drive off in such a sulk last night? You were acting like a right tool.'

'It was all an act,' he smiled. 'It's an old trick. When you want someone to do something particularly dangerous, you pretend to get all flustered. Then, just before you rush off, you say: "I'm sure you'll have no regrets when you die of old age." It always works.'

'You gave me a guilt trip.'

'Ah, you wouldn't be the first to fall for that one. Mind you, it usually it takes a day or two for the victim to give in. You caved in much quicker than I expected.'

'There didn't seem to be time to dally,' I said. 'You're a hard boiled shit, Hunter.'

'Oh, calm down,' he chuckled. 'I've fallen for it myself in the past. It worked so well on me that I employed itfor my own ends.'

'Who used it on you?'

'Jonathan Atkinson. Oh, he was shrewd that man.' Hunter smiled fondly. 'He could talk anyone into doing anything.' He dabbed his cigar into an ashtray on the window sill and looked at me. 'His daughter is just as persuasive.'

'Is she?'

'She convinced you to leave the Guild, didn't she?'

'I wanted to leave. There's a difference.'

'You didn't want to leave badly enough that it took me less than an hour to get you back in the saddle.'

'You just returned at the right time. A week earlier or later and I'd have told you to sling your hook ... Actually, your timing was impossibly good, Hunter. You've been watching me all along, haven't you? Ever since you tracked me down last December.'

'No.' He folded his arms and stared vacantly at the window. 'I don't know what you're talking about.'

'You have! It was too much of a coincidence that you showed up needing my help a day after Cathy left for France!'

'Do you honestly think I set this whole thing up just to get you back in the Guild? Come on. Don't be so paranoid.'

'I'm not paranoid.'

'Yes, you are. Now, shut up with all this nonsense. We've got a very serious issue that we need to discuss.'

'What's that?'

'I'm hungry. What are we going to do about it?'

'Room service?'

'That's what I was thinking …' He stood up from his chair and leaned against the window, staring across the street and pointing. '… until I saw that.'

I went to his side and followed his finger. He was pointing to a chipper next to the entrance to the apartment block. I was practically salivating within seconds.

'Yeah …' I said. 'Hotels don't do good chips …'

'No, they don't.'

'Is it worth the risk?'

'Here,' he said, handing me a couple of notes. 'Get me a battered cod and a bag of chips. Make sure they put loads of vinegar on both. I'll cloak you as you cross the street, but you'll be visible once you walk through that door. Don't hang around, don't make eye contact with anyone, don't do anything stupid, and get me a tub of garlic sauce while you're at it.'

My heart was in my mouth as I made my way across the grid-locked street. I was fighting back waves of that familiar anxiety even though I was invisible to everyone around me. Rain was pouring down and it made it difficult to focus on those walking on the pavement ahead or the people who had sought shelter under the shop front of the chipper. I then became acutely aware that I had no idea what Brofeldt looked like. By the time I reached the opposite pavement I had also realised that I wasn't cloaked at all; a cyclist thundering along the roadside had shouted at me to get out of his way.

Hunter was using me as bait. He really was an unscrupulous git!

I didn't linger on the pavement, and moved swiftly to the glass doors of the chipper. I couldn't help but stare at a middle-aged woman standing in the doorway chatting on her mobile phone. Her gaze met mine. My heart skipped a beat and I almost came to a stop right next to her. Was this Brofeldt?

Then she simply frowned and called me a freak before continuing her conversation. I let out a deep breath and pushed the door open and stepped into the noisy chipper. I was immediately smacked by the heat of the fryers, grills, ovens and the heaving mass of people on either side of the counter. I calmly threw back my hood, zipped down my jacket and strolled to the end of the queue. I tried not to make eye contact with anyone, despite feeling the urge to examine the faces of everyone sitting in the numerous booths on the far side of the room.

It felt like an hour had passed before one of the men behind the counter came to take my order. It was like an eternity before one of his co-workers called me forward to collect the large brown paper bag full of food. I felt the eyes of a teenage girl sitting in a booth by the window on me as I waiting by the till. Thanks to my precognitive gift I knew there was no danger, but like the clerk in the hotel, she had recognised my face. I didn't wait for her to place me and didn't wait for the teller to hand me my change.

'Keep it,' I said before hurrying outside to the embrace of chilled night air and the protection of darkness.

Despite the downpour I just stood outside the chipper staring at the fourth floor window of the hotel across the street. I knew Hunter would be watching me. He was going to pay for sending me into the firing line uncloaked. Oh, was he going to pay! I opened the bag and slowly lifted chip after chip into my mouth. I chewed as slowly as I could and smiled as broadly as humanly possible, so that he could see my pleasure from across the street. I really played it up. I knew he'd be over there drooling as I stuffed my face. I even tore a chunk from his precious battered fish and gobbled it down. I tore another piece off and raised it in the air to toast him and then lowered into my mouth then rubbed my stomach and nodded. Oh, he must have been going nuts!

Then I turned to my right to see Malcolm Wilson standing three yards away – staring straight at me. I almost died of shock right then and there. I remained perfectly still, silently gathered energy into my body in preparation for the fight that was surely to come.

The world seemed to be moving in slow motion around us. The people on the pavement faded away and all that was real was the stare that we shared. He looked so calm as he faced me. He must have had nerves of steel. I was bloody terrified and I'm sure it showed. Then he gave me a curious nod, as if he was saying: 'Aren't you man enough to attack?'. I couldn't think of anything else to do but nod back, as if to say, 'Your move.'

And that's exactly what I wanted to say; I wanted him to make the first move. I had never faced a mind-switcher in combat and didn't want to rush into this fight.

'We should get a move on,' he said. 'I don't want to be out in this rain all night.' He was so calm. There was even a hint of a smile on his face. Didn't he know of my reputation? Didn't he know I had fought Marianne Dolloway and Edward Zalech? He was actually courting combat with *me*? 'Don't just stand there staring at me.'

What the bloody hell was he talking about? Was he trying to trick me into dropping my guard?

'Why don't you shut up and watch the road?' a voice said over my shoulder. 'Look, here's one now.'

I spun around to see a smartly dressed woman with long blonde hair standing right behind me.

'Put out your arm, Malcolm!' she said. 'He'll drive right past!'

I looked back at Wilson to see him stepping to the side of the road with his arm in the air. 'Taxi,' he shouted. 'Stop, damn it! Taxi!'

Hunter had me cloaked. I had been standing in between the two killer spies as I ate and didn't even notice them. Thankfully Hunter had been on alert and used his light-tuning ability to make me invisible. They hadn't seen me and were now climbing into the back of a taxi. I was lucky that my mouth had been full of battered cod, otherwise I might have replied to Wilson, thinking he was actually talking to me and not Brofeldt. It had been a close call. A little too close for my liking.

❁ ❁ ❁

I threw the bag of food at Hunter as I stormed into the hotel room. Annoyingly, it didn't hit him; he used his gift to suspend the bag in mid-air and it floated harmlessly onto his lap. He was sitting in the chair by the window, where I'd left him, and was totally unperturbed by what had happened.

'That better taste good!' I shouted at him. 'That's the most expensive fish in the world. It almost cost me my life!'

Hunter calmly unravelled the sodden paper bag and stuffed a handful of chips into his gob. 'Don't get your knickers in a twist, Bentley,' he said with his mouth full, specks of food shooting from his mouth in all directions. 'I had you covered the whole time.'

'No, you didn't! I was uncloaked when I walked to the chipper. What purpose did that serve?'

'I simply wanted to see if anyone was following us. You would have sensed danger before anything happened anyway. You're precognitive, remember?'

'I don't like relying on that gift when my life is on the line – needlessly on the line.'

'Your life was on the line as soon as you stepped out of that cottage yesterday. Now, get your act together.'

'My act is together! In future you let me in on your plans before you throw me into a situation like that!'

'Okay, I admit it, that was a bit cruel.' He found a chicken burger at the bottom of the bag and threw it at me. 'Now eat up before it gets cold.'

'I've lost my appetite. Christ, you do know that was Wilson and Brofeldt standing next to me over there?'

'Yeah, I saw them before you left the chipper. I had you cloaked before you were out the door.'

'You play a dangerous game, Hunter.'

'The game has just begun, Bentley. Now we know for sure they are staying in the apartments across the street. We'll make our move soon enough.'

'They left in a taxi, Hunter. What if they don't come back?'

'They'll be back. They won't get away from me.'

'I don't know why you're so confident that you'll catch these two.'

'They call me Hunter for a good reason, Bentley. No prey ever escapes me.'

'You belong in a B-movie with all your one-liners!'

CHAPTER EIGHT

The Hit List

I sat on the bed sulking for a couple of hours and occasionally picked at the cold burger when Hunter wasn't looking. Windmill Street grew quieter as the night wore on, the traffic becoming sparse and the constant babbling of the pedestrians fizzling out, leaving only the sound of nocturnal revellers and the engine hum of parked cabs. Hunter had had enough by midnight and threw the binoculars at me and said it was my shift. We exchanged places and I settled into the lonely watch.

Most people would have found the task of monitoring an empty street excruciatingly boring, but I'd had a lot of practice at watching over lonely landscapes. It was still hard to keep my thoughts on the job, though. I kept thinking of Cathy, and how I wanted to hold her, let her perfume fill my nostrils, run my fingers through her soft hair and for us to fall asleep in one another's arms. I had not valued those simple things in the weeks before she left. They had become routine. It was only now that she was gone that I longed for them once more. Would I ever hold her again? Would the embrace still feel magical, as it once had? Would the magic fade once more? Would falling asleep with her become routine yet again? I knew I would never find out the answers. There was no going back for me.

I could never truly be content to hide away from the world, and it would be unfair to force Cathy into a life of constantly dealing with how hiding made me feel. We were too different, Cathy and I.

That still didn't stop me missing her, and missing the little things that had become part of my life. The thoughts of falling asleep with her had brought on fatigue quicker than I expected. I tried to fight it off by going to the bathroom and dousing my face with cold water. It helped only for a short while. By 3am I had surrendered. The soft caress of slumber sapped my strength. Then came *the* dream.

It was one of those dreams that trick you into thinking it's real by beginning in the exact same place you fell asleep. There were whispers in the hallway and I left the chair by the window to investigate. There was no one out there at first. Just an empty hallway. Then the whispers returned and I sought them once more. At first I could see the end of the corridor, that led to the stairwell, but it soon warped to become endless, stretching out into infinity with a million doors on both sides. I found myself racing forward in a panic and searching for a way out. I tried door after door. All were locked. There was no escape and I sprinted back to 408 to find it too was bolted. I screamed Hunter's name over and over, and pounded the door, until I noticed the shadow growing on the floor at my feet. I went silent and turned around.

A sallow-skinned man wearing a grey suit had appeared behind me. He spoke but I couldn't hear what he was saying. Then the dream went totally black and there were distant flashes of white and I felt compelled to chase these dancing lights, as if my life depended on it. Before I woke up there was only darkness and I heard Sarah Fisher whispering to me: 'He lives, Ross. He will find you soon.'

'Who?' I called out to the shadows. 'Who lives?'

Two glowing green eyes appeared deep in the empty blackness and became fixed on me. Then another voice spoke. A man this time.

'I am the Kematian. I am the shadow in the night. Allow me to show you what I am capable of.'

There were images flooding my mind. Too many and rotating too fast to focus on at first. Just before I woke up I identified a single image: Hunter lying on a tiled floor, surrounded by debris, his body bloodied and broken.

I fell right off the chair when I woke. My heart was jumping all over the place and I struggled to take air into my lungs. What the hell was going on? The dream felt more than just a dream. Dreams are never that clear when you wake up. I remembered every second of it. I could still hear the deep echoing voice of the Kematian. I'd seen Hunter dead. Why would my mind create such ghastly imagery? Was it a dream or was someone screwing with my mind? I had also heard Sarah Fisher's voice. Had she found a way to reach my mind to warn me of an impending doom?

'Bentley, what are doing lying on the floor?' Hunter bawled as he sprang off the bed. 'You're supposed to be watching the street!'

'Sorry,' I panted, lifting myself back to the chair. 'I dozed off.'

'I can see that.' He was absolutely furious with me. His fists were clenched and for a moment I thought he would start throwing punches at me. 'Now do you realise what a year as a civilian can do to an agent? Now do you understand why I don't take time off? The longer you're out of the game, the harder it is to get back into it. Look at you, you're a quivering mess!'

'I didn't ask to get back in, remember? You're the one who contacted me.'

'I'm starting to regret that decision.' He sat by the window and lifted the binoculars to his face. 'Damn it, they might have come back. We might have missed them!'

'Hunter, I had a terrible dream. I saw …'

'Shut up, Bentley. We're in business.'

'What?'

'They're back,' he said. 'Look! Third floor of the apartment building, the window on the far right.'

I took the binoculars from him and pressed my eyes into them. Through the furthest window to the right I had a clear view into one of the apartments. Wilson was sitting on a couch, writing in a notepad. Brofeldt was standing by the window smoking a cigarette. After a moment Wilson stood and flung the notepad aside and paced the floor, gesticulating. Before long they were screaming at one another.

'All's not well by the looks of things,' I said. 'They're really going at it.'

'Maybe their trip wasn't a successful one,' Hunter replied. 'I'd very much like to have a look at what he was writing into that notepad. Pass the binoculars.'

'Wait a minute.'

'What's happening?'

'Wilson has a sheet of paper in his hand and he's showing it to Brofeldt. He's still shouting by the looks of it.'

We watched as the two argued for the best part of an hour. Then things went quiet for a while, before Brofeldt appeared at the window once more, smoking again, but with a mobile phone pressed to her ear this time. She seemed quite animated as she spoke. I'd have given anything to eavesdrop on that conversation. Who was on the other end? Who was behind all the mysterious goings on? Who was our true enemy?

'I think this certainly proves that there are others involved in whatever these two are up to,' Hunter said. 'My theory might not have been that far-fetched at all.'

'Don't congratulate yourself just yet, Hunter. She could be talking to her boyfriend for all you know. Jeez, she could be talking to Paul Golding for all we know.'

'I told you already she would never work with Golding.'

'Well, either way, we don't know who she is talking to and we have no idea what they're really up to.'

'True. We won't know anything until we break into that apartment.'

'Are you absolutely, positively, out of your blinking mind?' I exclaimed. 'And you say I'm going nuts. You should take a long hard look at yourself. There's no way we're breaking into that apartment.'

'We can and will break into that apartment, Bentley. We simply have to wait for them to leave again.'

'What makes you think they'll leave together again?'

'Because it is obvious that whatever they were meant to do tonight didn't go according to plan. I'm betting they'll leave again at the same time tomorrow, to get whatever it is done.'

'Wouldn't it make more sense to follow them? That way we can find out where they're going and who they're meeting with. We can follow them on the kinetibike; that way we won't ever lose them. And you can keep us both cloaked. It the logical thing to do, Hunter.'

'No. At least not yet. Getting a look at those documents will tell us more about what's really happening here.' He took the binoculars from me and moved them to his face, restarting his vigil. 'Best you get some sleep now, Bentley. You'll need to be on your game tomorrow.'

'Why's that?'

'You're the one who's breaking into the apartment.'

I lay on the bed staring up at the glow the streetlights cast on the ceiling and fought to stay awake. Sleep was my enemy. Sleep brought thoughts and visions that I did not want in my mind. Anxiety was present once more. The excitement of the investigation had chased it away for a couple of days. It had returned when I had the dream earlier that night. I tried to be strong. Capitulating to this intangible dread would someday ruin me and in turn ruin all that was of value to me. I had to fight it off. I would not let this depression claim me. I had not fought the cruellest of villains just to surrender to a darkness my own mind was creating. It took hours, and a lot of determination, to conquer the anxiety that night. Most people will never know how wicked one's mind can be when it decides to go to war with itself. I wouldn't have wished it on my worst enemy.

The night was stubborn and only gave way to day around 9am. I lifted myself off the bed with my elbows and watched Hunter slumped in the chair by the window, a smoking cigar end hanging from his lower lip, his eyes rimmed red, the binoculars resting on one knee and an ashtray resting on the other. He looked a right mess.

'You want me to take over for a while?' I asked, snatching him from his thoughts. 'You look like you could sleep for a week.'

'I'm fine,' he said hoarsely. He stubbed the cigar into the ashtray, left the window and stretched his back with a loud click. 'I've done this a thousand times before.'

'I doubt you'll be able to do it a thousand times more. Get some sleep, Hunter.'

'Maybe in the afternoon,' he replied. 'I'm going downstairs to book the room for another night. I might get some toast and a strong coffee while I'm down there. You want some?'

'Yeah, get me the same.'

After he left I realised how similar we really were. Or how like him I was becoming. It wasn't simply our choice of breakfast that made us so similar; we had both killed people, lost loved ones at the hands of killers, neither of us could sleep properly because we were haunted by the ghosts of the past, and we were as grouchy as each other. All I was missing was the cigar smoking and the Scottish accent. I had often felt like that during the weeks that we hunted Edward Zalech. I didn't like the idea of ending up like Hunter back then. That was part of the reason why I left the Guild to be with Cathy. She had represented another possible future. A normal one. That started me thinking about her again. It had only been a couple of days since she left, but it seemed like months since we'd seen each other. I *did* miss her, but I didn't miss the cottage and the tedium at all. I was beginning to doubt whether I could return to that way of life. What was my future to be now that Cathy was gone? That was the question I pondered that morning as I watched the windows of the apartment building across the street.

There was no sign of either Wilson or Brofeldt. It was late afternoon when they finally surfaced. Hunter was asleep and I didn't bother to wake him. I kept myself a good distance from the window, as my colleague's invisibility shield was down, and watched their every move. They was no arguing this time. They spent most of their time sitting on the couch, Wilson consulting files that were laid out on the coffee table, Brofeldt typing into a laptop and occasionally moving to the other side of the room and returning with sheets that she handed to Wilson. I figured there was an inkjet printer in the room and she was printing out whatever she was writing, and Wilson was then working on these files with a biro. These two were involved in something big. I could feel it in my bones. I wasn't looking forward to risking my neck by breaking into their apartment. At the same time, though, I was sort of excited by the prospect and I was dying to know what they were involved in. Perhaps I was so eager to know because I would then likely bow out of the investigation and allow agents from the Guild to take my place. There was always that cushion of safety for me. There was always the escape route back to the loneliness of the west of Ireland.

Hunter rose late that afternoon and I gave my weary eyes a break and went to the bathroom for a very long shower. We spoke of our plan as the afternoon became evening and darkness claimed the street outside. It was a simple strategy; we would use our gifts to bypass the security door of the apartment building, locate Brofeldt's apartment, then Hunter would remain cloaked in the hallway and keep watch while I looked through the files the spies had been working on.

It was simple and it worked. I stepped inside the apartment at 9pm, only fifteen minutes after we had watched Wilson and Brofeldt leaving from the window of our hotel room.

After bypassing the main door, I trod along a short hallway that led me to the large, bland sitting room. Cheap wooden floor, magnolia walls and flat pack furniture. There was no TV, framed portraits, ornaments or books. There was nothing that would suggest this was a home to anyone. It was a safe house by the looks of it.

The laptop that Brofeldt had used was lying on the coffee table. The inkjet was standing on a cabinet on the opposite side of the room. There was no sign of the files they had been working on, though, and I feared they may have taken them away and this would be a waste of time.

I crossed the sitting room, staying clear of the windows, and went to another hallway. There were three doors. Two were closed and one was ajar with the light on inside. I could see enough through the crack in the door to tell it was the bathroom.

I leaned against the wall and heaved in deep breaths to stem a tide of anxiety that was washing over me. I was getting flashbacks of Rebecca Dunlow's house and the grizzly scene we had uncovered in that bathroom. Even one year later, every little detail of what I saw that night was etched into my memory. I'll never forget the revulsion I felt as I set eyes on her lifeless body, scorched and melted, and as the smell of her singed flesh met my nostrils. It was one of those moments that stays with a person until the end of their days.

'Calm down,' I whispered to myself. 'There are no dead bodies here. Everything is fine, Ross. Search the rooms and you'll be free of this place within ten minutes.'

I forced myself from the wall and opened one door to find a room with nothing in it except a single bed that was unmade. There were some clothes scattered on the floor. Wilson's, judging by the size and style. Nothing else.

I re-entered the hallway and went to the next room. I flicked on the light switch and saw it was an identical bedroom to the last. A single bed. Some women's clothes neatly folded and stacked on the floor. I let out a sigh of relief when my gaze met three binders full of sheets of A4 paper.

I sat on the bed and placed one of the binders on my lap and thumbed through the first collection of files to find them to be all gift related. Details and tricks and attacks for each of the fifteen true gifts. Someone had been doing a lot of research by the looks of it. These were certainly intriguing documents but were of little use to me. I placed the binder back on the floor and lifted another onto my lap.

These files were much more interesting. All were official government documentation. At first it seemed all were stolen from the British Ministry of Finance. Then as I flicked to the centre pages I found documents stamped by MI5, and others from the Ministry for Defence. Then to my surprise there was also a collection of files from Irish government departments. Mostly Department of Finance and a scattering from the Department of Justice. The final pages in the binder were official government documents from Iceland. They certainly had been busy. Too busy for two people to amass so many confidential files. Hunter was right when he claimed that more spies were involved. I was sure of that now. They had infiltrated the most sensitive areas of three separate governments. But to what end?

This was certainly a startling discovery. Nothing could prepare me for what was in the third and final binder. I couldn't quite believe what I was seeing as I flicked from one page to the next. I had borrowed Hunter's phone before I entered the apartment and I used its camera to take photos of as many pages as I could. It was impossible to look through them all; this one binder had more than a thousand pages in it. I couldn't quite grasp the enormity of the situation in that moment. There was too much fear and adrenalin in me to concentrate fully. Still, even in that instant, I knew these files would alter the course of my life. Maybe even alter the course of history.

Before I left the room, I noticed more files on a shelf by the window. I found them to be maps of Iceland, Scotland and northern England. Then another map of an area of India that was accompanied by a handful of photos – all of a tall office block. Another map of the isle of Unst, which was one of the Shetland Islands north of Scotland. This was stapled to blueprints for a massive industrial structure.

I took more photos of these maps then made a speedy exit from the apartment. Getting out of the building was even more nerve-racking than breaking in. I kept imagining that Brofeldt and Wilson would appear at the next bend in the corridor or behind the next door we pushed open. I didn't breathe properly until we were making our way up the stairs of the hotel.

'Well?' Hunter asked as we got back to room 408. 'Did you find anything of interest?'

I sat on the side of the bed, took the phone out and opened the photo gallery. 'I found lots of interesting stuff. I don't know what the hell we've stumbled on here, Hunter. This is big. This is far too big for the two of us. You need to contact the Guild immediately.'

'What did you find?'

'Collections of confidential documents from the British, Irish and Icelandic governments. Lots of information on the true gifts. Maps of remote areas with blueprints for office buildings and industrial premises.' I took the laptop from his bag and powered it up. 'That's not what has me concerned. It seems like *we're* the ones being hunted, not Brofeldt and Wilson.'

As soon as the laptop was powered up I uploaded the images from the phone and showed them to Hunter. The first five pages were filled with information on the Guild and its history. This could be easily explained away; Brofeldt had been a member of the organisation for a number of years and would have been aware of this information.

What came after that was what had me so worried.

Notice for all operatives.

11 December.

MAIN GUILD TARGETS.
All high priority targets are to be exterminated with immediate effect.

Target One
Name: Elizabeth Armitage.
Code name: Queen.
Age: 35.
Nationality: English.
Gift Level: 9.
Known Gifts: Mind-Switcher (Mutated).
Status: High Priority Target.
Location: Last sighted in London on the 3rd of August.
Guild Classification: Deep Black.

Target Two
Name: Michael Huntington.
Code name: Rogue.
Age: 43.
Nationality: Scottish.
Gift Level: 8.
Known Gifts: Psychokinesis (Partial). Electro-psych (Pure). Light-Tuner (Pure).

Status: High Priority Target.
Location: Last sighted in Ireland on the 9th of December.
Guild Classification: Deep Black.

Target Three
Name: Dominic Ballentine.
Code name: Chimera.
Age: 45.
Nationality: French.
Gift Level: 8.
Known Gifts: Psychokinesis (Pure).
Status: Undetermined.
Location: Last sighted in London on the 28th of November.
Guild Classification: Deep Black.

Target Four
Name: James Tucker.
Code name: Furnace.
Age: 30.
Nationality: American.
Gift Level: 7.
Known Gifts: Pyrokinesis (Pure).
Status: High Priority Target.
Location: Last sighted in Kiev, Ukraine on the 2nd of May.
Guild Classification: Deep Black.

Target Five
Name: Cathy Atkinson.
Code name: Dolittle.
Age: 20.

Nationality: English.
Gift Level: 7.
Known Gifts: Mind-Switcher (Pure).
Status: Mid Priority Target.
Location: Unconfirmed sighting in London, England on the 9th of December.
Guild Classification: White.

Target Six
Name: Amanda Ellenberger.
Code name: Singer.
Age: 51.
Nationality: Swiss.
Gift Level: 9.
Known Gifts: Precognitive (Pure), Siren (Pure).
Status: Mid Priority Target.
Location: Last sighted in Glasgow, Scotland on the 20th of November.
Guild Classification: Red.

Target Seven
Name: Joshua Carlebach.
Code name: Ranger.
Age: 22.
Nationality: Israeli.
Gift Level: 7.
Known Gifts: Emotomagnet (Pure), Light-Tuner (Pure).
Status: Mid Priority Target.
Location: Last sighted in New York, United States on the 8th of January.
Guild Classification: Black.

Target Eight
Name: Ross Bentley.
Code name: Devil.
Age: 19.
Nationality: Irish.
Gift Level: 9.
Known Gifts: Psychokinesis (Pure), Precognitive (Pure), Time-scanner (Pure).
Status: Mid Priority Target.
Location: No reported sightings in the last twelve months.
Guild Classification: Deep Black.

Target Nine
Name: Janice Powell.
Code name: Pilot.
Age:19.
Nationality: Unknown.
Gift Level: 7.
Gifts: Space Rupter (Pure).
Status: Mid Priority Target.
Location: Last sighted in London, England on the 15th of October.
Guild Classification: White.

Target Ten
Name: Anne Wilkins.
Code name: Thief.
Age: 18.
Nationality: Welsh.
Gift Level: 8.

Gifts: Electro-Psych (Pure), Light-Tuner (Pure), Siren (Pure).
Status: Undetermined.
Location: Last sighted in Cardiff, Wales on the 10th of November.
Guild Classification: White.

That was just the first page. There were four more pages that were filled with Guild profiles. I recognised a few of the names. The rest I had never heard of before. I didn't really care about most of the people mentioned; what had me so worried was that Cathy and I were both on the list. I couldn't understand why we would even feature on such a list.

'It's a hit list, right?' I asked Hunter while he examined the other pages. 'They're hunting everyone on that list.'

'That would appear to be the case. Some of the most important people in the Guild are included in these lists.'

'It says there are sightings of Guild agents as recently as yesterday. That means the list must have been made, or at least updated, today. They're watching everyone in the Guild and they know where the agents are. At the top it says an order went out to start killing us off!'

'I know. This is very worrying indeed …'

'And why am I on the list? I'm not even a part of the Guild anymore.'

'You're loosely allied to the Guild and you are very powerful when your head isn't stuck up your arse. If sides were to be chosen, you would likely side with us. That makes you a threat to these people.'

'And why on earth is Cathy a target? That makes no sense at all. Cathy wouldn't hurt a fly and she's dead set against the Guild – has been for a long time.'

'Perhaps some of their information is inaccurate.'

'It doesn't matter if it's accurate or not. Cathy is in grave danger because she's on that list.'

'We're all in danger. The entire Guild is under threat.'

'Why would they try to destroy the Guild?'

'Why do humans destroy anything? Usually because it's in the way of them getting what they want.'

'What do they want?'

'Impossible to say at this juncture. The only thing that's clear to me now is that Wilson and Brofeldt are part of another gifted organisation. And they seem to have a head start on us. They know a lot about the Guild. We know virtually nothing about them. They even have information that could have only come from within the Guild ...'

'You're talking about the Guild Classifications? What do they mean?'

'White indicates that the individual has never taken another human life. Yellow means the person has never killed and would refuse to kill under any circumstance. Those who are trained to kill but haven't actually taken anyone out are classed as Red. Code Black is reserved for agents who have killed numerous times.'

'And what the hell does *deep black* mean? You and I are both under that classification. Why am I deep black, Hunter?'

'As I said earlier, this document isn't entirely accurate, Bentley.'

'Seems very accurate to me. Now, tell me what it means.'

'Deep black means you're born to kill, not just trained to do it. It means you are a killer by instinct.'

'They know I've killed people in the past,' I sighed. I paced the room and cursed myself for getting involved with the Guild again. I was now in serious danger and couldn't see a way out. 'That information could get me a life sentence in prison. I don't want to go to prison.'

'Prison?' Hunter laughed. 'Prison is not what you should be concerning yourself with. Not when you're a top target for a group of gifted assassins.'

'I'm even more concerned for Cathy!'

'Cathy is well hidden.'

'It says in that file that she was seen in London a couple of days ago.'

'Wrong. It says reported sighting.'

'What if she went to London for something and didn't tell me? They could be following her, Hunter.'

'Don't let your imagination run wild, Bentley. I'm quite sure she's safe for the moment.'

'I'm not so sure. I should contact her. I need to warn her.'

'Let's calm down before we do anything stupid, eh? This is a very dangerous time and making phone calls can get people killed. You of all people should know that.'

'I'll never be allowed to forget that mistake, will I?'

'I'm not blaming you for Romand's death. I'm simply saying we need to think carefully about what we do next. All right?'

'Whatever you say.'

'Besides, this document is an order to assassinate all high priority targets. Cathy isn't classed as high priority.'

'It doesn't mean she's safe.'

'No one is safe. No one will be safe until we destroy these people. Just be calm for a while and don't do anything foolish.'

I was on the verge of losing control and Hunter was right; I needed to calm down and think rationally. Now was not the time to make decisions without thinking them through properly. I sat next to him by the window, and together we watched the street in silence. I couldn't stop myself from thinking of the dream I'd had. The vision of Hunter's dead body. I had to tell him about the dream. I couldn't keep it to myself any longer.

'Do you think dreams can come true, Hunter?' I asked. 'Or is that just childish superstition?'

'They can come true if you're a prophet. Otherwise it's simply your subconscious mind going wild because your conscious mind is taking some time off.'

'I had a dream last night,' I admitted. 'It didn't feel like a dream at all, though. It felt more like one of those strange hallucinations I've been having …'

'What did you see in this dream?'

'You were dead. It looked like you'd been beaten to death.'

'Lovely,' he snorted.

'I heard Sarah Fisher's voice.'

Hunter reacted differently to this piece of information. He turned to me and examined my face very carefully.

'Go on,' he said.

'She said: "He lives, Ross. He will find you soon."'

'Who lives?'

'She never said.' I looked him dead in the eye then. 'Then I heard another voice.'

'Whose voice?'

'A man. "I am the Kematian. I am the shadow in the night. Allow me to show you what I am capable of." That's when I saw you lying dead on the ground.'

'Just a dream. Pay it no heed.' He turned back to the window and watched the apartment across the road. 'Forget about all that. We have enough problems in the real world that need sorting out.'

There was a slight hint of worry in his expression as he turned away from me. I'd been in enough dangerous encounters with Hunter to know that he never displayed fear. This was the first time I'd ever seen Hunter afraid.

CHAPTER NINE

Fire & Light

It had been almost two hours since Hunter and I spoke. He claimed the dream had no significance, other than interrupting a much needed sleep, but I had identified a slight shift in his facial expression when I recalled the dream for him. His face had tightened when I told him I'd heard Sarah Fisher's voice. His eyes had widened ever so slightly when I told him the part about the Kematian. These subtle facial movements told me that he did believe that this was more than just a dream, and that he feared what it represented. I didn't bother trying to talk to him about it again; I knew when Hunter wasn't in a talkative mood and he would have ignored me if I pestered him. Instead we sat in silence and took turns at watching over Windmill Street. Nothing happened until deep in the night.

It was almost 4am when a taxi carrying Wilson and Brofeldt pulled up outside the apartment building. They got out and loitered on the pavement until another cab appeared. Two men exited the second vehicle and spoke with Brofeldt while Wilson unlocked the main doors. Within a couple of minutes they were all seated in the sitting room of the third floor apartment and were deep in discussion.

I had recognised one of the visitors immediately as the man in the grey suit from my dream. I didn't mention this to Hunter. I figured he'd simply say it was my imagination running wild again. I was sure it was him, though. He stood by the window at one point and I got a real good look at him. I guessed he was roughly forty years old and was muscular with dark skin and piercing black eyes. He had the look of a killer. I'd grown used to identifying them during my time in the Guild.

'We're out of our depth here,' Hunter said as he watched the tall stranger. 'We wouldn't be able to deal with the four of them if we were to be drawn into a fight.'

'You know these two men?'

'I know *of* them. The lunatic in the grey suit is Nayden Vanev. Bulgarian born, forty-three years of age, and one of the most brutal and efficient killers you will ever come across.'

'Another Guild runaway?'

'No, he was never friendly. Vanev started working as a street thug for a mafia in Sofia when he was just a teenager. His bosses were quick to realise he was a skilled killer, and someone who had the knack of evading the authorities even when he was cornered. By the age of twenty he was their top assassin. Most of his victims back then were underworld competitors or threats to the mafia: drug dealers, pimps, the odd police officer, politician and judge. Within five years his reputation became known outside Bulgaria and he was often hired by other mafia groups in eastern Europe and by some shady oligarchs in Russia. We became aware of him around that time and sent some agents to take care of him. None ever returned. We started taking him seriously after that. In 2001 the Guild sent a team of trained assassins to dispose of Vanev. They searched for him for many months and never managed to locate him. Most of us thought he'd fallen victim to one of the numerous mafias he worked for. Then we got word a couple of years ago that he was very much alive *and* off limits – he was working for an agency in the US.'

'What?' I asked incredulously. 'How could an American agency hire a man like that? Aren't government agencies supposed to lock up people like Vanev?'

'You'll find that the majority of western governments would turn a blind eye to a lot of crimes in order to have someone like Vanev in their employment.'

'If he was working for one of the agencies, it could link him to Brofeldt. You said there were rumours she was working for a shadow agency in the states.'

'Perhaps.'

'What's Vanev's gift?'

'He's a space-rupter.'

'He can make jumps through time and space?'

'He can,' Hunter nodded thoughtfully. 'It's not the purest form of the gift. He can easily make small jumps, but it would take a lot of time and concentration for him to make a significant jump.'

'What constitutes a significant jump?'

'From one continent to another.'

'No wonder he could never be cornered.'

'It would take hours for him to build up the strength to make a leap like that. Most of the time he's confined to more modest jumps: from one room to another, or from a standing position into a moving vehicle.'

'That would make him pretty hard to fight.'

'He's not got the pure gift, like Janice Powell, which does make it a little easier. When he makes a jump there will be a bright flash and he will leave a trail of light in the direction he travels. This means he can be tracked.'

'And who's the other guy that arrived with him?'

'Johan Verbannk. I don't know too much about him – other than the fact that he's an electro-psych. The Guild never saw him as much of a threat because he has no record and has never used his gifts for criminal purposes.'

'It would appear you were wrong to ignore him.'

'We ignored far too much. The Guild are supposed to be aware of any gifted groups on the rise – especially ones with known murderers in their ranks. I can't understand how they were blind to these people. Something feels very wrong about all this.'

'What are we going to do?'

'I'll make a call to Ballentine and ask him to send a hit squad immediately.'

'How long will that take?'

'Let's find out.'

Hunter took his mobile phone in hand and made a call to Dominic Ballentine, the man who had helped me to destroy the Golding Plaza hotel the year before. Ballentine seemed to spend most of his time operating as a trouble shooter for Guild agents. He was able to quickly organise squads of assassins and to relocate agents in time of peril. I was more than a little wary of the man; anyone who can so easily order a killing or send someone into a gifted duel is not to be taken lightly. Those who worked as full-time killers were even less appealing individuals, and I wanted to be long gone before the team of Guild assassins arrived. Taking human life in the heat of battle, or in self-defence, was hard enough for me to accept. Carrying out such tasks in cold blood was unnatural and more than a little sinister. I didn't like being a party to it.

Ballentine and Hunter despised each other, and there was usually a lot of shouting involved when they were forced to work together. Ballentine didn't trust Hunter at all. He believed the big Scot was irresponsible and old fashioned – which was true most of the time – and never took his advice or believed his theories on investigations.

Hunter began the conversation by telling Ballentine about what had happened at the hospital, then the gathering of spies on Windmill Street, and of the hit list we had found in Brofeldt's apartment. Ballentine was furious that Hunter hadn't called for help immediately after the incident at the hospital – I could hear him shouting down the phone from across the room.

Hunter told him to shut his mouth and to send in back-up. This was followed by more shouting from Ballentine. Then Hunter told him to shut up again and gave him the address of the hotel we were staying at and the room number. There was a moment of silence before he threw the phone on the bed.

'That went well by the sounds of it,' I snorted. 'You really hate that man, don't you?'

'He's an awful person to deal with,' Hunter grumbled as he returned to his chair by the window. 'Always telling me I'm wrong. He talks to me as if I'm a novice! Romand and I were hunting down gifted murderers long before Ballentine even knew he had a gift! And he thinks he can tell me what's what! Bloody fool!'

'Is he going to send help or not?'

'Four assassins who are stationed in Belfast will be sent to back us up. They should be here in about three hours.'

'I should leave soon,' I said. 'It wouldn't be wise for me to be here when they arrive.'

'Hmm,' Hunter grunted. 'Probably be for the best. You get your stuff together and you could make it back to your cottage by morning.'

'I don't intend to go back there,' I admitted. 'I'm going to France. I need to be sure that Cathy is safe.'

'She is safe.'

'Not until the Guild gets to the bottom of all this. I wouldn't be able to live with myself if anything happened to her. I have to go to her.'

'And what if you're followed? You could lead these people straight to her.'

'I'm not going back to that empty cottage, Hunter. I'd drive myself mad out there knowing that there are assassins searching for Cathy.'

'They are also searching for you.'

'I can look after myself.'

'I think it would be best if you remain here with me. Now that I think of it, you might not be safe in the cottage alone.'

'No way. I can't work for the Guild again. If the other agents see me here, the entire Guild will know about it within a day or two. I swore to myself, and Cathy, that I would never go back to this type of work.'

'You already broke that promise, Bentley.'

'But she doesn't know that.'

'Take an hour to think it over.' Hunter climbed onto the bed and rested his head on the pillows and let out a long, tired sigh. 'Wake me up when you decide what to do.'

I turned away from him and looked out over the street. I had three options: To remain with Hunter, to return to the isolated cottage, or to travel to France and protect Cathy. Remaining at the hotel was the safest, and probably the most sensible, course of action, but it would lead me back into the Guild. The other options represented serious danger, but I would at least be following my own path by choosing either of them. There was no easy way out for me. Why did I always end up in disasters like this?

An excruciating hour passed. At one point I was sure that leaving for France was the right option and was about to sneak away into the night. I couldn't bring myself to do it, though, and ended up sitting by the window once more. I raised the binoculars to my eyes and focused them on the apartment across the street. Wilson was standing by the window, talking and gesticulating. It seemed like he was arguing with someone again.

I twisted the rim of the binoculars and zoomed in on the window. Wilson filled most of the frame, but I could still make out the couch behind him. There was no one sitting on it. There didn't appear to be anyone else in the room. Who the hell was he arguing with? And where were Verbannk, Brofeldt and Vanev if they weren't in the apartment?

I drew back from the window and allowed the binoculars to slip from my hands. By the time they landed on the floor I was shivering. My precognitive gift had come alive. I was sensing extreme danger. My brain felt like it was on fire. My limbs were shaking uncontrollably. I was so disorientated that I barely heard the knock on the door.

'They're early,' Hunter groaned as he left the bed. 'They shouldn't be here for at least another hour.'

'Get away from the door!' I screamed. 'Get down!'

My body became energised as panic swamped my senses. I bolted out of my seat and flung my arms forward, releasing the immense power that was building inside me. A wave of psychokinetic energy rolled across the room, cracking the plaster of the walls, splitting the wooden floor and blasting the door into a hurricane of splinters. I heard Hunter cry out as debris showered him. He tumbled to the floor like a rag doll, then scrambled away hissing in agony, and disappeared through the open door to the bathroom.

In the hallway, as the dust settled, I saw Verbannk slumped against the far wall. His body was bent and soaked in blood, his eyes still wide with the shock he had experienced in the instant the blast had killed him. I stood in the centre of the room breathing heavily and staring at the dead man, when I really should have been preparing for what I knew was about to come.

My precognitive gift brought me to my senses. I sensed that the danger was yet to pass and that I would soon be under renewed attack. I looked through the shattered door frame and a warm light consumed the hallway … just before a thick funnel of flames twisted into the room. Brofeldt's gift of pyrokinesis was only supposed to be partial. Judging by the inferno she had created, it was clear Hunter's assessment of her abilities was very wrong – she was a master of that deadly gift.

The funnel of flame rose up and struck the ceiling of the hotel room, then exploded out above me in all directions. I created a spherical energy shield and it protected me as the furniture on all sides was set alight and the window behind me exploded from the intense heat that was rising in the room. I held the protective barrier in place for a few seconds, but the heat managed to radiate through it and there was steam rising from my clothes and sweat was leaking from my skin. I was slowly being cooked within the shield I had created, and all the while more and more flames were rolling into the room from the hallway. Within seconds I would pass out, the shield would collapse and I'd be burned alive. I looked through the doorway and saw that Brofeldt was standing in sight, laughing wildly as flames swept from her hands and incinerated everything in the room. I was losing control. The shield was slowly but surely giving way.

I did the only thing I could: I collapsed the shield and used the energy within me to blow a hole in the wall to my left. I dashed through the flames and leaped into the opening and landed on the floor of the next hotel room. There was no time to waste. Hesitating for even a few seconds would see this room under attack and I would find myself being cooked once more. My only option was to go on the offensive.

My temper was rising and with it came a tremendous power. I raced across the room and forced out a bolt of energy ahead of myself that slapped the door right out of its frame. I sprang forward into the hallway and fired out a slice of energy blindly to my right. I watched as Brofeldt was cut down, the psychokinetic slice chopping off her left arm above the elbow and opening a ragged wound across her chest.

Vanev stood next to the door to 408 and remained uninjured. Our eyes met and for a couple of seconds we just stood there staring at each other. He wasn't making the first move, so I went on the attack once more. I launched an invisible spear of energy directly at him. It moved along the hallway at mesmerising speed and struck the end of corridor. Vanev had disappeared in a flash of white light before the spear made contact.

A faint trail of white light shot forward and passed though my chest. Hunter had told me that space-rupters like Vanev often left trails of light as they made their jumps through time and space. It was the only way to track them.

I spun around and watched the light moving quickly away before there was another bright flash. When the light faded I saw Vanev had reappeared and was pointing a gun at me. I raised a simple barrier of energy to protect myself before he pulled the trigger. Three loud shots went off and, to my astonishment, the bullets shattered my shield. Two bullets embedded themselves in the wall next to me. The third sliced through the arm of my jacket, so close to my skin that I felt the heat of it in my bicep. Bullets that could penetrate psychokinetic shields? This would certainly level the playing field.

I couldn't stand there and face him. Even I, with my great powers, could not contend with this new weaponry. Again I had to attack. And in more creative ways.

I focused on the doorways either side of Vanev as he pulled the trigger again. The two heavy wooden doors were wrenched from their hinges and sandwiched him. Well, that's what I thought at first – until I saw a line of light darting away. He had disappeared again just before he was clattered from both sides.

I ran along the hallway, following the misty trail that Vanev left in his wake as he used his gift to slip through the barrier of reality. The trail arced along the hallway and through into a room on the right. He wasn't getting away from me. I sprinted along the hallway, launched a wave of energy ahead of myself that ripped a gaping hole in the wall, then bounded through the rubble into the room to see Vanev at the far wall firing shots at me. I jumped to the floor, one bullet missing me, another was so close that it severed a lock of hair from the top of my scalp. From the floor I shot out a small, precise burst of energy at him, but again he disappeared into a flash of light. This guy was really starting to annoy me!

I saw his wake of light spiralling around the room before sinking through the floor. I had to be relentless if I was to catch him. I climbed to my feet and fired a shot of energy at the floor that opened a hole to the room below. I quickly jumped through it and landed in the third floor room and saw the trail sinking through the wall into yet another room. I blasted my way into the next room then ducked to evade another flurry of gun fire. I rolled across the floor and released a burst of energy in all directions. Vanev was struck by it and bounced off a desk by the window. He was slowing down. I almost had him.

I clambered off the floor and prepared to attack, but to my frustration Vanev slipped away once more. This time the trail moved upward, back to the fourth floor. I fired energy downward and was lifted upward, though the hole in the ceiling to the fourth floor room again. I caught sight of the trail of light gliding across the room and through the ceiling. I raised my arms and screamed as I released a terrible wave of psychokinetic power. There was an almighty blast as the ceiling opened up to show the low clouds above.

I took one deep breath, levitated through the opening in the building and landed on the roof. I turned and saw a burst of light further across the rooftop. Vanev had finally made a mistake. He had gone to the roof where there was nowhere to conceal himself. He was out in the open at last. By the time he lifted the gun I had already shot an invisible burst of energy at him. He crumbled to his knees, clutching at a melon-sized hole in his stomach.

'You didn't do your homework, Mr Vanev,' I said confidently as I strode towards him. 'Didn't your friends tell you that I'm a born killer?'

'You …' Vanev gasped. He stumbled forward and looked up at me. 'You … are the devil …'

'Yeah, and you're an angel. Who are you working for?' I stooped to pick up the strange handgun that he'd armed himself with. 'Where did you get this bloody thing?'

'From the people …' he coughed out a mouthful of blood onto the rooftop, '… who will kill you and your kind. The world cannot be subjected … to the horror …'

He was dead before he finished the sentence. What on earth was he talking about? What horror could the Guild pose? It didn't make any sense at all. Perhaps he was the crazed fanatic that Hunter claimed he would be, after all.

'Crap,' I hissed. In the chaos of the battle I had forgotten all about Hunter. He'd scrambled into the bathroom to escape the inferno. He'd surely be dead by now if he hadn't managed to find a way out.

Sirens were wailing in the distance as I found my way back to

408. Flames were still spewing through the doorway and part of the hallway was on fire, thick smoke rippling along the ceiling and walls. Guests were screaming and shouting in the hallways below. Amid this chaos I saw that Hunter *had* managed to free himself. He had dragged Brofeldt along the corridor, away from the fire, and was looming over her, a tendril of electricity joining his hands with her face.

'Hunter, we have to get out of here,' I shouted at him as I approached. 'In a couple minutes this place will be crawling with police.'

'I'm extracting information, Bentley,' he shouted back. 'Shut up, will you? She's near death.'

I stood a few yards away, half watching Hunter electrocuting the spy, half watching the stairwell at the end of the corridor. I had just killed two people. That didn't weigh too heavily on me, though. I had taken the lives of Verbannk and Vanev in the heat of battle and I only did it to save myself. This, on the other hand, was torture and it wasn't easy to stand by and watch. To my shame, I did nothing. I could not intervene.

'Who are you working for?' Hunter shouted at Brofeldt. 'Tell me and I will bring this to an end. Don't put yourself through unnecessary pain. I can make this even worse if you don't talk!'

She screamed as the electricity became more intense and connected to her temples.

'Talk!' Hunter shouted at her. 'Talk, damn you!'

He took his hands away from her face and the stinging lines of electricity quickly fizzled away into thin air.

'Tell me who you are working for!'

'I'll tell you,' Brofeldt said weakly. She was almost dead, had been tortured and was facing a most brutal man in Hunter. Still she managed a defiant grin. 'I'll tell you that your time is coming to an end. You and your lot are finished. A new dawn is creeping up on the horizon.'

'Cut the crap!' Sparks of electricity began to spin around Hunter's fingers again. 'Tell me or else.'

'You're too late to stop us, you fool. The Master has been working against the Guild for decades. He has dozens of loyal soldiers and they have been in positions of power for years. We have people working in governments, in the police services of many countries, and we even have people inside the Guild. And we've all been very busy working on the revolution.'

'Who are you working for?' I couldn't stop myself from asking. 'Is it Golding?'

'*Golding*?' She tried to laugh. 'Golding works for us now. We seized control of his entire organisation three months ago. Now do you realise how hopeless your situation is? You are facing a legion of gifted soldiers, all dedicated to one cause, to one man, and we have the arsenal and finances of Golding Scientific at our disposal. And soon we'll merge Golding Scientific with the Guild of the True.'

'Lies,' Hunter insisted. He pressed his fist against her swollen cheek. 'Lies!'

'It's true,' she spat. 'You'll see.'

'We'll stop this master of yours,' I said.

'No, you won't,' Brofeldt boasted. 'The two of you will be dead soon. The Master will send his finest assassin after what you have done here tonight. He'll track you down and murder you both without breaking sweat.'

'Who is this master?' Hunter asked. 'Tell me his name.'

'Get ready for a surprise, Hunter,' she replied weakly.

'Who is it?'

Brofeldt's eyes rolled back in her head and she slumped to one side, dead. The floor all around her was soaked in her blood, as were Hunter's clothes and hands. He looked like a killer from a slasher movie as he straightened up and turned to me. Only now, that I could get a good look at him, did I see that one side of his face was riddled with splinters of various sizes, his eyes were bloodshot and his nose was badly busted.

'Bentley, I will beat you to death with my bare hands if you ever blow up a door in my face again.'

'I didn't have time to warn you properly,' I explained. 'And we don't have time to debate this right now.'

The hallway was filling with black smoke as the fire spread to other rooms. The sirens were screaming outside and raised voices were coming from the stairs. We were almost out of time.

'We need to get moving,' I said. 'Let's find a way out of here.'

'Just give me a moment,' Hunter said, leaning against the wall. 'I need to catch my breath.'

It was only then that I noticed a shard of wood, as thick as my forearm, sticking out of his stomach.

'Oh, my God,' I gasped. 'Hunter, you've got a –'

'I know,' he sighed. 'I know.'

'How deep in is it?'

'A few inches I would say.'

'We need to get you to a hospital.'

'No,' Hunter insisted. 'It's too much of a risk.'

'Too much of a risk? Hunter, that injury will kill you if you're not operated on.'

'I refuse to allow a piece of wood to kill me.' He forced himself off the wall and stood, rather unsteadily, in front of me. 'I'm using my powers to stem the blood loss. I'll be all right for a couple of hours.'

'And what happens when the couple of hours are up?'

'Then I use my gifts to operate on myself.'

'You *cannot* be serious!'

'I am serious,' he hissed at me. 'I've done this type of thing a thousand times before. Let's get going.'

Hunter waved his arms in the air and weaved a cloak for us both by using his light-tuning gift. As soon as we were invisible, we went in search of a way to escape both the flames and the emergency workers were who spilling into opposite ends of the hallway.

CHAPTER TEN

Safe Ground

During my year away from the Guild I became averse to taking risks. I'd grown ponderous, almost timid, in the absence of the danger I had endured in my previous stint in the Guild. I guess living a normal life means that you have the luxury to avoid life or death decisions, and that can make a person docile. I didn't think I'd ever take another risk for the rest of my life. That changed as soon as Hunter showed up at the cottage and presented me with a task that would interrupt the slow, wearying days in the wilderness. I took a big risk that day by going to the hospital with him. I'd taken another big risk when I followed him to Dublin. And in the hours that followed the attack on the hotel, I took two more risks – ones that could have gotten me, and others, killed.

Thanks to Hunter's light-tuning gift, we had managed to slip past the emergency workers and the police that filed up the staircase to the fourth floor. We found our way to a fire exit on the second floor and within moments we'd made it to the shelter of an underground car park nearby.

Hunter had been proud and stubborn about his injury back at the hotel. His strength had crumbled by the time we reached the kinetibike, which was parked in the darkest corner of the car park.

Sweat was streaming down his face, he was shaking, blood was steadily seeping from the wound and had dyed one leg of his trousers dark red. His stubbornness had not diminished; he still refused to go anywhere near a hospital and insisted that he could patch himself up once we got to safe ground.

What was safe ground, though? We were two agents who were being hunted by a gang of ruthless assassins. And we'd just partaken in a battle that had practically destroyed a city centre hotel and claimed a number of lives. Surely the hotel staff would have described us both to the police. Those descriptions had probably already been passed to every officer in the city. We were wanted men and there was nowhere and no one in Dublin that was friendly.

I helped Hunter onto the back of the bike then drove up the exit ramp and out into the cool night air. The police were everywhere. One end of the street was blocked by two squad cars and there were uniformed officers searching the opposite end on foot. I made sure Hunter had us cloaked before I slowly steered the bike around the parked squad cars and took to a road that led away from the heart of the city. We had escaped, but where were we going?

Hunter soon fell silent and I didn't know what to do. For a while I contemplated driving across country to my cottage by the west coast. Hunter was getting worse by the minute, though, and I probably wouldn't make it that far. There was only one realistic destination. I had accepted that by the time we reached the outskirts of the city. We were headed for Maybrook.

Hunter was out cold by the time I turned off the motorway onto the road that led to the sleepy suburb. We were now uncloaked, he was slumped over my back, spilling blood on the road, and I was driving at over 200kmph. The only bit of luck we had that night was that we weren't spotted by the local police.

The hour was late when I parked the bike in the lane at the back of Maybrook Avenue. The streets were empty, the houses were dark and silent, and sunrise was not yet near. I waited a short while and listened out for sirens that never came. When I was sure we had not been followed I killed the engine, flicked out the kickstand and climbed off the bike. I now had an opportunity to take a closer look at Hunter. I didn't like what I saw. He was still unconscious; he was bleeding very heavily and was as white as a sheet.

The high-speed journey certainly hadn't done him any good. Being slumped over the tank of a kinetibike in freezing temperatures was only making matters worse. I couldn't waste any more time. I had to get him indoors.

I carefully lifted him onto my shoulder and used my gift to wrench open the doorway to the back garden of my family home. It didn't take long to bypass the patio doors and to get Hunter upstairs to the master bedroom. I then went back outside and wheeled the bike into the back garden before making my way inside once more. All the furniture and framed pictures and knick-knacks were untouched. The house looked exactly as it had the night I left for London – apart from a little dust and a stale odour in the air.

I turned on the bedroom lights to see Hunter sprawled across the bed clutching his stomach and moaning. This was going to be a very difficult night. I almost puked when I got a closer look at his injury. Blood was spewing out around the sides of the piece of wood that was stuck in his stomach. It got worse every time he moved. His clothes were completely soaked through from perspiration, his face was bone white and every couple of minutes he went into a bout of intense shivering. He'd be dead within an hour or two and I had no idea how to save him. I couldn't even look at the wound without vomiting, never mind carrying out some rudimentary operation on him. I sat at the end of the bed, with my face in my hands, as my only friend slowly died right next to me. Why did everyone close to me have to die? Was I cursed? Was this all my fault?

'Bentley …' Hunter said weakly. 'Bentley, are you there?'

'Yeah, I'm here.' I rounded the bed and sat next to him. I leaned forward to look in his eyes and patted him on the shoulder. 'How are you feeling, pal?'

'Get your hands off me,' he grumbled. 'You need to listen, right? I want you to leave me here. I'm not going to last much longer. My insides are all cut up and I don't have the strength to operate on myself.'

'I can try, Hunter. I can try to use my gift to fix this.'

'No. You'd only mess it up, then blame yourself for killing me in some incredibly painful way. You just leave me here, lad. My race is run, and so will yours, if you stay with me. You need to get out of here and go somewhere off the beaten track. And you need to stay there until all this has blown over.'

'I don't want to do that, Hunter. I can't leave you here to die on your own.'

'Do as I say,' he said, wincing. He started shivering again, worse than before, and clutched at the piece of wood stuck in his gut. 'I'm going to pass out now. You get on that stupid bike of yours and clear off. And don't go searching for Cathy. You're too important to lose …'

He was out cold again as soon as he finished barking his last order at me. Romand, Dad, Peterson, and now Hunter. It seemed every mentor I would ever have was to meet this grim fate. And as usual, I could do nothing to prevent it.

Or could I …? There was one chance for Hunter. I had taken my first big risk of the night by going to Maybrook. Now I was contemplating the second big risk of the night.

Gemma Wright's house was only a few hundred yards away. Although she couldn't save Hunter, her dad was a medic in the army when he was a young man, and she had told me that he'd had to operate on injured soldiers a few times while serving in the Middle East. Surely he'd be able to help. To go there was reckless in the extreme. There were some very nasty people searching for me. I'd be endangering Gemma and her father by going anywhere near them.

No agent of the Guild would have even considered going to the Wrights' house if they were in my shoes. It was far too perilous. A sensible agent would have remained hidden that night, allowed Hunter to succumb to his injury, then moved on at first light. It was the sensible thing to do.

I wasn't a very sensible person, though, and within moments I was skulking along the avenue in the direction of the Maybrook Road. Hunter and I had shared too much, and faced too many dangers together, to let him slowly die from an injury I had inadvertently inflicted. I had to at least *try* to save him.

I paused at the end of the garden and saw one light on in the Wrights' house – Gemma's bedroom window. I was in luck. I picked up a pebble from the driveway and used my psychokinesis to make it float upward towards the window. When I was sure no one on the street was watching at me, I used my gift to tap the pebble against the window over and over until Gemma's face appeared between the curtains. Thankfully she was wearing her glasses and recognised me straight away.

'Ross Bentley, you are the strangest person I have ever known,' she hissed at me as soon as she'd gotten the window open. 'What on earth are you doing throwing pebbles at my window at this hour?'

'I need your help,' I said, keeping my voice as low as possible. 'I really need your help, Gemma.'

'Is that blood on your clothes?'

'Yeah. That's the reason I need your help.'

'You need my father's help.'

'I'll go if it's too much to ask ...'

'Stay there,' she insisted. 'I'll come down.'

Gemma pulled me into the hallway as soon as she had the door open. She thought I was hurt and that the blood that I was covered in was my own. I didn't correct her because this minor misconception made her dash upstairs and wake her father without hesitation. If I'd told her the truth she might have reacted very differently. Her father was a pleasant enough man, despite being rudely awoken in the middle of the night, and came plodding down the staircase wearing striped pyjamas and a pair of furry slippers.

'My God!' he gasped as he entered the hallway. 'Ross Bentley, what on earth have you done to yourself? Look at you, you're covered in blood!' Then he straightened up and a calmness came over him as he looked me up and down. 'Where is the injured person?'

'Ross is the one who's injured,' Gemma raised her voice. 'Can't you see he's badly hurt?'

'If Ross had lost that much blood,' he said to Gemma, 'he wouldn't be able to stand.'

'My friend is badly hurt,' I confessed. 'He's at my house. I couldn't think of anywhere else to bring him.'

'Most people would take an injured friend to a hospital,' Mr Wright said to me. 'You must be on the run if you brought him to an empty house.'

'He's going to die. And you need to believe me, he will be murdered if I bring him to a hospital. I wouldn't have come here if I wasn't desperate. It'll be my fault if he dies. I don't want that to happen. I *can't* let it happen.'

'All right, all right,' Mr Wright said after a moment's thought. 'What sort of injury are we talking about here?'

'Er …' I didn't want to tell him the exact injury, just in case he got spooked. I really didn't want to alarm him but still needed to portray a sense of urgency. 'You could say he's been stabbed.'

'And he's lost a lot of blood already,' he said, looking at my bloodstained clothes. 'This type of injury requires proper medical attention, Ross. I am advising you to bring your friend to a hospital immediately. I may not be able to patch him up.'

'He won't survive the journey to a hospital, Mr Wright. You have to help me save him. It's my fault that he got injured.'

'Right,' he said after a moment's thought. 'Give me a minute to gather some things.'

The short walk from the Wrights' house to mine seemed to take an eternity. All I could think of was that we'd get to the bedroom to find Hunter dead and as cold as the air of that winter night. The three of us entered the house as quietly as we could and found Hunter exactly how I'd left him; lying on his side and leaking blood all over the bed. Thankfully he was still breathing.

'Well, well, well,' Mr Wright said as he looked at the piece of wood sticking out of Hunter's stomach. 'How on earth did that get in there?'

'It's a really long story,' I replied. 'And I don't think we have time for long stories right now.'

'I think you're right. This man is very close to death.' He leaned over and took a closer look at Hunter's injury while mumbling to himself and nodding. 'Ross, put your hand over his mouth for a moment, would you.'

'Won't he suffocate?'

'He can breathe through his nose, don't worry.'

'All right.' I pressed the palm of my hand over Hunter's lips and looked quizzically at Mr Wright. 'Why do I need to cover his mouth?'

'You'll see in a moment.'

Mr Wright pulled on a pair of latex gloves, climbed onto the bed, straddled Hunter – which looked very bizarre – then pressed hard on his abdomen with one hand, and without warning, grabbed the shard with his other hand and tore it from his stomach with one pull. Hunter's screams would have woken half the street if they hadn't been muffled by my hands.

'Are you lucid?' Mr Wright asked Hunter. 'You there, can you hear my voice?'

'Who the bloody hell are you?' Hunter hissed. 'I'm in flaming agony here!'

'That's a good sign,' Mr Wright said quite calmly as he climbed off the bed. 'I'd have been worried if you couldn't feel anything.' He started pulling instruments from his medical bag and laying them on the bed. Then he took a bottle of whiskey and unscrewed it. He took a long swig from the bottle and then passed it to Hunter. 'What I'm about to do to you will be extremely painful and I have no anaesthetic – except for this.'

'Give it here.' Hunter was never one to pass on a shot of whiskey and raised the bottle to his face with trembling hands. He started drinking as Mr Wright began to remove his blood-soaked clothes.

'Gemma,' Mr Wright said, turning to his daughter. 'I'd rather you didn't have to look at a naked man drinking whiskey. I'll call you in if you're needed. Ross, you can remain here – I'll need an assistant. Press your hands on the wound. Keep pressure on it.'

Gemma's father waited for her to leave before removing the rest of Hunter's clothes, then used bed sheets to clear most of the blood from Hunter's body. The retired doctor gave me a sobering look when he'd cleared away the majority of the blood. Hunter was head to toe in old scars. God only knows what Mr Wright was thinking at that moment. To his credit, he didn't make a single comment, and got to work on his patient without delay. I'd seen my fair share of combat and had suffered quite a few bad cuts in my time, but this was a bridge too far for me. I'd never seen so much blood in all my life. Then I remembered how much Romand had bled before he died. The memory of him lying lifeless on Peterson's lawn awakened a deep fear in me and I stood there shaking as Hunter drifted into drunken unconsciousness. He was a right old grump, was Hunter, but I didn't want him to die. He was one of the few friends I had left in the world.

It was bright outside by the time the last stitch was sewn. The people of Maybrook were awake and going about their normal morning routine, oblivious to what had transpired in the house that night. I parted the curtains and looked along the avenue for any sign of unwelcome visitors. Nothing was out of place. The only ones who passed along the road were sleepy suburbanites venturing into another nine to five adventure.

'I've done all I can,' Mr Wright said as he draped a clean sheet over Hunter. 'He should live … I think.'

'I can't thank you enough, Mr Wright.'

'I know you can't,' he replied sharply.

'What happened, Ross?' Gemma asked. I hadn't even noticed her entering the room and had no idea how long she'd been standing there. 'How did this happen?'

'I wouldn't know where to begin, Gemma.'

'Try!' she demanded. 'We got you out of a right jam. I think you owe us an explanation.'

'Do you both remember those crazy videos of me moving things around at the big contest in London?'

'The videos from *The Million Dollar Gift*?' she asked. 'The fake videos?'

'Yeah …' I replied awkwardly. 'The *fake* videos …'

'They weren't fake, were they?' her father said. 'That's why you're on the run.'

'Yes.'

'We don't want to hear any more,' he said. 'I think what you have to say may be dangerous for us to know.'

'It is, Mr Wright,' I said. 'Thanks for understanding. Thanks for everything that you've done.'

'Stop thanking me,' he barked. 'You shouldn't stay here alone if there are evil people looking for you, Ross. This house would be a obvious place to look.'

'That's why I think the two of you should leave. I couldn't live with myself if anything happened to you. I shouldn't have even involved you in the first place. I was just so desperate last night.'

'You are still desperate if there are people searching for you and your injured friend – it will be quite some time before he is mobile again.'

'I have nowhere else to take him.'

'Well, I haven't spent half the night saving this man's life only for him to be gunned down in his sleep,' Mr Wright said. 'No, that won't do at all. You and your friend should hide at our house.'

CHAPTER ELEVEN

Fever

At first I refused Mr Wright's offer. He and Gemma wouldn't take no for an answer, though, and after a while I realised that they were right; staying in the house alone with Hunter was stupid and pointless. The assassins would eventually go to my family home in search of us, and I mightn't have been able to fend them off without Hunter's help. I wasn't even sure what I would be facing considering the advanced weaponry that Vanev, and the assassin at the hospital, had used. My gifts could even be rendered ineffective by such technology. It would have been foolish to remain.

After he'd gathered his instruments, Mr Wright walked back to his home then returned in his station wagon a few minutes later and parked in the lane at the back of the house. Gemma and I carried Hunter through the house and garden, then bundled him into the backseat. I watched them drive away then went back inside to clean up. I gathered everything that had so much as a speck of blood on it. Bloody tissues, bed clothes, towels and clothes all went into bin liners that I hid in the attic. I didn't want to leave any evidence of our brief but traumatic stay at the house. I then went to my old room to see if there was anything I could take with me that might come in handy. I found little of use. This was the room of a stranger, a youngster with too much time on his hands. A laptop, a games console, DVDs, earphones, an MP3 player. Most of it already outdated. Most of it was crap. Just worthless junk that serves only to distract people from living their lives. The boy who had left this house for a contest in London was a shallow stranger to me now. I had become someone different and more meaningful than who I once was. It made me feel like the early years of my life had been wasted. Leaving the suburban prison had unlocked the real me. For the first time in many, many months I didn't regret entering The Million Dollar Gift. If I had stayed here I would have amounted to nothing. I'd probably still be working at the same supermarket, and being bullied by my old boss.

Before I left the house I wandered into the sitting room. I shouldn't have gone there. I knew there was only hurt for me in that room but I couldn't stop myself. I had to go in. I had to look upon this room that had occupied my thoughts for so much of the last year.

There was enough light creeping in through the crack in the curtains to see the black circular stain on the carpet. It was the crusty remnants of the putrid liquid that Zalech had summoned from the roadside or the sewer or the garden – who knows. He had used it to drown my father. The carpet was a mirror of my soul; stained forever by that one moment of cruelty.

I sat on the couch and gazed around the cold, dim room and recalled so many moments from my childhood. I used to stay up late watching TV with my parents then drift off on that same couch. I'd wake to find my mother carrying me to bed. I remembered it all quite clearly, but the feelings of that time were gone. Impossible to recapture that sense of security and contentment. I was so happy back then. I had no idea of the horrors that roamed this world. I could have no comprehension of the trials I would face. I only began to realise how difficult life can be when my mother lost hers. Everything went wrong when she died. The grief I suffered had stirred the gift for the first time. I'd been trapped on an emotional rollercoaster ever since.

The memories of my mother and father were so painful to experience that they unleashed a ferocious headache, one so potent that the faint light slicing in through the curtains hurt my eyes. I turned my face from the light and slowly rose from the couch and staggered towards the door. The pain quickly became unbearable. I had crumbled to my knees before I got to the doorway and I hunched over groaning as the throbbing inside my skull grew more and more intense.

Then suddenly there was no pain at all. There was no chill in the air. The shadows that haunted every corner of the room had been chased away by the warmth of the lamp hanging from the ceiling. I slowly got to my feet as voices emanated from the speakers of the TV in the corner. Was this a dream? Was it a momentary lapse of sanity brought on by the ferocity of the headache?

'Don't just stand there, Ross. Sit down, would you. And close the door, you're letting the heat out.'

I turned around to see my father sitting in his favourite armchair, a mug of tea in one hand, the remote for the TV in the other.

'Da?'

'You don't recognise me?' he laughed. 'I know we don't talk as often as we used to but surely you haven't forgotten what I look like?'

It wasn't real. It couldn't be real. But here I was, standing there looking into his eyes, hearing his voice, feeling the warmth of the room, hearing the voices from the TV, the low rumble of cars passing on the road outside.

'I'm sorry,' I said to him. 'Da, I'm sorry.'

'What are you sorry for?'

'For not being there to save you …'

'Save me from what?' He rested the mug of tea on a side table and stared at me, a look of deep concern dulling his features. 'Ross, are you sure you're okay? I think those headaches you've been having are worse than you've admitted.'

'The headaches?'

'You've been having them for weeks.'

'I don't remember any headaches …'

I looked up and caught my reflection in the mirror above the mantelpiece. I was fifteen years old. The shock of seeing my younger self staring back at me seemed to shatter the illusion. The room immediately plunged into shadow and I saw myself in the mirror as I should have been; a scarred nineteen year old who looked like he'd lived a hundred years. I was going insane. I was sure of that as I walked to the back garden for clean air.

What had just happened? It was just like when my time–scan of Detective Clarke had been invaded by the illusion of being in the English countryside with Romand. Were they visions? Hallucinations? Dreams? Or were they memories? And if they were memories, what was unlocking them and why did I not remember having these headaches over the years? Not for the first time in my life I was plagued by questions that could not be answered. My life was a mystery to me. Sometimes I felt like I didn't know myself, like my conscious mind was a casual passenger in my body.

Then another vision seized control of me without any warning. I was sitting by the fireplace in the cottage by the coast, one hand clutching the side of my head, the other wrapped tightly around the neck of a beer bottle. Cathy was watching me from across the room, a look of intense worry screwing up her face.

'Don't drink, Ross,' she pleaded. 'Alcohol won't make it any better.'

'Cathy, you can't understand the pain in my head. I can't take it anymore.'

'It's because of what you are, Ross. Soon it will pass. It always goes away.'

'What do you mean by that? I've never had a headache like this before.'

'You have them nearly every day now, Ross. You just don't remember having them. You black out or something. You won't remember this conversation either.' She left her seat, took the bottle from my hand and pressed her lips against my cheek. 'One day it will all make sense. One day it will be worth it.'

One day it will be worth it … those seven words unlocked another alien memory. I was unsteady on my feet and was being helped around the winding paths of the animal sanctuary by Peter Williams.

'Greatness can only come with some measure of sacrifice, my lad.'

'It feels like my skull is cracking open.'

'Some day in the not too distant future it will be worth the pain you are going through.'

I looked up to find myself standing in the back garden – where I should have been. Romand, Dad, Cathy and Williams. I now had memories of being with each of them while I endured cruel headaches and bouts of terrible anxiety. Why was I not aware of these headaches? What did they mean when they said it would be worth it one day? Williams and Cathy must have known what was causing the headaches. Unfortunately I couldn't quiz Williams about the memories, he was long in his grave, but Cathy was only a phone call away. I had to contact her soon. I had to know she was all right, but I also needed to understand what was happening to me. This was a mystery that could not go unsolved.

I pulled the patio doors shut and locked them. My family home was not the place to linger, not with the type of people that I had fought at the hotel still looking for me. I wasted no time in wheeling the kinetibike to the end of the laneway. Then I drove carefully to Maybrook Road, down the side of the Wrights' house and parked it in their garage out back. Before I made my way to the house, I stuffed the gun I'd taken from Vanev into one of the bike's sidebags. It had been concealed under my jacket all night and I didn't want it to fall out in front of Gemma or her dad – I think their welcome would wear thin very quick if that happened.

Gemma made me a brew and a sandwich when I got inside the house and we chatted about nothing important for a while, before her father told me I could get some sleep on the fold-down bed in the sitting room. It was midday when I pulled the blanket up to my chest and nestled my face in the cushions. I was out cold in minutes.

❀❀❀

I woke up late in the evening and heard Gemma and her father having a heated discussion in the kitchen and low moans coming from upstairs. I just lay there listening to what the Wrights were talking about, unwilling to rise from the comfort of the bed. Mr Wright was saying that he should call one of his old colleagues to inspect Hunter's wound and to help treat the infection that was setting in. Gemma urged him to tell no one. Eventually her father relented and I heard him climbing the stairs and entering the room above me. He spoke to Hunter. The only reply he got was coughing and groaning. It went on like that all night before there was a period of silence around dawn. That's when I finally rose and went to the kitchen to raid the fridge.

Within a couple of hours Hunter was making noises again and I finally had to help the Wrights in looking after him. The injury had become infected and that brought on a fever that disrupted his senses and made him act like a raving lunatic. That first night was calm enough. The second day it got gradually worse. Hunter made so much noise that a neighbour called at the door to see if everything was all right. Gemma said her father was in bed with a bad dose of the flu and to ignore the coughing and moaning. I don't know if the neighbour believed it or not.

The third day was as bad as the one before it. I started to wonder if Hunter would ever recover. How long could I remain hidden at the Wrights' house when there was so much trouble plaguing the world of the gifted? The pressure was mounting. Hunter was still delirious and the war between the Guild of the True and the mysterious organisation that Brofeldt claimed she worked for was about to break out. That was one the longest days of my life and I fell onto the fold down bed around midnight and was as tired as I had ever been.

I didn't get any sleep. Before I drifted off, Mr Wright came into the room and told me to follow him upstairs. He led me up into the attic, that had been converted into an office, and ushered me to the window that looked out on the street.

'What am I supposed to be looking at?' I asked, as I looked up and down the road beyond the garden.

'Take a step back from the window,' he replied quietly. 'Keep your voice down. I don't want Gemma getting wind of this.'

'Wind of what exactly?'

'There,' he said, motioning towards the window with his head.

I stepped back to the window and watched a dark coloured saloon rolling slowly along the road. There were two men in the front and another two in the back. They were clearly examining the houses and gardens as they went along the road.

'I first noticed them about an hour ago. They keep showing up as if they are doing laps of Maybrook.'

'Stay away from the windows tonight,' I told him. 'They'll move along soon enough.'

'You don't sound very certain.'

'Nothing in my life is certain, Mr Wright.'

'Ross, I have seen my fair share of war wounds over the years. And I can see by the scars that you and your friend bear that you are leading a violent life –'

'I can handle myself in a fight.'

'I don't doubt it – I saw those videos from the contest. That's not what I want to warn you about. I also treated countless people who had been emotionally dismantled by years of strain and stress. I can see that same look on your face right now.'

'What am I supposed to do, take a chill pill?'

'No. What you need to do is distance yourself from whatever it is you are involved in. Get away from all this, Ross, before it dismantles you.'

I didn't sleep a wink that night. I roamed the house like a tormented ghost, thinking over all the troubles and doubts that surrounded me. I also contemplated Mr Wright's advice. I knew he was right about not being able to deal with stress for years on end. Someday I would have to escape the world of the gifted or else face being consumed by the hurt it caused me.

It was 5am when I heard Hunter calling for me. I welcomed the distraction from my grim thoughts and went to the spare room and sat on the bed next to him. His eyelids hung lazily over his eyes and his skin was dashed with sweat. The fever still refused to relinquish its grip on him.

'Bentley, don't tell them about yourself,' he said in a conspiratorial voice. 'You can't tell anyone about your gifts. They'll kill you if you do! Promise me that you'll stay quiet.'

'I'm all right, Hunter. I haven't told them anything.'

'You're far too important,' he whispered. 'Way too important for us to lose. The Guild needs you more than you know.'

'Peter Williams once said something similar to me. You know,' I snorted, 'he believed that one day I would lead the Guild.'

'Of course he did. It's only natural.' He tried to lift himself from the bed but was too weak and fell back onto the pillows, hissing in sharp breaths.

'Don't get yourself so worked up,' I told him. 'You'll be better tomorrow.'

'If tomorrow comes ...' Hunter was staring into the shadows that filled the corners of the ceiling. 'I know what's out there ... Bentley, you have to be ready when the time comes. You have to be strong. Those demons that Romand and I found in the underground all those years ago are still out there. Don't you realise that? They're out there waiting in the shadows for their moment.'

'What demons are you talking about?' At first I thought he'd been babbling aimlessly. Now I believed there was some hint of truth in what he was saying. I recalled the speech he gave at Romand's funeral. Hunter said that he and Romand had searched the world for the Kematian.

'Who are the demons, Hunter? Are you talking about the Kematian?'

'That's not what we have to worry about.' He reached out and grabbed a fistful of jumper. 'It's the other ones. They're the ones who'll destroy everything. No one can know, Bentley. Never say a word.'

'What demons, Hunter?'

'Monsters that have no place in the natural world. They'll kill everyone ...'

I was about to question him further when I was interrupted by Mr Wright. He paced into the room and sat next to me, wrenching Hunter's arms away from me and feeding him more tablets.

'He's out of his mind,' Mr Wright said to me. 'He's been rambling on about demons and the underworld all day. He'll snap out of it soon enough. It's the fever that's talking.'

'He's been like this for days,' I said. 'Are you sure he'll come through this?'

'He's as strong as any man I've ever come across,' Mr Wright said thoughtfully. 'Most would have succumbed to either the injury or the infection by now. He's through the worst of it. Another day or two and he'll be more like himself.'

The medication took an almost immediate effect on Hunter. He was snoring within a few minutes and I went to the silence of my room to rest. I didn't quite know what to make of what he had told me. None of it made any sense really. But I did suspect that a great evil was hidden from me by Hunter and the other leading members of the Guild. I also got a feeling that it wouldn't be long before this dark secret of theirs would be revealed to me. Did I want to know? That was the question I pondered before I fell asleep.

I had breakfast with Gemma the next morning. Then we sat on deck chairs in the back garden and chatted for almost two hours. I never told her anything about my new life. I never once mentioned Cathy. Never a word about the Guild. And I never uttered Zalech's name, even though she asked me about my father's death more than once. She could not know of these things. I did tell her a little about my psychokinesis, and even used the gift to entertain her – just simple tricks like levitating her chair by a few inches, and making her hair curl into extravagant shapes. I was giving her just a glimpse of what I was capable of. I kept most of what was going on a secret, though. Sharing information with her was dangerous, but it wasn't only that; I didn't want her to see too much of the bigger world – the world of the gifted – because it might ruin her perspective on life. I wanted her to have a happy life, untainted by stories of gifted murderers and assassins. And by all accounts her life was a happy one.

She told me countless stories about college and all the interesting people she'd met and the places she planned to visit. There was a time when stories like this would have bored me. Now, I just sat there listening to her. It was nice to hear about the everyday things that people my age did. I sat there imagining that I had gone to college and played pranks on the friends that I might have made. It certainly was nice to be around her again. I still felt so comfortable in her company, as if there had been no break in our friendship, as if nothing had been altered between us. A lot had changed for us both, though. I had become a different person. Gemma had grown into a beautiful young woman with the world at her feet. It was almost strange that we still had such a strong connection. I was glad to have shared that time with her.

I had left my family home three days earlier thinking that my earlier life had little meaning. Talking with Gemma brought back all the little things that did give it meaning. Talking with her had introduced a sense of normality that had been lacking in my life of late. All traces of that fleeting moment of normality were instantly banished as soon as Hunter woke up …

'Bentley!' I heard him shouting from upstairs. 'Bentley, where are you? Where the bloody hell are you? And where are my clothes, damn it?'

'Sounds like the patient is conscious,' Gemma smiled. 'You better get up there. He sounds pissed!'

'He always sounds like that.'

'Feeling better?' I asked him when I opened the door to the spare room. I knew the second I looked at Hunter that he was back to himself. He was sitting upright, his shoulders were tensed up and that familiar frown of his had taken over his face again. 'How are you feeling?'

'Never mind how I'm feeling. Where are we?'

'This house belongs to a friend of mine.'

'What are you talking about? You don't have any friends!'

'A friend from my former life.'

'Don't tell me you brought me to the place you grew up.' He slowly climbed from the bed with a groan then returned his focus to me. 'That was a stupid thing to do.'

'It was either that or let you die.'

'Die? I could have fixed the wound myself.'

'You don't remember telling me to escape and leave you to die?'

'I would never have said that. Your imagination is running wild again.'

'Yeah, I must have dreamed the whole thing up.'

'Well, don't beat yourself up about it.' He parted his pyjama top and examined the rough scar on his stomach. 'That's not a bad job. Who did it?'

'The man who owns this house. He is the man who saved your life and risked his neck to protect us both. Don't you forget to thank him.'

'Oh, enough of all this,' he moaned. He staggered to the window, parted the curtains and squinted at the sky. 'It's late in the day...'

'Almost 3pm,' I told him.

'3pm? Christ! That means I've been out for over twelve hours. We've wasted far too much time. We have to get going.'

'Hunter, you've been unconscious for over four days.'

'Four days?' he asked incredulously. 'Four days! Half the bloody Guild might have been wiped out by now. I can't believe you left me unconscious for that long. We have to get moving immediately.'

'Hunter, you'll need another couple of days before you can travel. You nearly died more than once since the fight at the hotel.'

'I'll live,' he grumbled. 'Now fetch me my clothes! I refuse to leave the house in silk pyjamas that are two sizes too small for me!'

'And where are we supposed to be going? Are you intending to catch a flight to London to see your friends in the Palatium?'

'No ...' A veil of doubt fell over his face and he eased himself back on to the bed and sat in silence for a long while. 'No ... we can't go there ... It's all coming back to me now.' His brow hung low over his eyes and his hands became fists. 'We were betrayed. Someone sold us out to Vanev and Brofeldt.'

'What are you talking about?'

'I made a call to Ballentine. Don't you remember? I told him exactly where we were staying. Then within the hour those goons were trying to kill us. We were betrayed, Bentley.'

'You think Ballentine told them we were at the hotel?'

'Someone did.'

'I don't believe that. One of the spies must have seen us or something. Maybe they caught a glimpse of one of us standing by the window. Maybe they saw me when I left the chipper with the food.'

'No, Bentley. They didn't see us. They were told where we were.'

'Maybe they had Ballentine's phone tapped or something. Remember Brofeldt said they had people everywhere – in government agencies.'

'All Guild phones are encrypted. They can't be tapped. And yes, she did say they had people everywhere. She also admitted to us that they had people in the Guild.'

'She was full of crap. She was just trying to scare us.'

'A dying woman doesn't tell lies,' he assured me. 'They have people planted in the Guild. One of those people sold us out.'

'And if what you say is true, who betrayed us? Surely Ballentine would never work for a group like this.'

'Ballentine's an arsehole.'

'That doesn't automatically make him a traitor.'

'I know. He might have passed the order to someone else … Maybe it was the agents based in Belfast that he called. It's impossible to know right now.'

'If we don't know who the traitor is, then we can't seek help from the Guild. We don't really know who we're asking for help.'

'Exactly,' he nodded. 'We are on our own for now.'

'There's nothing we can do if we're on our own.'

'I'm not going to sit here hiding while the Guild is destroyed. Too many people have sacrificed themselves for the Guild for it to end up like this. There are too many good people still within the group to abandon it now. We have to try to stop this *master* that Brofeldt talked about.'

'Do you have any idea who he is?'

'None.'

'Are you sure? Hunter, you were running a fever last night and you kept going on and on about demons who are allied to the Kematian.'

'I never said that!' he almost shouted. A look of shock took over his face as he turned to me. 'I would never say something so idiotic.'

'You did say it.' I stepped closer to him and lowered my voice. 'Listen, I know you're not supposed to be telling me about the Kematian, but if he is out there and you think he's responsible for all this, you have to tell me. I must know what I'm facing before I risk my life again.'

'You are not facing the Kematian,' he replied. 'That man is dead to the world.'

'Then who the hell is this master?'

'I told you I don't know,' he said angrily. 'We need to contact people who know more about this before we make our next move.'

'What about the Council? Sterling? He can't be a spy working against the Guild, he's running the show! How can we contact him?'

'We can't. I told you the entire Council goes into hiding when war is brewing. No one outside the Council knows where they go ...'

'That's bloody great!' I moaned. 'So we can't contact anyone. We don't even know who is genuine and who is a traitor.'

'There are two people in the Guild who simply cannot be spies.'

'Who?'

'Marie Canavan and Elizabeth Armitage. Other than Sterling, those are the only two people who I would entrust my life to.'

'I hope you memorised their phone numbers because your mobile phone was in the hotel room – the hotel room that was turned into a furnace.'

'I remember their numbers. I won't make any calls from a civilian's house, though. I have to get moving, Bentley.'

'We have to be careful before we leave. There's been a car full of very suspicious looking dudes doing laps of this housing estate.'

'Now?'

'Last night. There's been no sign of them today.'

'We will have to be extra cautious.'

'We'll need more than caution. We'll need a fair amount of luck to survive this time.'

'Yes, this is indeed a wicked time. The next few days will be the most perilous we've ever faced.'

CHAPTER TWELVE

The Wrong Luggage

I had no idea what we were going to face when we entered the fray once more. I was understandably apprehensive about leaving the safety of the Wrights' house after the vision I'd had of Hunter being killed. If that vision was accurate I would lose my best friend and would have to countenance a very lonely future. I could feel my anxiety levels rising by the minute and I doubted I had the stomach for the fight. There was no backing out, though. I was going to be a part of this gifted war whether I liked it or not. I had been targeted by the enemy, even though I had been inactive for more than a year. They would come for me one way or another, and I thought it best that I at least do my bit for the Guild rather than try to hide.

After my conversation with Hunter I went to tell Gemma and her father that the time had come for us to leave. Mr Wright fetched some of his old clothes for Hunter to wear, then insisted that we stay for dinner before we hit the road again. To my surprise Hunter accepted the offer; he told me it could be a long time before we got a square meal again, and from experience I knew this was a definite possibility.

To my surprise, Mr Wright was quite the cook. We even had starters before the main course – which was quite delicious as well as filling. Then he laid out some homemade rhubarb pie and custard for dessert. It was quite the meal. I doubted I'd see the like of it again for a long time to come.

The conversation had been friendly through the evening. Then as Mr Wright poured coffees for us all the chatter died down. Most of the talking was done by Gemma's dad; he was advising Hunter on how to treat his injury if it became infected again. He also advised him not to be doing anything strenuous. Hunter assured him he would take it easy. I sat there listening to my colleague and was fascinated by how comfortable he was with lying and how convincing it sounded. I didn't blame him for lying. It was part of his survival technique in a way. All gifted people grow accustomed to hiding the truth from others.

Gemma barely said a single word and merely picked at her dinner. She didn't look at me once for the entire time we were seated. Occasionally her gaze rose from her plate and focused on Hunter. She stared at him like he was a monster from a fairy tale. In truth, he was far worse than any ghoul that a writer could dream up to scare impressionable minds. Hunter had killed, or murdered, depending on your point of view, countless people throughout his life. I knew some of those people didn't exactly deserve the punishment he delivered. I tried to convince myself that the world needed people like him – those who could set aside feelings and conscience to protect society. His view of the world and the threats that often face it was a narrow one: Stamp out the threat before it becomes too great. If that meant killing someone, then so be it. I too had taken human life, but my perspective on the world and the people and villains who filled it was polarised with Hunter's; I could never neglect conscience, even if killing was for the greater good. There was always a price to pay for taking a human life. For me the effects of killing were hardly ever immediate; it would be weeks after the event that the guilt and revulsion would set in and linger. But for all of Hunter's flaws, he'd probably fight to death to protect Gemma and her father if our enemies tried to harm them. It was this that made him rather odd and endearing: he could take human life at times like it meant nothing to him, then on other occasions he would risk his neck to save people he didn't even know.

Gemma would have been terrified of both Hunter and me if she knew even a fraction of our true nature. I think her father had a better grasp on what we were. I hadn't told him of the Guild or that we were agents who tracked down criminals, but I did get a feeling that he knew we were killers as soon as he'd laid eyes on Hunter's scarred body. That look he gave me before he started the operation spoke volumes.

Hunter excused himself as soon as we were finished eating and went to the back garden for a cigar as the sun set over Maybrook. Gemma went to her room without so much as a word. I didn't want to leave without talking to her one last time, and so after I helped her father clear the table, I went upstairs and rapped my knuckles on her bedroom door.

'Go away, Ross,' she answered from within. 'I don't feel like talking right now.'

'Yes, you do. You just don't want to say what's on your mind.'

'Stop twisting my words.'

'Open the door, Gemma. I'd rather we had this chat face to face.'

'We're not having a chat.'

'We are actually.'

The door swung inward and she stood facing me with sadness clouding her eyes. She reluctantly stepped to one side and ushered me inside with a tired sweep of her arm.

'Why don't you want to talk to me all of a sudden?' I asked as she shut the door behind me. 'What's wrong?'

'I don't like that you're leaving.'

'I have to leave, Gemma. I can't stay here.'

She nodded pensively as she took a seat on the end of her bed. She took an old teddy bear from a shelf next to her and massaged its tattered ears and stared at the floor. 'Never mind me. I'm just being silly.'

'What's really on your mind, Gemma?'

'I'm wondering what the hell is out there, Ross? Where are you going? Why are you running?'

'It's nothing too serious, believe me. I have to hide this power of psychokinesis that I have. There are people who will do anything to have control over me because of the things I can do. That's why I move around from place to place. I refuse to allow this gift to be used for evil.'

'You're not as good at lying as your Scottish friend.'

'What do you mean?'

'Of course it's serious, Ross. I'm not stupid.'

'I know you're not.'

'Then stop treating me like I am. You disappeared into thin air, no one hears from you for two long years and then you show up at my door, your friend almost dead with a piece of wood stuck in his gut. Do you think I don't know how it got there?'

'How could you know?'

'I know because I watch the news, Ross. You came to Maybrook looking like you'd been in a war only hours after a terrorist attack on a hotel in Dublin. The police have been looking for two men who are supposed to be responsible. One is Irish and in his early twenties, the other is in his mid-forties with an accent that is either Scottish or northern English.' She rose from the bed and wrapped her hand around mine and forced a smile. 'I know you're not a bad person, Ross. You can't be. But I know you're involved in something really dangerous.'

'I guess there's no fooling you,' I said, giving her hands a squeeze. 'I won't tell you what's going on in my life, though. You can't know. You don't want to know. I would prefer if these last few days became an oddity in your life that soon becomes nothing more than a curious memory. I don't want my presence here to alter your future.'

'It's too late for that,' she said quietly. She turned away from me and sat on her bed again, running her hands through her long chestnut hair, as she often did when she was agitated.

'How has it altered your life?'

'Never mind.'

'Tell me, Gemma. I want to understand.'

'We were always good friends, Ross,' she said, almost embarrassed. 'Good friends … but maybe there could be a little something more than just friends …'

'What?' I almost laughed. 'You think there is more to us than simply friendship?'

'You used to have a crush on me …'

'Yeah, I did. And I let that go when I found out that you didn't feel the same.'

'Things can change.'

'Have your feelings changed?'

'I always liked you, Ross. You were a good friend and fun to be around. I didn't feel attracted to you, but we're older now and you're very different. You're not the silly fool who just made me laugh anymore. You're quite mysterious and you've got these amazing abilities.'

'I can't have this conversation, Gemma.'

'I told you I didn't want to talk. You're the one who insisted on knowing my mind.'

'I'm seeing someone.'

'So am I.'

'Well then,' I said, suddenly grinning like a tool, 'that settles that. This conversation is out of bounds. There's no reason to discuss our feelings.'

'You being here the last few days has given me these feelings.'

I had dreamed of this for countless nights when I lived in Maybrook. Gemma was the hottest girl I had ever set eyes on. A glance, a smile or simply a kind word from her was enough to brighten the darkest day. My infatuation with her was mostly frustrating because I was under the impression that the attraction wasn't mutual. But now she had the same feelings? It had been a long time since I thought of anyone other than Cathy in a romantic way. Now there was a sliver of the old attraction to Gemma showing through. My heart was beating just a little faster than usual as I sat next to her on the bed. The faint aroma of her perfume being sucked into me with every breath was like a magnet drawing me to her. It was like magic.

The same magic that had abandoned Cathy and me months earlier.

'Try to stay alive,' she whispered to me. 'I would like to think that you're alive and that someday you might show that ugly face of yours here again.'

'I intend to stay alive,' I replied. 'It might be nice to come back here again and look at your ugly face one more time.'

'That would be very nice …'

We leaned into each other and our lips met. I couldn't describe what we did as kissing because there was no movement on our lips. It was more like we breathed each other in for a few seconds before we drew back and took one last look into one another's eyes.

I fought back the rising desire and hid my eyes from hers by wrapping my arms around her shoulders and giving her a hug. This confusion of the heart was not the luggage I wanted on the journey that was ahead of me. For the first time in my life I was glad to hear Hunter shouting my name from the hallway below. It allowed me to avoid dealing with feelings that had no place in my life at that time.

There was no long goodbye. Within moments I had pushed the kinetibike along the laneway at the side of the house and mounted it by the gates. Hunter stood next to me and zipped up his new coat before he climbed on the back.

'Right, Casanova,' he said, smirking. 'Let's get moving.'

'She's just a friend.'

'She's too good-looking to be a friend.'

'We just talked.'

'Frankly, I don't care about your love life, Bentley. I'd like to get moving before those suspicious dudes of yours show up again.'

'Where to?'

'The nearest port.'

As always, Hunter's plan seemed a simple one. We were to go to Dublin port and he would cloak us as we sneaked onto the first liner that was headed to Britain. From there we were to search out either Canavan or Armitage – these were the only two people that Hunter could be sure about. Everyone else in the Guild was to be treated as an enemy.

In truth, Hunter's plans were never straightforward and this one was no different. No plan is simple when everyone is your enemy. We were wanted by the police after the battle at the Windmill Hotel, and because it was thought to be terrorism, every police force in the western world was on the lookout for us. The Guild was not safe for us anymore; there were people in the organisation who were traitors and had already tried to have us murdered. Then there was the shadowy group that Malcolm Wilson was a part of. They appeared to have moles planted everywhere and there was the unseen threat of the assassin that Brofeldt had warned us about. There was so much danger surrounding us that I felt claustrophobic even in the open air.

It took less than an hour to get from Maybrook to the docklands in Dublin. Hunter used his light-tuning gift to render us invisible to everyone around us and we were able to navigate right past the lines of cars waiting to drive onto the ferry to Liverpool. The fear that I felt as we neared the boat was in stark contrast to the elation I experienced the last time I boarded a boat in this port and left Ireland to enter *The Million Dollar Gift*. I was full of hope back then. Now I just wanted to get through the night with my life.

I steered the bike to the front of the line of vehicles and drove alongside an eighteen wheeler as it parked in the car deck, which was below the passenger levels. We were well hidden away and the hold was empty and silent by the time the ferry pulled away from the port. This allowed Hunter to relinquish the cloak and he was able to rest properly. We intended to stay there hidden next to the truck for the entire journey. We would have if Hunter hadn't fallen asleep. He still wasn't back to full health and after almost two hours of swaying in silence he drifted off.

With no one to talk to I soon grew restless and started to wander the tight spaces between the vehicles. I had no intention of doing anything apart from wandering until I saw an open door that led into a narrow service corridor. I took a glance through the open door out of sheer boredom and saw there was a telephone mounted on the wall at the far end. I wouldn't have much time to myself after we reached Liverpool so this was my one and only opportunity to disobey Hunter's orders and contact Cathy. I think it was a mixture of guilt for being intimate with Gemma and genuine concern for Cathy that forced me to walk forward and pick up the receiver. Our relationship was finished, but I still wanted to hear her voice and for it to sound friendly. I still worried about her constantly and this one phone call would allay most of my fears and allow me to concentrate fully on the dangerous tasks that lay ahead – or so I thought.

I punched in the number to the house in France and waited as the phone rang and rang. I expected that the call would wake her up and that I would hear the familiar gravel that was always in her voice when she was tired. What I heard was something very different.

'Hello?' It was June Atkinson. There was still a slight delay between each word she spoke that betrayed the damage done to her mind by the attack on her home by Marianne Dolloway. June was but a shadow of the person she once was. 'Who is this?'

'June, it's Ross. I'm sorry to ring so late. I hope I didn't wake you.'

'You didn't wake me, Ross,' she said distantly. 'I was just getting ready for bed.'

'Listen, I can't stay on this line for very long. Could I speak to Cathy?'

'Cathy?' she asked in a high pitched voice, as if it was strange to make such a request. 'Why would you ring here for Cathy?'

'Because she's staying there …'

'But Cathy's not here.'

'She's out quite late,' I said, looking warily along the corridor. 'When do you expect her back?'

'Back? Cathy is in London doing work for the Guild. Lord only knows when she'll come here again.'

'Working for the Guild?' I asked, trying to keep my voice low. 'Cathy would never work for the Guild again. She hated being part of the group.'

'Cathy is in London working for the Guild,' she insisted. 'And I don't know what could ever possess you to think she hated the Guild. Cathy is a valued member and has been for many years.'

June had been like a mother to me after I escaped the clutches of Golding and Shaw. It was cruel that such a cultured, caring and confident person could be reduced to this timid and confused woman on the other end of the phone. It broke my heart to listen to her. I was thinking she'd completely lost her mind. Cathy simply had to be there with her. She could not be working for the Guild!

'June,' I raised my voice. 'Cathy ran away from the Guild with me. Don't you remember?'

'She didn't run away.'

'June, where is she?'

'Cathy is far away from here.'

I was about to question her further when a door slammed somewhere nearby. People were talking in an adjoining corridor and their voices were growing closer by the second. I couldn't risk staying on the line and placed the receiver back down without another word to June.

I quietly made my way back to Hunter, who was still sleeping. I slid down against one of the wheels of the truck and sat on the cold metal floor, trying to figure out what just happened. June Atkinson had just told me that Cathy was not in France as she had claimed to be. And that she was doing important work for the Guild of the True. This made no sense at all. Cathy was dead set against the Guild. She had turned her back on the organisation over a year ago and vowed never to even have contact with them again – never mind work for them. June's mind was never the same after Romand's death and I thought that she might still be confused and had dreamed the whole thing up. The fact remained that Cathy was not in France. She had lied to me. She had left me and had lied about where she was going to be. Where was she if not in France tending to her mother? June Atkinson was hardly a reliable source but the information on Brofeldt's files saying that Cathy had been sighted in London seemed to corroborate her claim. The Palatium was in London. Everything pointed to Cathy being back in league with the Guild of the True. This truly was a stunning revelation.

I wanted to wake Hunter and confide in him but he'd go nuts if he knew I'd made that phone call. No, I'd have to keep this mystery to myself for the time being. I'd have to wait until things had calmed down before I could go looking for Cathy.

'How long was I out?' Hunter asked as he groggily peeled his face from the tank of the bike.

'Not long enough,' I grunted back at him.

'Christ,' he sighed as he stretched his back. 'You're a real bundle of laughs tonight. You know, I'd kill for a cup of coffee.'

'I wouldn't be surprised if that was actually true.'

'Oh, what's eating you?' he snapped. 'You're acting like a little girl again!'

'I have a right to.'

'Why?'

'I'm not telling you.'

'Good because I don't want to hear it.'

'Enough talking about my mood,' I said. 'What are we going to do once we get ashore?'

'We make some calls. We have to find someone friendly in the Guild to go to and who can fill us in on what's been going on. Then we go in search of the traitors in the Guild and torture the hell out of them until they rat out all their friends.'

'And what about this assassin that's supposed to be hunting us? Have you given him any thought?'

'Not much. We have no idea who he is or where he is, so we can't do anything about him. I'll think about him if he manages to find us.'

'Do you have any idea who he might be? If he's such a great assassin then the Guild would surely know about him, right?'

'There are a few assassins out there who might fit the bill,' Hunter said, folding his arms and nodding. 'There's a Peruvian woman who works for the south American drug cartels. She's an emotomagnet and a pyrokinetic. A very potent mix of gifts for an assassin. She could be the person Brofeldt was talking about. Then there's Gutierrez – he's based in Los Angeles. He is a very skilful electro-psych and could also be classed as a master assassin. There are other possibilities but most of them have been out of action for a long time.'

'Will we be able to deal with Gutierrez or the Peruvian if they find us?'

'Neither would represent a threat like Dolloway or Zalech did.' He looked down at me and shrugged. 'We managed to deal with them, didn't we?'

'Yes, we did. They basically destroyed my life but we did *deal* with them.'

'Forget the assassin for now,' Hunter said. 'Chances are that the trouble we face will come from Guild agents who have aligned themselves with our mysterious new enemy.'

'I hope the war hasn't already kicked off. These traitors in the Guild could be supplying Golding Scientific with the whereabouts of countless Guild members. They'll be slaughtered if they're not warned.'

'We can do little to save them right now. Our only choice is to stick to my plan. I just hope that we can contact Armitage. She might be able to contact the Council and that could bring a swift conclusion to this entire affair.'

'Why would she be able to get in touch with them? I thought no one knew their location.'

'Elizabeth Armitage is very tight with Jim Sterling.'

'I don't see what good Jim Sterling could do. He'll only make himself a target if he raises his head above the parapet.'

'Jim Sterling is strong enough to tip the balance in our favour.'

'I doubt he's that strong, Hunter. We're facing a well organised group that has control over Paul Golding. That means they have an advanced army at their command and that tips the balance in their favour. Golding Scientific has been developing some very interesting weaponry for use in a gifted war, remember? The armour that Zalech wore, the kinetibike, Vanev's gun and the gauntlet that the assassin used against us in the hospital. Lord only know what other technological horrors they have dreamed up in the labs of Golding Scientific. I think the only way to stop them is to kill this master that Brofeldt mentioned.'

'Yes, you may just be right.' He sat down next to me and scratched at the grey stubble on his chin. 'I've been thinking a lot about what she said and I still have no clue who it could be.'

'Maybe it's someone who has been hidden from the Guild their whole life. Or someone who appears to be just another gifted person who poses no threat, like Verbannk was.'

'I suppose both are plausible,' he said. 'There's no point in guessing. What we need are answers. Facts.'

I could see in Hunter's eyes that he did have an idea who the leader was but that he didn't want to tell me for some reason. I didn't probe any further. I didn't dwell on it either. It was best to keep my mind on staying alive rather than dreaming up images of some mysterious dark lord that had been waiting in the shadows his whole life for the right moment to cast his wickedness upon the world.

I was beginning to feel sea sick.

CHAPTER THIRTEEN

The Chase

The port in Liverpool was swarming with police that morning. I guess it was to be expected considering there had been a terrorist attack in the city only two weeks earlier, and the supposed act of terrorism at the Windmill Hotel probably set them on high alert again. The uniformed officers scrutinised every person getting off the boat and were stopping all the vehicles that rolled out of the parking deck. We didn't suffer their attentions because Hunter had made us invisible with the trick of body refraction. We slipped past the cops and the barriers without anyone ever knowing we were there.

The city was no different to the port; there were officers on every street corner and we also saw a few army vehicles that were packed with armed soldiers sitting inside. It looked like a war was about to break out and it felt like it too; there was an uneasiness in the air that clung to me as we journeyed through the rush hour traffic. It made me paranoid and I started thinking that people could see through the cloak and were watching our every move. I even thought for a while that a helicopter that hovered high above the rooftops of the city was following us. I didn't take a comfortable breath until we were outside the city centre.

It didn't take us long to break free of the suburbs and find a road that would take us east of the country. Hunter removed the cloak when we got to the first strip of empty road then told me to stop at a filling station that was further along the route. He'd obviously come this way before and felt it was a safe place for us to stop to figure out our next move.

Within half an hour we had reached the filling station. There was a large forecourt at the back that Hunter instructed me to park in, and on the opposite side of the road was a diner that he claimed had great grub. As I steered off the road towards the small car park I realised why Hunter had chosen this location to stop; there was an old-fashioned telephone box at the side of the building. I figured he'd take this opportunity to try contact his friends.

'Let me know if that precognitive gift of yours starts acting up,' he said as we left the bike parked between two SUVs. 'I don't really feel comfortable being out in the open like this.'

'I'll give you as much warning as I can.'

'You better. I don't want a repeat of what happened at the hotel.'

'Sorry about that,' I said, thinking about the terrible injury that he'd sustained during the fight with the spies. 'How are you feeling?'

'I've been better.'

'Maybe it's not such a good idea for us to go to the diner. You're not in good shape and you're obviously not comfortable with this location.'

'We'll just stay long enough to fill our bellies with fried food and to sink a strong coffee or two.'

Hunter walked to the telephone box and simply shook his head when I pointed out that we had no coins. He sent a spark of electricity into the phone before using his psychokinesis to both lift the receiver to his ear and to press the appropriate buttons.

'We're gifted, remember?'

'Okay, using your power to make a free call is fine,' I said. 'Using it to press buttons is just plain lazy.'

'It's not lazy at all. I like to use my powers as often as possible, so that I can maintain total control over them.' He smiled and gave me a wink. 'Practice makes perfect.'

'I say you're lazy.'

'I say you're a novice who shouldn't question my experience.'

He tried the same number over and over again but there was no answer and he finally accepted that Armitage wasn't going to pick up. This left him with one only option: Marie Canavan. He seemed reluctant to make this call and waited for more than a minute before dialling. It was risky to contact anyone in the Guild because there was always a chance the call might be somehow traced. I could understand his trepidation in calling Canavan because she wasn't just anyone, she was the woman who had been his mentor and foster parent for many years. He was obviously worried about putting her at risk by making the call.

'Yes?' I heard Canavan's strong voice over the drone of the cars as they passed the filling station. 'Who is this?'

'How's the weather in the city?' Hunter asked.

'It's appalling,' Canavan answered. 'Although I hear there are clear skies by the coast.'

'Might be nice to have dinner there.'

Hunter hung up then turned and walked towards the road. He really was a strange bugger at times, but the brief conversation with

Canavan was on a whole new level of weird.

'What the hell was that all about?' I asked as I walked with him to the roadside. 'Why were you asking her about the weather, dumbass?'

'I wasn't.' There was a break in the traffic and I followed Hunter as he strode cautiously across the road towards the diner. 'It's a simple code we use, just in case there was anyone listening in. Asking about the weather in the city is really asking what the situation at the Palatium is like. She answered by saying it's appalling, which means it's not safe for me to go there. Clear skies by the coast means I should head for a little house on the east coast that Canavan and I bought a few years ago – one we didn't tell the Guild about. And by saying it would be nice to have dinner there means I will be there by dinner time – approximately 6pm. If I'd said it would be nice to have supper there it would mean I'd arrive at 9pm. Breakfast at 8am and so on. Anything else you would like to know?'

'Yeah, how are we paying for lunch?'

'Don't worry, I'll think of something. Remember, I've done this type of thing a thousand times before.'

'So you've stolen a lot of money over the years, yeah?'

'Yes,' he laughed. 'Only because it was absolutely necessary.'

'Coffee is not a necessity.'

'It is to me.'

I was surprised to find the diner practically empty as we entered. I figured the reason was because it was too late for breakfast and too early for lunch. There were only two members of staff behind the counter, a waitress wiping down a tabletop and just four customers: A young man who was busy with his cell phone, two older men, probably truckers, who were deep in conversation, and one woman who was reading a newspaper while tucking into a muffin. Hunter looked to me as we got inside. I knew by his eyes that he wanted to know if I was sensing any danger. I wasn't, and gave a shrug of my shoulders to indicate so.

We sat at the table nearest the door and read through the menus before the waitress asked us what we wanted. We both ordered a full breakfast and black coffee.

'So, tell me' I said to my companion, 'why do you and Canavan have a house that the Guild doesn't know about? It seems quite strange to me.'

'Technically it's my house. I bought it with some money I've gained over the years. But it was always intended for Marie. She's getting on in years and I thought the clean air by the coast would be good for her whenever she decided to go into full retirement. I didn't tell the Guild about it because agents aren't supposed to have large stashes of money hidden away from them.'

'Where did you get so much money?'

'I got it about five years ago. Romand and I were investigating a rumour that a major drug dealer in Birmingham was actually gifted and using that gift to rise to the top of the criminal class. We eventually cornered him in a flat complex and he came out fighting. We had no choice but to take extreme measures.'

'You killed him?'

'Romand was the one who struck the final blow. We were about to move on when we discovered the reason why he'd decided that a fight against two Guild agents was a good idea. He'd hidden a lot of drug money in the bedroom of the flat.'

'How much?'

'Just over five hundred thousand pounds.'

'And you took it all?'

'I took half. Romand took half. It was during a time that the Guild was awash with money and we felt they wouldn't need it. If we'd left the cash at the apartment, the police would have taken it and chucked it into the black hole of the government coffers. It was a golden opportunity for us to have a pension that the Guild couldn't dig into whenever it needed to finance some expedition or survey or study. We'd risked our lives more times than I care to remember and we bloody well deserved that money.'

'What did Romand do with his half?'

'He never told me. Although, I suspect he squandered it on his private quest to capture Marianne Dolloway. I was more sensible with my share. I sat on it for a couple of years then used a portion of it to buy the house near Hornsea.'

'I was right about you, Hunter. You are a common criminal.'

'More like Robin Hood actually.'

'He used to give his money away, not purchase beach front property with it.'

'I didn't spend it all on the house. The rest of the cash is buried under the shed in the back garden. Remember that in case you're ever in dire straits.'

Our conversation was interrupted when the waitress brought us our breakfast and coffee. I don't think I'd ever eaten so much in such a short space of time. Hunter was only half way through his as I'd pushed my plate to the centre of the table and washed down the last mouthful of beans with my coffee.

'You'll give yourself indigestion eating that fast,' Hunter mumbled. 'You need to learn patience in everything you do. The way you use your gifts, the way you deal with your personal life and the manner in which you fight.'

'Spare me your advice, Hunter. I bet you were just as bad when you were my age.'

'I was,' he nodded. 'That's what qualifies me to lecture you on such matters. I can help you to avoid the mistakes I made.'

'Lecture me some other time.' I took a sip from my cup and leaned back into the leather couch. 'What are we going to do if Canavan can't shed any light on what's been going on?'

'We'll track down Ballentine and make him talk.'

'So you've decided that he's the traitor?'

'Remember the hit list?'

'Yes.'

'Obviously you don't remember it as well as I do.' He laid down his knife and fork, wiped his mouth with a napkin then leaned forward and lowered his voice. 'Everyone on the list had a status. Each agent was either a high or mid priority target. Everyone except Ballentine, that is. He was classed as undetermined.'

'I suppose that is quite incriminating.'

'It's damning, Bentley. Damning. There were also code names that the enemy created for each person on the list. Ballentine's was Chimera.'

'What's a Chimera?'

'Two-headed beast from Greek mythology.'

'Two-headed is different than two-faced.'

'I took it to mean that he is playing both sides.'

'Then why would he be on the list in the first place?'

'He might have been on the original list, before they turned him.'

'This is becoming very far-fetched, Hunter.'

'I'm quite sure he's our man.'

'Can we handle him?'

'Yes,' he nodded. 'We can handle him together. But let's not concern ourselves with all that right now. First we go to Canavan and see what she knows. Now is not the time to get worked up for a fight.'

'It might be ...'

'Hmm?'

'Look at that.' I pointed out the window at a helicopter that was high up over the filling station. It was just hovering in the one spot, hundreds of feet above the road outside. 'I had a strange feeling back in Liverpool that a helicopter was following us. Then it disappeared from sight and I didn't give it any more thought.'

'It's the same helicopter?'

'I can't say for certain. It is definitely the same model and colour.' I turned from the window and looked Hunter dead in the eye. 'It's too much of a coincidence, right?'

'I would say so.' Hunter finished his coffee as he watched the helicopter circling like a vulture waiting for an injured animal to finally collapse so it could swoop down to feast. 'I know a little about helicopters. That model is usually used by television stations. It's not fast. I doubt it could manage more than 150kmph.'

'Then we should be able to outrun it on the kinetibike.'

'That sounds like a good plan.' I could tell by the way he shook his left hand that he had created a cloak for us. 'Come on,' he said quietly, 'let's get the hell out of here.'

We made our way to the door as the staff stared at the empty booth, shaking their heads and pointing. Normally Hunter wouldn't have been so blatant in his use of light-tuning, but the arrival of the helicopter made such things seem trivial. We had been followed from the port, despite being cloaked for much of the way. Our situation was becoming precarious.

By the time we reached the side of the road we saw how precarious it truly was.

There were two more helicopters approaching fast from the east. These were lower to the ground and larger, certainly not the type of craft used by TV stations. These had the unmistakable characteristics of military helicopters. Hunter seemed stunned. He stopped in the centre of the road and watched them gliding over the landscape with wide eyes.

'This is not good,' he breathed. 'Not good at all.'

'British army?'

'No, they're not used by the British military. They're KA50 Black Sharks. We're in big trouble here. They'll have heat sensitive cameras and will be able to see through any invisibility cloak.'

'We can't hide from them?'

'No.'

'How fast can they travel?'

'Over 320kmph.'

'I might not be able to outrun them.'

'You'll have to. We certainly won't stand a chance if we try to fight them.'

We were so preoccupied by the helicopters that we didn't pay much attention to a dark coloured 4x4 speeding up the road. My attention turned to the approaching vehicle when my precognitive gift became active once again. My entire body tingled with fear as I watched it slide to a halt about twenty metres away. My blood ran cold as I watched an unusually tall and robust man climb out of the passenger seat.

'Hunter, look!' I gasped. 'What the hell is that?'

We both watched as the figure came into full view. He must have been seven feet tall and was built like a house. His attire was military in style and on his head he wore a black cowl that cast a deep shadow over his face and accentuated his glowing green eyes. I couldn't even believe it at first. His eyes were actually glowing.

'Bentley,' Hunter said to me quietly. 'I'll hold him off while you make a run for the kinetibike.'

'No, it'd be better to fight him together.'

'You can't fight him!' he snapped. 'Neither of us can. All I can do is delay him.'

The tall figure was striding confidently along the road towards us. Then he spoke, and for a moment I thought I was hearing the sick mechanical voice of Edward Zalech; it had that same emotionless and robotic tone as my old nemesis. It wasn't him, though. This was someone, or *something*, altogether new to me.

'Ah, this is a moment to savour,' the monster called out as he drew near. 'I finally come face to face with the infamous Michael Huntington.'

'You should have stayed in hiding,' Hunter shouted defiantly. 'You just made a big mistake, pal.'

'I have no need to hide from anyone. You should know that by now.'

'I've already had enough of this conversation,' Hunter spat. 'Let's see if you live up to your reputation.'

Hunter's reactions were lightning fast. He used his psychokinesis to pull down the power lines that criss-crossed above the road. They rolled and whipped through the air as if they had a life of their own. Within seconds they had wrapped themselves around the tall stranger and an immense burst of electricity flowed through them that brought him to his knees. Hunter was using his gift of electro-psyching to channel so much electricity through the cables that the assassin should have been set alight. Yet he was still alive and struggling with all his strength.

'Bentley,' Hunter shouted over the zapping sounds of the electrical cloud, 'get to the bike. I can't hold him much longer!'

I ran as fast as I could across the courtyard of the filling station. There were people standing by their cars staring at Hunter and the giant, others looked disbelievingly at the two Black Sharks that were now only a few hundred feet away. I barged them out of my way and sprinted to the car park at the rear of the building and dragged the kinetibike off its kickstand.

By the time I jumped on the saddle there was a shuddering sound in the air. The helicopters had opened fire and a line of bullets swept across the ground next to me and peppered the side of the building. I reacted out of instinct and shot out a slice of energy at the approaching crafts. I actually saw the air in front of the lead helicopter rippling as the kinetic slice struck what appeared to be an invisible barrier of some kind. These were no normal helicopters. These were specifically designed to hunt and kill the gifted. Golding Scientific had indeed been busy.

Another volley of bullets ripped up the concrete car park and almost sent me off the bike. Once more I shot out a bolt of energy at the lead helicopter, and once more my assault was deflected. I was in luck this time. The bolt of energy ricocheted off the shield and shot towards the second of the Black Sharks. I saw its tail snapping away from the main body and it went into a violent spin, almost taking out the lead helicopter. This was my opportunity to escape. I channelled energy into the kinetibike and it skidded forward across the car park as the Black Shark nosedived onto the road. There was a powerful explosion on impact and I barely evaded the flames as they spewed along the road.

The tall assassin was back on his feet and, although his arms were still braced against his body by the tangle of power lines, he was stalking forward once more. I yelled out at Hunter as I drove towards them and he released the heavy metal cables and leaped onto the back of the bike as I made my pass. I pushed as much energy into the bike as I could and we accelerated so fast that I thought my face would be left behind. We were just fast enough to evade our attacker as he snapped the cables with his powerful arms and reached out for us.

We hit top speed in under a minute but the remaining Black Shark was catching up fast. Hunter instructed me to drive onto the motorway and I foolishly thought that the helicopter wouldn't attack us on a roadway as busy as the M62. I was very wrong. We'd only gotten a few miles away from the filling station when the first line of bullets darted over our heads and cut a number of vehicles to shreds. We powered past the cars as they spun and broke apart, the drivers and passengers helplessly tossed onto the road, their screams quenched when a petrol tank of one of the cars exploded.

Then another blast went off just behind us. I instinctively knew this was no exploding car. There were missiles being fired on us. I screamed at Hunter to use his powers to bring down the helicopter. He tried everything he could and still the terror in the sky remained. Its shield had repelled Hunter's every effort to destroy it.

'Hunter, look up ahead,' I shouted. 'The pylons!'

'I'll try!' he roared back. 'I'm all out of ideas if this fails.'

There was a line of mighty electrical pylons ahead, with one standing no more than twenty yards from the edge of the road. I glanced in the side mirror to see the Black Shark bearing down on us. My precognitive gift was warning me of imminent danger. I was just about to close my eyes and get ready to meet my maker when the pylon to the right cracked in half – Hunter was using his gifts to drag it down onto the road.

There was an almighty blast as the helicopter slammed into the metal pylon and its twin rotors got entangled in the power lines. It spun through the air as it caught fire and smashed onto the road with a terrible bang. We were travelling at such speed that the flames disappeared from the side mirror within seconds. Then for a fleeting moment I thought we were out of harm's way. I was wrong.

I glanced in the side mirror again and saw a black shape speeding along the motorway. It was growing bigger in the mirror which meant it was gaining on us, despite the fact that I was driving the bike at its top speed. There was only one type of vehicle that could move as fast a kinetibike. Another kinetibike.

The kinetirider was catching up on us. His bike had to be a more advanced model than my own. And I had a feeling that it might even be shielded by the same type of defence system as the Black Sharks.

'Bentley,' Hunter shouted in my ear, 'we've got company!'

'I know. See if you can discourage him.'

I could feel the reverberations of Hunter's assaults and could also see in the mirrors that they had little or no effect on the kinetirider. He was much closer now, and I could see he was wearing black clothing which was very similar to the outfit that Irena Hofer wore when I fought her under the Golding Plaza hotel. This meant the rider was immune to psychokinetic strikes. It seemed we were hopelessly outmatched. And before long I realised that the good guys are always at a disadvantage. We didn't use civilians as weapons. Our foe did.

I watched a car far up ahead wobbling across the road before it leaned to one side and toppled over. It was an unnatural movement and obviously the psychokinetic rider had used his gift to force the car into our path. I was skilful enough to dodge the tumbling vehicle. It was much more difficult to evade the next vehicle that spun into my path. Eventually I had to use my powers to brush the vehicles aside as they were thrown directly at me. I could hear the passengers screaming as I shot out power to knock them out of our way. For a moment I considered giving in and allowing one of the vehicles to hit us; how many people would have to suffer and die so we could survive for a few seconds more?

'Look,' Hunter shouted. 'Up ahead. The bridge!'

I stared at an overpass that we were approaching. This would be our only chance of escape. Out of nowhere a motorcycle ahead of us rose up on its front wheel and the driver fell off as it left the ground and came spinning right at me. I raised one finger and sent out a slight cushion of energy that deflected the motorcycle above my head. Our pursuer had to act fast to avoid the flying bike. He had been distracted for a couple of seconds and that's all I needed.

The kinetirider never even saw the end coming. While he was distracted I shot as much energy I had into the bike and we powered ahead of our pursuer as we drove through the overpasses. As we were swallowed by its shadow I used my gift to crack the concrete above and it crumbled just as we met sunlight again. The black rider was crushed as the overpass collapsed under its own weight.

There was open road ahead and no more assassins behind. I didn't slow down until we were by the coast – on the other side of the country.

CHAPTER FOURTEEN

War

Canavan's home was a few miles north of Hornsea and overlooked a strip of sandy beach that was being battered by a turbulent sea crashing in from the east. It was a small, two-storey abode with white washed walls and a terracotta roof, and was surrounded by a circle of rowan trees. A fitting retirement home for someone who had dedicated her life to the Guild. It was peaceful and seemed safe enough, although nowhere was truly safe for us that day, not with the type of evil that was searching for us.

I wheeled the bike into the shade of the trees to hide it from view, then followed Hunter inside. Darkness was setting in and the house was frigid and unwelcoming. That didn't bother me in the slightest; I was more concerned that we might have been followed and I remained by the sitting room window for a long while, watching the sky and the road for any unwanted visitors. When I felt sure that we'd escaped our enemy for the time being I went to the kitchen to find Hunter rummaging through the cupboards. He was complaining that there was no coffee. Sometimes I felt as if I didn't know him at all. We'd just been chased across England by attack helicopters and a kinetirider, many innocent people had been either killed or seriously injured and all Hunter cared about was having a cup of coffee. And that wasn't the worst of it! We'd faced some sort of monster on the road outside the filling station. He barely looked human. No man has glowing eyes. No one could withstand the electricity that had been driven into him. This was an enemy like no other, and I had a good idea as to his real identity. I wasn't going to be a fool any longer. I wanted answers and I wanted them right away.

'Ah, I think a shot of whiskey is in order,' Hunter said as pulled a dusty bottle of scotch from a cabinet over the sink. 'I knew this would come in handy some day.'

I used my gift to pull the bottle from his grasp and it flew across the kitchen into my hands. Then I summoned a much more potent power and knocked Hunter off his feet and across the room. The crush layer was so strong that he couldn't peel himself more than an inch from the wall.

'You better tell me right now what's going on or I'll kill you,' I snapped. 'You've led me into the heart of this war and you've been lying all along.'

'I don't know what you're talking about, Bentley,' he hissed at me. 'Release me before I lose my temper.'

'Go ahead and lose it. You'll be dead before you know what hits you.'

'I haven't been lying to you.' He knew full well that he couldn't break through the layer and that I was naturally stronger than him. His struggling quickly subsided as did his temper. 'I swear I have not lied to you.'

'You haven't been entirely honest either, have you?' I replied. 'What was that *thing* on the road today? No bullshit. I want the truth.'

'He's an assassin.'

'Don't give me that crap!'

'Well, what do you think it was if not an assassin?'

'It was no ordinary assassin. I believe he's the master Brofeldt talked about. I think I just saw the Kematian. Glowing green eyes. Immune to everything you hit him with. There's no one on this earth who would survived being electrocuted like that. Admit it, Hunter. Just tell me the truth!'

'It was not the Kematian,' he shouted. 'Now you bloody well release me.'

'I will if you tell me all that you know.'

'Release me!'

I reluctantly drew down my power and Hunter slid down the wall and stared at me, shaking his head. The bottle of booze flew across the room into his hand and he unscrewed it and took a long drink.

'I told you before you need to put a cap on that temper of yours,' he snarled. He took a seat at the table and knocked back another mouthful of whiskey.

'I tend to lose my temper when I realise I've been tricked into risking my life. No more lies,' I told him. 'I want to know what we're up against.'

'I was not lying to you, Bentley. The assassin we encountered on the road was Jermaine Scott. Well, that's the name he went under when we first came across him – Lord only knows what his real name is. And I'm quite certain he's not Brofeldt's leader. He's the assassin she warned us about before she died.'

'Jermaine Scott? I've heard that name before.'

'Perhaps his nickname will be more familiar to you. He's known affectionately as *Boxer* by the agents of the Guild. We call him that because he likes to beat his victims to death with his bare fists.'

'He's just a man?'

'Of course he's just a man. What did you think he was? An alien?'

'But his eyes. I saw his eyes. They were glowing!'

'I got a better look at him during the fight. Those weren't his eyes. He was wearing a mask. The green lights you saw were some sort of visual aid, probably dreamed up by Golding's scientists. I reckon it was manufactured to enable him to see through body refractions and to protect his eyes from light orbs.' Hunter slammed his fist against the counter in an unexpected instant of rage. 'It was designed to help him fight and kill light-tuners like me.'

'Why would he have a mask designed with light-tuners in mind?'

'Boxer has few weaknesses,' Hunter admitted before he took another shot of scotch. 'The Guild always felt a light-tuner would stand a chance against him because they could blind him. That's the only way we believed he could be hurt.'

'I remember hearing about him,' I said as I took a seat next to Hunter. 'He was one of Armamenti Tal-Future's soldiers, right? He was said to be indestructible.'

'He was their *best* soldier. They were an organisation who put together a small army of gifted mercenaries who would fight on the side of anyone who could afford to pay them. It was a repulsive notion. Supremely gifted individuals who were trained to maximise their gifts in combat being sent to fight third world armies for oil companies or greedy nations who wanted to expand their borders, or fanatics who wanted to wipe out communities who didn't agree with their politics or religion. They were the Guild's main adversary for many years until the late 1980s when we managed to find their base in Malta and assassinate their entire leadership. After their organisation was dismantled, the mercenaries were hunted down one by one. All were given the same choice: Join the Guild, retire or die. A handful joined our ranks and contributed a lot to our cause. Most retired because they had been forced to butcher innocents and no longer wanted to be a part of the gifted world. There were, however, a couple of them who enjoyed such butchery. Melissa Nijinska was one. She opted to work for Golding and she caused a great deal of suffering and in some ways she changed the world … and not for the better. The other mercenary who refused our offer was Jermaine Scott. It's not his real name. I don't even know if he has a real name. What I do know is he was born into extreme poverty in the South African townships. His parents abandoned him when he was six years old and he had to fend for himself. As you can imagine, he's a rather thick-skinned individual who knows how to look after himself in a fight. He also has the gift of psychokinesis. What sets Boxer apart from others with that power is that when he was growing up, he didn't understand the power he possessed and he learned to use it in a totally unique manner …' Hunter sighed and rubbed his forehead. 'He truly is an abomination.'

'How does he use his power?'

'It's called kinetic fusion. He doesn't – and can't – use the gift to move objects without physical connection, as we do. Instead he draws energy into his body, contains it there and it fuses with his bones and muscles. Can you imagine a physical form that is intertwined with psychokinetic energy?'

'Not really,' I said. 'What does it do for him?'

'It makes his body almost impossible to break down. His limbs, his bones, sinews, muscles and skin are held together and protected and fuelled by the energy that we know so well – and we know how potent it is, right? Boxer may not be able move things as we do, but he's capable of lifting a vehicle with one hand without breaking a sweat. His body cannot be pierced or damaged by any known force or weapon. And the kinetic fusion makes his muscles supercharged and allows him to react and move at unbelievable speeds – I heard a story that he once chased down a speeding car on foot during one of his missions for Armamenti Tal-Future. We'll be finished if he manages to corner us.'

'I was able to destroy a block of metaliglass with my psychokinesis. That's the hardest substance known to man. I'm sure I can break him.'

'If you use that gift on Boxer he will simply absorb your strike and it will only serve to make him stronger. That's why I wouldn't allow you to fight him on the road today. One of your temper tantrums would have made him unstoppable. I barely held him as it was.'

'He must have a weakness of some kind. Everyone has a weakness.'

'Yes, you're right. Boxer's weakness are his eyes. And with the help of Golding Scientific, he has been able to eliminate that one weakness. Now he really is indestructible!'

'How do you know he's not the Master? I would think that someone so strong would be able to dominate others quite easily.'

'No, Boxer is a loner. By all accounts he wasn't very reliable when he worked for Armamenti. He's doesn't have the qualities or the inclination to lead others. He's a chaotic killer who sees himself as a free spirit, travelling here and there unchallenged and unknown. Sometimes he goes on killing sprees. Then he disappears for years at a time. He's not the type of man to believe in anything, to have a purpose or direction. He's spent most of his adult life roaming from one place to another, doing as he pleases. That's why I doubt he's officially part of this rogue group. I'm leaning towards the idea that he's simply doing this for money or the pleasure of killing other gifted people.'

'We have to find a way to stop him. He'll track us down sooner or later.'

'It would be wiser to avoid him. Fighting him will cost us our lives.'

'I don't feel very safe here all of a sudden.'

'This place is as safe as any,' Hunter said. 'Mind you, I don't think we should remain beyond tomorrow morning. It would be best to keep to the road. At least that way we'll have a chance to outrun anyone who tries to kill us.'

'We need to be moving in a definite direction, Hunter. I'm getting the feeling that we're aimlessly wandering from one hiding place to another and sooner or later they'll guess our next step and our luck will run out.'

'Our luck almost ran out today,' Hunter said. 'That was as close as I've come to death for quite some time – I must admit it was exhilarating.'

'No, it was terrifying,' I corrected him. 'I still can't figure out how they found us. We were out in the middle of nowhere then suddenly we're surrounded!'

'They must have been watching the ports since we disappeared from the Windmill Hotel. It was a fair bet that we'd travel over here and look for help. The surveillance chopper must have had a heat sensitive camera on board and that's how they saw us. Then it was simply a case of waiting until our guard was down.'

'They've proved rather resourceful, haven't they?'

'They've got us all figured out by the looks of things. Brofeldt wasn't lying when she said they had been planning this for many years. They seem to have every angle covered. I think the key to all of this is in formation. They have lots on us, we have hardly any on them. We can't hope to fight them until we know more.'

The adrenalin of the chase was now dissipating. Tiredness filled the void that it left. Perhaps it was this momentary weakness that brought on the latest headache. It didn't matter what the cause, I was soon wincing at the lights of the kitchen and went to the darkness of the sitting room for relief. Hunter soon joined me and stood watch by the window watching the narrow road that led from the house to the open country, knowing that we were vulnerable while I was debilitated.

'These headaches of yours are becoming a nuisance,' he said. 'You won't be much good in a fight if you're suffering one if the enemy finally finds us.'

'It's hardly my fault.'

'I know it's not.'

'I had these headaches a lot while we lived in Scotland, didn't I?'

'So your memories are returning,' he said without turning to me. 'How much do you recall?'

'Just brief moments. You've known about the memory loss that accompanies my headaches?'

'You used to get those headaches from time to time and never remembered them the next day. Apparently you had them before you came to live with me. Peter Williams told me about them before I agreed to protect you.'

'And what did he say?'

'He described them as growing pains for the gifted.'

'Did you ever experience such headaches?'

'No.'

'And neither has any other gifted person you know.'

'Everyone deals with it in their own way, Bentley.'

'I have two new memories that bother me greatly. One with Cathy and another with Williams. They were both saying the same thing to me …'

'And what was that?'

'That I was enduring the headaches for a good reason and that one day it would be worth it. Williams also believed I was destined to lead the Guild of the True.'

'I don't know why Williams would think you worthy of the role, especially seeing as though you didn't want to be a part of the Guild at all. Perhaps he saw something in you that I cannot.'

'I agree with you. I'm far too reckless for such responsibility.'

'You are indeed.'

'More than you know …'

Hunter turned slowly from the window and narrowed his eyes at me.

'What have you done?' he growled.

'I called Cathy while you were asleep on the ferry.'

'You fool!'

'What's so foolish about making a simple phone call?'

'You don't know the risk? You, the one who led Marianne to the Atkinson house, do not know why making such a call is foolish?'

'She wasn't at the house, Hunter.' I stared back at him through the gloom and remained composed despite how aggressive he was becoming. 'Cathy is not even in France. She's actually in London, just like Brofeldt's notes said she was.'

'And who told you this?'

'Her mother.'

'June Atkinson has a few too many screws loose, Bentley, didn't you know?'

'That may or may not be true. It doesn't change the fact that Cathy was not there.'

'Maybe she's found a new boyfriend in France and was out on a steamy date.'

'You know where she is.'

'There goes that imagination of yours again. You're becoming a very paranoid, annoying and dangerous person. It's quite a chore keeping an eye on you.'

'Keeping an eye on me? You say that like you're still under orders to be protecting me.'

'I have no orders concerning you. As far as the Guild knows, you're still living on the west coast of Ireland.'

'I'm starting to doubt everything you say.'

'That's not my problem. I'm not going to try and convince you of my honesty, Bentley. In fact, I'd rather this conversation ended right now.'

'Fair enough.'

He returned his attentions to the window and the room fell silent. I hadn't the strength to demand he talk to me. I would not get the answers I needed from Hunter, anyway – that much was obvious. I would have to wait until I found Cathy. She too had been lying to me, but she would tell me the truth if we were face to face. At least I hoped she would.

The pain inside my skull became so severe that I lost consciousness. I don't know how long I was out, maybe an hour, maybe no more than a few minutes. I was dragged from sleep by the beams of car headlights illuminating the room. I was still groggy but the sleep had sent the headache into retreat and I was able to push myself from the chair and go to Hunter's side.

When the headlights died I could clearly see the car and recognised it immediately as Canavan's red hatchback. I gave her a wave as she stepped into the garden. She just stared back as if I was an unwelcome stranger. I followed Hunter to the hall and kept my distance as he opened the door for his old mentor. She entered quite cautiously, watching us both with suspicious eyes. It was hardly a happy reunion. Even Hunter seemed perturbed by her manner.

'Good to see you,' Hunter dared to say.

'Is it?' she said flatly. 'I can't say the same because I'm putting my life in jeopardy by being near you.'

'Why would you be risking your life by talking to us?' Hunter asked.

'We'll get to that soon enough.' She made her way along the hallway to the kitchen and Hunter and I exchanged a look of bewilderment as we followed her. 'I take it the two of you were responsible for the carnage on the M62.'

'We weren't responsible for it.' Hunter pulled a chair from the table for her and continued after she sat. 'We're being hunted by some very well equipped assassins.'

'You're being hunted by more than just assassins.'

'What do you mean?'

'Every agent, tutor, mole and apprentice in the Guild has been ordered to kill you on sight – both of you!'

'What?' I almost shouted. 'Why would they be after us?'

'Because you called in help from the Guild and four agents from Belfast were sent to your aid. The same four agents were found murdered in the back of a van four days ago, parked at the back of a Dublin hotel – the same hotel in which a gifted civilian, Johan Verbannk, was found murdered.'

'Now hold on a minute!' Hunter snapped. 'We are not –'

'And there's more,' Canavan raised her voice. 'Three of our agents went missing two days ago. Their bodies were discovered in your highland cottage when it was searched last night. You're just lucky that there aren't many agents free to search for you right now. Not with all the other troubles that are facing the Guild.'

'What troubles are you talking about?' Hunter asked.

'Where have you two been the last week?'

'It's a long story.'

'Well, you've missed out on quite a bit. The Guild's plan to attack Golding Scientific was pushed forward. The first strike took place three days ago.'

'Who pushed it forward?' Hunter demanded. 'It wasn't supposed to start for another few weeks.'

'I don't know where the order came from. I do know it was an epic failure. Ten agents went to Iceland to kill off some of the high-ranking personnel within Golding's organisation and they were ambushed. All of them are dead. It was as if Golding had been tipped off. Then yesterday there was an all-out gifted battle in central London. One of our safe houses was attacked without warning by assassins. The fighting lasted hours and spilled into the heart of the city.'

Canavan switched on a TV set on the kitchen counter and flicked through the channels until she reached a news report. There was a bold headline running under the image of a newsreader that read: *Terrifying scenes in London as violence claims dozens of lives.* There was a banner at the top of the screen that was even more worrying: *No official comment from government on mysterious footage of violence.*

'If you've just tuned in,' the newsreader began, 'we do advise viewer discretion, as there are some graphics scenes of death and violence in the footage we are about to show you. And do bear in mind that this is not a clip from a movie. The footage has not been doctored. What you are about to see actually took place on York Road this afternoon.'

The news channel then cut directly to footage that had been filmed by a helicopter crew. It was looking down on York Road and there were thumping explosions in the distance. There was fire spewing out across the road and as the helicopter banked to one side, it became clear what was causing the flames. It was a single individual pacing out onto the road and shooting streams of fire from his hands. Then the camera focused on two women who were approaching from the Thames. One of them was waving her arms about and seemed to be raising parked vehicles and sending them through the air at the pyrokinetic. Her companion was firing white bolts of energy that were setting off explosions all around her. It was a full-on gifted duel. In broad daylight. All captured on camera.

'And this,' the newsreader said as the picture switched to footage that had been recorded on a cell phone. 'Words fail me ...'

There were over a dozen gifted people fighting in a shopping mall. Numerous gifts were clearly identifiable. This would change everything for the gifted people of the world. Hunter and I sat in silence as more footage was shown. Some of it was recorded by film crews, some on phones and some were still images captured by cctv cameras.

'And if this street battle was not enough,' the newsreader said soberly, 'dozens more innocent people were killed today in the north. Again, this footage is genuine. It has not been altered in any fashion.'

We then watched a montage of short clips that had been recorded by those who had been unfortunate enough to be on the M62 that afternoon. The gifted world had been revealed at last to the public.

'This stuff is on every news channel across the world,' Canavan said as she turned the TV off.

'Then the war has begun,' Hunter said, 'whether we like it or not.'

'It won't last long if it continues in this vein,' Canavan sighed. 'This week has been an unmitigated disaster for us.'

'That's because there are traitors in our group who are supplying the enemy with inside information. We've been tricked into waging this war, Marie. Sending agents to attack Golding is as good as sending them to their death.'

'Traitors?' Canavan asked, leaning over the table towards Hunter. 'Who are these traitors?'

'That remains unclear. It started when Bentley and myself were working on an investigation that led us to Dublin. We set ourselves up at a hotel and were watching two gifted people who'd been working as spies.'

'Yes, I remember,' Canavan nodded, 'you were sent out to track down Malcolm Wilson.'

'Wilson, yeah. We picked up his trail, thanks to Bentley's time-scanning trick, and followed him to Dublin. It didn't take long to find out that he was allied with Elina Brofeldt.'

'I remember her,' Canavan said. 'She was a very talented mind-switcher.'

'Her gift of pyrokinesis is far more impressive,' I added.

'After a couple of days,' Hunter continued, 'Brofeldt and Wilson were joined by Vanev and your gifted *civilian*, Verbannk. I felt at that point we were outmatched and I called Ballentine for help. He said he'd send in the Belfast team to take over from us. The next thing we know we're under attack.'

'You think Dominic betrayed you?'

'There's a strong possibility that he's the one who sold us out.'

'Michael, are you sure you're not allowing your personal feelings about Ballentine to cloud your judgement?'

'I've given you the basic facts of what transpired. What's your opinion?'

'You might be right. I would still rather be certain of his guilt before calling for his head.'

'We are running out of time, Marie. Bentley found some documents at Brofeldt's apartment. One set of files contained a hit list. Dozens of the top Guild agents were on the list, and it included information that could only have come from within the highest ranks of our group. When we questioned Brofeldt she said that she and many others are in league with *The Master* and that he has been plotting against us for years. She also claimed that they are now in control of Golding Scientific.'

'Not to mention the assassin who nearly killed us both on the M62,' I added.

'Yes, they've employed Boxer. He's the one who was behind the carnage on the motorway this afternoon.'

Canavan was quiet for a long while. She'd been cautious, even fearful, as she entered the house and had become more and more agitated as Hunter told her of the rogue group that were working against us. But she'd held up pretty well until Boxer was mentioned. Now she was just sitting there staring into space, hunched over, hands quivering.

'I don't know what to do, Marie,' Hunter admitted. He was pacing the tiled floor and had a pained expression on his worn face. 'For the first time in my life I can't protect the Guild and the people who are dear to me. There are enemies hidden everywhere. And the ones I face cannot easily be destroyed.'

'You cannot destroy Boxer,' she said. 'There are only two people I know of who would stand a chance: Armitage and Sterling.'

'And Sterling is hidden away and can't be contacted,' Hunter replied. 'I've tried Armitage and there's been no answer.'

'Armitage has been working on a very important case.'

'What could be more important that this war?'

'She's been hunting Janice Powell ...'

'Janice?' I said incredulously. 'Janice Powell is one of us. She's a really good person.'

'She used to be,' Canavan said dryly as she turned to look me in the eye. 'She is no longer herself, though. Janice has been doing intense training with her tutor, Martina Kuhr, and has been pushing her gift of space-rupting to the limits.' Canavan swallowed hard and gave a slight shake of her head. 'Three weeks ago she went beyond the known limits of that gift.'

'That gift is dangerous,' Hunter said. He'd stopped pacing and was standing next to me, his eyes wide and fixed on Canavan. 'Kuhr should know that!'

'Kuhr craves notoriety. She always has. I fear now that she will become notorious because of what happened.'

'What happened?' I asked.

'The most gifted space-rupters can break the barrier of the known universe, slip through it into an alternate existence – a parallel universe. There are no restrictions in terms of time and space in that parallel universe and that allows them to move great distances in a split second, before they re-enter our universe. That's how the pure gift is used. The problem is that we know very little of the other side that they enter momentarily. Even the best space-rupters only enter that place for a second or two.'

'There's a five second rule, right?' Hunter asked. 'Anything over five seconds in the parallel existence is deemed unsafe.'

'That *was* the rule. In truth, very few are strong enough to remain there even that long. Janice is different. She's the best space-rupter we've ever encountered.'

'She went beyond the five seconds?' I asked.

'Way beyond. Janice, under duress from Kuhr, spent three minutes on the other side.'

'A three-minute jump?' Hunter bawled. 'I'm surprised it didn't kill her.'

'It would have been better if it had. Janice returned from the jump and was … not herself. She murdered Kuhr and some of the other students she had been with. The ones that survived said she had peculiar powers and was crazed and violent.'

'So, the jump broke her mind,' Hunter said. 'That's hardly surprising.'

'Her mind was not broken. Her mind was overcome by some unknown force. The Guild believe that a life force from the other side latched itself onto her and gained control over her mind.'

'An alien?' I asked, stupidly.

'We have no idea what it is. All we know is that she has powers that have never before been witnessed and that she is bent on destruction.'

'Seems far-fetched to me,' I said. 'There has to be a more plausible explanation.'

'Elizabeth Armitage believed it. And she is not the whimsical kind.'

'Do you know where Armitage is now?' Hunter interrupted. 'We need her with us if we have any hope to bring this to a successful conclusion.'

'I have no idea where she could be.'

'Then there is little hope for the Guild.'

'I never thought I'd see you give in so easily.'

'I like a straight fight!' Hunter shouted. 'All this cloak and dagger nonsense makes me weary.'

'They will lose in a straight fight,' Canavan said with a smile. 'They work in the shadow because they fear warriors like you.'

'Stop trying to make me feel better,' Hunter said. 'I'll only feel better when this is at an end.'

'How can we bring this to an end?' Canavan asked. 'It's too much for the three of us to contend with.'

'You know,' Hunter grunted, 'I think I preferred when you were trying to make me feel better.'

CHAPTER FIFTEEN

Secrets in the Dark

All the talk of betrayal, plots and super villains made Canavan very agitated. By midnight she was so stressed that she cut off the conversation and used her masterful skills of light-tuning to weave a cloak around the house and the surrounding grounds. We would still be visible to thermal imaging devices but it would provide us with some added security. I felt confident enough that we would not be tracked down that night. Beyond morning was a different story; I knew our enemy was clever and determined enough to find us sooner or later, whether we were cloaked or not.

Later we convened in the sitting room and discussed the shadowy group that had waged the clandestine war against the Guild. Hunter and Canavan argued over who they really were. My Scottish friend claimed they were nothing more than a band of lost souls and mercenaries that had been joined together and galvanised by a charismatic leader. Canavan believed there had to be a more structured organisation responsible for it all. She went on to suggest that JNCOR might be the ones who had orchestrated the attacks. She also thought that some remnant of the Eastern Shadow could have been responsible. Hunter dismissed her suggestions. I remained silent until they discussed the identity of the mysterious leader.

'I've given this question quite a lot of thought,' Hunter mused. 'I can't figure out how someone that strong, persuasive and evil could go unnoticed.'

'He must be very cunning,' Canavan added. 'Anyone who could infiltrate and seize control of an organisation like Golding's must be a master of disguise and extremely intelligent. Let's not forget that Golding is very calculating, suspicious and ruthless. The Guild have tried to place a spy in his organisation for years. We failed every single time thanks to Derek Shaw.'

'But he's been dead for a couple of years,' I pointed out.

'He has,' Canavan answered, 'but he had set up a complex system of security checks that still remains. Golding Scientific is as impenetrable as it's always been.'

'So how could the enemy do it if we could not?' Hunter wondered. 'This leader must be a bloody genius.'

'This person must be known to us,' his mentor replied. 'It has to be someone we've encountered before. It would take influence to be capable of placing spies in both Golding Scientific and the Guild of the True. Could it be Kondo? He liked to place his minions in competitor groups.'

'Who's Kondo?' I asked.

'Former leader of the Jin Assassins,' Hunter answered. 'He's a brutal man – so brutal that his own followers turned on him and sent him into exile. He hasn't been heard of for almost five years. He does have a maniacal streak and is very persuasive. He never had much of an influence or an interest in the west, though.'

'There could be a more obvious explanation,' Canavan said. 'Perhaps this *master* is the traitor within the Guild.'

'I have considered this,' Hunter nodded. 'It is plausible. That makes it imperative that we identify and execute this traitor. It'll be like killing two birds with one stone.'

'Maybe it's the Kematian,' I blurted out. 'Everything would point to him. I can't see why you don't discuss that possibility.'

'That's not a name I thought I would hear today.' Canavan gave a nervous chuckle then cast her worried gaze at Hunter. 'I can safely say it's not him.'

'Why are you so sure?'

'He's dead, Bentley,' Hunter answered for her. 'And so will you be if you mention his name again! Anyway, I'm sick of guessing the name of this phantom. He'll reveal himself soon enough. What's more important right now is that we plan our next move.'

'What can we do?' I asked.

'We have to find out if Ballentine is the traitor or not. If he is, then we can kill him and wrench the Guild from the grip of these spies. If he turns out to be clean, we will have a powerful ally in the heart of the Guild.'

'How can we uncover his true motives?' asked Canavan.

'We go fishing,' Hunter smiled mischievously. 'Bentley and I will be the bait.'

'I don't like the sound of this,' I said, nervously rubbing my forehead. I hated when Hunter smiled like that. It usually meant we were to put our lives at risk.

'Marie, you will travel to the Palatium at dawn. Go there and do everything you can to find Armitage. I will contact Ballentine again. I will tell him exactly where we are and to come alone.'

'Fat chance of him coming here alone,' I said. 'Why would he?'

'He will come here alone if he is genuine. If he is the traitor, then Boxer will be the one who shows up.'

'That's not a good plan!' I exclaimed. 'We lure Boxer here so he can kill us both?'

'We can evade Boxer if he does arrive. Then we will go to the Palatium and deal with Ballentine.'

'The Palatium is full of people who believe you to be an enemy assassin,' Canavan argued. 'It would not be wise for you to go there and challenge a high ranking agent.'

'That's why I need you to find Armitage. She will trust me over Ballentine.'

'Sounds like a fantastic plan,' I said, getting to my feet. 'Now, I'm going upstairs for a nap. Wake me up in the morning.'

'A nap?' Hunter asked. 'How can you nap at a time like this?'

'I'm tired and will be stronger in the morning with a good sleep behind me.'

'Let him go,' Canavan told her former pupil. 'The boy probably hasn't slept properly in days.'

'In almost a week,' I corrected her as I left the room. I gave an exaggerated yawn as I passed into the hallway just for good measure. 'See you in the morning.'

I was not in the least bit tired. It would have been impossible to sleep in such a circumstance, but I wanted them to believe I was exhausted. I knew they were holding things back from me and would not speak openly in my presence. I needed to hear what they truly wanted to say to each other. I needed the truth about what was really going on.

I stomped noisily up the stairs and into the bedroom above the sitting room. I then made quite a racket as I climbed onto the bed. I sat motionless for almost half an hour before using my gift to levitate into the air and across the room to the door. I never once made the slightest sound as I hovered over the banisters and stairs into the hallway below. I'd performed this manoeuvre before, when I was living in Scotland. That time I overheard Ballentine and Hunter talking about the Zalechs. This time I was hoping I'd eavesdrop on a more revealing conversation.

I floated along the hallway then gently eased myself onto the floor, right next to the door that I had purposely left ajar.

'A dark time,' Hunter was saying. 'I've never known such evil days.'

'Nor I,' I heard Canavan say. 'There is evil everywhere. I am starting to think those apocalyptic prophecies of Sarah Fisher's may actually be true.'

'She's had more?'

'I won't burden you with them. They are too dark to contemplate right now.'

'Yeah,' Hunter sighed. 'I don't need any more on my plate.'

'You have too much on your plate, Michael.'

'You mean Bentley?'

'Yes, I do …' There was a long pause before she spoke again and for a moment I thought I'd been busted. I was just about to levitate back to the staircase when she spoke once more. 'He keeps speaking of the Kematian. Why is he so hung up on it?'

'He's grown obsessed with that tale. I curse Romand for having told him in the first place.'

'That was part of Romand's orders. He had to say that to the boy.'

'I know, I know. It's just very unsettling. For Bentley, of all people, to keep asking about the Kematian. I'm starting to think he knows more than he admits.'

'You think he knows the truth?'

'No. There aren't many who know, and none of them would tell Bentley.'

'So why does he keep asking?'

'I don't know why! Sometimes I think he's more trouble than he's worth, Marie.'

'He's worth all the trouble in the word, Michael.'

'Is he? Is he really?'

'You would rather him dead?'

'I didn't say I want him dead. He's like a little brother to me now. I would fight to the death to keep him safe. I argue with him constantly, but that's only because we spend almost all of our time in peril. We'd be the best of friends if we saw a few months of peace.'

'He's very fond of you. I can see it every time he watches you speak.'

'Bentley's a good kid to have around. But the pressure of protecting him is becoming too great for me, Marie. You cannot begin to understand the strain I've been under since I took him under my wing. He should have been brought to the Palatium two years ago. It's too much of a burden for one person to bear.'

'He has to find his own way in the world, Michael. You know this. If he had lived at the Palatium he might have come under the influence of the traitors. Hasn't it worked out better that he has lived uninfluenced?'

'He's hardly uninfluenced, Marie. His every step has been guarded and guided.'

'But he is becoming his own man. It had to be that way.'

'I know. He'll be a good man, too. I'm sure of it.'

'And the headaches you spoke of, are they getting worse?'

'He's starting to remember things now. That worries me.'

'It will be all over soon. I know it will.'

'It better! And I will need a long vacation after it is done.'

'And you'll get it. The Guild owes you a great deal for the service you have given this last year.'

'The Guild may fall before it pays me back.'

'We'll get through this. Even if we have to rebuild the Guild.'

'I hope I live to see it … The injury I sustained in Dublin pains me greatly. I busted a few of the stitches when I fought with Boxer today. It'll only get worse if I have to stay on the move.'

'You must hold out for a few more days.'

'A few more days will seem like an eternity!' Hunter cursed. 'There are too many enemies. Damn it, why will Sterling not come out of hiding? We need him now more than ever.'

'The king does not fight alongside the pawns.'

'I'd rather you didn't refer to me as a pawn.'

'You know what I mean. There's too much to risk for him. There is more at stake here than the war with Golding and our mysterious enemy. There is more at stake than the Guild itself. You know of the threat that waits in the shadow. If we lose Sterling, we would lose everything. The entire world would be in danger.'

'I don't want to think about all that.'

'We've talked too much of darkness,' Canavan said softly. 'I think we both need to take some rest before the busy day that awaits us both.'

'I think you might be right. You take the room upstairs. I'll sleep here on the couch.'

'Keep one eye open.'

'I always sleep with one eye open,' Hunter chuckled. 'It's because of an old injury I picked up when I was on the trail of a murderous pyrokinetic.'

'I've heard all your war stories.'

'Not this one!'

'It'll keep for an easier day.'

There was movement in the room and I sent a soft pulse of energy at my feet and was lifted into the air. I had just floated to the landing when Canavan pulled open the sitting room door and stepped into the hall. I was in bed before her foot met the first step of the staircase.

I lay there in the silence of the room and thought hard about the discussion I had overheard. Why had I been such a burden to them? I hadn't even been part of the Guild for the previous year. And what was this great shadow that threatened the world? It sounded awfully similar to Sarah Fisher's prophecy that described the Kematian's shadow that still loomed over the Guild. And it appeared she'd had more of these dark prophecies. I felt so sorry for her. She was a loveable young child who'd had a torturous few years and was not given the chance to live properly because of the visions she'd had. It pained me to know that she continued to see the horrors of the future. I'd have done anything to see her again. Just to give her a hug and tell her everything was going to be all right.

Everything was not all right, though. There was so much danger in the world, and it was growing by the day. The Guild was under serious threat and the gifted were openly fighting in the streets, the rest of the world now knew about us. And while all this was going on, my closest friends were keeping important knowledge from me. I hated that they were so secretive. I hated the way they had talked about me. It was as if I was an object to them. Why did they speak of me in such a way? It was clear that they liked and cared for me – just listening to the way Hunter had spoken of our friendship confirmed that. Yet still they did not trust me enough to reveal the full truth of what was going on.

There was too much to figure out. Everything was a mystery to me. I should have stayed in the cottage in Ireland and never returned to the Guild. I no longer knew who and what I was. I no longer knew who my friends were, and why they had befriended me in the first place. For a while I contemplated sneaking out the back of the house and fleeing into the night. I wanted to go far away, somewhere that they would never find me. I just wanted to be normal. I wanted no more mysteries.

When the house fell completely silent I walked downstairs and went to the back door. I could take to the kinetibike and be hundreds of miles away before they woke. They would never find me.

CHAPTER SIXTEEN

Snow

I was sitting by the kitchen table when Hunter appeared by the door. At one point in the night I had wheeled the bike along the driveway and was ready to drive off and to turn my back on them forever. I sat on the saddle and was ready to fire energy from my fingertips into its engine when I resisted and saw sense. It would be too cowardly to run. Not when they were in their most desperate hour. I could have escaped it all, but never would I have been comfortable with what I had done. I would have been haunted for the rest of my days if I had fled and they had died and the Guild crumbled under the weight of the evil it faced. I grudgingly wheeled the bike back under the trees and returned to the house. I'd been sitting near the back window since then, gazing out over the ocean as the sun chased the darkness from the morning sky.

'How was your nap?' Hunter asked as he lit his first cigar of the morning. 'Comfy?'

'It was all right. I managed to sleep for a couple of hours.'

'Then you slept better than I did,' he said, arching his back with a loud click. 'That couch is even less comfortable than the bed in my old cottage!'

'Miss your old bed?'

'I'll miss it forever,' he grumbled. 'I doubt I'll ever return to that place after what Marie told us last night.'

'I guess it would be difficult to sleep in a house where your colleagues' bodies were stashed – in order to frame you for their murder.'

'It would be impossible. When I find the one responsible for their deaths, so help me God, they will know the true meaning of suffering.'

'Because they murdered the agents or because they desecrated your home?'

'What sort of question is that?'

'Just a question.'

'Come off it.' He took a seat at the table and watched me carefully. 'I know when you're in one of your moods.'

'I'm just a bit stressed.'

'Stressed?' He took a deep pull from the cigar and grinned at me. 'Is that why you left the house last night?'

'What are you talking about?'

'Don't deny it. I was watching you the whole time. You were on your bike and just about to leave.'

'I didn't leave, though.'

'No, you didn't.' He reached over and clapped me on the shoulder. This was momentous. Hunter making physical contact with another living being in a gesture of friendship and thanks. I was stunned. 'I'm glad you came back, Bentley.'

'Would you have let me leave?'

'Probably not. I wouldn't want you to miss out on all the fun.'

'Today will not be fun.'

'You're right, it won't. But we'll go a long way to concluding all this trouble.'

'You still want to go through with that plan of yours?'

'There is no other way.'

'Perhaps there is …'

'Oh?'

'It came to me while I was sitting next to the window, watching the sun slowly burn up the ocean. It was so tranquil that my mind went still and all the thoughts and worries that usually dog me were lifted. That's when it came to me. I got to thinking about that hit list we found in Brofeldt's apartment. I thought of all the names that were on it and how tragic it would be to lose them. How much of a loss to the world it would be if so many gifted people were murdered –'

'This is all very poetic, Bentley, but would you please get to the point!'

'I realised there were two names missing from the list. Names that should have been on it.'

'Who?'

'Angela and John Portman.'

Hunter sat there with the cigar hanging precariously from his lower lip and stared into space for what seemed an eternity. It was clear that he had not considered this until now. Eventually he looked at me, a hint of excitement in his cold eyes and a rueful grin on his stubbly face. 'What would I do without you, Bentley?'

'Probably get yourself killed.'

'Why didn't I see this?' he said, shaking his head. 'I never felt those two were trustworthy. I should have seen this!'

'There's been too much going on to think straight,' I said. 'Do you think they could be involved?'

'They're friends of Ballentine's. They never risk themselves for the Guild. They are not on the hit list. Yes! I think there's a very good chance they could be working for the enemy.'

'Then it would make more sense to hunt them down rather than walking into the hornet's nest to face Ballentine. They may have the answers we seek.'

'That's a very good plan.' He puffed heavily on his cigar and his face was brighter than it had been for many days. 'And I know where they live.'

'Where who lives?' Canavan asked as she entered the kitchen.

It didn't take long for us to devise a new plan with the help of Marie Canavan. We still needed to know if Ballentine was a traitor, so we would still have to contact him one way or another. But once we were sure of his true motives, we would hunt down the Portmans instead of travelling to the Palatium. I was much happier with this scenario and felt a little more confident that I might see another sunrise.

At 8am we saw Canavan to her car and before we went our separate ways, she retrieved a sports bag from the boot and handed it to Hunter.

'I had a feeling that you'd have nothing but the clothes on your back, so I packed a bag that might come in handy.'

'Ah, you are a genius, Marie Canavan,' Hunter said as he unzipped the bag and examined its contents. 'Binoculars … bottle of scotch … a mobile phone … spare pair of boots …'

'Anything in there for me?' I joked.

'I didn't know you were with him until I arrived,' Canavan said apologetically.

'I'll live.'

'You better,' she said, giving me a hug. 'Stay close to Hunter at all times, Ross,' she whispered in my ear. 'Run if you lose him. Don't look back.'

'What was that?' Hunter asked.

'I told him I didn't want the Guild to lose him. I have the number of that mobile phone in the bag. My number is saved in the contacts. Call me if there are any developments.'

'I will.'

Canavan wished us luck before she took to her little hatchback and started her journey for London. Hunter and I watched her disappear down the narrow road, then we took to the bike and he instructed me to drive to some high ground that was almost a mile to the north of the house. From there he contacted Ballentine. It was a short conversation. Both men weren't eager to give the other much information on what had been going on. Hunter said that we were alone at the house by the coast, that I was gravely ill and he couldn't risk leaving me alone, then gave him the address and told him to come alone. Ballentine agreed. There was no fuss from him, as there usually was. He told Hunter to stay put and that he would be there within two hours. It was very suspicious; Ballentine always argued with Hunter and always demanded as much information as could be provided. He hadn't even asked what was wrong with me.

We took a spot on the high ground that was thick with long grass and bushes, got low to the frozen ground and Hunter pressed his binoculars to his face and our latest stakeout began.

Only an hour had passed when a vehicle appeared on the winding road that led to Canavan's house. It looked awfully similar to the 4x4 that Boxer had emerged from during the battle at the filling station the day before. Hunter remained silent as the vehicle slowly drove along the driveway and came to a halt at the side of the house.

'Who is it?' I asked, tugging at his sleeve. 'Is it Ballentine or Boxer?'

'Take a look for yourself,' he said as he passed the binoculars to me. 'It's exactly as I said it would be.'

It appeared Ballentine was the traitor after all. I was looking down on the property to see Boxer and another man, who was much younger and had his arm in a sling, standing either side of the vehicle, watching the house.

'Once they go inside we should make a hasty retreat,' Hunter said to me. 'We can't linger here.'

'Agreed.'

I watched Boxer closely as he scouted around to the rear of the house. He wore no hood this time, and I could now clearly see the mask that Hunter had told me about. It looked to be a mixture of leather and carbon fibre plates and covered his entire head. There was a diamond shaped panel at the front covering his nose and mouth – I figured this helped him breathe – and there was a visor stretching from ear to ear, that covered his eyes. On this visor were two circular buttons that were glowing green. Hunter's hypothesis seemed to be on the money; the mask was probably constructed to protect his eyes, and to allow him to see what the naked eye could not.

'I want to be the one who kills Ballentine,' Hunter said under his breath. 'Many honest men and women have been murdered because of his treachery.'

'I won't stop you. I wonder why he turned on the Guild? What could possibly make him side with the likes of Boxer.'

'Probably money.'

'That's too obvious. Money is not always the chief motivator for people.'

'The obvious explanation is usually correct, from my experience.'

'I'm sure we'll discover his motives in time.'

I returned my attention to Boxer's companion. He was tall and slender with dark skin; he had an air of arrogance about him. He had remained at the 4x4 and simply watched the surrounding grounds while his partner patrolled the house. His left arm was in a sling and I noticed he moved gingerly when he turned. This weakness could be his downfall if we were to face him at some point.

'I wonder where he picked up the injured arm,' Hunter said quietly.

'Probably when he killed the other Guild agents.'

'He'll get his comeuppance soon enough.'

'I'm sure he will. How far to the Portmans' house?'

'They live on the outskirts of Manchester. Shouldn't take us too long to reach them on the kinetibike.'

'I'm not taking the M62.'

'Yes, let's not tempt faith. We can take a longer route and still be there at 5pm.'

'What's so important about 5pm?'

'You'll see when we get there.'

'Why do you insist on withholding information from me?' I

asked, unable to hide the insult I felt from the night before. 'You're always keeping secrets from me.'

'I can't answer that.'

'Why not?'

'Because I like keeping you in the dark,' he smiled. 'You'll be the one to keep the secrets in a few years, and you'll then understand why it's not wise to tell young men everything before they are ready.'

'Don't think so,' I shrugged. 'I'll be living by a golden beach in a very warm country when I'm your age. I'll be long retired by then.'

'You're planning on winning the lottery?'

'Yes. I'm going to track down Sarah Fisher and make her tell me the winning numbers.' I took the binoculars from my face and turned to Hunter, smiling. 'And you're not getting a share of my winnings.'

'I wouldn't want your stinking money, Bentley. I'd rather remain a working class hero, thank you very much.'

'They've gone inside,' I said as I gazed down the grassy slope. 'We should get going.'

We wasted no time in leaving the high ground and soon found our way onto a road that led away from the coast. We avoided the M62, opting this time for the road to Harrogate, where we stopped for half an hour. It was a bitterly cold morning, by far the coldest day of that year. There had been showers of sleet and bone splitting winds to endure for over an hour and we decided it was worth the risk of stopping at a coffee shop near the town. We defrosted while we ate a modest lunch with piping hot coffee. By midday we were on the road once more. We drove straight to Blackburn, through an ever strengthening snowfall. I don't know if it was the extreme cold that brought on the headache or not, but by the time we passed Blackburn for Manchester I could barely think straight with the pain that pulsed against my skull. At 2pm I was in so much agony that we had to pull over to the side of the road and Hunter and I switched positions, and he drove us the rest of the way.

The Portmans lived in the suburbs of Prestwich, a town to the north of Manchester city. It took Hunter quite some time to find the right street, and he cursed endlessly about the snowfall and all the houses looking the same. At 3pm he had located the correct street and we parked about fifty yards from number 87 – the house that belonged to Angela and John Portman.

The road was typical suburbia: two identical rows of red brick semi-detached houses either side of a narrow two lane road. Most of the gardens had two cars. There were a scattering of SUVs parked on the roadside. Normally there would have been kids playing in the street, but the bad weather had driven them into their homes. There was nothing extravagant about the place. This was hardly surprising; most Guild agents lived in rather unglamorous settings.

I was suffering badly as I climbed off the bike to stretch my legs – they were almost numb from the sub-zero temperatures. I couldn't move my toes at all, and stomped my feet into the fresh snow on the pavement to circulate some blood into them. The headache had softened a bit and I was at least able to think straight.

'Stay close to the bike,' Hunter told me. He remained in the seat and watched the road for any sign of the Portmans. 'I have a small cloak set up around me and I don't want you straying outside it and giving us away.'

'Why are we waiting? Shouldn't we get this over with before we both freeze to death?'

'They don't usually arrive home on weekdays until 5pm.'

'What time is it now?'

'Almost that time.'

'Good. I don't want to prolong this.' I stepped to the roadside and stood next to the warm tank of the bike and rubbed my hands together furiously. 'Why do they arrive home at the same time every day?'

'Because they work five days a week.'

'What, normal work?'

'Yes. They're both accountants. They have a little tax consulting business in Manchester city. They only work for the Guild on a part-time basis, whenever we need accountancy work done, or if there's a serious emergency.'

'Aren't accountants supposed to be well off?' I asked as I examined the façade of 87. It was the most rundown house on the entire street.

'The Portmans probably should be well off. But they have given a lot of their time to the Guild over the years. That means they aren't seen as very reliable accountants and struggle to find repeat work.'

'Doesn't the Guild pay them?'

'The Guild doesn't have an endless supply of cash, Bentley. I work for them twenty four seven. Do I look like I have a lot of money?'

'No. You do steal from drug dealers, though.'

'Maybe I should actually change my name to Robin Hood.'

I managed to laugh, despite my face being stiff with cold. Hunter wasn't laughing with me; he had leaned forward and was staring at a silver station wagon that crawled up the road. I watched it turning into the driveway of 87, where it remained, engine running and lights on, for quite some time.

'Is that them?'

'It's him.'

'Do we wait for both of them before we attack?'

'To hell with that,' Hunter spat. 'I'm too cold to wait.'

Finally John Portman killed the engine and climbed out of the station wagon. He stood in his garden, under the heavy snow and looked up and down the street four times before making his way to the door. He thought he was being vigilant by monitoring the street. In truth, he'd stared right at us more than once as we made our approach. He hadn't expected a light-tuner to come calling that evening.

'I forgot to ask,' I said quietly to Hunter, 'what gifts does he have?'

'Partial emotomagnet and pure ink-seer.'

'That doesn't make him dangerous, right?'

'Right. His wife is the dangerous one. Hopefully she doesn't stumble in on us while we're torturing him.'

'You can do the torturing,' I replied, teeth almost chattering. 'I don't have the stomach for it.'

'Leave it to me. You just make sure you stay on the alert. This could get ugly.'

'I don't want to depend on my precognitive abilities while I'm fighting this headache.'

'Just keep your eyes open.'

We plodded up the driveway to the front door and could see Portman through the frosted glass of the side porch window. He was sitting on the bottom step of the stairs and was pulling off his shoes. It seemed like as good a time as any to confront him. Hunter took the lead by snapping the lock of the front door and pouncing into the hallway, his hands surrounded by blue lines of electricity that latched onto Portman's face as soon as he was inside. I stepped into the threshold and turned back to glance along the road. No one had seen a thing, and there was no sign of Angela. I eased the door shut then used my gift to fracture the frame so it would stay shut despite having no lock.

'No, Hunter,' Portman moaned as the big Scot dragged him by his feet to the kitchen. 'Please, Hunter! Why are you doing this?'

'Why?' Hunter barked. 'Because I fancy a cup of coffee.'

'I don't think he means why are you going to the kitchen, Hunter,' I said, following them along the hallway. 'I think he wants to know why you're roughing him up.'

'Ah, I see,' Hunter laughed. He lifted Portman off the floor with one hand and slammed him up against the kitchen counter. 'I will explain it all very shortly.'

'What do you want?' Portman asked. He was shivering head to toe, and I was half expecting him to wet himself at any moment.

'I want a cup of coffee. Go make one, black with lots of sugar. Bentley will have the same, won't you?'

'I will.'

'Don't give me any cheap stuff either, Portman,' Hunter growled. He leaned his backside against the counter and never took his eyes of the reluctant host for an instant. 'Any biscuits?'

'Got a few chocolate ones ...'

'Don't tell me about them. Fetch them, man.'

Portman pulled open a cupboard above the counter and passed a tin to Hunter. His face was bone white and sweat poured from his forehead. He was surely aware of how vicious Hunter could be. He had the look of a man who knew he was about to die.

'Nice,' Hunter said as he crunched into a biscuit. 'How's that coffee coming along?'

I stayed by the door to the hallway and watched the front door for any sign of trouble. I cared little for Hunter's toying with the man. A hot cup of coffee was welcome, but I doubted I'd keep it down once the violence started. And there *would* be violence; Hunter was in that scary mode that made him kill people – even those who didn't really deserve it. I was in for an eventful night by the looks of it.

CHAPTER SEVENTEEN

The Master's Identity

'That's not a bad coffee,' Hunter said, taking the rim of the cup from his mouth. 'Finally we've discovered something you're good at.'

'I'll speak to Ballentine about this,' Portman replied nervously. 'He won't like agents being roughed up. You have no right to treat me like this, Hunter.'

'Ah, yes, your good friend Ballentine.' Hunter used his psychokinesis to push Portman away from the counter and into a chair that swung out from under the table. 'First of all, you are not an agent of the Guild of the True. You're a walking calculator who never gets his hands dirty. Your wife is the one who could be classed as an agent.' Hunter placed his cup on the counter and loomed over Portman. 'Where is your wife this evening?'

'I'm not telling you anything.'

'Mr Portman,' I called from the other side of the kitchen, 'you should tell him what he wants to know. I've seen what happens when prisoners resist.'

'Oh, so that's what I am? A prisoner?'

'I just want some information,' Hunter said. 'That's all.'

'I'm not saying another word.'

'Pity.'

That's when the electrocuting started. I thought what he'd done to Brofeldt was bad. I always felt that a man should never physically hurt a woman, even in desperate times, but now I could see that Hunter had gone easy on her. The pain Portman went through for almost half an hour was sickening. Hunter wasn't even questioning him. He just kept shocking him over and over again, and appeared to be taking great pleasure from it.

'Hunter,' I shouted. I used my gift to pull him away from his captive and to turn him towards me. 'You're losing control. We need answers. All you're doing is torturing the poor man.'

'Poor man? This scumbag is partly responsible for dozens of agents being killed.'

I stepped close to him and whispered: 'We still don't actually know if he's a traitor or not.'

'Hmm, that's true,' he nodded. 'I think you're right. I should start quizzing him now.'

'I can't take anymore,' Portman screamed as Hunter turned back to him. 'Please. Bentley, I implore you to put an end to this. You're a good lad. Don't let this animal hurt me again.'

'I can't help you, Mr Portman. He'll only stop when you answer his questions.'

'He hasn't asked me any questions yet!'

'Here's a question for you,' Hunter said casually. 'Who turned you?'

'I don't know what you're talking about.'

'Listen to me, Portman. My good friends Burrows and Armitage smoked out Ballentine this morning,' Hunter lied. 'They killed him in a most brutal fashion. But before they did, he told them the names of the other traitors. He named you and your wife. Let's stop messing around here. I've got all night to keep zapping you.' A ball of electricity grew above Hunter's outstretched hand. 'Who turned you?'

'Ballentine …' Portman admitted. He winced as he said the name, as if it caused him physical pain to betray his fellow conspirator. It was followed by a sigh – seemingly one of relief. It felt like he wanted to admit his guilt, and would have done even if Hunter hadn't roughed him up.

'Now we're making progress. You admit to being a traitor?'

'Yes.'

'Why did you turn?'

'Why the bloody hell do you think? Money! Look at where I live! I bust my ass all day working and I still can't get anywhere. The Guild make me work for them and never even pay me for expenses. I'm sick of it. I have one of the rarest gifts in all the world and I live like a slave. I'm no better than any of the other saps in the world who works a nine to five. I'm the best ink-seer on the planet! Don't you remember the things I did for the Guild? All the times I had to break into government offices to read their files on gifted people. Thousands of pages at a time being sucked up by my mind, and then endless late nights rewriting the knowledge I'd stolen for the Guild. Half the files in the archives of the Palatium were written by me! No one even thanked me for all that! I deserved a better life than the one the Guild has given me. They promised me the moon and the stars when I signed up fifteen years ago. In all that time I never let them down, Hunter. I didn't fail them. They failed me.'

Hunter allowed the ball of electricity to fizzle out. I think some of Portman's plight struck a chord with him. How could it not? Hunter lived like a pauper even though he constantly risked his life for the Guild. He had even stolen money before and hidden it from the Guild.

'You didn't have to lead such a mundane life, John,' Hunter said. He sat on the table in front of Portman and his body language became less aggressive. 'You could have done something else. Betraying your colleagues has cost a lot of lives.'

'I'm sorry.' Portman was weeping now. He slumped into the chair as if his bones had melted. 'Ballentine gave me twenty grand in cash. He told me there would be larger payments every month. It was too late to turn back when I realised what I'd done.'

'Where is your wife, John?'

'I haven't seen her in three days.'

'Don't lie to me.'

'I'm not lying to you. It's the truth. We were at the office and she said she was going out to buy some lunch for us both. Said she'd be back in twenty minutes. I haven't seen or heard from her since. Her phone is dead. None of her friends have heard from her. I don't know if she's run away or if she was murdered.'

'She was always smarter than you,' Hunter said, his eyebrows raised and a sympathetic grin on his lips. 'If she did indeed run.'

'I've always been a fool. I'll die a fool.'

'I haven't decided to kill you yet.'

'I'd rather you did. There's no life for me now. I have destroyed my own future.'

'You don't mean that, John. Now tell me about the people

Ballentine is working for.'

'The shadow Guild ...' There was no more fight in Portman. It was clear by the look in his eyes that he was about to reveal everything he knew. 'I was in before I knew who they were, Hunter. I promise you I would never have worked with them if I'd known.'

'Tell me what you know.'

'They're in control of Golding Scientific. They planted one of their spies in the corporation almost two years ago. She's a very powerful mind-switcher. Her name is Aubrey Pearson. She worked in their security division at first. After Derek Shaw was killed, she was elected to take his place, even though there were better candidates.'

'She used her gift to get the job?' I asked.

'Of course she did. As soon as she was head of the division, she was real close to Golding. That's when she started influencing him directly.'

'How did she influence him?' Hunter asked.

'She didn't take full control of him at first,' Portman replied. 'She used her gift to plant ideas in his head that slowly grew, so that Golding began to question his own sanity. After a time his mind became vulnerable, and that's when Pearson performed regular mind-switches. Within weeks she was dictating important financial decisions as well as security matters. Three months ago Golding signed everything into her name in the event of his death.'

'She will control the organisation when he dies,' Hunter said. 'Now I understand.'

'He's already dead,' Portman said. 'Golding has been murdered. They poisoned him two days ago.'

Portman was not lying. I could see it in his eyes. Paul Golding had been murdered. The man who had caused me so much strife over the years was no more. I should have been jumping for joy, but I just stood there, my heart as cold as the wind that rattled the windows of the kitchen. The incident with Zalech prevented me from taking any pleasure in death – even the demise of my worst enemy.

'Pearson is the one behind all this?' I asked Portman. 'She's the leader? The one they call The Master?'

'Nonsense,' Hunter insisted. 'She's not the leader, is she, Portman?'

'No.'

'Who is it? Give me a name!'

'The Master is an old friend of yours ...' Portman couldn't bring himself to look Hunter in the eye. He stared at the floor and sucked in deep breaths as the tall Scot stood over him. 'Remember, Hunter, if I'd known who it was I never would have considered siding with them. I would have gone straight to Sterling and told him everything.'

'Who is The Master?'

'It's ...' Portman finally looked up at Hunter with glistening eyes. 'It's Brian Blake.'

I thought Hunter was going to literally explode right then and there. His face went purple with rage and he struck Portman a punch that was so ferocious I felt the force of it in my gut. Brian Blake was the mysterious leader of the shadow group that was causing so much trouble. Blake was the bane of Hunter's life. He had tracked Hunter down when he was a teenager and tried to kill him, simply because he displayed his powers in public. Hunter had survived the assassination attempt. His aunt – the only family he had – was not as fortunate. Blake had burned her alive. To make matters worse, Hunter was blamed for her death and incarcerated. He was fortunate that Peter Williams and Jonathan Atkinson were aware of his suffering and broke him out of prison. He'd been living as a ghost ever since. I could not imagine the mix of emotions he was now experiencing.

'Who told you this?' I asked Portman.

'Ballentine did.'

Hunter struck Portman again, without warning. He was about to electrocute him when I stepped in and pulled him away. Only then did I see his eyes filled with tears.

'The bastard!' he shouted. 'I will kill him. I will kill him slowly. I will make him experience pain like no other human has ever endured.'

Blake had gone into exile two decades ago, when Jonathan Atkinson had waged a civil war against him and his cohorts. Most of Blake's allies had been killed. *He* had survived and fled, but not before a fight with one of the old Guild agents – an expert in pyrokinesis, just like Blake. It had been a titanic struggle by all accounts. Blake lost the duel and was burned beyond recognition. He did escape, despite his injuries, but most were happy with that outcome, thinking the life he would have would be a living hell. They had underestimated him. He had returned to exact his revenge on those who had overthrown him all those years before. The plot was cunning and ruthless, reflecting the man who had designed it.

'Brofeldt told us that Blake planned to unite the Guild and Golding Scientific,' I said to our captive. 'Is that correct?'

'He's a crazed fascist,' Portman explained. 'He wants to merge the two organisations and to control numerous governments by using mind-switchers. He wants to be at the helm of a global superpower.'

'The Guild would never allow him to rule again,' Hunter insisted. 'He's a hated figure within our group. Why on earth would he believe that to be achievable?'

'He claims to know a terrible secret about the Guild. I wasn't told what it is. Ballentine knew. He believed that if Blake revealed it to the Guild members they would turn on the Council and willingly invite Blake to lead once more.'

'Who knows of this secret?' Hunter grabbed Portman by the lapels of his jacket and wrenched him out of the chair so that they were eye to eye. 'Who knows?'

'I don't know, Hunter.'

'Who has Blake told?'

'I don't know! He was waiting until the senior agents of the Guild were wiped out. He's almost ready. That's why he needed spies in the Guild. He had to get details on all the members, active, retired, trainees, moles, the lot. Once he had the likes of you out of the way and had control of Golding Scientific, he would inform all the Guild members of this secret. That's when the whole plan would fall into place.'

'I'll do a deal with you, Portman,' Hunter snarled. 'Tell me where Blake is and I'll let you live. I need to know where he is right now! You're not a fool, John. You know what will happen if that type of power is in Blake's hands. He'd be Hitler with an army of gifted soldiers. The world could be ruined by him. You must tell me.'

'He's only a few miles from here,' Portman confessed. 'In the centre of Manchester. It's called the Imperium Building. It looks like a normal office tower from the street, but inside they use it as an experimental lab for Golding's scientists. It's where they rebuilt that lunatic Edward Zalech.'

'Tell me more about this building.'

'It's practically empty now. They built a much larger facility on an island in the North Sea. I don't know which one. They've been moving the operation to the island for weeks now. There's only a skeleton crew left at the Imperium.'

'And Blake remained?'

'He's being treated there. I don't know what treatment it is before you ask. They planned to move him when the new labs are fully functional.'

'And when will that be?'

'I believe he is to be moved tomorrow morning by helicopter.'

'We can be there in less than an hour,' I said to Hunter. 'We can put a stop to this if we can get to Blake before he's moved.'

'We'll leave shortly,' Hunter replied. He turned to our captive and electricity sparked around his fingers. 'Night, night, John.' There was a bright flash and Portman was sent jolting back into the chair before he slumped to one side, motionless.

'Did you kill him?'

'No. He'll be out for at least twenty-four hours. We can come back here and get him after we've dealt with Blake. I have to contact Canavan, in case we don't survive the night.'

The seriousness with which he said it was disturbing. I became aware that this would probably be the most dangerous mission of all. I felt pangs of anxiety in my gut and the headache I'd suffered that afternoon returned with a vengeance. I winced and rubbed my temples. I felt unsteady on my feet and my stomach was twirling.

'Bentley, this would not be a good time for you to have one of your headaches.'

'I don't choose when to have them.'

'Go upstairs and soak your face in the sink or something. We'll be on the road again in less than an hour. I'll need you to be at your best tonight.'

I listened in to Hunter's call with Marie Canavan. He told her of Portman's confession and said that we would travel to the Imperium Building without delay. She informed him that she had been able to contact Elizabeth Armitage, who had been in Copenhagen, and that she was already on a flight to England. It appeared that Canavan had also secured the capture of Ballentine, with the help of someone called Burrows, who I'd never heard of before that day. They would try to get to Manchester as soon as possible, but we could not risk waiting for them. Blake could be transported at any moment. We had to get to the building before that happened.

After the call, I took Hunter's advice and went to the bathroom and soaked my head in a sink of warm water. I felt truly ill. Nothing would make the headache go away this time and as I sat on the side of the tub I saw the ghostly figures of Romand and Williams standing either side of me. For the first time their hallucinations had sound. Every previous occasion they simply stood there silent and ethereal. Now they were more tangible and had voices.

'… it made a monster of a good man …' I heard Romand saying.

'We know you have great power, Ross,' Williams said, 'and you have so much potential …'

I thought for a moment they were speaking to me or to each other. They weren't. These were memories of my time with them. I recalled Romand saying those exact words while we were together at the Atkinsons' house. What Williams said was one year earlier, when he was about to give me the papers written by Rudolph Klein.

Somehow obscure memories were playing out in the bathroom as if they were being projected by my mind into some form of reality. I felt my sanity was giving way. At least I was now sure that what I was seeing were not ghosts. Simple memories only.

I doused my face with water again and the apparitions were no more. The headache was excruciating now and I struggled to even open the door. It was twinned with an overwhelming sense of dread. I couldn't tell if it was the anxiety I often suffered with, or if this was my precognitive gift ringing the alarm bell. I eased myself down the staircase and back into the kitchen to find Hunter tying up Portman, who was still unconscious.

I stood in the doorway to the hallway and tried to clear my mind. I heaved in deep breaths. Hunter was saying something but his words did not register with me. I was too focused on the floor of the kitchen. I was staring at the tiles in the corner. I had seen this room before. I gasped when I recognised it as the room from the vision I had the week before – the one in which Hunter was lying dead on the floor of shattered tiles, bloodied and battered. The anxiety I was experiencing *was* my precognitive gift. We were in mortal danger!

'Hunter, they're coming for us,' I screamed. 'We have to get out of here.'

'Who is coming for us?'

'My precognitive gift …' I panted. 'Someone is coming ...'

'How long do we have?'

I didn't even have time to answer him. The hall door was smashed inward and I turned lethargically to see Boxer's injured companion stepping over the threshold. His left arm was in a sling; in his right he was holding an automatic weapon. The sound was deafening as he pulled the trigger. The muzzle ignited and a volley of bullets was fired along the hallway at me. My attempt to deflect the shots was unsuccessful. Two bullets made their way through, one striking me clean in the right shoulder, another hit the wall and a part of the bullet ricocheted off it and struck me in the stomach. I collapsed onto my back, reeling in shock. The pain and the heat of the bullets raged inside me and I fought to pull air into my lungs.

I tried to get away before he pulled the trigger once more. I turned and dragged myself towards the kitchen as bullets whizzed over my head and shattered the tiles on the floor. I thought I was done for. I would have been if Hunter hadn't intervened. He sent out a pulse of electricity that bounced off the walls of the hallway and blasted our attacker through the open doorway, and sent him smashing through the windscreen of Portman's car.

'Are you all right, Bentley?' Hunter asked as he kneeled over me. 'Where are you hit?'

'Leave me,' I panted. 'This isn't over. You'll die if you stay.'

'Peter Williams gave me an order two years ago. It was to protect you with my life and I mean to obey that order to whatever end. I will never leave you.'

'Hunter, you *have* to get out of here!'

CHAPTER EIGHTEEN

The Last Fight

Hunter clamped his hand over my injured shoulder to stem the blood loss. It didn't do much good. There was blood spouting from my stomach, too. I felt dreadfully cold – cold from the inside out.

'I'm going to die,' I kept saying. I couldn't stop myself from saying it over and over. 'I'm going to die, Hunter.'

'You're not going to die,' he said. 'Concentrate on the bullets in your body, draw on your psychokinetic gift, and force them out the way they went in. I've done it before. It'll hurt like hell, but it'll save your life. Do it now.'

I could actually feel the metal of the bullets inside me. My body ached for them to be repelled. I focused my mind completely and concentrated on the bullet in my shoulder. I felt the cold metal grating against my muscles. My gift was rising. I channelled it within myself and pushed the mangled bullet out of the wound. I went to my knees with a cry as it tapped the wooden floor in the hall. I was just about to repeat this process with the fragment in my stomach when an almighty crash came from the back of the house. I looked up to see the furniture of the kitchen being blasted against the wall. Portman's body was sent upward and smacked off the cupboards above the counter. I doubted anyone could survive such an impact.

'I'll buy you some time,' Hunter said as he strode back to the kitchen. 'Now get on that bike and get to the Imperium and finish this.'

'Hunter, you can't beat him!'

I hunched over and sucked in energy to my body and pushed out the other bullet. The fighting had already begun by the time I'd managed to get to my feet. I saw Hunter being thrown against the wall, only for him to pounce forward and fire out a bolt of electricity. I staggered forward to the doorway, blood pouring down my clothes and dashing the floor. Boxer and Hunter had a grip of one another on the other side of the room, lines of electricity stretched out and licked the walls and ceiling. Boxer towered over my friend – he seemed to fill the room.

Hunter was thrown to the floor and I used my gift to build a protective barrier around him. It was ineffective. Boxer reached straight through it and grabbed hold of Hunter's coat then tossed him through a gaping hole at the back of the house. He landed half way down the back garden with a loud thump and he was very slow in getting to his knees.

'Fight me!' I screamed at Boxer. 'Come on, I'm not afraid of you!'

He turned around and his artificial green eyes were set on me. He placed his hands on his hips and shook his head, laughing.

'You *will* be afraid of me,' he said. 'As soon as I'm done with your friend.'

'Fight me.'

'I've already beaten you, Bentley. You will realise that soon enough.'

He stomped over the rubble and into the back garden. Hunter was back on his feet again and was swaying from side to side. I hoped he was playing possum. He was about to take another pounding because Boxer was not tired and still uninjured. There was seemingly no way of fighting him or even slowing him down.

That's when I realised just how powerful Hunter really was. All the occasions I had fought with him, the times we'd been at each other's throats, when I thought I was more powerful than him, I was really utterly outmatched. He had allowed me to get the better of him when we battled in the woods near his home and when I threw him against the wall at Canavan's house. I never believed he possessed such devastating power.

He raised his arms above his head and pointed his fingers together at the sky. There was light all around him, swirling like fireflies, then far above the earth, deep within the low swirling clouds another light appeared. This one broke the clouds apart. There were flashes above the houses before an immense streak of lightning was drawn from the heavens and fizzed into the garden. Boxer took the full force of it. This was no random streak of lightning. No, this was constant. An unwavering line of blinding power that brought Boxer to his knees, screaming. The thick line of electricity stretched down from the sky and stung Boxer for more than a minute. Then the garden was instantly plunged into darkness.

Hunter swayed on unsteady legs. Boxer was lying on his back, with sparks of electricity still dancing around him and smoke twirling from his body. My friend staggered forward a few steps and nudged the stricken giant with his boot. There was no reaction. Hunter let out a sigh of relief. He was covered in blood, his face bashed, one of hands distorted and broken. Lord knows how many new scars he had under his coat. At least he had finished off Boxer …

A hand reached through the falling snowflakes and gripped Hunter's leg. Boxer rose ominously from the grass and Hunter was tossed across the garden and smashed through the window and landed on the floor next to me. He was barely conscious. He posed no further defence against the tall assassin, who was stalking up the garden towards me, green eyes glowing through the snowfall. I fired blasts and waves at him. Nothing I did had any influence. When Boxer reached me he simply swiped me away with one arm. It felt like I'd been hit by a car. I was sent tumbling onto the floor and knocked my head against part of the broken wall.

He had a hold of Hunter when I managed to straighten myself. One hand on the back of his head, the other wrapped around his neck.

'Don't!' I pleaded. 'You don't have to kill him.'

'I know I don't have to,' he replied. 'But I *want* to.'

'You're a coward,' Hunter spat. 'I'd have kicked your head in if you hadn't got that mask on. You only beat me because Golding and Blake paid the scientists to build that stupid looking thing.'

'I agree,' Boxer laughed. 'You would certainly have beaten me if they hadn't made this ugly looking mask.' His grip tightened around Hunter's neck. 'Ain't technology a bitch?'

'Bentley,' Hunter hissed at me. 'Run!'

With one swift movement the giant twisted both arms and snapped Hunter's neck like a twig. Boxer tossed his lifeless body aside and I saw him land on the broken tiles in the corner, just as I had seen in the vision days earlier. It had been a premonition of this terrible moment in time. Hunter wasn't moving. Surely he could not survive such an injury.

Everything that Hunter and I had shared was now nothing more than memories in the caverns of my mind. I did not scream. I did not cry. I simply watched him, stupidly hoping he would return to life and spring back to his feet. He didn't. I was alone with this monster who I could not fight.

Boxer pulled the mask off his head and let it fall at his feet. He no longer had any need for it. His dark face was weathered and grim. His eyes more lifeless than the mechanical ones he'd just shed. How could the human race spawn such abominations? Marianne, Zalech, Boxer, Golding, Shaw. I had faced them all. I suppose it was only a matter of time before one of them got the better of me. I was just a normal lad from a quiet suburb. How could I hope to contend with villains of this calibre?

'You just gonna stand there like a statue while I kill you?' Boxer asked, a smile twitching one of his cheeks. 'Or are you at least going to make a run for your bike?'

'I can't outrun you.'

'I'll give you a head start.'

I knew he was impossibly swift. Hunter had told me that kinetic fusion enables a person to move at speeds that should have been impossible. I couldn't hope to outrun him, not with the injuries I had. I would have to give *myself* a head start.

I pulled in as much energy as I possibly could, and with it came the ceiling of the kitchen and contents of the bathroom, all crashing down upon my foe. It wouldn't hurt him in the slightest, but it distracted him for a few seconds and I used that time to race through to the front of the house.

The cool air met my face and snow scratched my eyes as I ran. I bounded over the garden wall and onto the icy pavement. He was behind me, I could hear him barging through the front of the house. I kept on forcing myself forward until the bike was in sight. I still had time. I could make it.

I pounded across the slippery road and slid on my knees to the bike. The snowfall had obscured my view of the kinetibike as I had approached it. Only now that I was close to the bike could I see it had been torn to pieces. The engine was smashed, the handlebar bent, the exhausts ripped open. He had sabotaged it before entering the house, just in case one of us escaped. He'd beaten me before the fighting had even started.

'Looks like you have nowhere left to run,' Boxer said. He was standing right behind me. He probably could have caught me before I reached the bike. He was simply toying with me.

'What are you waiting for?' I asked, without turning to him. 'End this now.'

'I've heard so many great things about you, Bentley. I was actually expecting you to be the one to give me the fight, not Huntington. I must say I am disappointed in you. My employer, though, thinks you are most valuable. That means they'll pay me a handsome sum to bring you in alive.'

'Why would they want me?'

'They probably want you to work for them. Just like I do. They'll make you a very wealthy man. Isn't that what you were after in the first place? Isn't that why you entered the *Million Dollar Gift*?'

'Yes.'

'On your feet, then. Don't bother trying anything stupid. You'll only get yourself killed.'

'What could I possibly try?' I replied as I stood and stuffed my hands into my jacket pockets. 'You're indestructible after all.'

'And don't ever forget it.' He raised his arm and beckoned a car from the other end of the street. It came speeding up and slid to a halt right next to us. 'Get in,' Boxer ordered. 'I'll take you to meet Blake.'

I was pushed into the back seat and Boxer squeezed in next to me and shouted at the driver in a foreign tongue. We sped away from the street and were soon on a busy road leading to Manchester. I wasn't bleeding as much as before; I was using my gift to close the wounds, as Hunter had described for me many times. I would always raise my eyes to the heavens when he told me about the technique. I never actually thought I'd be caught out by a bullet. Thankfully some of his advice had gotten through to me. I was still in bad shape, though. I'd bleed to death sooner or later because I simply couldn't use my gifts for a prolonged amount of time in such a weakened state.

I actually found it difficult to focus my gifts to stem the bleeding because of the two young men sitting in the front. They were alarmed by something. They kept shouting at each other in a language I didn't understand, and the passenger turned to me more than once and gave me a look as if I was the grim reaper. Then he returned to shouting at his companion and the word 'diablo' was repeated many times.

'My Brazilian friends here think you are the devil himself.'

I remembered the hit list I'd found in Brofeldt's apartment. They had given me the code name of Devil. Did these people actually believe there was a supernatural explanation behind my powers?

'Why do you people call me that?' I asked Boxer.

'Maybe because you look like death,' he tittered. 'You're as pale as a ghost.'

'So would you be if you'd been shot.'

'Shot?' This amused Boxer. He spoke to the others in what I guessed was Portuguese, considering they were from Brazil. They all laughed. 'I'll never have to worry about being shot,' he said, turning back to me. 'It would be about as much use as throwing salt at me.'

'Hunter said to me once that we all pay for our sins in the fullness of time.'

'He certainly paid for his.'

'At least he died fighting,' I said bitterly.

'Yes. He had a relatively honourable death. I'm surprised by you.' He was watching me with those emotionless black eyes of his. 'You surrendered without much of a struggle.'

'I didn't have much of a choice.'

'There is always choice. You could stop using your gift and you would bleed out before we reach our destination. Some would consider that an honourable way to die. I would consider that honourable.'

'I'm quite happy to disappoint you.'

'The desire for wealth overcomes your sense of honour. That is common these days.'

'Where's your honour? You work for Blake because he gives you money. You said so yourself.'

'I am not in your situation. I joined him of my own free will. You, on the other hand, will go to him injured, frightened and captured. You go to him in an effort to save your life, or to get rich quick.'

'Maybe I have reasons you're not aware of.'

'Make sure killing is not on your agenda. I would not be pleased if you became violent in front of my employer. I do not think you would enjoy my company as much as you do now if I was displeased with your behaviour.'

He was out of his mind. He might have been born crazy, or been driven over the edge by his upbringing, or the years of killing for Armamenti Tal-Future, or the decades in wandering the world. It didn't matter what the cause, he had me in the palm of his hand and there was no escape.

The chatter died off as we entered the city. It was then, when I had time to think, that I was overcome with sorrow for my fallen friend. I couldn't believe he was gone. The world would be a greyer place without him. My life would certainly be a lot less eventful. At least he died the way he would have wanted. There was no long goodbye. He would have hated that. Hunter went out on his shield, like Romand had. He never wanted to die of old age. That didn't make me feel any better. I was lost without him. An unbeatable monster was leading me to the most evil man in the world. Blake. The bane of the Guild. There could be no worse situation to find myself in.

The Imperium was a ten-storey building, its exterior almost completely covered in glass. It stood isolated from the smaller and older office blocks of an industrial area in Manchester. Only a few windows on the top floor were illuminated. The rest showed only shadow. The ground floor also seemed to be deserted, apart from the reception area, which was brightly lit and full of uniformed guards. There was also a large warehouse situated at the rear of the building and there were two trucks parked at its loading bays, which were being filled with machinery.

It looked like Portman was telling the truth; they were only hours from relocating the operation to the North Sea. Was there still time to stop them? That was the question I pondered as Boxer wrenched me out of the car and pushed me across the pavement and forecourt to the glass entrance. I was getting the distinct feeling that I would not leave this building alive.

The doors automatically parted as I drew near and when I passed through them there was a loud wailing that made me jump with fright. Some of the uniformed guards rushed at me, pointing their guns.

'Back off,' Boxer told them. He pulled an automatic pistol from inside his coat and showed it to the guards. 'I set off the alarms.'

The guards holstered their weapons and gave Boxer a wide berth as he led me across the marble foyer.

'You want to see Ms Pearson?' a woman at the reception desk shouted to Boxer. 'I can call her down if you like.'

'Please do. She'll think Christmas has come early when she sees what I've brought to the party.' He chuckled as he looked down at me. 'They believe you to be quite the prize, Bentley.'

I wanted to make a wise crack, in the hope it would irritate him, anything just to wipe that wicked smile from his face. I couldn't think of a witty riposte, though. I was all out of ideas, humour and strength. The wound in my stomach was terribly sore and I was struggling to keep it closed. My right arm was going numb from the shot I'd taken in the shoulder and my head felt like a balloon. Simply remaining upright took a great deal of effort.

The elevator doors parted and a muscular, mean looking woman stepped out and came pacing across the marble floor towards us. Her beady eyes were directed right at me, never looking away for an instant. She was also smiling. Smiling like it was indeed Christmas morning and I was an unexpected present.

'Well, Ms Pearson,' Boxer said. 'Look what I caught in Prestwich.'

'Well, well, well,' she said, looking me up and down. 'This is a surprise. Mr Blake will be most pleased.'

'I don't give a damn if he's pleased or not.' Boxer stood between me and Pearson. 'The price for this one is a million pounds.'

'You'll get your money in time.'

'When?'

'You think we have that type of cash lying around?'

'When?'

'As soon as we've moved to the new facility. No more than two days. I'm sure you can hold out until then.'

'I've killed more agents. One of them high priority. That's another hundred thousand.'

'Who?'

'The Scottish killer. Huntington.'

'Good work, Jermaine. You might even get a bonus for taking care of that one – Mr Blake was quite eager for him to be removed for some reason.'

Money is the root of all evil. Or so they say. I believed in that old saying as I listened to them bargaining for the heads of Guild agents. I was sick just thinking that Hunter had been killed just to top up Boxer's bank account. They were loathsome characters. But there was worse awaiting me. Brian Blake. I knew his motivation was not financial. He had more sinister reasons for doing all this. He'd often been described as a fascist who believed all non-gifted were a lower form of humanity. The future he wanted to bring about belonged to those born with true gifts. The rest of society was to serve us as slaves. I knew that was his ultimate goal. A horrible prospect. The death and suffering that he could inflict would overshadow any war, famine, dictatorship or depression that mankind had ever endured. And he was now very close to realising his vision of domination.

'He's been shot twice,' Boxer told Pearson. 'At least he's clever enough to use his gift to stop the blood. I'd give him three hours before he's dead.'

'We have one or two doctors knocking about the place. We can patch him up before shipping him out to the new facility.' She moved to me and placed her hand on my uninjured shoulder. 'You'll be all right, Ross.' Her smile made me want to puke all over her manly face. 'I think you deserve a bonus, too. What with you killing that Zalech person last year. I wasn't too keen on him.'

'Join the club,' I said, forcing a smile. 'How much would something like that earn me?'

'Oh, I think I could sanction a six-figure sum.'

'Sweet.' I played along as best I could. 'How much do I get if I tell you where two agents will be tonight?'

'Another six figures.'

'Where do I sign up?'

'We can arrange all that after you've spoken to Mr Blake.' She turned stiffly on her heel and nudged me forward. 'This way. I'll bring you up to see him.'

CHAPTER NINETEEN

Blake

Boxer was practically glued to my side as we left the elevator and strode along the corridor on the top floor of the building. He knew I could still put up a serious fight if I wanted to. He was strong enough to stop me with a single blow, and this was the only reason why I was to be brought in front of Blake. Boxer wasn't the only protection, there were six armed guards outside one of the doors ahead, and a seventh guard at the opposite end of the corridor. Pearson was also armed. She walked behind us and I could feel her eyes burning holes in the back of my head. She eventually moved ahead of me when the armed guards blocked our way.

'Stand aside,' she ordered. 'Mr Blake has a visitor.'

I don't know who pushed the door open. My mind was too confused to focus. Boxer placed his monstrous hand on my injured shoulder, squeezing slightly, before shoving me inside.

The room was poorly lit and it took my eyes a moment to adjust. Blake was lying on a wide bed, his arms fixed by his side, his head propped up with a mound of pillows. His face was gruesome to behold. The bottom half of it was melted – probably from the fight with the pyrokinetic all those years before. No lips, no nose, no chin, no cheeks, just melted flesh draped thinly over his skull. The upper half of his head was relatively intact. He was ancient. Dull eyes hooded with drooping lids, a grid of lines across his forehead, thin strands of white hair spilling into the pillows. I had imagined he was being treated here to bolster his gifts, like the procedures Zalech had undergone in this very building. I had been wrong. They were keeping him alive. Machines either side of the bed were attached to his arms with wires and tubes. A nurse sat at a computer in the corner of the room, closely monitoring the screen.

Blake's head never budged as I moved across the room. Only his eyes followed me. There might have been a smile if he had a proper mouth. Boxer grabbed my arm, pulled me to the end of the bed and told me not to move. Pearson had her gun drawn and was pointing it directly at my face.

'I killed Huntington,' Boxer told his employer. 'He suffered greatly before I broke his neck. I found this one with him. He is injured, but will most likely live if he is operated on soon.'

'Good.'

The voice had emanated from some speakers that were connected to the computer the nurse was sitting at. I saw now that there was a mechanical device on Blake's throat that was attached to the hard drive with two wires.

'It is a great relief to me that Huntington is no more,' Blake continued. 'Alas, my only regret is that I lacked the vigour of youth in order to rid this world of his presence with my own two hands. You have done well, Jermaine, and will be rewarded accordingly. And you, boy,' his eyes focused on me, 'you have played on my mind so very often in recent times. You are such a talent. You could be the one who finally destroys the Guild once and for all.'

'Yeah …' I said awkwardly. 'As I was saying to Pearson downstairs, I'd be happy to help you out if you're paying a hefty reward.'

'Your reward will be a future of limitless possibilities. You do not yet realise your true potential at all, do you? And I am quite sure you do not realise that you have been fighting on the wrong side since you were kidnapped by that French meddler, Marcus Romand.'

It took a lot of restraint to hold my tongue. I didn't like anyone speaking ill of Romand. Especially this withered piece of Nazi filth. I would have liked to put a crush layer on him right then and watch him squirm as the life was slowly pushed out of his decaying body.

'You serve evil, Ross Bentley,' he continued. 'I am your salvation. You see, I am the great liberator of the gifted. I intend to free all the gifted people of the world. First, it will be those within the Guild of the True. Then I will move on to Der Orden der Befahigen and then finally JNCOR. A world of gifted united under one banner. A collection of the most wondrous people who walk this earth. We could lead humanity into a new era of peace and prosperity. No longer would the course of our societies be dictated by banks and corrupt capitalist whores, military commanders who bow to weapons manufacturers, socialists who cringe in the face of globalist corporations. No, their time is at an end. The world and everyone in it will have to unite and serve our new, gifted regime.'

'Sounds cool.'

'You do not take me seriously. I can see that by simply looking into those innocent eyes of yours. They see little, your eyes. I think perhaps I should show you something that would force you to take me seriously. Something that may incinerate that innocence that lives in those pretty eyes of yours.' His left hand slid slowly to a table next to the bed. Pearson lowered her gun and helped Blake to lift a collection of papers from the table top. 'I have here the truth about the Guild. This should be enough for you to see clearly that you have been duped by the Council. You believed you were a freedom fighter. In truth, you were nothing more than an agent of evil all along. The Guild is not what you thought it to be. You have been surrounded by lying scoundrels from day one. Marcus Romand, Peter Williams, Michael Huntington. All of them responsible for the deaths of countless gifted individuals. All of them at the behest of the greatest villain of all.'

'I always knew they were killers. What you're telling me isn't news.'

'I am sure they told you that the killing was a necessity, yes? That they had to do it to preserve the Guild? That it was for the sake of the common good?'

I nodded.

'They lied. It is an organisation that is built on untruths. Did you know that I was once the Primicerius of the Guild? Yes, many years ago I tried to lead them from their dubious origins and to mould them into a group that could withstand the test of time and the coming of a new millennium. It would, and should, have been a golden age for the gifted. Sadly, I was betrayed by those who lied to achieve their goals. I was cast out. They did this…' He waved his hand weakly over his burned face. 'Thankfully my will has always been stronger than my flesh could ever be. And now I have returned to ruin their kingdom of dishonesty.'

He held out the papers.

'Take them,' he insisted. 'See for yourself.'

'Careful,' Boxer grunted as I leaned forward to take the papers from Blake. 'Don't do anything foolish.'

I took the papers from Blake and walked to the other side of the room, to the soft glare of one of the lamps. I tore off the binding and gazed upon the first page. I was sure this was the great secret that Blake had used to turn the likes of Ballentine against the Guild. I honestly had no interest in reading these secrets, but I had to stall them. I had to buy myself more time. The opening page had official watermarks and stamps that made me believe it was genuine. But more than that, for some reason I knew it was real as soon as I laid eyes on it.

Ship Itinerary – Private Cruiser.
Vessel: The Blue Fin
Sale Date: 5 – 6 – 1989
Departure Time: 11am (Singaraja)
Passenger List:
Ian Garrott
Daniel Shelser
Katherine Kinlan
Stephanie Parker
Li Woo Sung
Suzana Fuentez
Sebastian Kowatich
James Barkley
Angus Robertson
Henrik Valstrom
Luigi DiVadino
Sarah Washington
Jerome Happer

I recognised only one name from the list of passengers: James Barkley. The man who was to achieve the sixteenth gift. The man who was to become insane. The Kematian. It was all very familiar to me. I knew of this story. Barkley and twelve gifted friends had been travelling the world on some sort of hippy voyage of exploration. Golding knew of his powers and wanted him to work for the fledgling Golding Scientific as an assassin. Barkley refused him time and time again. Golding had eventually lost patience and hired Melissa Nijinska – Boxer's old colleague from Armamenti Tal-Future – to track Barkley down and kill him. She had found them on a tropical island in south-east Asia. The document I was looking at seemed to confirm all that I had learned of this tale. Barkley and twelve others. Travelling to an island. The date was a good match for the story that Romand and Hunter had mentioned.

Nijinska was a mageleton and had created a tsunami that wiped out almost every living thing on the island. Barkley survived, though, and in his rage over the murder of his friends he achieved a higher power, killed the assassin and became the crazed and all powerful Kematian. But why show me this? I knew about what had happened all those years ago. This simply confirmed the story as fact – or at least part of it.

I was about to toss the sheets back at Blake when I paused. I held the paper close to my face and examined the passengers' names once again. There was a name missing. Hunter had told me that Jim Sterling had been on that boat. He was one of Barkley's closest friends. He had fought the monster that Barkley became. Why was he not on the list?

'It is genuine,' Blake said. 'Those were the only people who went to the island that day.'

'Wrong,' I replied. 'There's one name missing.'

'You refer to Jim Sterling?'

'He fought Barkley. They were friends before they travelled to that island. They were the only two that made it out alive.'

'No.'

'Two of them survived!'

'No.'

'This is not real. You made this up.'

'One man left that island. The great enemy. The great shadow. He went there as James Barkley and he left it as James Sterling. He changed his name after what happened so he could disappear into obscurity. He eventually found his way into the Guild. You now know him as Jim Sterling, the Primicerius of the Guild. Your leader. The man who orders you and your friends about. The man who orders you to kill. The Kematian.'

'It's lies. You're lying.'

'Turn the page if you doubt me.'

I said I didn't believe it, but in my heart I knew it was true. I could just feel it. I slowly turned the page and it confirmed my gut instinct. The heading explained that this was part of Nijinska's team's surveillance on Barkley. There were four photographs. A youthful Jim Sterling was in each, smiling and laughing as he boarded the boat. The name 'The Blue Fin' was visible on the side of the old cruise ship.

'We found those documents when we infiltrated Golding Scientific. They were locked deep in their vaults. Golding's people never knew the full story of the Kematian. They never knew that

Jim Sterling was the leader of the Guild – he has remained so well hidden over the years that they never even knew of his existence. It was simply useless information to Golding. I, on the other hand, recognised its significance as soon as I saw it.'

'It's quite significant ...'

'Now do you believe?' Blake asked. 'Now do you see why we had to wipe them out? All of those who mentored you have been protecting him for years. Williams, along with Jonathan Atkinson, who found him, protected Sterling and projected him into the highest rank of the Guild. They believed he was the future. Your life has been a lie, Ross Bentley. You have been working and living alongside despicable villains since you left the Golding Plaza Hotel two years ago. They brainwashed you. Eventually Sterling would have told you the truth and you would have been so deep under the layers of lies that you would have willingly accepted whatever he told you.'

The shock of what I had just learned seemed to weaken my knees and I staggered to the window and supported myself with the sill. I had always known they were withholding information from me. The strange conversation I'd overheard between Hunter and Canavan. All the mystery surrounding the Kematian story. How Hunter used to get mad every time I mentioned Barkley's name. How violent he became when Portman said that Blake knew of a great secret about the Guild. They kept those things from me, but could they have knowingly served the great villain? Could they have been faking it all along? How does one fake friendship? How can a person imitate love?

If they were aware of Sterling's true identity, then they were not the heroes I believed them to be. No. They had tricked me. The people who surrounded me in this room were more genuine than the Guild had ever truly been. It would have made sense for me to join them and to help them hunt and kill the senior members of the Guild of the True. That was the only sensible thing to do …

I turned to face them. Blake was staring right at me. Boxer stood by the wall, arms folded and grinning. Pearson watched me and nodded, as if to say: 'You're doing the right thing by joining us'.

'Help us to rid the world of this terror,' Blake continued. 'Do you feel no insult that they have manipulated you?'

'I am very insulted,' I replied. 'I would like nothing more than to kill Jim Sterling right now. But before I make my decision, I have just one question.'

'Ask your one question,' Blake replied.

'It's one that I want to put to Boxer.'

'Go ahead,' the giant killer smirked. 'Ask away.'

'What did you say to Hunter before you killed him?'

'Hmm?'

'The exact words. What were the exact words you said to him before you broke his neck?'

'Ain't technology a bitch …'

'Yes,' I smiled. 'It certainly is.'

I drew Vanev's gun from my jacket. I had stuffed it into the pocket when I'd gotten to the kinetibike back in Prestwich. It had been in the sidebag since I went to the Wrights' house. I'd almost been caught with it when I entered the Imperium and the siren sounded. Boxer, the fool, had allowed me to smuggle it inside by telling the guards that it had been his gun that had set off the alarm.

I had intended to use it against Boxer when he caught up with me in Prestwich, after he'd killed Hunter. Then he offered to take me to Blake. It was an opportunity that I could not pass up. The gun was designed to fire rounds that could break through psychokinetic energy – the same energy that made Boxer indestructible.

'Technology is a bitch,' I continued.

I lifted the weapon and pointed it directly at him. I waited just long enough to see the smile disappear from his face before I pulled the trigger. Three bullets left the gun and burrowed into Boxer's chest. Blood exploded into the air as he tumbled back and crashed against the wall.

'Technology like this gun that Golding's scientists invented is a real bitch for people like us,' I said.

I fired the last round through Pearson's forehead. By the time she hit the ground the guards had burst through the door and were lifting their guns. I raised my uninjured arm and a wave of energy blasted them back into the corridor. Some died from the blast, others simply got to their feet and fled.

'It would be prudent to run,' I told the nurse sitting by the computer. 'Don't stop until you're home. Forget everything you heard here. Forget what you saw. Forget there are gifted people. Go.'

She nervously pushed back her chair from the computer then took a few hesitant steps across the room. She was running by the time she passed the guards' bodies.

I took my time unplugging the machines that were keeping Blake alive. I made sure the computer was the first to be shut down – I was sick of listening to his crap. His eyes darted left and right as I moved around the bed, unplugging wires and tubes. There was nothing he could do. I guessed he was far too frail to use his gifts and I was safe enough to take my time.

'I'm sorry, Mr Blake. I will have to reject your offer. I may be a fool who believes lies too easily, but I would never be foolish enough to believe in your vision of the world. I'm a Bentley. We're ordinary, decent people, the Bentleys. We don't like cruel and greedy people like you. That's why I think it would be better if you were to die now. I'm not going to kill you. I'm simply going to allow nature to take its course with you. Let's not depend on technology. As you have just seen, it can certainly come back to bite you in the arse when you least expect it. The time to pay for your many sins has arrived. I'm going to wrestle the Guild from the liars. I'm going to kill Jim Sterling myself and put an end to all this. It's time a new generation took charge, one that is not tainted by the actions of the one that preceded it. I'm going to end this tonight.'

I turned out the lights before I left the room, leaving Blake to twitch and squirm in the darkness, alone and helpless as death overcame him.

I made my way along the corridor to the elevator, only to find that it had been disabled. Obviously the guards didn't want me following them as they made their escape. I turned back and staggered towards the opposite end of the corridor, where the stairwell was. I never made it. The pain of my injuries became too great and I stopped. I leaned against the wall and tried desperately to keep the wounds shut. I wasn't doing a good job; there was blood trickling down my body and tapping the floor. I couldn't go any further. I would not face down Sterling, after all. At least I had dealt with Blake, Pearson and Boxer. The shadow Guild, as Portman called it, was as good as finished. Blake had been the driving force behind it. His twisted vision of how the world should be was what glued it all together. That and the money he offered to his many minions.

Blake had succeeded in one of his boasts: Killing the innocence in me. I had a newfound cynicism about the world and all in it. No one was to be taken at face value. Everyone had secrets. Everyone had an agenda of their own.

I slid down the wall and sat, sucking in deep breaths. I was dying. My journey, that had started when I left my home for London two years before, was now at an end. I wasn't proud of a lot of the things I'd done. I hated that I ever got involved with other gifted people. It had all been for nothing because it was all lies. Williams had lied to me. Romand had lied to me. Hunter had lied to me. Even Cathy had been lying to me. She had run away and told me she was going to see her mother, when she had actually travelled back to England, for what reason I would never know. I hated them all.

I should have stayed at home with the people who genuinely cared about me. My dad. Gemma. They didn't have feelings for me because I was gifted. They cared about me for who I was. Only now, in my darkest hour, did I see the true value of genuine love.

Boxer said that releasing my gift and bleeding to death would be an honourable way to bow out. I could now see his point. I had stood up to evil. I remained true to myself and to what I felt was right. I'd done the best I could. There was no shame in allowing it to end. I let out a deep breath, released my gift, the wounds opened and I became still. I probably would have died soon after if they hadn't barged onto the corridor from the stairwell.

I turned and watched them approach. The woman was short,

had long curly blonde hair and a stern face. The man was stocky and tall, rugged looking and had serious eyes. The senior agents of the Guild all looked like this. Every last one of them had that unmistakable battle hardened appearance. They rushed along the corridor then slowed as they neared me, wary of me for some reason.

'Let me guess,' I said, managing a chuckle to myself, 'Armitage and Burrows?'

'We got here as soon as we could,' Armitage told me. 'We are friends of Hunter. Where is he?'

'He's lying dead in John Portman's house in Prestwich.'

They didn't look as upset as friends should be on hearing such tragic news. Perhaps they were too far gone into the world of death and deception to feel properly for humans – even those who are supposed to be friends.

'Who killed him?' Burrows asked.

'Boxer,' I said. 'Don't worry, you won't need to avenge your friend. I already did it for you.'

'And Blake?'

'I'd say he's dead by now. I've done all your dirty work for you.'

'Did Blake tell you some secret about the Guild?' Armitage asked as she cautiously stepped towards me. 'Marie Canavan said that Hunter had mentioned some secret that Blake was going to tell us. What was it?'

I pressed the palms of my hands on the cold floor and pushed myself back up the wall, just about managing to stand so I could face them properly. I had no idea if they were friend or foe. If they were enemies, though, I was not going to die sitting on my arse.

'Tell us if you know, Ross,' Burrows pleaded. 'We must protect the Guild at all costs. If there is some evil within it, we must know so that we can weed it out and destroy it once and for all.'

'We are loyal to no one but the ethics of the Guild,' Armitage assured me.

'The essence of the Guild is built on lies,' I replied. 'Blake did reveal the secret to me. Jim Sterling is not who he claims to be.'

'Go on.'

'He is the Kematian.' I forced myself off the wall and stepped towards them. 'But you already knew that, didn't you? You're Elizabeth Armitage, Sterling's right hand.'

'We don't have time for this,' she said to Burrows. 'Put him down now. Let's finish it.'

My precognitive gift was not warning of danger. Then I tried to use my psychokinetic powers to protect myself and could not. I was totally powerless. My gifts were gone. I was utterly defenceless.

'Burrows,' Armitage demanded. 'Take him down now! Finish this!'

Burrows moved his arms towards me and I felt a terrible impact. It was like my body was being ground into dust. I fell back and banged my head off the floor. The wounds on my body burst open and blood spurted over my clothes. I couldn't catch my breath. My heart was pounding harder than ever just to keep me conscious. Then the sense of death fell over me. Blackness was cast over my eyes and an empty sensation followed it. This was what it felt like to die.

CHAPTER TWENTY

Facing Death

I opened my eyes to find myself lying awkwardly on a leather couch. My shoulder and stomach were still aching and my right arm remained numb. I was wearing a clean shirt that was a few sizes too big for me and tracksuit pants that were intended for a man much taller than I was. I carefully pulled the shirt open to find my injuries had been treated; black stitches had been freshly knitted into my skin. I was alive, although I still had no sense of my gifts. It was as if they had been stolen away from me. I hadn't felt this powerless since I was a child – long before the gifts had revealed themselves.

I pushed myself up on my left elbow and examined my surroundings. It was a cavernous space – it was too big to be described as a room, too small to be considered a hall. The ceiling was low, not much higher than six feet, and arced downward as it met the walls. On the opposite side of the glossy wooden floor were extensive book shelves – floor to ceiling and crammed with books numbering in their thousands. To my left the wall showed many portrait paintings of people I didn't recognise, and a few exotic landscapes depicted in vibrant oils. The only space that didn't have a painting was filled with the only door. To my right was a large and ornate walnut desk that had stacks of paper on it. There was one chair in front of it, and another, grander one one the other side. On the wall behind the desk was a fine mosaic of the Guild's logo – the wolf head surrounded by the Latin initials of each of the true gifts. I noticed instantly that this logo had sixteen sets of initials instead of the fifteen that usually adorned the crest. 'SM' I recognised as the fabled Seductor Mortis gift. I knew I was in the lair of the Kematian. I still remembered Romand's exact words when he first told me of the dreaded sixteenth gift: 'The power to bring death to the living and life to those who have passed.'

I was contemplating climbing off the couch and making a dash for the door when I heard footsteps. There was someone moving in the shadows of the far corner by the book shelves.

'Show yourself!' I demanded as I straightened up. 'Face me, you damned coward!'

Sterling emerged slowly from the shadow, one hand holding a walking cane, the other holding a book. He casually made his way towards his desk then placed the book down and looked at me. He was dressed in black – appropriately – and looked a good deal older than he had when I last saw him the previous winter.

'I wasn't hiding,' he said. 'I have no reason to hide in my own home.'

'That's what you've been doing for years. You've been hiding behind a cloak of lies. You're a monster.'

'A monster who patches you up and saves your life? Allows you to sleep safely on my couch for two days without harming you?'

'I know who and what you are.'

'Blake's great secret, eh. The fool. He thought he could turn my own people against me and reinstate himself so he could wreak havoc once more. Thank you for killing him for me, Ross. He was proving to be quite the thorn in the side. And as for who and what I am,' he stepped towards me and dramatically raised his arms above his head. 'I am Jim Sterling. I am James Barkley. I am the Kematian. I am all three rolled into one. They are me, the man who stands before you now.'

'You're a lunatic who needs to be stopped.'

'Am I indeed? And how do you know of my true nature?'

'Romand told me all about you.'

'Oh, the same Marcus Romand who was one of my chief agents for many years? My trusted confidant? My good friend?'

'So, he was another traitor. Another who protected you.'

'He protected me as all my friends have. We have shared many friends, you and I. Peter Williams, Marcus, Hunter …'

'You bastard. You somehow tricked them all into working for you. I know you did. You let Hunter die.'

'Hunter isn't dead.'

'You're a liar!'

I raised myself from the couch and moved at him, my hands as fists, ready to beat him to a pulp.

'Sit down!' he shouted at me. I was drawn back by an invisible force. I landed on the couch and my arms were pulled tight against my body, my feet rooted to the ground. 'You would attack me? Do you have any idea what I am capable of?'

'Murder. That's what you're capable of.'

'Murder,' he scoffed. 'I am the Kematian. I am the shadow in the night. Allow me to show you what I am capable of.' He paced to the centre of the floor and turned on his heel to face me. 'You are a novice in every sense of the word when compared with me. Do you think you know of the true gifts? You know only what we've taught you, of what we allowed you to know.'

He bowed his head and lifted his arms, his hands twisting slowly, fingers livid like claws. 'Gift one: The prophet.' After a few seconds there were wisps of white mist falling over his shoulders and dancing through the air between us, slowly and gracefully mingling together to form one shape that became almost human. The mist evaporated to leave a translucent figure standing before me, staring and smiling fondly. It was me. I was much older, perhaps fifty years of age, carrying a few too many pounds around the midriff and sporting a goatee. 'Prophecy is not simply seeing future events,' Sterling told me. 'It is a transmitter of what may come. Images travel back in time to rest within my mind. But those, like me, who have mastered the gift can pull a part of a person from the future or the past into the present.'

Sterling clapped his hands and the glowing figure of my future self collapsed into a cloud of white smoke that was gone within seconds. Sterling looked at me for a brief moment, a cold stare that made my heart sink and the hairs stand on end. He turned to his desk and once more raised his hands.

'Gift two: The Psychokinetic.' His fingers moved fluidly, like typing in slow motion, and suddenly the legion of tiles that made up the Guild mosaic were torn from the wall and moved around Sterling like a swarm of multi-coloured wasps. He walked towards me again and was smiling proudly as our eyes met. The swarm moved away from him and flew around the walls at great speed before they slowed, floating rather peacefully through the air and forming a large sphere behind him. Sterling shut his eyes and his body became strained. The tiles fluttered furiously at his back, gradually reforming into the Guild crest without him even looking. Within a moment the mosaic was perfectly replicated and rotated in mid-air. I could not imagine a more impressive display of psychokinesis. My own ability was clumsy and obvious in comparison to his. The mosaic floated across the room and attached itself to the wall, as if it had never been disturbed.

'Gift three: The Pyrokinetic.' Sterling revealed a handkerchief from his jacket pocket and allowed it to move from his hand and sail above his head. He clicked his fingers and it was set alight. The flames grew and fanned out across the ceiling then dripped to the floor and the fire raged there before he moved hands in a languid gesture. The flames spilled across the floor and then rolled into a ball that spun right past my feet. As it neared the door, the ball was transformed into the shape of a cat. The flames perfectly mimicked the feline form as it hopped around the room, sometimes racing across the floor, at times dancing along the book shelves. Sterling threw his hands down and the fiery cat disappeared into a puff of smoke.

'Gift four: The Metallisir.' This time he revealed a silver coin from his trouser pocket, balancing it on his thumb before flipping it into the air. As it came back down, the coin was enlarged into a thin silver plate that came towards me very slowly then stopped right in front of my face. It was a perfect circle. The surface highly polished enough that I could clearly see my reflection in it. This was a most impressive trick, but he wasn't finished. A lump formed in the centre of the plate and grew into the shape of a face. My face. Perfectly rendered in the silver. It even managed to mimic the subtle movements of my eyes and forehead. The plate then disintegrated and dripped all over the floor before moving together like mercury and forming the original coin.

'Gift five: The Ink-Seer.' Sterling lifted his right hand and a book came flying off the shelf behind him. It moved rapidly through the air and froze right in front of my face. I just had time to read the cover of the thin and tattered book before the pages parted: *King Henry VI* by *William Shakespeare*. The pages flicked over and over as Sterling approached me. He placed his index finger on the cover, shut his eyes and read:

'I have not stopp'd mine ears to their demands,
Nor posted off their suits with slow delays;
My pity hath been balm to heal their wounds,
My mildness hath allay'd their swelling griefs
My mercy dried their water-flowing tears;
I have not been desirous of their wealth,
Nor much oppress'd them with great subsidies,
Nor forward of revenge, though they much err'd:
Then why should they love Edward more than me?
No, Exeter, these graces challenge grace:
And when the lion fawns upon the lamb,
The lamb will never cease to follow him.'

He had read one of the passages on the page word for word. A random extract, without ever seeing the text. The ink-seeing gift at its very best. The book fell harmlessly onto my lap as Sterling returned to the centre of the floor.

'Will I show you more?' he asked. 'Gift six: The electro-psych.'

The lights dimmed as a flurry of sparks ran over Sterling's body. There was bright lines shooting out from his hands and his eyes, snapping at the floor and the low ceiling. Then they suddenly disappeared, and Sterling grinned at me malignly. The hairs on my head stood on end and my skin began to tingle all over.

'You are now surrounded by enough electricity to kill a hundred men. It has actually made contact with your body, yet you are unharmed. It is impressive to electrocute someone, or to summon lightning from the sky, but the hardest trick is to negate the effects of electricity as I am now doing.'

'Gift seven,' he said, disappearing before reappearing by the desk. 'The space-rupter.' Again he disappeared. Within an instant he was sitting right next to me on the couch. 'The ability to pass out of our reality in order to move great distances in the blink of an eye.' He was standing back in the centre of the room before he had finished his sentence.

The coin at my feet flew across the room at mesmerising speed and he caught it without looking. 'Gift Eight: The Warper.' He threw the coin towards the door then caught it before it impacted. He'd moved so fast that he was nothing more than a blur. He repeated the trick over and over again, crossing from one side of the floor to the next with blinding speed. 'Forgive me,' he said. 'I cannot give you a more impressive display in such a confined place.'

'Gift nine: The light-tuner.' The room went black and a myriad of light orbs twinkled as they moved closer to the centre of the floor to form a galaxy that spun hypnotically. The ability to create light orbs was one thing, to manipulate them in such a complex manner was another thing entirely. Even Hunter and Canavan were incapable of such a trick. He didn't just possess these powers, he had mastered them.

'The rest of the fifteen true gifts are difficult to display. I assure you, though, that I can use them in ways that others can only dream of. When you challenge me, Ross, you do not face a simple gift. With me you face *all* of the true gifts. That is what my true power is. But I am even more than that. I also possess the Seductor Mortis. A gift you have little or no understanding of. Shall I give a little taste of what is possible with the sixteenth gift? Yes, let me show you how it works.'

I felt a burning sensation growing all over my body. It was followed by severe pain in my shoulder and stomach. I was still clenched in the invisible grip and could do nothing to protect myself. The pain grew and grew. My body felt like it was on fire – as if someone was stabbing me in the shoulder and stomach with white hot pokers. I tried to contain myself, not wanting to show weakness in front of Sterling. I didn't hold out long, I was soon screaming in agony. The stitches were torn out of my flesh and I almost passed out, such was the pain. Then without warning it subsided. The heat within me fell, as did the pain. I was released from the grip and I opened my shirt to see that my wounds were no more. It was as if I had never been shot.

I looked to Sterling as his arms fell limply by his side. He sucked in deep breaths and leaned on the walking stick as he clumsily made his way behind the desk.

'Now do you understand what I can do?' he panted. 'Well?'

'The power to give life and the power to take it ...'

'Yes. A living man with the power of a god.' He fell into the chair behind the desk and sighed. 'Forgive me, it has been many years since I used that gift. The wound on your stomach is not entirely healed. It will take a few weeks more for your body to fully recover. I have already pushed myself too far. I dare not use the Seductor Mortis again.'

'Why would you fear to use such a gift?'

'Because it is more dangerous than you can comprehend.'

'Why did you save my life? Why are you healing me? I won't work for you again if that's what you're thinking. I won't fall for your lies.'

'I saved your life for more than one reason. I healed you to prove a point, and also because I don't want you to suffer. Whether you work for me again is your own decision. I will allow you to leave this place very soon. Your life is your own to lead. As for the lies, I apologise. There have been many lies told to you. There was little malice in the deception, I promise you. We were only trying to protect you.'

'From what?'

'Mainly from yourself.'

'Enough with the riddles,' I demanded as I rose from the couch. I stomped across the floor to the desk and demanded that he tell me the truth.

'Sit,' he pointed at the second chair. 'Please, Ross.'

'No.'

'Sit! You know I can force you to if I wish. Give me a couple of hours of your time. That is all I ask. I will tell you everything you need to know. There is no longer any need to hide the truth from you.'

I reluctantly sat. I still had no power within me and thought it would be best not to test his patience. I would at least hear him out before trying to find a way out.

'We have crossed paths a few times, haven't we?'

'Yes,' I answered. 'Usually in sinister or tragic circumstances.'

'Did you think me a villain on those occasions?'

'I thought you to be a commanding figure,' I admitted. 'Someone who deserved respect. A decent person. But appearances can be very deceiving.'

'Yes, I agree. They can be. And you said Romand told you about the real me. James Barkley. What did he say about my former self?'

'That you were supremely gifted.'

'And?'

'That you were setting up a group like the Guild. Said you were a good man.'

'I was a good man. If not somewhat foolish, as most young men are. It is also true that I was setting up a modest version of the Guild. I guess it's as good a place as any to begin the story. It's a story you need to hear. I promise it will be factual. And you play a leading role in it.'

'How could I play a lead part in your story?'

'Perhaps a lead role only in the latter chapters.' He clasped his hands together and stared at the ceiling, a hint of a smile on his lined face. 'My story begins when I was twelve years old. It is a time in a person's life when they start to learn about the world and make discoveries about themselves. The discoveries I made would mean that my life was to be very different than I thought it would be. I was a skinny kid and a bit shy, not the sporting type that makes you popular in school. Some of the other kids called me a nerd because I enjoyed mathematics and chemistry. They stole my lunch money. Occasionally there was a Chinese burn or a punch in the arm. I put up with it until one day I lost my temper with one of my classmates. He made fun of me in front of a group of girls and I lost my temper. I swung for him and missed, falling flat on my face. Embarrassed, I jumped up immediately and swung at him once more. Again I missed. My fist passed his face without ever making contact. Everyone else thought I had hit him, because his nose was shattered as I threw the punch. It was the first time I used psychokinesis. That one moment changed everything in my life.

'As my teenage years passed by I realised that I had more than one power. I could create fire at will, and manipulate it in any manner I saw fit. I had a measure of control over electricity and I could also sense things before they happened. In later years I would realise that I possessed four of the true gifts: psychokinesis, pyrokinesis, electro-psyching and precognition. A combination of abilities that made me a very powerful young man. It also made me a very sought after young man.

'I was around your age when I became aware of the gifted world. It was Peter Williams who made first contact with me. I was living in Chicago at the time and never realised that one of the Guild's American agents had been keeping an eye on me since my early teenage years. When I reached nineteen years of age they decided it was time to approach me. Williams struck up a conversation with me at a bar. At first I thought he was a strange English gent with dubious motives. It was only when he discreetly displayed his powers that I took him seriously. He told me that the Guild had been greatly impressed by the gifts that I had, and my control over them, and even by the manner in which I used them. He invited me to travel back to England with him and to learn of the Guild and train to be an agent.

'It was a tantalising prospect. But one I ultimately declined. I was a content young man, you see. I liked my life and had lots planned for the years ahead. I told Williams that perhaps one day I would visit him in England, but for the moment I wanted to see some of the world. Williams, dear fellow that he was, didn't take offence. Instead he gave me the names and addresses of other gifted young people who lived in the United States. He believed it would be beneficial for us to get to know one another – strength in numbers and all that. It took me twelve months to track them all down. Some didn't want to know me; they feared their gifts and only wished for a normal life. Others, twelve in total, were like me; they wanted to learn more about the gifts and to be around people like themselves. Our merry little band travelled across the United States then through Mexico into South America. I'd never been so content before … or since ...

'In the spring of 1989 we went back to the United States and went our separate ways for a few months. It was during this time that I noticed changes in me. I was enduring dreadful headaches and memory loss. I was seeing phantoms appear in the night. Ghostly white figures watched me in silence. I thought I was going mad. In reality, though, my mind was struggling to cope with the coming of more gifts – the phantoms are symptomatic of pure prophecy.'

This part of his story stunned me. I too had suffered with the headaches, memory loss and seeing white phantoms. I was about to ask him to explain it further when he went on with his story.

'I also became aware that I could see into the past and future when I touched objects and I was also capable of sensing the emotions of others. It was a lot to deal with. And I was struggling to deal with it all. That was when I was at my most vulnerable, and as is often the case, this was the time when my life came under threat.

'I had another visitor. This one was not as pleasant as Peter Williams. Her name was Rita Mitchell. She was a director of a little-known company called Golding Scientific at the time. Somehow they found out about my powers and she asked if I would work for the company. The money she offered was quite an eye opener for a man of my age. It wasn't tempting enough. Something felt very wrong about Mitchell, and I saw her true self when I rejected her offer. She told me that Paul Golding would not be taking no for an answer and that she would return with some of her colleagues in a few weeks to see if I had changed my mind.

'A month passed and, true to her word, she returned. This time she had two men with her – both partially gifted and armed to the teeth. I was adamant that I would not work for the company and when they tried to rough me up, I killed one of the men, injured the other, and told Mitchell it would be wise to forget about me.'

'Golding wouldn't have liked that answer,' I said.

'No, he didn't. More of his henchmen came. Each time they were more violent and demanding. I repelled them as best I could before going on the run. I gathered my friends together, told them about Golding and the danger he represented, and we left the United States for France. Together we rented a chateau near Toulouse for a little over a month and kept a very low profile. We spent endless nights debating about what to do. Eventually it was decided that we should join the Guild. They could protect us from Golding or anyone else who threatened us. I phoned Williams and asked if we could meet with him, with a view to signing up to the Guild. To my surprise he refused my request. He went on to warn me not to approach the Guild and to stay clear of England. Apparently the Guild had a new leader. He was a tyrant who was trying to turn the organisation into the beginnings of a fascist army.'

'Blake?'

'Yes, it was our troublesome friend Brian Blake. Williams also warned me off entering China, Japan or Korea. These nations were occupied by JNCOR, the modern incarnation of the Jin Assassins. There seemed to be danger everywhere. While I spoke to Williams, I also confided in him that I had developed more of the true gifts. He said it was an extremely rare phenomena, and that he only knew of one such person who had ever displayed more than three gifts. He advised me to travel to the Strahov Monastery Library in the former Czechoslovakia. There lay the only copy of an ancient text that would help me to understand what was possible by having so many of the true gifts.'

Sterling held out his hand and a book flew from the shelf across the room into his grasp. He placed it on the desk and pushed it towards me. The title embossed on the tarnished leather cover read: *The Vinlorn Chronicle.*

'This is the book. I broke into the library and stole it as soon as we reached Prague. It's been in my possession ever since. This dates back to the fifth century, however, the story it tells is much older. The events that it describes were recorded by a Greek historian in the third century BC. It tells the tale of a young man, Vinlorn, who lived in ancient Egypt. He was a renowned soldier that came to notoriety when he displayed many supernatural powers. It is easy, with our current knowledge of the true gifts, to identify what these powers were. He was elevated to the highest reaches of Egyptian society. Finally becoming chief advisor and protector to the pharaoh. This is not an uplifting story, though. Vinlorn became a troubled man, dogged by phantoms, suffered bouts of paranoia, often flew into tantrums and had cruel pains in his skull. Those around him claimed he was descending into madness, and understandably that caused a lot of panic because of the powers he possessed. They imprisoned him while he was at his most vulnerable. Not a wise course of action on their part. When he overcame his troubles he broke free and it was said that he had the power to take life at will. A simple glance or a mere touch could wither the strongest of men. The scribe who translated the original story from Greek to Latin called it the Seductor Mortis. The fabled sixteenth gift.

'After reading the book I grew wary of the transformation I was undergoing. I feared that I might give in to madness and use this mysterious power to hurt others. I hoped that I would never attain it, or that it was nothing more than an obscure myth from ancient times.

'My friends and I felt unsafe in eastern Europe and opted to travel to India, before moving onto the Indonesian islands that summer. It felt safe at first. We were immature, though, and ignorant to the lengths to which unscrupulous bastards like Golding would go to in order to get what they wanted. Then came that fateful day…

'I think Golding viewed me and my friends as a threat to him.

Not an immediate threat, but as his influence and wealth was growing, he probably believed that we collectively had the strength to destroy all that he was building, if we set our minds to it. That's why he decided at that point to have us tracked and killed. We were unaware that a team of assassins had been hunting us for weeks. They caught up with us in Bali. They didn't reveal themselves at first. They waited until we were out in the open, and that opportunity came when we hired a boat and set sail for a small, deserted island to the north. It was a particularly hot day – sweltering even at 8am. The mood among us was optimistic and jovial. We intended to stay at that island for a couple of months, far away from the world and all the threats and violence within it – this was supposed to be the beginning of a wonderful time in our lives. We never suspected what was going to come for us later that day.

'By this time the Guild had chased out Blake and reformed under the guidance of Jonathan Atkinson. He was a fine man with a keen intellect. But he was not without a ruthless streak. Soon after he assumed control of the Guild he led an attack against Armamenti Tal-Future. They were a private military company who hired and trained gifted soldiers, and supplied them to whoever was willing to pay for their services. The Guild found the headquarters of the operation in Malta and assassinated all the directors. The company fell into disarray and the Guild welcomed in the stray mercenaries. Two of them slipped through the net. Boxer was one of them. Melissa Nijinska was the other. She was the strongest mageleton in the world at that time. And she was the one who Golding had sent to Indonesia to murder my friends and me. She also had the assistance of a team of partially gifted assassins – most were ex-military types who had no problems in murdering innocent young people.

'It's funny how the human mind works … I couldn't tell you what I had for breakfast yesterday, yet I can recall every single detail about that summer afternoon on the island. We arrived on the eastern shore at precisely 3.04pm – I remember looking at my watch before diving over the side of the boat into the turquoise waters. The others guided the boat to the shore and unloaded the crates of beer, the tents and food for a barbecue we intended to have that evening. It was a perfect moment in a perfect place, with perfect people.' Sterling smiled fondly as he stared at nothing. 'Perfection.'

'Perfection didn't last long.' His smile quickly evaporated. His brow became furrowed. His eyes went narrow with bitterness. 'I made my way onto the beach and stood next to my good friend, Henrik Valstrom. He had a keen eye, did Henrik, and it was he who noticed a small boat anchored about a mile off shore. I started to feel dreadfully ill. My precognitive power was in full flow, warning me that a great threat was upon me. I didn't have time to alert the others. I was jogging along the beach towards them when Henrik shouted at me.

'I never caught his exact words. It was something like: "the ocean is going out" or "the ocean is being pulled out". I stalled on the beach to see the tide was indeed receding away from the beach at an unnatural pace. I looked out to sea, to where the mysterious boat had been, and could no longer see it. The ocean had risen up. A mighty wave was flowing towards the island.

'I can't begin to describe the speed and ferocity of the tsunami. I managed to protect myself as it struck by wrapping myself in a shell of psychokinetic energy. Eventually the rush of the ocean proved too strong even for me and the shield caved in. I almost died. Still to this day I have nightmares of drowning, salt water forcing itself down my throat and filling my lungs.

'I latched onto a tree as the waters flooded inland and held on for dear life. Then the waves died down and I went in search of my friends. I found their bodies in the hour that followed and brought them to a clearing at the centre of the island. None had survived. I was battered and heartbroken. I was almost out of my mind with grief – certainly not prepared for the fighting that was to come. The following days saw the rise of pure evil.'

Listening to Sterling describe the loss of his friends, and seeing the obvious grief in his expression, made me think his story was true, and that he wasn't the villain I first thought him to be. How could anyone who cared for others so much be a villain? And Sterling and I had befriended many of the same people over the years: Romand, Williams, Hunter, June Atkinson to name but a few. Slowly I was becoming more comfortable in his presence. The initial fear of him was dissipating.

'Where do I even begin to describe the horrors that I faced after the tsunami?' he sighed. 'You and I have both fought great terrors. Golding, Shaw, Zalech, Nijinska, and Dolloway to name but a few. But all of these pale in comparison to the evil that rose on the day my friends died.'

CHAPTER TWENTY-ONE

The Darkest Hour

I listened closely as Sterling began to describe what happened next.

'I gathered the bodies of my fallen friends as the waters seeped from the island back to the ocean. It was gruesome work. Some had sustained severe head injuries when the wave bashed them against the rocks and trees of the island. I think I tuned out of reality that afternoon, perhaps a defence mechanism of the mind that allows us to cope with such tragedy and horror. That's why I had no sense of the threat that drew close.

'Nijinska, like most wicked people, didn't put herself in harm's way. She remained on the boat and sent her mercenaries to the island. I fled when I saw them coming ashore. I ran through the flooded jungle until I reached the far side of the island as darkness fell. There was nowhere left to run. I was cornered. I had to put aside any fear or inhibition and come out fighting. They surrounded me on the beach and opened fire. I used my numerous gifts to protect myself from the bullets, and to use them against my attackers. It didn't take long to cut them all down. Foolishly I lowered my guard when the last of them was killed.'

Sterling pushed back his chair and threw his left leg up on the desk, then rolled up the trouser and showed me an horrific scar on his calf. I'd sustained serious injuries in my time and knew how painful it must have been.

'Not all of the mercenaries were dead. Two of them had remained in the cover of the jungle – two snipers. I remember that moment clearly. The bullet tore through my leg before I even heard the shot. I fell forward onto the sodden sand, clutching my injured leg, and screaming with the pain coursing through my body. That was the moment when it happened. I felt a new power stirring. It was like nothing I had experienced before. The sixteenth gift probably would have been developed naturally at some point in my life, but the pain, stress and the anger of that instant had awoken it from its hibernation and I became only the second person in history to attain all sixteen of the gifts. The power of the Seductor Mortis shocked even me ...

'I couldn't see the snipers. It was pitch black at this time and they were well buried in the undergrowth. I could feel them, though. This new gift allowed me to sense any life force and to snuff it out if I wished. All I did was think of them dying and seconds later I could hear their screams from deep within the trees. It didn't take them long to die. Then the island was deathly silent. Those few peaceful moments allowed me to think straight and to devise a plan ... The mageleton was still alive, you see. I knew she wouldn't flee. She would remain nearby until her mission was complete.

'I went to the south of the island, to the top of a high cliff, so I could get a good view of the ocean to the east. Nijinska was clever enough not to have any lights on the boat and I could not see her. I could feel her, though. She was out there somewhere.'

'Why didn't you just use the sixteenth gift again?' I asked. 'Like you had with the snipers?'

'I tried. I was running on empty though, and could not seem to replicate what I'd done before. I had to wait out the night and hope that by daybreak I would have renewed strength – just enough to kill her. She too must have been exhausted; raising a tsunami is quite a draining feat. The night seemed to last forever and I never slept a wink thanks to the injury to my leg. I curse myself for not having tried to end the fight that night … I had too much time to think … In the silent darkness I began to contemplate what I had read in *The Vinlorn Chronicle*. Ross, the sixteenth gift works in four different ways: It gives you the power to sense the life force of others, it allows you to heal injury, it allows you to remove life by willing it alone, *and* it empowers you to give life where there is none.'

'So you really can bring people back from the dead?'

'You could say that. I had read in the chronicle that Vinlorn had been able to raise the dead. And in one case he had revived a fellow slave who had succumbed to fever. I believed that I could do the same. I could bring my friends back from the dead! I used the cover of darkness to travel back to the centre of the island and there I used the Seductor Mortis to revive all eleven of them. Their terrible injuries I healed as best I could, in order to give them a chance at survival. They could barely speak at first, only one could manage to stand upright, but as the hours slipped by they slowly recovered – although not enough to face Nijinska in combat. I left them at first light and went to the eastern shore. I was exhausted at this point. I could hardly even stand. I still don't quite know how I managed to defend the island from the inevitable attack.

'The tide retreated fast from the beach and far out to sea the horizon climbed the sky. Another, more powerful, wave had been created. The water rose up hundreds of feet and began to roll west towards the island. It took every ounce of my power to halt its momentum and to reverse its course so that the full weight of the wave came back at Nijinska. I sensed her life force disappearing as a massive white explosion rocked the sea. She had used all her strength in creating the wave, saving none to protect herself. She was no more. I believed that I was safe. I believed that I had won. My enemies were dead. I was alive. So too were my beloved troupe of friends.

'I went to them when I had the strength to walk again. They were where I had left them, sitting in the shade of the jungle, watching each other with empty eyes. That was when I started thinking I had made a mistake in bringing them back. There seemed to be very little, other than the physical, that remained of the people they were. Foolishly, I clung to the hope that they would come back to themselves in time. It took me two hours to get them to the shore and to use my gifts to draw in the boat we had hired from far out on the sea. I got them onboard and set sail for another island that was some miles to the west. This was an inhabited island. I thought that I might be able to get them medical treatment there. To feed them. Fresh water. Anything that would return us to some form of normality.

'Along the way there were whispers between them that ceased when I turned to look at them. They returned my stares with empty ones of their own. I was very uncomfortable by the time we docked on the next island. The locals flocked around us, full of questions about the giant waves that had been seen. I told them that it was caused by an earthquake, that we had survived it and that my friends needed rest and food. Some of the older people didn't believe me. No, they weren't buying my story at all. They needed only to look upon my old friends to know there was something very wrong. My friends had suffered broken limbs, terrible cuts, fractured skulls and so on. I had healed these injuries, so that they were no longer life threatening, but the dreadful scars marred their skin and deep indentations could be seen on their heads and limbs. They were monstrosities. When the commotion died down I was brought to a nearby house where I got some food before I fell into a much needed sleep.

'When I awoke I was in the middle of utter chaos. The family who had allowed me to stay in their home were screaming: "Orangmati, Orangmati, Orangmati." This was a local term for *The Dead*. I quickly learned that evening that my friends had grouped together and used their gifts to start systematically wiping out all the people of the island. I was responsible for what they were doing – I had brought them to the island! I went and faced them, pleading with them to stop the killing. That's when they turned on me. I realised then what I had done. The fourth stage of the Seductor Mortis is a power not of this world. It should never have been used. You see, when you bring someone back from the dead it is as if you put their soul into reverse. They come back as the opposite of what died. Good people become vicious and maniacal. My friends were beautiful in life. Now they had returned as monsters. Evil to the core and bent on murder and destruction. And when they were brought back, their gifts were also inverted, or mutated. They used mysterious powers against me. I found it next to impossible to defend myself, and tragically I could do nothing for the poor folk who called that island paradise home.

'I surrendered to fear and stole one of the fishing boats and set sail for the islands to the south. My friends – the Orangmati – were in pursuit. They were coming for me. The love they felt for me in life had been reversed. It became hatred of me. They would stop at nothing to see me dead. They were right on me as soon as I reached the next island. I fought as hard as I could, and managed to kill two of them that night before I was pushed into retreat. I hid for an entire day before they caught up with me again. There was more fighting before I reached the port on the other side of the island where I saw some friendly faces. It was Jonathan Atkinson and Fiona Taylor.

'Taylor was the Guild's representative in that part of the world and she had contacted Atkinson as soon as she heard about the tidal wave. He'd left England with great haste when she told him about the talk of "Orangmati". The locals who spoke English told her that undead were stalking through the islands, hunting a westerner who had super powers. They had found me just in time. I was practically delirious at this point. I'd been on the run and fighting, while injured, for days. I was always outnumbered and often outmatched. When Atkinson and Taylor found me I was at breaking point.'

I knew what Sterling was telling me was true. It made sense now that he told me the other side of the tale that I had read in Jonathan Atkinson's own diary.

'Atkinson was wonderfully gifted, cunning and courageous. Taylor was a born fighter, tenacious and vicious in combat. They managed to hold off the enemy for more than twenty-four hours. By that time I had regained my strength, and the stomach for the battle. We faced my friends and cut down three of them in the battle that ensued. Alas, Taylor was lost that night. Atkinson was injured badly and I was all out of ideas by dawn. I believed the end was coming … It never came. The military arrived instead. I created a body refraction for Atkinson and myself and we stowed away on a boat headed for Australia. There we met another Guild agent, Georgia Murray, who hid us at her home. We stayed there until our injuries had healed, then we journeyed to England, to the home of the Guild.'

'What happened to the Orangmati?' I asked. 'Were they killed by the army or something?'

'If only,' Sterling said as he lifted himself from the chair. 'Six of them had survived. They simply disappeared.'

He pointed at the far wall and I watched as one of the large framed portraits became detached and floated away from the wall. Behind it was a metal safe that became unlocked. The door swung open and a stack of cards, each a little bigger than a standard playing card, levitated across the room and landed neatly on the desk. There was a symbol that covered the top card. It was similar to the Guild logo, but had a skull and dressings instead of the usual wolf head. The number 37 was just above the emblem. Sterling took the cards and began flicking through them. Occasionally he'd crunch one up and it would disintegrate to dust.

'There were thirty-seven until recently,' he said. 'You and Hunter have killed four of them over the last few days: Boxer, Blake, Brofeldt and Vanev. That leaves thirty four … He took four of the cards and placed them before me, all face down, with only the skull crest and the numbers showing. These were numbered: 1, 2, 3 & 4.

'Each of the cards represents an enemy of the Guild. Not troublesome thieves. These are all extremely dangerous individuals who pose a threat to us and the world. The lower the number, the higher the threat level. Most of the senior agents are given their own set of cards – usually no more than ten at any one time. The vast majority of our agents have no idea who the top four enemies are. These four cards are a secret that only a few people know of.'

Sterling sat again, facing me, as a smile grew on his face.

'What's there to smile about?' I asked.

'I am happy that you've calmed down a little and don't believe me to be the devil.'

'I'm the devil here …'

'What do you mean?'

'Vanev and Brofeldt referred to me as the devil.'

'Ah, I see. I'm sure I can explain that to you shortly. First, I will continue *my* story. So that you are in full possession of the facts.'

'Hold on,' I said. 'Why did Romand and the others tell me that you were a monster? How did you become known as the Kematian?'

'It's quite simple really. It could not be common knowledge that I had survived. James Barkley had to be gone. That's why I changed my name to James Sterling. The Guild were told that I was one of Barkley's friends and that I fought him when he attained the highest power.'

'That doesn't make any sense at all.'

'Oh, but it does. Many people knew of Barkley's abilities. Many had also heard of the terrible acts carried out on the islands, and the rumours of an undead that claimed many lives. Atkinson and I felt that no one should ever go looking for me or my friends, for it might restart a battle that could consume the world. We then invented the story that I had gone mad when my friends were killed and that in my madness I gained the Seductor Mortis, became a ghoul and went on a murderous rampage. This explained away the atrocities that occurred. It was such an evil tale that it would scare off anyone who would come looking for me, or into the story that we cooked up. You see, from the moment we arrived in London, we knew that I could never be put at risk. I could never go about the work of a Guild agent. I could never masquerade as a normal person. I could never be found by anyone seeking to avenge what had happened in south-east Asia. I could never be found out by Golding or his ilk. My life was far too precious. I could still sense those of my friends who had survived. I could feel the six of them, and I understood that they could also sense me. I would have to remain hidden and safe in case they ever went on the rampage again. I was the only one who could fight them properly. And so Jim Sterling was born. The story of the Kematian was born. The story was told to all members of the Guild. Every time a youngster is recruited, we tell them anecdotally of the story that you were told by Romand. It would keep from going looking for me – the real me.'

'I don't get it. If you could still sense your friends, why not track them down and kill them? Why not bring an end to it all?'

'The reason is simple: because I do not know if I, even with the help of the Guild, can defeat them. And I think that they remain hidden because they fear me. It's a very uneasy peace.'

'So you've been hiding out all this time?'

'I guess you could say that. You now sit in the basement of the Palatium. We're in the heart of London. It actually used to be a hospital for convalescent soldiers before it fell into disrepair. The Guild bought it in the early 1970s, fixed it up and we've used it as our HQ ever since. I was given this basement when I arrived in 1990. It's been my home from that day on. Although it was more like a prison than a home in those early years. Books were my only true companions. I read every book I could find that related to the gifts, so that I could maximise my abilities. Within a couple of short years I had perfected most of the true gifts, despite ignoring the sixteenth for the most part. I still feared to use it. At one point I tried to heal up this awful wound on my leg and discovered that the healing part of the gift only works on others.'

'You can't heal yourself?'

'Unfortunately not. After a couple of quiet years the world of the gifted became active again. Golding was growing in power and was hiring more efficient killers and intensifying his search for gifted recruits. One such recruit contacted us and told us of his plans to escape the clutches of Golding. He wanted us to take him in.'

'Romand?'

'Yes. We helped him to flee Golding's organisation and drafted him into the Guild. That was when he told us of Marianne Dolloway – she was just a young girl at that time. Romand insisted that she had more than three gifts, and that despite her youth, she had an unsound mind and could grow to become a vicious killer. We knew that she had the potential to reach my level, and that posed great danger to everyone. Can you imagine if Marianne had developed my skills?'

'I'd rather not.'

'We made a decision to have her assassinated. Not a decision we made lightly, mind. We're not in the business of killing children. There were only a handful who volunteered for the task. Romand, though, insisted that she was his responsibility. He felt he should have killed her when he found out she had four gifts. It became his life work to track her down and end her life. It wasn't easy. Golding guarded her closely when she was growing up. She only emerged in her late teens and she proved to be ever elusive.

'But I'm getting ahead of myself. It wasn't long after Romand joined us that Jonathan Atkinson fell ill. He had been hurt badly during the fighting in Indonesia years before and never truly recovered. The strain of rebuilding the Guild and dealing with those injuries eventually took its toll on him. In his final days he elected me as his successor. The senior members of the Guild agreed; they felt I was the only one strong enough to deal with the Orangmati if they returned and the strongest should always lead. My accession caused a lot of controversy amongst those who did not know of my true identity and power. It was a difficult time for me. The pressure was immense.

'Gradually I became used to the position of Primicerius and surrounded myself with a small group of people who I had great faith in. I admitted to these trusted allies the truth of my life and swore them to secrecy. They have been loyal to me ever since.'

'Hunter and Romand?'

'Hunter, Romand, Canavan, Williams, Armitage, Burrows, Powell, June Atkinson and Sakamoto to name a few. These were the agents that took on the most dangerous of missions for me …'

'Did they hunt for your old friends? I'm guessing that the four cards before me represent the only four Orangmati that remain?'

'Only four remain, yes.'

'What happened to the other two?'

'As I said before, I could feel their life force at all times. In 1996 one of them faded and I could no longer get any sense of her. That was Suzana Fuentez. I'm not sure how she died. I doubt I will ever know what happened to her. The next one died in 1999. Hunter and Romand were tracking down an assassin at the time. The trail led them to Paris, and ultimately into the vast catacombs that lie beneath the city. They cornered the assassin and a gifted battle broke out. They managed to overcome their opponent, but the battle had disturbed something far more dangerous. One of the five remaining Orangmati had been resting in that dark and foul place. It was Daniel Shelser. He chased Hunter and Romand around those shadowy passages for two whole days before they managed to get the better of him.'

'How could they kill him? I thought you were the only one who could fight them?'

'I worded it wrong. Shelser got the better of himself really. Romand had been in the catacombs before and knew of a certain tunnel that had a weak floor. He led Shelser there and the ground gave way and he was cast into a chasm that opened up. In truth, your mentors were very lucky to have survived. The other four Orangmati have kept themselves well hidden since then. They remain at the top of our hit list, but we are apprehensive in searching for them.'

'May I?' I reached out for the cards.

'Allow me,' Sterling replied as he clicked his fingers. The cards floated off the desk and turned over to reveal the information on the other side of the skull logos. 'Number four is Ian Garrott – known now as *Shocker*. Garrot was once a light-tuner. A peaceful and caring man. When he was brought back from the dead his gift was terribly mutated. It allowed him to change the molecular composition of elements. He used this as a weapon by changing the air itself into volatile elements, such as phosphorus. It is quite devastating...'

'Phosphorus ...' I breathed. 'So that's why the others were so worried last year when Hunter told them about the reporter that had been tortured with what looked like weaponised phosphorus. I always felt that it wasn't Ania Zalech who had done it.'

'And I think you were right,' Sterling nodded. 'I, and the senior members of the Council, believe that it was indeed the work of Garrot.'

'But why would he risk revealing himself to torture a reporter?'

'Probably because he wanted the same thing that Zalech wanted. The same thing that we in the Guild wanted.'

'He was after Sarah Fisher?'

'Yes.'

'But why?'

'She has the power to see the future, Ross. She might one day predict my death. And that would be something the Orangmati would be most interested in.'

'Did you search for Garrot?'

'I had my most trusted colleagues on his trail, yes. Alas, that trail went cold and Garrot has faded into obscurity once more. Card three is Sarah Washington,' Sterling said as the next card floated close to my face. 'She has the ability to create viruses at will. We've given her the nickname of *Plague*. Number two on the list is Sebastian Kowatich. His gift of mind-switching was mutated into what's known as *Examen Aminos*. He can control literally thousands of minds at one time. He's known as *Piper* – after the Pied Piper of the old tale. And last but not least is a man who was once my best friend. Henrik Valstrom. We call him *Wizard*, on account of his ability to create objects out of thin air and to shift his body into any shape imaginable.'

'They sound like a quartet I'd rather avoid.'

'They have been dormant for more than thirteen years. I doubt you will ever have to face them.'

'So,' I sighed. 'It seems I have wronged you, Mr Sterling. You aren't the monster I believed you to be.'

'No, I'm not. And our mutual friends were never protecting a monster. They never would. They are far too honest to do such a thing. They served the Guild with great honour over the years. You know, for a while there I believed that I would live out my life in hiding, hoping to outlive the Orangmati, that the peace would remain in place. Then you came along and everything changed …'

'I don't see how I could play a part in this.'

'Don't try to fool me, Ross. We both know you have more than three gifts. We both know you have headaches, see phantoms, memory loss – the first signs of pure prophecy being developed.'

'How much do you know?'

'Let's start with the *Million Dollar Gift*, shall we?'

CHAPTER TWENTY-TWO

The Pieces of the Puzzle

'I mentioned that Romand had warned us about Marianne when he joined the Guild,' Sterling went on. 'We quickly made the decision to have her assassinated, and Romand insisted that he, and he alone, would be the one to track and kill her. For years he tried to catch up with her. He failed every time. She was often protected by Golding and she was a very cunning young woman when she was travelling alone. It seemed at one stage that we would never catch her. Then a couple of years ago we got a tip off that her relationship with Golding had fallen apart. Her wage demands and her general psychotic behaviour was impossible to deal with, and Golding was trying to find a replacement. That's when he came up with the idea for The Million Dollar Gift. Romand, knowing Marianne like he did, believed that she would be insulted by this obvious attempt to replace her. He thought there was a good chance she'd show up at the Golding Plaza and he stationed himself nearby.'

'I believed he was there to free anyone who proved to have a gift.'

'No,' Sterling answered. 'He was there primarily to watch for Marianne. His brief changed when the footage of you using your gifts was leaked onto the internet. I remember the shock I felt as I noticed you had displayed four of the true gifts.'

'I didn't display four gifts,' I insisted. 'There were only three back then. It's only now that I realise that I have a fourth gift – prophecy.'

'Prophecy is the fifth gift that you used in your life. You showed the other four in those test videos.'

'What gift are you talking about? I only used three during the tests: psychokinesis, precognition and time-scanning.'

'Do you remember when you were asked to break the block of metaliglass?'

'I do.'

'Give me your account of what took place.'

'I broke it apart. It's as simple as that.'

'Think carefully, Ross. How exactly did it break?'

'The scientists were giving me electric shocks. It kept breaking my concentration and I was struggling to make any impression on the metaliglass with my psychokinetic power. I remember being frustrated to the point of losing my temper. That's when the block was shattered.'

'What happened right before it shattered?'

I thought back to the moment when I lost my temper and used the anger within me to break the metaliglass apart. It hadn't simply shattered. No, something else took place just before that. *The centre of the block of metaliglass bloated and melted for a split second.* My gaze met Sterling's.

'Do you remember now?'

'Yes,' I nodded. 'The metal melted before I blasted it apart.'

'Exactly. You have the metallisir gift. And you never even knew.'

'I've had this gift all along and no one told me?'

'You were very new to the world of the gifted, Ross. It would have been a great burden to place on you. Anyone who can have four gifts can go on to develop *all* of the gifts. After my experience, we didn't want anyone else going on to attain the sixteenth gift. We weren't even sure about you back then. There was no way we were going to tell you about the true powers you had. Remember that you were under the control of Golding and Shaw at that time. It would have been a disaster if they could control such a power. It was a stroke of luck that your videos caused such furore and that the originals were destroyed after they'd been doctored to look like fakes; Golding's people never had time to properly analyse them. They would have realised you had that fourth gift if they'd been given more time.'

'So that's when you ordered Romand to get me out of the hotel?'

'Not exactly. I called a meeting with my most trusted colleagues and we discussed what to do with you. There was talk of assassinating you at first. After a few hours of debate, though, we decided to give you a chance to prove yourself. We told Romand to contact you again and try to get you out. It was also decided that you were too inexperienced to be brought into the Palatium. We felt it would be too much of a shock to a young man, and you would be better if you spent a year or two in a family environment. This is why Romand brought you to his home. June was a kind person who could fulfil the role of mother. Romand could be your mentor and protector. Cathy was around the same age as you and could be a close friend. We didn't foresee that the two of you would become more than friends, but that was fine by us. It should have been a wonderful couple of years for you, slowly learning about the gifts and settling into a new and peaceful life.'

'It didn't exactly work out like you planned.'

'No. We never expected that Marianne would track you down.'

'It was my fault …'

'We all make mistakes, Ross.'

'That mistake cost Romand his life.'

'Stop beating yourself up about it. Romand knew the risks that were involved. He took on the responsibility with his eyes wide open.'

'Did June Atkinson know the risks that were involved? She also paid a heavy price. As did Cathy …'

'June had been a member of the Guild for many, many years. She knew the risk better than anyone.'

'Did Cathy know about my four gifts? Was she in on all of this from the start?'

'She wasn't aware of it at that time. After what happened to Romand I felt that it would be best to get you away from it all for a year. Hunter's home in the Scottish highlands was ideal. There was little chance of anyone finding you out there and you could have peace and quiet to recover and improve your powers. Hunter was reluctant to take you on at that time. He preferred to spend most of his time on the road searching for enemies. Babysitting, as he called it, wouldn't come easy to him. He trusted my judgement, though, and after a few quiet months he was to ease you into the life of an agent. Your first task was to be a very simple one: finding Sarah Fisher. Tracking down gifted children is the most common task for all agents. It's usually a safe one. Mundane even.'

'It was far from safe.'

'We could never have known that Edward Zalech would get involved in the search for the child. What followed was a total disaster and I understand how hurt you were. That's when I revealed the truth to Cathy. I asked her to pretend she wanted to leave the Guild and to take you away from here as soon as Zalech was out of the picture. I gave her money, which she told you was an inheritance, and I found a location for you both in the west of Ireland.'

'She lied to me all along,' I said. I was burning with insult. I hated her in that moment. 'I can't believe it was all a lie!'

'Her love was not a lie. She kept things from you for your own sake. She was doing it all for you, Ross. Cathy kept the secret because she cared so much about you.'

'I should have been told the truth!'

'You weren't in the right frame of mind, Ross. The truth would have been revealed to you if it hadn't been for the depression that you fell into. You were also struggling with the headaches while you were living with Cathy. From what I've been told, one night back in September you got a headache that was so bad that Cathy broke down and told you of the powers hidden within you. The next day, as was often the case after a headache, you didn't remember what she had revealed to you.'

'That's why Hunter and Canavan were worried that I was starting to remember things ...'

'Indeed. Cathy had been under too much strain and gave in after that particular night. There was too much pressure in your budding relationship for it to survive. She contacted me about a month ago and said she needed a break from it all. I told her to return to the Palatium and that I would send Hunter to watch over you. And once more you found your way into a lethal situation.'

'Why do you think Blake and his cohorts referred to me as the devil? Do you think they knew about me having more than three gifts?'

'I think that he had warned them all that you could become a Kematian. That's why they feared you so much. Devil was quite an appropriate name to give you.'

'And what now of my gifts? I have no powers left at all. I feel weak. Empty.'

'Your gifts remain. My good friend, Elizabeth Armitage, whom you met the other night, has a very unusual form of mind-switching. It's a mutation. One of the first mutated gifts we've ever come across. She has the ability to switch her mind into the bodies of others, like all who posses that gift. But she has an added power that makes her very unique: She can prevent the gifted from using their powers.'

'That's why I couldn't fight back.'

'It was a tense situation and Elizabeth knows how strong you are when you feel threatened. Removing your powers was the sensible thing to do.'

'She told Burrows to take me down! That wasn't exactly friendly behaviour.'

'Yes … she's always been a little jumpy in situations like that.'

'She is still using her gift on me now?'

'She is. Remember, my friends would do anything to keep me safe.'

'I'm not going to try to kill you!'

'You were when you woke up. Let's not get into that. Elizabeth's heart was in the right place. She did you no lasting harm. Do you have any more questions for me?'

'Do you think I'll develop all of the gifts?'

'It's hard to say. You certainly have the potential to develop all sixteen of them. Whether you fulfil that potential is a different matter. If you're asking my personal opinion, I would say that you will have all the gifts some day. You know, Ross, it was as if a great weight was lifted from my shoulders when we first found you. I knew then that if something was to happen to me, there would be another capable of standing up to the Orangmati – if they were to return.'

'You want me to take your place, don't you?'

'I would be pleased if you chose to become my successor when I decided to step down.'

'I'm not sure I want to be your successor, Mr Sterling. There's been too many lies told to me. How could I ever truly trust you again?'

'There were a lot of mistakes made, yes. I did what I thought was best by you. I could have done it differently, but who's to say that would have worked out better. I could have ordered Romand to take you from the hotel and to bring you here. I could have told you the truth that first day. And you might have snapped under the pressure of that truth. Who knows what might have happened if you couldn't handle the pressure. There's no template to follow in life, Ross. I tried my best.'

'I don't want the responsibility of leading the Guild,' I said. 'I don't blame you for everything that has happened. I know the blame belongs to the enemies we faced. I know the Guild is not malign. I know most of the agents are good people. It still doesn't make me want to remain here.'

'I would prefer if you remained, Ross. However, I will not force you to stay here. The decision is yours.'

'I think I'm much like the young man that you were before the death of your friends,' I said after a moment's contemplation. 'I want to live a little, as you did back then. I want to see more of the world. I want to enjoy myself for a change. There's been too much misery over the last couple of years. I really need a change of scenery.'

'You can take some time to think about this, if you wish.'

'I don't need to think it over. I must decline your offer, as you once declined the offer that Williams made to you. I don't want this anymore. I don't want to end up living in this dungeon.'

'I will not stop you if that's your decision.'

'Is that the truth?' I asked. 'Will you really let me leave? You promise there won't be someone following me again?'

'You are free, Ross. There will be no one following you.'

'Thank you,' I said. 'I do need to know one thing before I leave here ...'

'And that is?'

'Hunter. Were you telling the truth when you said he was still alive?'

'I was. After he knocked you unconscious, Burrows left you with Armitage and travelled to the Portmans' house. There he found Hunter, unconscious, barely breathing, a broken neck, and a thousand minor injuries.'

'I can't believe it,' I breathed. 'That old bugger managed to survive.'

'Barely,' Sterling said. 'Burrows got him to a hospital in time and his life was saved. He is far from healthy, though. Hunter is paralysed from the neck down. I visited him yesterday and used my gift in an attempt to heal his wounds. It was not successful. There was some improvement, yes, but the damage to his nervous system is so complex that not even I could rebuild him.'

'Has he woken up?'

'Not yet. We don't know if he ever will.'

'Maybe he shouldn't ...'

'You can't actually mean that, Ross.'

'Hunter wouldn't be capable of living life like that. Some people are strong enough to deal with physical disability, but not my old friend. He's a man of action. He's the type that should die in action.'

'Perhaps you are right,' Sterling said. 'I for one will not give up on him just yet. I will do everything I can to restore him to the man he once was.'

'I hope you're successful.' I didn't want to remain any longer. I wanted out. I wanted fresh air. I pushed back my chair and got to my feet. 'I wish you and the Guild the best of luck.'

'We'll need it,' he smiled. 'We've lost a lot of good people over the last few weeks. I am certain that now we've weeded out the traitors and imprisoned them we can rebuild. The Guild will survive. Oh, before you go ...' Sterling pulled open a drawer under the desktop and revealed a silver ring with two keys dangling from it. 'Take these.'

'What do they unlock?'

'The larger of the two opens the door to a lock-up two blocks from here. It's the same lock-up that you got the kinetibike from last year.'

'And the smaller key?'

'Some of our agents went to the Imperium yesterday to gather up any documents, equipment or weapons. They found a lot of remarkable items stored in a warehouse at the back of the main building. One of them struck me as something you would enjoy. I'd like you to have it. The lock-up is a short walk from here, no more than ten minutes. There is a hallway on the other side of that door.' He pointed across the room. 'In the last room on the left there are some clothes that will fit you. I also put a briefcase there. It's full of cash – enough to get you by for a month or two.'

'So you packed some clothes and money for me. You knew I wasn't going to remain, didn't you?'

'There was always a chance that you'd refuse to stay here. I didn't want to stand in your way if you wanted out. One last thing,' Sterling said before I turned away. He gathered the death cards into a neat stack and pushed them towards me. 'Take these with you. Just in case.'

'I don't want to bring those things with me into a new life.'

'Indulge me. Please ...'

'I'll see you around, Mr Sterling.'

There were no more words between us. I had enough to think over and couldn't continue the conversation any longer. I left him in that dark, subterranean cavern and strolled to the end of the hallway where I found the clothes and money he said he had left out for me. The clothes were a good fit, although they smelled of damp. The shoes were a size too big, but I wasn't complaining or delaying. I wasted no time in grabbing the briefcase and ascended a winding iron staircase that rose to the ground floor of the Palatium.

I climbed up into another corridor with only one door at its end. There was a surly looking man guarding it and I kept my distance from him until he unbolted the door – I was still powerless and felt very vulnerable around these people now. I walked through the doorway to yet another corridor that led to a reception area. It was bizarre to behold; it looked like any normal business premises. There were a few people fluttering about the place, and all glowered at me like I was a leper.

'Over here!' a woman called from a doorway on the opposite side of the room. It was Elizabeth Armitage. She watched me with her harsh eyes then motioned for me to follow her along yet another corridor. 'I don't want you leaving by the front door.'

'Whatever you say.'

There were offices either side of me; some of the doors were open and I glanced in at people in suits sitting at desks, typing on keyboards and speaking on phones. No one would ever suspect this was the headquarters of an organisation of gifted people. It was the perfect disguise.

'Your gifts will return shortly after you leave this building,' Armitage said without looking at me. 'I would advise you to take an hour before using them again. Sometimes people get bad nosebleeds after I have suppressed their powers.'

'I'll keep that in mind.'

'There,' she said as we came to the end of the corridor. She was pointing down a short staircase. 'There's a door down there that will lead you out the back way.'

'Don't get too emotional on me,' I joked. 'I can't stand long goodbyes.'

'Get out of my sight,' she sneered. 'We don't need you.'

'What the hell is that supposed to mean?'

'The Guild has lost a lot of experienced people recently. We're short staffed. We're hurting. We're in a time of need. But what we don't need are people as strong as you who would turn their back and flee in such a time.'

'My conscience is clear. I don't want trouble in my life anymore.'

'Trouble,' she said, frowning. 'Make sure you stay out of trouble in the future. Otherwise myself and Burrows will come visit you again.'

'You're a wonderful woman, you know that. I wish I had someone like you to wake up next to each morning.'

'Get out!' she snapped. 'You're still the immature fool that Romand scooped up two years ago.'

'You're damn right I am,' I said as I made my way down the stairs. 'I like being an immature fool!'

I got to the bottom of the stairs and the back door of the building was in sight. I felt a surge of relief. I was almost out. Freedom was on the other side of that door. A new life awaited me. Then I heard my name being called from the top of the stairs and cursed under my breath. This was the last thing I needed.

'Where the hell do you think you're going, Ross Bentley?'

'I think I'm going through this door, Cathy.'

She came stomping down the steps right to my face. She looked mighty pissed off with me. I probably looked even more pissed off with her.

'So this is it? You're planning on running away?'

'No, I'm planning on walking away.'

'Don't.' Her features softened a little. Her eyes glazed over with sadness and her lips trembled. 'Don't leave like this, Ross.'

'Like what?'

'Without at least talking.'

'Why do women always want to talk?' I moaned. 'Talking complicates things.'

'Things *are* complicated.'

'Too right they are. That's why I don't want to talk!'

'Come back upstairs. I don't want us to part ways like this.'

'Cathy you lied to me. It didn't work out between us. We broke up when you left. You even lied about leaving me! There is no going back. We're finished.'

'I know there's no going back for us, Ross. I just wanted to tell you that I wasn't with you because Sterling ordered me to. I was with you because I loved you.'

'Love? I doubt you know the meaning of the word.'

'Don't you dare say that to me!' My precognitive gift was still suppressed and I didn't sense the slap across the face that was coming. 'You don't have any idea of what I went through when we lived together. You can't understand what it was like to be around you, knowing what you were. You can't begin to imagine the pressure I was under every minute of every day in that cottage. Dealing with your depression. Watching you in agony at night with those damned headaches. I didn't know what the hell to do. I thought you were going out of your mind! I was afraid of you by the time I decided to come back here. I allowed our relationship to die to keep the secret that I was sworn to. It cut me up inside. I'm still hurting, Ross.'

'And you think I feel good about myself? I had to watch Hunter have his neck broken right before my eyes a couple of days ago. My best friend, Cathy. He's paralysed from the neck down. And you people have the nerve to question me for leaving all of this!'

'Hunter is my friend, too! What happened to him isn't easy for me to deal with, Ross.'

'I don't want to end up like he has. And I definitely don't want to end up like Sterling hiding in that basement down there. That's not for me. I want a different life.'

'Did he tell you everything?'

'Oh, he told me a great deal of disturbing things.'

'Then you know that you're the only one who can take his place.'

'There's no need for me to take his place, Cathy. All Sterling needs to do is outlive those monsters he created and everything will be fine. Golding is dead. Blake is dead. There's no more threats to the Guild now. They don't need me. They don't need that horrible sixteenth gift – it brings nothing but evil. All they need is a good person with a good vision. Someone like your dad.'

'And if Sterling dies before the Orangmati?'

'If that happens, and I doubt it will, the Guild will have to reveal itself to the rest of the world and ask for their help. I think eight billion people can deal with those four ghouls.'

'It's not that easy.'

'It's as easy as you make it.' I reached out and ran my fingertips along her cheek. 'I don't hate you. I'm not leaving because of you. I just can't take this anymore. I'm not cut out for working as an agent.

I'm certainly not cut out to take Sterling's place. I have to go my own way, Cathy. I have to leave.'

'I'll miss you …'

'Cathy, you'll only miss the time when we were happy. And I'll miss that time, too. We'll never be happy together again. We had our chance and it didn't work. Go live your life and try to enjoy it.'

'Where are you going to go?'

'I'm not telling you. I don't want anyone from this building knowing my destination.'

'Why?'

'Because I don't want to be taking a bath some evening then discover there's a light-tuner standing right next to me. The Guild should forget about me. I'm never coming back here again.'

'Ross …'

'No! I want no more of this talk. I can't trust you anymore. I can't trust any of you again.'

I turned my back on her and pulled open the door. The clean, cool air of December embraced me and I took a long, deep breath. It tasted of freedom. Cathy remained by the door but I didn't turn back. I paced across a car park that was surrounded with high walls. There was one metal gate and it was opened for me by a security guard sitting in a hut in the corner of the grounds. By the time I got to the street I had regretted being so short tempered with Cathy. I kept walking, despite wanting to go back and apologise. I'd said too much. It was best that I leave and never come back. My time with the Guild was over.

I'd walked these same streets the year before when I went to collect Zalech's kinetibike. I recognised the buildings and apartment blocks around me. This did nothing to alter my foul mood. I actually felt even more insulted that I had actually walked right past the Palatium with Cathy that morning before we left for Ireland. I'd been such a fool. How could I have been blind to it all? I certainly would not be a fool for her or them ever again.

By the time I'd reached the laneway where the lock-up was, I was convinced I was doing the right thing. I used the key Sterling had given me to unlock the iron door, then fumbled about in the darkness of the lock-up until I found the light switch. The overhead lamps blinked on and I took a sharp intake of breath when I saw what was in front of me.

'Wow,' I breathed. 'Now that's what I call a bike!'

Sterling had been right about it being something I would appreciate. I circled it, almost afraid to touch such a magnificent piece of engineering. It was slightly smaller than my old bike, but was more aerodynamic, sleeker and aggressive looking. Its panels were black with gold trim, the engine parts chrome, the leather of the seat unblemished. This was the Ferrari of kinetibikes. I must have circled it for half an hour before I dared climb onto the saddle, which was a lot more comfortable than the previous one. I ran my hand over the tank, the grips and the embossed name on one of the side panels: GSK20. My mood had lightened quite a bit as I wheeled the bike into the sunlight.

Now that I was out of the dimness of the lock-up I could clearly see a dial in the centre of the dashboard. There were only two settings. Turning the dial to the left initiated *Drive Mode.* I took a look at the second setting and grinned.

'It can't be ...' I said to myself, laughing. 'I couldn't get this lucky, could I?'

The second setting on the dial read, *Flight Mode.* I didn't use the latter until I was free of the city. I'm sure there were lots of reported sightings of a UFO over the south of England that evening. There were probably even more sightings of the same mysterious craft crossing the skies over Europe in the weeks that followed. Because that's what I did in the weeks that followed. I flew from country to country, seeing the sights, and simply enjoying myself. One night I'd be living it up on the Cote d'Azur, the next morning I'd be chilling out in the Dalmatian Islands. I travelled to so many places in such a short space of time. Then I ventured further afield, to places I'd always dreamed of going: the Bay of Kotor, the fjords of Norway, the Andes, Egypt, Tokyo, California, Antarctica. Visiting such exciting destinations was thrilling at the start. But after a few months I longed to settle in one place. Eventually I found my new home in Thailand. I rented a small house near a picturesque beach and began a rather lazy life. One couldn't ask for a more beautiful and peaceful setting.

Two years passed before I began to seriously consider how I would spend the rest of my life. Thanks to my numerous gifts, I could have anything in life that I desired. I could have been anyone I wanted to be. There were so many places I could have gone. However, in the end I chose the most unlikely destination of all.

CHAPTER TWENTY-THREE

The Odd Couple

The tranquillity of morning was shattered suddenly and I leaped from the bed with fright. I looked to the far wall of my room to see the clock reading 7am. I'd barely time to curse him before he screamed again.

'Bentley! Get in here quickly, Bentley!'

I stomped my feet into a pair of slippers, pulled open my bedroom door and plodded out into the hallway. He'd screamed my name twice more before I reached the kitchen.

'Bentley, come in here and help me. Hurry up, would you!'

'Hunter, is your sole purpose in life to shout my name at me all day?'

'Get over here!'

'Why have you woken me up so early?'

'I want you to take that *thing* out of here.' He was pointing at Nightshade, who was sitting close to his feet, staring right at him. 'It's trying to talk to me again.'

'Nightshade, would you please behave yourself,' I said to the cat as I opened the back door. 'Out with you. There's plenty of mice in that field that need catching.'

The cat almost smiled at Hunter, as if it enjoyed antagonising him, before it sauntered out to the back porch.

'Close the door, damn it. I don't want it getting back in here,' Hunter insisted. 'I don't see why you had to bring that horrible creature here. You should have left it in Ireland! It doesn't belong here.'

'I could hardly leave the cat to starve to death.'

'Starve?' Hunter bawled. 'That cat would never starve. It's smart enough to rob a bank! I'm quite certain it could have fended for itself. It's been tormenting me night and day for the last six months. I can't even have my morning cigar in peace.'

'I told you not to be smoking so early,' I said, moving to the counter to fill the kettle. 'You'll need your lungs in good working order for the months ahead.'

'Oh, stop fussing!'

Hunter jerked back one of the wheels of his wheelchair then pushed himself forward to the table where he lit a cigar. Even after six months living with him, it still saddened me to see him confined to the chair. But I tried not to let him see pity in my eyes. He hated that. It made him grouchier than he usually was. He'd always been a right grump, but his disability now made him worse than ever. Life in the cottage was far from serene.

One thing made up for all the hardship and moaning, though. Hunter was without the use of his legs, and his arms weren't what they used to be, and that meant he depended almost entirely on me. I was the only reason he was not living in Hornsea, being tended to by Marie Canavan. She never would have allowed him to return to his cottage if I hadn't offered to look after him. He only had freedom because I was his live-in orderly. All this meant I was now in the position of power, and that allowed me to torment him, as he once had tormented me in this very same cottage years before. I wasn't exactly cruel to him. I simply annoyed him to make him more determined to get better so that one day he could look after himself.

'You want some porridge?' I asked, placing a hot cup of tea on the table for him.

'I want a coffee.'

'Coffee is out of the question. You remember what the doctor said about too much caffeine?'

'Vaguely.'

'Do you want some porridge or not?'

'No. I don't feel good this morning. The air's getting chilly.'

'It's almost October, Hunter. Winter is on its way.'

'Cold makes my body stiff,' he said. 'Can't get the blood circulating, you know. Can't move around anymore,' he raised his voice. 'Stuck in this blasted chair!'

'Calm down.'

'I can't calm down. It's all right for you to say calm down. You can go for a walk, or a jog, make yourself a meal, visit the town. I'm stuck here all day and night! And that cat of yours! Oh, that cat is determined to make my life even more miserable.'

Such temper tantrums were common for Hunter. Especially in the mornings. He tended to calm down gradually as the day wore on. He was particularly grouchy, and upset, that day so I took his tea to the sink and emptied it. I made him a coffee to take his mind off his troubles, and told him to take it to the other room. I followed him down the hallway and to the sitting room where he relit his cigar and sipped his coffee as he stared out the window.

Being disabled wasn't easy for him. It wouldn't be easy for anyone to lose their mobility. But Hunter had lived life as a warrior. He'd been constantly in and out of fights, and travelled the world hunting for dangerous villains. Being confined to the chair, and to the cottage, was incredibly frustrating for a man like him. When I first moved back to the cottage with him I actually cried a few times when he wasn't looking. That's how upset I was to see him so down and so weak.

It had gotten easier over time to be around him, not just through familiarity, but because I knew he was gradually improving. When I returned from Thailand I went to Canavan's house to see how he was doing. At first he refused to talk to me, or even to make eye contact with me. Canavan told me that he had been crestfallen that I had gone away to travel the world while he was lying in a bed, paralysed from the neck down. He was right to be angry. Only when I returned did I see how selfish I had been.

I was determined to wait around until Hunter spoke to me, and was left waiting for five weeks. Hunter's stubbornness had not been dented by the ordeal he had gone through. During my stay in Hornsea I was reunited with Jim Sterling. He paid regular visits to Hunter and used his sixteenth gift to try to repair the damage that had been done by Boxer. There was no immediate improvement, but over the five weeks I noticed that he regained the use of three fingers on his right hand. And Sterling was confident that Hunter would recovery fully someday.

As soon as Hunter could lift his right arm he was insisting that he be allowed to return to his home in the Scottish wilderness. Canavan refused. That was when Hunter started to talk to me again, and soon he had convinced me to live with him in his cottage. I only agreed because I owed him in a big way, and was able to convince Canavan and Sterling that he would be safe with me. In the six months that followed, Hunter regained the use of both arms and a slight movement in his toes. It was enough to allow him to move about in a wheelchair. There were also subtle hints of his gifts returning. He had no psychokinetic ability since the accident, but his electro-psyching was slowly returning. He was on the slow and painful road to recovery, and would likely be back on his feet within a year. After that, he'd soon be champing at the bit to revive his career as an agent.

I left him to his cigar and went to my room to listen to some music – an old passion of mine that I'd rediscovered since I'd left the Guild. It was nice to enjoy the simple things in life again. Most days I would spend a couple of hours listening to my favourite tunes, relaxing, thinking of nothing more important than what to make for dinner. On that day even the dry serenade of Nick Drake could not calm my soul. There was a busy night ahead for me, and my mind was growing busy. By midday I'd left my bed to light a fire in the sitting room and sat in the armchair watching it in silence.

'Any word from the Guild?' Hunter asked without drawing his gaze from the window.

'None,' I answered. 'They know better than to contact me.'

'The least they could do is keep me up to date with what's going on in the world. It's like they've forgotten all about me.'

'I'm sure you'd know about it if there was anything important going on.'

'Anything could be happening out there,' he said. 'And I wouldn't know about it.'

'Why would they tell you anyway? You're of no use to them anymore, Hunter.'

'I can still do my bit.'

'Really?' I chuckled. 'I can just see you now, *rolling* into action.'

'You've a terrible sense of humour, Bentley.'

'Yeah, it's something I developed over the years. I wonder where I would learn such a thing ...?'

'I must have done something awful in a previous life to have ended up like this.'

'In a previous life?' I laughed. 'You've done enough awful things in this life to deserve a lot worse that you're suffering now.'

'It's hell.'

'Oh, stop. You know full well that you'll be up walking around again in time.'

'It can't come soon enough. I hate being trapped here, depending on you, and putting up with that evil cat of yours.'

'Oh, be quiet, would you? Keep this up and I'll have to send you to bed for your afternoon nap.'

He turned to me and raised his middle finger.

'Mature,' I said, rolling my eyes. 'That's very mature of you.'

A line of electricity pulsed around his raised finger and he gave a defiant grin.

'Any more of your jokes, Bentley, and you'll be the one who'll be taking a nap.'

That's how we spent most of that day, bickering and poking fun at one another. To some it would seem like a hellish existence. To us it was normal. It's the way we'd always been. It was the way we liked it.

Most days were the same in the cottage. The nights were unpredictable, though. Sometimes Hunter would be exhausted by 8pm and would sleep soundly until morning. Other nights he suffered with pains and could not sleep. On those nights I'd sit by the fire with him, sharing a few measures of whiskey and talking over the old times. The problem with that was that our old times were in fact dark times that weren't always nice to recount. There was often mention of our friends who had died in battle. Of the love I had for Cathy. Of the love that Hunter had once shared with Linda Farrier. Of the lunatics we had fought. These were not easy conversations to have.

Some nights the discussion would turn to the future. What might happen to the Guild and the gifted people around the world. We even discussed the demons that Sterling had accidentally made of his murdered friends. We discussed the four Orangmati that remained at large. Where they could be. What they were doing. I claimed that they were terrified of Sterling and would never again reveal themselves. Hunter, being an argumentative soul, would always counter this claim by reminding me of Ian Garrot's search for Sarah Fisher years before – back when we were trying to save her from the clutches of Edward Zalech. 'They are not as dormant as we would like to believe,' Hunter would say. And he was probably right.

Any talk of the Orangmati, or of Jim Sterling, would force me to ponder my own destiny. I had developed many of the true gifts, and the coming of the sixteenth gift seemed inevitable. Sterling was getting old and might not be strong enough to face his old foes if they returned. I could not escape the fact that I would have to be the one to confront them if that time ever came.

'Are you off out on one of your mysterious excursions tonight?' Hunter asked.

'Nothing mysterious about it.'

'It's a mystery to me. The last Saturday of each month you leave here for God knows where on that bike of yours, and don't return for nearly two days.'

'I told you before, Hunter. I'm seeing a girl who lives in Aberdeen. She works most weekends, and the last weekend of each month she has free. Nothing wrong or mysterious about it.'

'You're a terrible liar, Bentley. I know you're up to something.'

'I'm not lying to you.'

'Yes, you are.'

'Why do you think I'm lying?'

'Because you look worried each time before you leave. A young man going to see his girlfriend wouldn't look like you do now.'

'I'm nervous around girls.'

'Ah, keep your secrets!' he spat. 'I don't care what you're doing.'

'Don't ask if you don't care,' I said. 'But will you be all right on your own for the night?'

'Don't talk to me like I'm an …' He was about to say 'invalid', but stopped himself short.

'Will you be okay until I return, Hunter?'

'I will.'

Hunter fell asleep in his chair early that evening and I used my psychokinetic power to levitate him into the air and through the hallway to his bed. I then brought the wheelchair to his room and left it within reach. I felt a little guilty about leaving him alone so I gathered three cigars – one more than he was allowed in one day – and placed them on his bedside locker. I then made sure everything in the kitchen was within reach for him the next morning before I prepared to leave. I never thought I'd actually grow so attached to him. It actually made me laugh when I thought back to when we'd first met and how much we hated each other. I was glad we'd sorted out our differences. I was glad I'd come back. I was glad he was my best friend.

CHAPTER TWENTY-FOUR

All the Time in the World

As soon as I had gotten everything ready for Hunter, I went straight to my bedroom and pulled up one of the floorboards under my bed. In the dark space beneath the floor was a small wooden jewellery box that I lifted onto the bed. I gazed at the contents for a long while before taking them out. I slipped one into my jacket and placed the rest back into the box. As soon as I'd put the floorboard back in place I made my way to the back of the cottage and climbed onto my kinetibike.

I drove slowly away from the cottage until I found a long, narrow road that cut through the wild grasslands. The road was perfectly straight for over a mile and was a good place to launch the bike into flight mode.

I stalled the bike on the roadside so that I could prepare myself for the flight. It took a lot of concentration and a lot of energy to fly the GKS20, especially a long flight to continental Europe. I sucked in deep breaths and reached into my jacket pocket to gaze upon what I'd taken from the jewellery box.

The Guild death cards that Sterling had asked me to take from the Palatium two and a half years earlier had been with me throughout my long journey and my stay in Scotland. Thirty-two of them had been put back inside the box. I'd taken only one with me that night and was staring at it as I prepared to take flight No.27.

I turned the card around and gazed on Malcolm Wilson's mug-shot. His treachery had led to many deaths that I wanted desperately to avenge – none more so than Detective Clarke. Wilson had been walking free for far too long. I'd been searching for him one weekend of every month since I'd been living with Hunter. Each time I got a little further along the trail. A little closer to catching him. I was patient in my hunt for this elusive murderer. I was patient because time was on my side for a change. I started the engine of the GSK20 and looked out over the highlands to see the sun slipping beneath the horizon.

Night was fast approaching and I had all the time in the world.

PD * II * FV * LF * VV * TC * ML * M * ME * DA * PR * LM * PS * V * DM *

Read more of
Ross Bentley's
adventures ...

The first Ross Bentley book

Million Dollar Gift

by Ian Somers

Ross Bentley has a gift – he can move things with his mind.

Ross has always known he was different, but he's kept his talent secret, even from those closest to him. Everything changes when he hears about a contest called The Million Dollar Gift – a wealthy businessman has pledged a million dollars to anyone who can prove they have superhuman powers. It's too good a chance to miss ...

But Ross finds himself drawn ever deeper into a world of corruption and peril. His gift puts him in danger from powerful foes, but also introduces him to people and talents he can hardly believe exist ...

A fast-paced ride into a hidden world of extraordinary gifts and deadly enemies.

The second Ross Bentley book

The Hidden Gift

by Ian Somers

Ross Bentley has supernatural gifts, but they don't stop him feeling alone and miserable when he's cut off from family and friends in a remote farmhouse with Hunter, the taciturn but powerful Guild-member tasked with protecting and training him. But suddenly Hunter is summoned by the Guild. A gifted child has been kidnapped. Hunter needs to track her down, and he has no choice but to take Ross with him. The search for the missing child, and the dangers it uncovers, take Ross to the darkest place he's ever been. He must face danger and great grief and learn to harness his powers to face down his greatest nemesis yet ...

www.obrien.ie